DAWN LAND

ALSO BY TESS CALLAHAN

April & Oliver

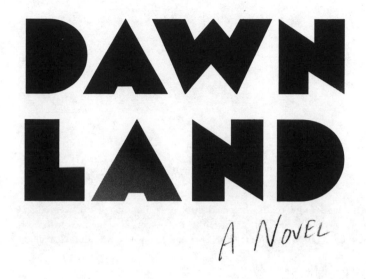

DAWN LAND

A Novel

TESS CALLAHAN

Little a

Published by Little A, New York

www.apub.com

Amazon, the Amazon logo, and Little A are trademarks of Amazon.com, Inc., or its affiliates.

ISBN-13: 9781662517594 (hardcover)
ISBN-13: 9781662517570 (paperback)
ISBN-13: 9781662517587 (digital)

Cover design by Kathleen Lynch/Black Kat Design
Cover images: © Lindsay Basson / Arcangel; © Matthew Smith / Getty;
© SteveBosselman / Getty

Printed in the United States of America
First edition

For you, dear reader.
May you make great sky-circles of your freedom.

The way of love is not
a subtle argument.

The door there
is devastation.

Birds make great sky-circles
of their freedom.

How do they learn it?
They fall, and falling,
they're given wings.

—*Rūmī, from Birdsong (translated by Coleman Barks)*

PROLOGUE

August 2018

When Lochlann hits the cold, dark water, his first thought is that his mother will think he did it on purpose. The surface smacks him sidelong, and he's under, shirt around his face, shoes like bowling balls. He tries to kick them off, propel himself up, but he can't see his arms, the water black with night. He's a good swimmer. Fifteen years old. Unkillable. A fall from a skiff can't do him in. But the whirlpool pulls him down, salt in his nose, eyes stinging. Something thumps him, big and rubbery, its wake hurtling him in a somersault, blurring up and down until his lungs scream for air. His chest convulses. He fights a spasm. *Do. Not. Inhale!*

Abruptly the clamor in his head ceases, a sluicing silence. Pain in his eardrums dissolves into stillness so vivid a strand of hair caresses his face—his mother's touch. His gut unclenches, his body an anchor cut loose from a ship. Warmth rushes his groin. He's peed himself. Darkness enters him, shocking and vast. Something is here with him, moving in the shadows, its centrifugal wake sucking him down faster and faster until he is hurtling back through time toward the moment of his conception. Two luminous orbs appear, faces so young he hardly recognizes them as his parents. He screams at them to get out of the way, his impact will destroy them, but they open their arms and wait.

1

Talking would be risky. Even a glance will likely offend her long-limbed teenager captive in the passenger seat like a rock in a slingshot. "Grandpa says he saw a fin last week," April ventures.

Lochlann's face tightens, headphones on, knees rammed into the dashboard.

"Sunfish or shark?" Nula asks from the back seat, twelve years old, not yet impervious to enthusiasm.

"Shark." April turns to Lochlann. "Sunfish are the ones with big floppy fins, right?" She knows but hopes to appeal to her son's vault of marine facts.

He gives his best eye roll.

Hidden in the center console is the little stuffed mouse April packed to remind her not to slug him, her firstborn, who recently turned from a boy who saved spiders to the poison-quilled riddle beside her. Tattered and oozing stuffing, Mousy had slept with Lochlann through childhood. He'd be galled to know it's here, en route to their family vacation, but April is banking on the one-eyed sack of cotton—or the memory of Locky's tenderness toward it—to keep her civil for seven days straight.

Nula's phone dings. "Uncle Oliver's not far behind us. Phoebe wants to know if we can stop at the same service plaza." Nula glances back in search of her cousin.

"No," April says. "We're making good time." Since their incident on a Manhattan sidewalk last month, she and her husband's brother have not exchanged a word.

A staticky voice on the radio forecasts a week of rain. "Noooo!" Nula says. "The Perseids!" She's been counting the days to the meteor shower.

"Would you chill already?" says Lochlann. "Iron dust disintegrating in the atmosphere. Like, wow."

"Obviously you can hear us, Loch." April clicks off the radio. "Take off your headphones."

Her darling munchkin—tart apple of her eye, silk-skinned, cinnamon-scented miracle of birth—lifts one ear pad a fraction from his skull.

"I think we should talk about summer school before Dad arrives. We'll have to tell him what happened. It's better if it comes from you."

He eyes Nula. "Looks like Mom got kicked in the head by that horse again."

"Dad won't be mad," April says, though of course Al *will* be. "He'll just want to see you own up."

"Fine. I got suspended because some bitch—"

"Knock it off. We don't call young women—"

"Fifteen's not a woman."

"She was fourteen. Try to be honest, at least with yourself."

"Did it ever occur to you that she was the one who cornered me? I know you live in la-la land, Mom, but there are girls out there who'll jump you just to get laid."

"Jesus, Loch." April glimpses in the mirror. Nula is sharpening her drawing pencil. Loch adjusts his headphones, scrolling on his phone. "We're not finished," April says.

"Grandpa texted," Nula says. "Wants to know if we'll be there in time for five o'clock Mass." Her face knots in the rearview. "Church on Saturday?"

"Tell him another three hours at least."

"And while you're at it," Lochlann says, "tell him we don't *do* church."

"We do for him." April clutches the wheel.

"You should let me drive. I'll get us there in an hour."

"Great. Fantastic. Who needs a learner's permit."

"You're not funny when you're sarcastic. You think you are, but you're not."

She nearly clocks him but feels the beady mouse eye in the console staring her down. "What about your father? When are we going to tell him?"

"I don't see how it's any of Allen Night's effing business."

"Lochlann, don't talk to me like that. And with your sister in the car."

"Oh, her virgin ears."

"You want me to pull over? Because that's where we're headed."

"Pull over. I don't give a shit."

She swerves onto the shoulder, the pickup juddering over rumble strips. She pictures opening his door, shoving him into the ravine.

"Mommy," Nula says. "Deep breaths."

April's laugh comes out as a snort. Her daughter is feeding her own lines back to her. An eerie percussion reverberates from Loch's headphones like the soundtrack of a horror film. She parks on the shoulder and grabs her phone. His glance emits a cold draft. "What're you doing?"

"Canceling your Spotify. That's what I said I'd do, and that's what I just did."

He checks his phone.

"Next, I take your headphones. You want to be rude, that's your choice, but don't expect privileges."

"Who cares," he says. "There's a free version."

"Not on mobile devices."

He looks at the roof. "Fine, I'm sorry. The last time you canceled it, I lost all my music." He searches his phone and drops an f-bomb.

"That makes two weeks. One more and it's three."

"Thought you wanted me to express myself more," he mutters.

"Don't act like self-expression and disrespect are the same thing. I don't care who started it. Fourteen is too young to give consent. Fifteen is too young to ask for it. People get hurt." April never told him what happened to her at that age. If there was a brief window between the time he was too innocent to know and too jaded, she missed it.

"I guess this is where we're supposed to pretend the whole school isn't going at it. Tell her, Nula. Last spring two seventh graders got caught in the utility closet."

"I'm talking about *you*, Lochlann. I want you to treat girls with respect. Where do you go when you disappear at night? I hope you're not climbing in windows."

"Yeah, Mom. I've got a harem out there."

"And why in God's name did you sneak the chain saw into the pickup bed? What are you planning to do with that thing?"

"Forgot to tell you. Cape Cod massacre in the works."

The back draft of a semi rocks the car. April takes a breath, tries to soften. "We only want you to be happy. Obviously you're not."

"I was, till you canceled my Spotify." He groans. "Just drive. I'll be good."

"You're already a good person," she says, her stock response, woodened by use. "It's your decisions we're talking about. You're a young man now. Your choices matter, every one of them."

"So do yours."

She stiffens. "What's that supposed to mean?" Flames lick the inside of her skull. The dull voice that used to warn when she was too loaded to drive now tells her she's too livid. She has to find a rest stop, cool down. But she can't help herself. "Tell me, Loch."

"Why should people respect you if you don't respect yourself?" he says. "No wonder Dad doesn't come home anymore."

Her blood ices. It would be dangerous to get physical in the car. He's taller than she is. "Lochlann Night," she says, "if you're talking about your father—"

"I'm talking about you. The sound of your voice makes me want to shoot myself. If I'm dead by the end of the week, you'll know why."

"Locky, stop!" Nula kicks the back of his seat. Her phone dings. "Grandpa again. Says church will be crowded. And he spotted whale blow from the outer cliff. C'mon, Mommy. Let's go."

April's hand trembles on the gearshift. She tries to remember holding Loch as a baby, the down of his hair, the way he liked to nuzzle his head under her chin, that intoxicating sense of purpose. Her only job, to protect him. She pulls into traffic, five thousand pounds of metal in her grip, and prays for the strength not to kill him.

2

In the fast-food line, slim young arms hug April from behind. Her niece's silken black hair gleams under the fluorescent lights. "Phoebe, you found us!" April embraces her, glancing around for her brother-in-law, Oliver. "Your parents?"

"Still in the car. My mom's got a work emergency." She rolls her eyes, dark as April's own. "She's having a fit."

"Poor Meredith," April says.

"How's your drive?" Phoebe asks. "You look like a shaken-up seltzer bottle."

"That's about right." April laughs, running her hand through her tangled hair. She drove with the window down, hoping to blow bad energy out of the car.

Across the lobby, Meredith darts to the restroom, sandals flapping, blonde hair bouncing—the kind of woman people turn to look at.

"I'll show you where your cousins are sitting," April says. "This line's not moving, anyway."

Phoebe sneaks up on Lochlann and Nula. "Boo," she says. "Nula, your hair looks dope. I've never seen a cut like that."

Nula blushes, pressing down the part that stands on end.

"She did it herself," Loch says. "Can you tell?"

"And yours is a hot mess." Phoebe ruffles Lochlann's shoulder-length mop. He gives her a bruised look without removing his headphones. "What the hell." She slaps his shoulder.

"Do you have to be so cheerful?" he says. "It's annoying."

April checks her phone, staying within earshot.

"I've never cut my own hair." Phoebe sits beside Nula. "Do you like it short?"

"When my mom goes long, Nula goes short," Loch says. "It's an inverse equation. If they come down in the morning wearing the same color shirt, Nula runs back up and changes."

"So what? I wouldn't want to wear the same shirt as my mom, either," Phoebe says. "Both my boobs wouldn't fill one of hers."

"Didn't anyone ever tell you size doesn't matter?" he says.

They laugh, Lochlann's voice sounding more like himself.

Nula flips open her sketch pad. "What're you drawing?" Phoebe asks. "That's creepy." A Medusa-like figure fills the page with snaky hair and a cavernous mouth.

"Nula's into Gorgons now," Loch says. "And my parents think *I'm* the disturbed one."

"Those jaws are scary," Phoebe says. "Hey, you get the shark speech yet?"

"My mom printed it out." Nula pulls a paper from her sketchbook. "Where that lady got bit last year? That's Grandpa's beach." She shows her the list.

Shark Precautions:
1. Avoid murky or turbulent water.
2. Don't swim with seals. They attract sharks.
3. Stay close to the shore, in less than five feet of water.
4. Avoid areas where birds are feeding heavily on fish.
5. Avoid brightly colored clothing and high-contrast tan lines.
6. Don't swim near sandbars or steep drop-offs where sharks hide out.
7. Never enter the water if you are bleeding.
8. Don't swim at dawn or dusk.

9. Never swim alone.
10. If you suddenly become uneasy in the water, leave immediately.

"Like someone would be stupid enough to swim with an open wound," Loch says.

"Sometimes people don't notice when they're bleeding," Nula says.

"Then they deserve to die," Loch says.

"Harsh!" Phoebe laughs. "Hey, where's your dad?"

"Who the hell knows," Lochlann says.

"He's coming later," Nula says.

When April catches sight of Oliver's long stride coming in the door, she returns to the food line. She hears him approach, a soft tread for a tall man. Her brother-in-law's feet have the same confident grace as his fingers on the piano. He stands behind her like an electric charge. She pretends not to notice. He exhales slowly, as if gathering strength. "Hey," he says.

She turns. "Oh, hey."

There is a flash of ice in his blue eyes. "Look, I'm sorry about what happened in New York. I don't want to ruin this week before it's begun."

A prickle of heat shoots up her spine. "Already forgotten." She sees Meredith approaching and spins away from him.

"April!" calls her sister-in-law. "It's been too long. How's the farm? We have to catch up, girl. You look terrific!"

April is certain she does not look terrific. She'd rather not talk about her slumping fiber sales and rising hay costs. "Heard about your work crisis." She hugs Meredith.

"Don't get me started," Meredith says, and launches into a speech about whiny customers and a potential product recall. Oliver casts his gaze to the floor. They bring bags of food to the kids.

"Locky, why do you hide in there?" Meredith tugs his hoodie.

"Hi, Aunt Meredith." He doesn't look up.

"Brave haircut, Nulie," she says. "Makes you look confident."

"She did it herself with the alpaca shears," Loch says.

April massages her temple. Nula jabs Loch and globs ketchup onto her veggie burger. Meredith eyes Oliver.

"The salon straightened it out." April makes her voice bright, caressing Nula's hair. "It's growing out nice."

"No Al?" Meredith says. "Where's my illustrious brother-in-law?"

"Separate cars," April says. "He was in New York this weekend."

"'This weekend'?" Lochlann scoffs. They haven't seen Al in weeks.

Oliver and Meredith cast each other another glance.

April smiles tensely. "Grandpa's anxious to see us. You guys go ahead. I need to rest my eyes a little longer."

"Can I go in their car?" Phoebe asks.

"Yes, yes!" Nula grabs her arm.

"Angel, they don't have room," Meredith says.

"We can make room," April says. "Phoebe's always welcome."

Meredith looks at Oliver uneasily.

"Fine," he says. "Don't cause any trouble, Bee." He winks.

Meredith visibly bristles. They leave, Oliver holding the door for his wife, her gait edgy. "My backpack!" Phoebe runs after them. In a moment she returns, frowning. "Never mind. My mom wants me to go with them. See you at Grandpa's."

Once she's gone, Lochlann crushes the rest of his burger inside its bag. "Who cares?" He goes to the men's room.

"Aunt Meredith thinks Loch's becoming a bad influence," Nula says.

"That's not true," April says. "Where'd you get that?"

Nula holds up a text from Phoebe.

April gathers up the trash. It's going to be a long week.

For the rest of the drive, Lochlann is so somber she wishes for one of his outbursts. His dejection scares her more than his anger.

"Mommy," Nula says. "Grandpa sent one of his mile-long speech-to-texts." She scrolls. "This one's a record!"

"Read it to me, honey."

Lochlann shifts his headphones to listen.

"Hope traffic is not too bad. I'm here on the outer cliff. You know, my favorite spot, Dawnland, a better name for this coast than Cape Cod, if you ask me, especially now that there are no cards left."

Nula pauses. "'Cards'?"

"Cods." April smiles. She hears Hal's signature delight in the sweet clunkiness of his text. "Go on," she tells Nula.

"Just now I saw a plume on the horizon. Pretty sure it was not one of our resident humpbacks or fin whales. It looked blue—I mean really blue, like your grandma's eyes. I wish you could have known her. Hard to believe it's been twenty years since she passed. Seems like yesterday. There it is again! I haven't seen a blue whale in this water since before you were born, but I've heard they can wander through on their first migration. They navigate by magnetism. Mind boggling, really. It's skim feeding the surface now. Definitely blue. Wow. It's like a visitation. Maybe you think your old grandpa is a little woo-woo, but when you have the privilege of spotting a creature like this—any creature, for that matter—it connects you to it in a way that changes you both. I hope we can all walk here this week. Can you believe this will be our eleventh summer vacation? I have some news. Can't wait to see you. Love, Grandpa/Dad/How."

"'How'?" Nula asks.

"Hal," April says. "Love that man." She pictures him on the cliff top, binoculars lifted. Dawnland, he's told them, is the Indigenous name for this coastline, Wampanoag land, the place of the first sunrise. When the kids were younger, they would beg to accompany Hal on his predawn walks. April glances at Loch slumped beside her and searches for traces of that old zeal. He hugs his sweatshirt tighter.

3

It's dusk as Oliver turns up the long, curved driveway to his father's house, the car bouncing over ruts, the encroaching woodland batting the chassis until they emerge into sloping meadow, vast and sweeping as an ocean swell. Across the field wild grasses undulate as if breathing. A bluebird flits from a birdhouse. Beside Oliver, Meredith scrolls on her phone. Phoebe is in the pickup, materializing now in his rearview, April navigating the gullies. At Mass she switched places with Nula in the pew in an obvious move to avoid sitting beside Oliver. He wondered if anyone noticed but him. They'd arrived in the middle of the first reading, Jonah imploring his crew to cast him overboard because his sins had caused a tempest. Oliver's middle name is Jonah, a metaphor that has already played out once in his life. Years ago, law school spit him out onto the shores of musicianship.

High atop the knoll, surrounded by pine barrens, the cedar shake house looks like a ship riding a wave, its windows aflame with evening sun. It seems to Oliver a living thing, all fury and grace, daring him to board. He has been coming here for a decade, yet the five-acre property feels more mysterious than ever. There isn't a neighbor in sight. No artificial lights. No traffic sounds. After growing up in their tidy Long Island suburb, his dad's retirement here surprised Oliver. Another man might be spooked by so much solitude, the depth of stars overhead, the perpetual surf sound pulsing the walls. Being here, even for a week, requires an inner reckoning most people would run from.

Meredith looks at her reflection in the visor mirror. "My hair always looks like a feather duster here."

"I like it this way," Oliver says. He means it, too.

She frowns, stroking his arm. "That's just you being you."

The tension he noticed at the service plaza has quickly evaporated. By some fluke of temperament or missing gene, Meredith lacks the propensity to brood. Ink-stained blazers, stock market losses—she shakes everything off. Oliver envies that. There's a lot he has yet to shake.

The pickup has more rust since he saw it at Christmas, the alpaca-farm logo peeling off the door. Before he unbuckles, April is already opening her tailgate, handing luggage to the children, and hauling a chain saw case out of the back. "Shoes off!" she calls as the kids run up the porch steps. "Don't make the house into a sandbox!"

Nula, lean and strong, looks like she's wearing a Joan of Arc helmet, hair spiking and flopping at the will of her cowlick, as if fending off a beauty she cannot outrun. She has her mother's features. With his voluminous mane and penetrating gaze, Lochlann could pass for a young George Harrison if not for his crystal-blue eyes. Phoebe's velvet black tresses fall loose to her shoulder blades, her brilliant smile lighting the porch.

April carries a crate of peaches she brought from her land, the dark sheath of her hair as long now as when they were kids. She's always been slender, but years of farmwork have defined her muscles, like a photo coming into focus. By contrast, the soft parts of her seem softer.

"Oliver." Meredith rubs her forehead. "How am I going to survive this week? I'm so overwhelmed."

He wishes that, for once, she could treat this like a real vacation, yet he understands. He himself never stops thinking about his music. "Take the time you need." He kisses her temple as "Flight of the Bumblebee," Meredith's tune, skitters through his mind. Rimsky-Korsakov. The songs rarely change. His father is a Gregorian chant.

Phoebe, a cello suite. Some people see auras; Oliver hears a person. April has always been Beethoven, Symphony no. 7, the second movement, that sensuous allegretto. But as he catches a flash of her bare calf entering the door, a whisper of Coltrane slips into his mind, smoky and unfathomable.

4

At dinner, April sits as far from Oliver as her father-in-law's table will allow. The room looks different, she thinks. The floorboard tabletop has been refinished, the wine rings erased. Sheer curtains billow where heavy drapes had hung, and the portrait of Hal's late wife, Avila, that stood on the side table is missing.

The aroma of striped bass grilled in herb butter fills the room. Hal adds garlands of parsley and basil from his garden. It's unlike him to fuss. His friend Beryl Eldridge is athletic looking, with skin patchy from sun and dark-blonde hair streaked with white. She has an astute, observant air as she studies Nula's drawing.

"No sketch pads at the table," April says. Nula's Gorgons might send the poor woman running.

"You drew that yourself?" Beryl asks. "That's quite a creature. I'd like to be that powerful."

"You are," Hal says with a quick smile. How strange that he's never mentioned her. His elaborate introduction—a professor at Boston College, master gardener, and cross-country cyclist—makes it clear they are being instructed to like her.

"Tenured professor. That's a big career," Meredith says. "What subject?"

"Sociology." Beryl angles her chair toward the kids, apparently preferring them to the adults. Meredith gives Oliver a look to acknowledge the slight. They have a complex nonverbal language, those two—ninjas of the subtle gesture. April's communication with Al is not so nuanced.

"April, heard from Al?" Hal asks. "This fish won't taste half as good later."

Oliver perks up.

Nula checks her phone. "He's almost here." Al has taken to bypassing April. Perhaps she sent one too many blistering texts this summer. Honey gets the bee, they say, but April is out of honey.

"I saw his photos online from the Press Club award ceremony," Hal says. "Nice suit. Is it new?"

"Um, yeah." April forks a tomato. How is she supposed to know the status of Al's wardrobe? She motions for Loch to put away his phone. He nods toward Meredith, who is texting. She tends to spin her diamond backward in her fist when she's concentrating. April wonders what it feels like, that sharp rock pressing into her palm. April has no engagement ring. She and Al skipped that part.

Beryl pages through Nula's sketchbook. "Nula Night. Snappy name," she says. "I like the alliteration."

"I've got alliteration, too," Phoebe says. "Phoebe Fontaine."

"Oh, you have your mom's name."

Meredith looks up. "Phoebe and I were a family before I met Oliver."

"But then Dad adopted me, too. I'm both of theirs."

"How lucky for him," Beryl says. "Two for one."

"Phoebe clinched the deal." Oliver winks at his daughter.

"Daddy's little girl knows how to turn him to mush," Meredith says. "If she asked for an elephant, you'd see one in the yard tomorrow."

"Only because she hardly asks for anything," he says.

Evening light slants through the window, creating a nimbus glow around Meredith.

"Why adopt as a single woman?" Beryl asks. "With your looks and success, I bet you had proposals right and left."

"I never wanted to get married until—"

"Until she realized what a bitch parenting is," Loch says.

"Loch!" April says, though she wonders if he's onto something.

"Until I met Oliver. Locky, why such a noodge?" Meredith gives a gentle tsk. "Why do the potluck of pregnancy when you can handpick a gem like Phoebe?" She smiles at her daughter.

"Meredith Fontaine," Beryl says. "You are like a fountain. Bubbly and at the center of things." She turns to April. "How about you? Keep your name?"

"Yep," she answers. "April Francesca Simone."

"Ah, I have a print on my wall of that Rossetti painting, Francesca and Paolo."

"I don't know that one," April says. Her end of the table is growing darker.

"True story. Francesca da Rimini was a twelfth-century noblewoman forced into marriage to a violent older man. She fell in love with his younger brother Paolo, also married. They kept their affair secret for ten years before the husband surprised them in the bedroom and savagely murdered them both."

April winces. Oliver takes a swallow of wine.

"They were contemporaries of Dante," Hal says. "He wrote them into *The Divine Comedy*. I used to teach it in my Epic Poetry class."

"They were the inspiration for Rodin's *The Kiss*," Beryl says.

Oliver wipes his mouth. The setting sun burns orange, glinting off his wineglass.

"It's a gorgeous painting. They're holding a book in their lap." Hal gives Beryl a warm look, some shared memory in their eyes. "They fell for each other while reading."

April winds her napkin around her fist.

"At least they had ten years." Meredith raises her glass as if toasting them.

"Dante wrote that they were condemned to hell forever," Hal says.

"That's ridiculous," Meredith says. "Was the crime theirs or their society's? Clearly she was murdered for exercising personal agency in a time when women were property. It would be as shocking as if this chair decided to get up and walk out of the room."

"You mean if this chair decided to hump that one," Loch mumbles.

"Lochlann!" April says.

Phoebe elbows him. "It must've been about more than just that," she says. "Ten years is a long time."

"I see what you mean." Beryl glances at Hal. "Deep, like her dad."

Loch nods in agreement, a fleeting spark of sincerity that lifts April's heart. He's in there somewhere, her boy.

"Loch resembles you, Hal," Beryl says. "The high cheekbones and pensive eyes."

"The blue comes from Avila," Hal says. "Like a summer sky. Same as Oliver."

Loch casts a glance at Nula, chewing his cheek, a message April can't read.

Oliver clears his throat. "How about we talk about our plans for the week?"

"Yes, perfect." Hal rubs his hands. "Oliver, you're our mastermind. What's on the schedule?"

"I was thinking our usual," he says. "Bike riding tomorrow, the beach on Monday . . ."

"But not to swim," Beryl says. "You've heard about the spike in—"

"White sharks. Yes, the kids have been indoctrinated." Oliver continues, "Canoeing Tuesday, plus my performance that night. We have a fishing charter Wednesday."

"All this is usual?" asks Beryl.

"Oliver squeezes in more every year," Meredith says.

"Whale watching Thursday. Sea kayaking Friday. Sadly, back home on Saturday."

"Late Saturday, I hope." Hal glances at Beryl.

"Not too late," says Meredith. "I have a trade show."

"I can't wait for your performance Tuesday, Oliver," Beryl says. "Preservation Hall is our Carnegie Hall, even if it is just a little revamped church."

"Oliver played at Carnegie Hall," Hal says.

"Dad," Oliver says. "That was a million years ago."

"Three," April says. Oliver glances at her over the rim of his wine-glass. She averts her eyes. Fading light dapples the tablecloth, the room dimming.

"Two sons with their own Wikipedia pages," Beryl says. "Not bad, Hal."

"Hitler's got his own wiki page," Lochlann says.

"Lochlann Night!" April says.

"Meredith's the real talent in the family," Oliver says. "She started her own business—earbuds that double as jewelry. They're quite lovely."

"Except they're packaged in Styrofoam," Nula says.

"No other way with electronics, Nulie," Meredith says. Lochlann rolls his eyes.

Tires grind on the oystershell gravel. "He's here!" Nula says. April glances at the empty seat beside her, her stomach a fist.

5

Al clicks off sports radio when the gully scrapes the Tesla's undercarriage. A Range Rover Sport would've had better clearance, but Nula wouldn't have forgiven him if he bought a gas-powered car. He's been telling his father for years that the driveway needs to be leveled. His dad likes things rustic. Another winter of erosion and it will take a helicopter to reach the house. Hal bought the place for a song after the housing bubble popped in 2008 and hasn't done a thing with it since. Al suggested a pickleball court, a hot tub, an in-ground pool—hell, there's room for a football field—but his father won't even bend on a dishwasher. "Why, when I enjoy looking out the window as I scrub?" he said. As for the precipitous, untamed field, his father contends it must be kept wild for the bluebirds.

Achy from the six-hour drive, Al extracts himself from the car, his body a crushed ball of paper that refuses to smooth out. He reminds himself that Tom Brady is still throwing footballs at his age. "Buck up, Allen," he says aloud. He takes out his suitcase and liquor luggage—his dad can't be trusted to buy quality—and lights up. All day he's been picturing a glass of scotch, amber clarity scented with woody vanilla, but he draws the line at drinking and driving. He saw what happened to April's family, done in by accidents one by one. The final crash, her brother's, was a fluke of black ice. Life hasn't cut April any breaks.

Through the window he sees the dinner table. Nula looks like someone took a hacksaw to her hair, yet she's adorable as ever. He wonders how long before adolescence turns her against him, as it's done so efficiently with Loch. Why hasn't April told him to pull down his hood at the table? He looks like a dropout next to Phoebe, who is, as usual, all sparkle. At that age, Al was catching passes in the end zone. He wasn't fast for a wide receiver, but he always knew how to get open. Loch can barely catch a Frisbee. Al takes a drag. Endless locker room interviews have taught him to get a quick read on body language. His dad is square shouldered at seventy, his hair more salt than pepper. Beside him sits a female guest—that's a first—the ease between them evident. Meredith appraises the woman with veiled skepticism. His brother is doing the talking, seemingly confident, yet Al sees from his measured gestures that he is still prisoner to his sense of caution. Oliver will never learn.

Al rests his gaze on the one he's been avoiding. April is passing a platter of fish. She has the arms of a person who does strenuous work. Beneath her surface weariness, she looks stronger than before. His stomach flutters. He'll have to explain why he's been out of touch. He can't lie, but neither can he tell the truth. He snuffs out his cigarette and, lifting his bags, begins to cough.

6

April hears Al clear his lungs in the driveway, a sound more guttural than usual.

"My eldest son." Hal smiles. "Never on time."

The door flings open. It's dusky outside. Nula runs and throws her arms around Al's neck. He twirls her in a circle—though she's getting big for that—and sets her down. "What happened to your hair?" he says. "Not to mention your braces. Looks like San Quentin in there." She thwacks him.

April reads hunger in Al's voice, fatigue in his eyes, hands antsy for a drink. Hal gives him a solid pat on the back. "Son, we would've come to the Press Club ceremony if only you'd told us." He grins at Beryl. "Good thing I follow him online."

Al greets Oliver with his usual fraternal shove. Oliver doesn't push back. Al grips Lochlann's shoulder, but the boy twitches him off. He comes to April last, stands beside her shyly until she looks up into his face, a question in his road-weary eyes, an ache of sincerity she'd rather not acknowledge. He bends to kiss her, breath scented with cigarette smoke. She gives him her cheek.

"Allen," Hal says, "I'd like you to meet my friend Beryl."

She extends her hand. "I hear you're working on a new book."

"Brought the manuscript." He sits down heavily and reaches for a platter. "Anyone feel like critiquing?"

"Is this the NFL one?" Nula asks.

"Yep. Repetitive brain injury. Not happy stuff, Nulie."

The room has grown dark. April flips on a light switch.

"Candles too?" Hal asks.

April circles the table, striking matches. She squeezes past Oliver, brushing his arm, a buzz of energy.

"So, Beryl," Al says, composing a question. He has a habit of taking over conversations.

Beryl cuts him off. "Your daughter's quite the artist. And I hear your son is a terrific bassist."

Eyes on his phone, Lochlann wags his head as if they are all foul-smelling passengers on a bus he can't get off.

"True. His room is full of awards," Al says.

"When was the last time you saw my room?" Loch asks.

"Don't be rude," April says.

"Have you noticed everything you say to me starts with *'Don't'*?"

She blows out a match. Hal dabs moisture from his lip.

"Actually, his room is full of whale posters," Nula says. "He knows all the species."

"Have you heard what's happening with the blue whales?" Beryl asks. "Their song has been getting deeper."

Loch shifts in his chair, picks up a fork. April sits back down beside him, candles flickering.

"The tonal frequency of their vocalizations has fallen by a few fractions of a hertz every year," Beryl says. "The pitch has dropped by thirty percent since the 1960s."

Lochlann glances up, unable to conceal curiosity.

"Probably noise pollution," Nula says. "They can't hear each other."

"Good theory," Beryl says, "except sound carries farther when the frequency is higher, not lower."

"They can't find each other anymore," Nula says. "We killed like ninety percent of them—right, Loch?"

"Ninety-seven," he says.

"Do you know only two centuries ago, the bay was teeming with sperm whales?" Beryl says. "For thousands of years the Wampanoag hunted judiciously. Then the colonists arrived and slaughtered all the whales. I'll bet you a hundred bucks some kid back then said, 'Hey, what happens when there are no whales left?' And some adult said, 'Sonny, there's no other way to fill the oil lamps.'"

"Exactly," Lochlann says. "It's called fucking lack of imagination."

"Loch!" April says.

Al leans on the table. "You're right about the whales, son. But don't fucking curse at the table." He winks.

Hal presses his eyes shut.

"We can't solve the world's problems tonight," Al says gently. "Come watch the game with me, Locky. It's do or die for the Mets."

Lochlann pushes fish around on his plate. April senses he both wants to sit with his dad and doesn't. To Al's heartbreak, the boy doesn't care about sports.

The windows darken, the outside world invisible. A quiet whirring sound fills the room. "Hal, is your washing machine off-balance?" Meredith asks.

Beryl laughs. "That's a whip-poor-will, dear."

"They sing after sunset, Mom," Phoebe says. "We hear it every year."

Meredith flusters. "I've never heard it before."

Oliver takes her hand, massaging it.

"You're a good soul, aren't you, Oliver," Beryl says. "I hear you do charity work."

"He's on the exec board of a music nonprofit," Hal says. "Last month they took a bunch of kids up to Al's farm."

Al's farm. April creases her napkin.

"Oh yeah?" Al lifts his head. "When was this?"

"When I was at that alpaca show," April says. "The farmhand took care of them."

"Was this in the works for a while?" Al looks at Oliver. "No one mentioned it."

"'Cause you haven't been home, Daddy," Nula says.

Al turns to April. She's seen his televised interviews. When he wants an athlete to be more forthcoming, he goes silent. The whip-poor-will gets louder and faster.

"Mommy and Uncle Oliver planned it," Nula says. "She took the train down to New York."

April's chest tightens.

"You were in Manhattan?" Meredith says. "We could've had drinks."

"I barely had time for coffee," April says. "Had to fly back for the school bus."

"But she was late," Nula says.

April's face heats. "You know Metro North."

Oliver wipes his mouth with his napkin.

Al taps the table. The whip-poor-will whistles its name in an endless dizzying loop. "Charity has its limits," Al says. "Oliver's never going to get his Grammy as long as he keeps tripping over his own goody two-shoes. Picasso didn't volunteer at the dog shelter, bro."

Oliver lifts his chin at Al, code from boyhood that he's being an asshole. "It was just one field trip. And the kids loved it. Right, Loch?"

"Yeah," Loch says without sarcasm. "They dug it."

"What the nonprofit needs is funding, not field trips," Meredith says. "If you really want to help them, you should use your fame to schmooze, Oliver. Find Mr. Big."

"Or Mrs. Big," says Phoebe.

"I'd hardly say I'm famous," Oliver says.

"Case in point. You suck at sucking up," Al says. "That *New York Times* critic got it right. You need to think bigger. You've outgrown the trio. You need an ensemble, touring, music videos. You weren't born to be the opening act."

"I don't read reviews."

"Well, obviously you should," Al says. "That B-list manager of yours is an idiot. He wants you to narrow down your genre when it's the opposite. The fact that you can't be pigeonholed is your ace. You've got to be more aggressive." He turns to Beryl. "This is the kid who let the class bully pluck his Oreos out of his lunch box every day. If I wasn't around, he would've starved."

Oliver's jaw tightens. "I'll pass on the psychoanalysis."

"Let's play Parcheesi." Nula tugs Phoebe's arm.

Al assesses the table the way he might a team after a blundering loss and leaves to watch the game. "Dad," he calls out, "why don't you let me buy you a new TV? This one's made for a dollhouse."

"Because I don't watch it," Hal says.

"I can't even get it out of the cabinet. You hide it like it's contraband."

"Let Nula help you. It takes finesse." Hal smiles at Beryl. "It's the same conversation every visit."

The whip-poor-will's crescendo heightens. Normally April finds the song enchanting, but tonight it quickens her heart. She pours tea for the remaining adults and rushes Oliver's cup, spilling it into the saucer.

Beryl takes them all in with a shrewd eye. "I have three boys," she says to April. "Nice that you have one of each. The girl will be the one who calls."

"I have two boys, and they both call," Hal says.

"How about you?" Beryl asks Meredith. "Didn't want another?"

Meredith stiffens. "Excuse me?"

"Another child, I mean."

Meredith glances open-mouthed at Oliver.

"I didn't mean anything by it," Beryl says. "It's lovely that you adopted, and as a single woman at the time. More people should be so generous. A professor in my department spent tens of thousands on infertility and still—"

"I don't have infertility," Meredith says. "Does that fricking bird have an off button?"

"Beryl," Oliver says gently, "Meredith was a senior director at Bose when she adopted Phoebe. A single man with that level job would never—I mean, to adopt was quite extraordinary."

"So true," Beryl says. "Forgive me. And such a wonderful child. Phoebe will take good care of you when you're old. She'll be the equivalent of five children."

Meredith's eyes flash. "You mean because she's Chinese?"

"I mean because she looks at you so adoringly."

"She's fifteen. Give her time," Meredith says. "Phoebe gets the brunt of a lot of assumptions. People expect her to be quiet and studious, good at math, deferential to men. She's none of those."

"She's got a good role model," Beryl says.

Meredith fans herself. "Did someone turn off the AC?"

"I thought the sea breeze was enough," Hal says. "But if you're too—"

"Hot flashes already?" Beryl says. "You can't be more than forty."

Meredith gives a hard laugh. "I'm forty-six. And I don't have hot flashes."

"I wouldn't have guessed. You could pass for thirties."

"I'm seven years older than Oliver," Meredith says. "Age doesn't matter to me."

Beryl smiles. "Me neither. I'm ten years younger than Hal, and my first husband was twenty years older than me."

April can't help but shoot Oliver a glance. "And your *second* husband?" she asks.

"I told you." She touches Hal's arm. "We're ten years apart."

Oliver leaps to his feet. "Sorry, I think I missed something. Are you two—"

"Goodness," Beryl says. "What a clumsy announcement. I'm sorry, Hal."

He takes her hand. "I meant to say something before everyone left the table. This Saturday, a week from today. I hope you weren't planning to leave early."

"Saturday?" Oliver says. "You're getting married on Saturday?"

The whip-poor-will ceases abruptly, filling the room with awkward silence. Nula and Phoebe poke their heads up from the couch. Al clicks off the television.

"We didn't want you to make a fuss." Hal reddens.

"Hold on," Al says. "You two are getting spliced?"

Hal's blush deepens. "I was afraid you'd get gifts and whatnot. We're keeping it simple. Little ceremony on the outer cliff, Dawnland. Just you and us. Beryl's sons can't make it. One in Texas and two in California."

The room stalls. April is the first to stand and hug them.

7

April sits at the dining room table, the windows black with night, and leafs through Al's manuscript, taking in the lean sentences and no-nonsense style. She once told him he was better on paper than in life. Mean, and not true. Oliver sits at the other end of the table, headphones on, and opens a book of poetry he's been browsing in preparation for his performance, a gig with a famous poet whose usual pianist is away. The room is hushed except for the crisp turn of pages and a murmur of voices from the kitchen—Beryl and Hal deconstructing the evening. She seems to be reassuring him that his family is wonderful.

Meredith walks in, searching for her water bottle. "Hey, love," Oliver says.

She motions in the direction of Beryl's voice. He shakes his head, the stenography of gestures suggesting they will discuss Beryl Eldridge when their bedroom door is shut.

The kettle goes quiet, and the voices in the kitchen become audible. "Now there's an interesting marriage," Beryl says.

Oliver slips off his headphones, glances at April.

Al jaunts into the kitchen. "Whose marriage?" He opens the refrigerator.

"Your brother and his wife," Beryl answers.

April's nape prickles. "Match made in heaven," Al says. "Any more french bread?"

"Didn't we just finish eating?" Hal says.

"In the bread drawer next to the fridge," Beryl says. "'Made in heaven' how?"

The slide of a drawer. The rustle of plastic. "Meredith found someone to raise her kid. Oliver found someone to support his music."

Oliver casts April a heated look as if the comment came from her.

"That's terrible," Hal says. "Who made you so cynical?"

"How about you and April, then?" Beryl asks.

Al has apparently stuffed food in his mouth, his voice muffled. "True love," he says, and leaves the kitchen without acknowledging April and Oliver in the dining room.

"I can't tell when he's kidding, that one," Beryl says. The screen door clatters as Hal walks her to her car.

Oliver turns a page and spins his wedding ring. April remembers the first time she heard Meredith's name. Locky had climbed out of his crib early one morning and was playing with April's eyebrows, giggling when he could get them to stand on end. Pregnant with Nula, she'd tried to go back to sleep, but the caller ID jolted her. "Al." She nudged him. "It's your brother."

Al answered groggily. April listened for traces of Oliver's voice, but Lochlann was tittering. "You're shitting me." Al turned to her with a shrug. "Meredith who? Dude, you might've mentioned you were dating."

The dog pushed open the door, put his scruffy chin on the bed. Dubious had a way of showing up when April needed him. A wave of morning sickness washed through her.

"Tax Day? That's one way to remember your anniversary," Al said. "Seems impulsive," he added without irony.

Al had forgotten the other significance of April 15. Her birthday.

Al's footsteps return to the kitchen, pulling April back to the present. Oliver pops up and follows him in. "I'd appreciate it if you'd keep your opinions about my marriage to yourself."

The snap of a beer can. "I was joking," Al says. "Don't be so sensitive."

"I'm serious, Al. We barely know Beryl."

"What's wrong, bro? Scared your secrets will come out?"

"Not all of us keep secrets," Oliver says. *"Bro."*

The screen door sounds. Hal's voice. "Boys, it's a stunning night. You should go look."

"Beryl's lovely," Oliver says. "We're so happy for you, Dad."

"I hope Meredith didn't take offense. Beryl can be direct, but she means well."

"You could say the same of Meredith. She has a trade show next weekend. If only we'd known about the wedding."

"We're planning the ceremony for dawn. You can be on the road by nine," Hal says. "Look, boys, I can see you have a lot on your minds. Just don't get so distracted that you lose touch with your wives. No matter how busy you are, you can manage to look in their eyes once a day. I mean, really look."

April lolls her head. Dear Hal. His suggestion is sweet, starry-eyed, the admonition of a man in love. Also cheesy and impractical. She picks up Al's manuscript and retreats to the living room. The shadow box coffee table is filled with shells the children have collected over the years. On top of it, the dog-eared *Secrets of the Sea* lies open to an image of a vampire squid. Having abandoned Parcheesi, the kids slump shoulder to shoulder on the floppy couch, each on their phones. April settles into an armchair.

When Oliver enters, Meredith motions toward the kids nestled like puppies—too close for Meredith, apparently. Oliver shrugs, his spar with Al still brewing on his face, but life never waits for one moment to be processed before missile launching the next. Meredith gives him a command with her eyes.

"Hey, Loch." Oliver nods toward the piano. "Let's tune her up."

Loch dislodges himself. So easily Oliver gets a yes! Satisfaction lights his face. He whacks a tuning fork against his knee. "Have you done the tuning fork experiment in physics yet?" He holds another fork near the first, silences the original, and brings the second to Lochlann's ear.

"Weird," Loch says. "It picked up the vibration through the air?"

"Just think," Oliver says, "whether we realize it or not, every time we walk into a room, that's what we do for each other."

"Or *to* each other," Nula says.

Lochlann flips her off with his eyes, but Nula only smiles.

As they remove the photos from on top, April sees Avila's picture is not gone, merely moved to a less prominent spot. They unhinge the panel and test the keys low to high, wincing simultaneously on the middle C, clearly pleased by this shared recognition.

"And we just did a touch-up at Christmas," Loch says.

"The salt air," Oliver says. "Sorry for the noise, everyone." They work up the row, examining hammers and strings. Lochlann drops his sweatshirt to the floor. "Better, but there's still a warble," Oliver says. "Take it more out of tune, then bring it back." Lochlann pushes hair out of his face, concentrating. "Perfect," Oliver says. "Now the one to the left." They work methodically, animated. "They can use some help tuning pianos at the nonprofit. Want to come to Brooklyn for a few days?"

Meredith's head flies up.

"Sure," Lochlann says, his face cast down to the housing.

April feels a cold front traverse the room from Meredith to Oliver. On a scale of one to ten, her sister-in-law is Level 8 pissed. It appears Oliver has set a timer on a nice fat argument. "Let's test her out," he says.

"Uh, haven't played in a while," Loch says.

"I was thinking a duet. 'Für Elise,' like we used to. Did you bring an instrument? Phoebe brought three."

"The bass was too big."

"Your violin," Nula says. "Mommy brought it. It's next to the couch."

April doodles on Al's manuscript as if absorbed.

"No pressure." Oliver tests a key.

Smooth, April thinks. She turns a page.

"Doubt this thing's in tune." As Loch lifts the violin, his spine straightens, shoulders squared.

"How long we been playing this one?" Oliver asks. "Since you were ten?"

"Eight," Lochlann says, tuning.

"Half your life." They signal each other with a nod. Lochlann's bow arcs over the violin, dipping and swaying, the weight of insecurity lifted. The room vibrates, photos quivering in their frames, glasses reverberating. Buoyancy swells in April's heart. Oliver has tossed a mooring line, and somehow the boy has caught it. Just before the room has a chance to break into applause that would make Loch uncomfortable, Oliver calls out, "Now a quartet. Phoebe. Nula."

"Only thing I play is basketball," Nula says.

"We need you for percussion. Think of it as dribbling." He turns to Loch. "Your fingering's gotten better. Now, concentrate on your phrasing. Let your breathing guide you."

"Sax?" Phoebe asks.

"Horn."

"This is going to be one weird quartet." Phoebe uncrates her French horn.

"Let's do this piece I've been arranging," Oliver says. "I want to hear how it sounds." He pulls out a sheet of music. "Like this, Nula." He taps time on the bench. "Keep it steady for me. Ready?"

"No," the children say together.

They play, bumbling, smiling in exasperation. "I have no idea what we're doing," Lochlann says.

"Good," Oliver says. "Get messy. Find the groove."

"A bit hard to concentrate on the game," Al says, but everyone ignores him.

Oliver quiets the piano and nods at Phoebe. She closes her eyes, solos a few bars.

"That's it," Oliver says. "Let it get up inside you. You can't do it wrong."

Phoebe pulls back and Lochlann solos. Everyone claps, but April wishes they would tone it down, the moment too tenuous. Any second now Loch will feel duped, his help not needed, hooked to the puppeteer strings of the family. Oliver cuts short the applause. "Time for bed, Phoebe." He stands. "It's late." The man is brilliant.

"What?" Phoebe says. "We're on vacation."

"Bike riding in the morning. Brush your teeth." Oliver puts his tools away. Nula scoots up the stairs.

"You too," April says before Lochlann can settle on the couch. "Bedtime."

Phoebe shoves him up the steps. "We sounded dope."

"You mean *like* dopes." He laughs.

"Bring your double bass when you come to Brooklyn," she says. "We can jam."

Oliver turns to face Meredith's glare, some attempt at reassurance in his eyes, apology or promise. Meredith's mouth hardens.

With the girls tucked in, April sits on Nula's mattress. The twin beds are covered with faded patchwork quilts made by Avila when Al and Oliver were little. Over the years the blocks shrank unevenly, puckering the fragile seams. "Is your retainer in?" April asks.

"You already asked me." Nula pushes her with her foot. "Mommy, go to bed."

Phoebe gives April a sympathetic look. April snaps off the light.

April and Al's is the darkest of the bedrooms, the knotty pine paneling adorned with family photos. The blackness of the window reflects April's image, wary and distorted. She assembles a wall of pillows down the middle of the mattress. Al coughs in the hallway and comes in, his clothes scented with his last smoke of the day. He looks at the pillow arrangement. "Beautiful," he says.

"I haven't seen you in six weeks," April says. "What did you expect?"

"Managed to see my brother, though," he says, hurt in his voice.

"I would have mentioned it if you bothered to call," she says, but wonders if that's true.

"Thought you said all I do is splash lighter fluid around the place," he says.

"I didn't mean not to come home," she says. "Obviously I'm doing a crappy job, but at least I show up."

"Fine. Buy me another goddamn self-help book, why don't you?" He sits on the bed with his back to her. "Nula looks like a punker and Loch looks like a hippie," Al says. "Why didn't you make him get a haircut before you came up?"

"Their hair is the least of my worries."

"You're too soft on him. I could've gotten him an internship in a newsroom this summer, and instead he's hanging out in the band room doing nothing."

"Did you actually offer that to him?"

"He doesn't talk to me."

"He might if you tried," she says.

He rubs his face.

"Why have you ignored us?" April asks. "If I hadn't seen you on Twitter, I might've thought you were dead."

"I had a rough summer," he says. "The World Cup and Tour de France were back-to-back."

"You used to include us on those trips. You used to at least call."

"I've got more pressure now with the book."

"You're making excuses. Tell me the truth." She feels queasy, her voice tremulous. "If we're over, I'd rather not put on a show for your dad."

"What?" He turns to her. "No, Rosie," he says, his old nickname from when they were teens and he used to make fun of her rosy dollar store perfume. "It's not about you. I had some stuff I had to deal with, but it's done now," he says. "Come sit next to me."

She sits cautiously. "What stuff?"

"It's personal."

"Al, couples talk about personal things. That's what couples do."

"You don't tell me personal stuff."

"Of course I do. You know my worst secrets. You know everything."

"That was back then. You don't tell me anything now."

"It might help if you answered my freaking texts."

He exhales heavily and reaches for her hand. "I'm sorry, April."

She returns his grip. His hands are strong and blunt, yet softer than hers, which have grown calloused from farmwork. He once told her that playing football in high school taught him to have receptive fingers, flexibility in his wrists, springy elbows. You have to give a little when you catch the ball. His hands look younger than the rest of him. They have typed columns read by millions, carried luggage through countless airports, touched who knew how many women's bodies.

"I'm here now," he says. "Tell me about Loch and summer school. What happened in the classroom?"

"He won't say. Maybe you can find out. No boy wants to talk to his mother about sex," she says. "Will you come bike riding tomorrow?"

"You know I don't see the point of bike riding."

"The point is to spend time with your kids."

"I'll find another way. I hear Beryl has a boat." His voice softens. "Lie down with me, April. I just want to hold you."

Sex was Al's cure for everything—arguments, toothaches, boredom. As much as she could use it right now, she doesn't want another temporary fix. "You still haven't told me what happened this summer."

"Maybe later in the week," he says. "I'm too tired to think."

She sighs, releasing his hand. "I'm going downstairs for a glass of water."

"Sure." He closes his fist. "Catch you later."

8

Phoebe hears the scritch of Nula's pencil point against paper, drawing by moonlight, until her breath deepens and the pencil clatters to the floor. Angry voices penetrate the wall. Phoebe slips out of bed, compelled by the sharpness of their tones, and listens at their door, winding the edge of her pajama sleeve around her pinkie. They sit on the bed with their backs to each other as if each talking to a different person. Uncle Al's voice rises: ". . . buy me another goddamn self-help . . ."

Phoebe bolts, afraid she's been seen. She sails downstairs rather than risk the creak of her doorknob and burrows into the couch, heart racing. From the ceiling their muffled voices get louder. A few weeks ago, her parents had the first roaring blowup she'd ever overheard. Still, if arguments had a Richter scale, her parents' was a tremor compared to her aunt and uncle's earthquakes.

Snug on the sofa, she grabs her phone—her father forbids her to bring it to bed—and checks her email. She's been waiting on two big things: her ancestry DNA results, which should come any day now, and news from the finder in Beijing, which might never happen. She doesn't actually want to meet her birth parents, she's just curious what they look like and if she has siblings and . . . well, why they gave her up. There's only one new email: a notice about a college essay-writing workshop. Ugh. She hears movement from the dining room, her grandfather closing windows. "Still up, princess?"

"Dinner was yummy, Grandpa." She hides her phone.

"You're too nice." He settles beside her. "Loved hearing you play tonight."

"We sounded atrocious."

"What's up with Loch?" he asks.

She shrugs. "Mad, I guess."

"At?"

"Everything. Everyone. Nothing."

The sound of quarreling gets louder, Aunt April's voice punctuated by indistinct responses from Uncle Al. "Don't mind them," Grandpa says. "They're like Frank Sinatra and Ava Gardner—except you probably don't know who they were, do you?"

Aunt April's soft tread descends the stairs and disappears into the kitchen. "Your friend Beryl asked me why he doesn't wear a wedding ring," Phoebe says softly. "Uncle Al, I mean. Do you know?"

"Beryl asked you that?" He looks in the direction of the driveway. "Something about Uncle Al's thick fingers."

Phoebe looks away, blushing that Hal thinks her so gullible.

"I'm sorry. I don't know why. I wish I did." Lightness goes out of his face.

"It's okay. There's lots of stuff I wish I knew."

"Tell me one." He puts his arm around her.

She glances at the mirror over the end table. "Like, what I look like."

"What do you mean?"

She wants to ask if she looks like Lucy Liu or Constance Wu, but it seems wrong to compare herself to an actress. How to explain that when she looks in the mirror, she sees nothing identifiable? "Is my hair the same color as Aunt April's?"

"Hmm. Let's see. I guess you'd say hers is a very dark brown—mahogany—and yours is like midnight, a deep night sky."

"Oh, Grandpa."

"Like velvet. Like mink. A black filly standing on a hill, with wind in her mane."

"All right." She giggles. "That's enough."

"And your face? Well, there's no one to compare. No one as pretty."

She stills. "Well, my mom's pretty, isn't she?" She looks up the stairs.

"Yes, your mom's very pretty, like a daffodil. You? You're a lotus."

"Humph. Who's too nice now?"

"Just make sure once you start dating, you pick someone kind, like your dad."

She reddens. "He won't be too kind if he finds out how late I stayed up."

He hugs her good night.

9

April leans in the kitchen doorframe, sipping her water and listening to Hal's and Phoebe's voices. How lucky the kids are to have him. How lucky April was to have had her grandmother, the one steady force in her life.

Their footsteps recede up the stairs. April looks at the stove clock—Al is no doubt still awake—and takes her sweatshirt from the hook. Out beyond the tree house, she descends the wild slope of the meadow, salt grass and bluestem swishing her thighs. The sound is symphonic, the grasses below calling the grasses above, layered with the swoosh of pines and a rhythmic percussion of crickets. Oliver taught her to hear the world this way. Above the house, the incandescent blush of the Milky Way parts the darkness, so immense she thinks it might break her open. She continues down and slips through an archway of trees into a quiet hollow, a spot she has gravitated to in summers past. She settles on a stump within a ring of five tupelo trees. They whisper to each other as if sensing her return. Fireflies blink like fairies transmitting a code. Through branches, the house is dark except for Oliver and Meredith's window. April wonders what they are talking about, what most couples talk about. She and Al were best when traveling, she thinks, when the woman he brought back to his hotel room was her. She remembers the Iditarod, the Great Barrier Reef, the Beijing Olympics, where he pushed the kids to try sea cucumbers, their faces morphing from dread to delight. They were happy in those moments.

They felt like a family—not a typical family, but a curious one. She looks up at the house, Al's darkened window. It could have been a good marriage. Maybe it still can. She tries to picture it.

A blanket of cloud cover swallows the stars, the breeze in the tupelos ruffling her hair. She thanks the wind, the trees, the house on the hill—even the raindrops striking her skin. She will survive this week as long as she keeps her balance. After dinner, Beryl announced that she'd googled April Francesca Simone and found three words: *Allen Night's wife*. It ought to have said *Woman on a tightrope*.

Rain wets her hair as she starts up the hill. She's surprised that Oliver and Meredith's light still shines. April wonders what kind of things they tell each other. For all she knows, he is, at this very moment, confessing what happened in New York.

10

Oliver hears the clink of a C-sharp—Meredith's earrings flung onto the dresser—followed by the one-two of a snare drum as she kicks her sandals into the closet. "I can't believe you invited him. I never agreed to have Loch stay with us."

"It would only be for a few days." Oliver scoops up the earrings. "He needs—"

"What about *my* needs? You know what's at stake. Everything rides on these next few weeks. This is life or death for me."

"Which means you won't even be around." He slips the earrings into a bowl on the bureau. "You'll be traveling with Dixon or on the phone twenty-four seven like you are now."

"That's exactly why my downtime is precious. You think I'm an extrovert, but I'm not. I need headspace, Oliver. We're already on top of each other in that shoebox of an apartment." She takes the earrings out of the bowl. "And why do you always move my stuff? This is why I can never find anything." She hurls them back onto the dresser.

He tries to rinse his mind of orchestral substrate, a frenzied tinnitus of notes. The room doesn't help—starkly lit, the walls aggressively yellow. "I know I should have cleared it with you, but I promise you won't even know he's there," he says. "Look, why don't you ask your co-packer what could have caused—"

"Just because I tell you my problems doesn't mean I want you to fix them. Why do all men feel the need to—"

"Please don't do the *all men* thing."

"I only want you to listen."

"Don't I?"

"If you understood what I'm going through, you wouldn't have invited Loch."

"I get that, but—"

"You don't get it," she says. "Can you at least admit that? That would be a start."

"I'm sorry. But can we at least—"

"'Sorry but' is 'sorry bullshit.'"

He resists the urge to push the earrings back from the dresser's edge.

"And it's not just this one incident. You've got poor Phoebe asking every day if we've found her so-called parents."

"It was the only thing she asked for for her birthday."

"And I said we'd think about it. Next thing I know, you've hired a finder."

"I've tried to talk to you," he says. "To be honest, sometimes it's hard to get your attention."

"So we're back to that? If a man is preoccupied with work, it makes him a good provider, but a woman—"

"I understand how busy—"

"Then why don't I feel understood?" She rubs her temples. The harshness of the overhead light gives the air of an interrogation room. "And the genetic testing? Whose idea was that?"

"It's harmless. She wants to know her ancestry."

"As if she doesn't already?"

"Not everything has to be logical. She wanted all of us to do it, remember? We bought three kits, but you never had time to spit in the vial."

Her eyes flash.

"Because you're overwhelmed. I get that."

"My point is that you keep making decisions without me. Teenagers are fragile, Oliver. Lochlann is in a dark place. I don't want *dark* for

Phoebe. I don't want her glued to him this week. I don't want them alone at night in that spooky tree house."

He glances out the window blurred by rain. "The tree house?"

"Alone? Two fifteen-year-olds?"

"Please. They're cousins." But as soon as he says it, he sees himself and April at fifteen, when she turned from someone he grew up with to a stranger his friends stole glances at. The spiritual smoke of Coltrane's sax fills his mind, washing away a frenetic strain of Rimsky-Korsakov. "Fine, I'll tell Phoebe no tree house unless with Nula."

"And the finder? What if they tell us her parents gave her up because she's a girl or because she has a heart murmur?"

He puts his hands on her shoulders. "There's value in knowing our stories, don't you think?"

She softens, kneading her forehead.

"Give her credit. She's a great kid, thanks to you."

She sits on the bed. "That's a lie. We both know you do the heavy lifting."

"No, you're an amazing mother. You're teaching her to be a strong, independent woman. She won't have to rely on anyone."

She looks up. "You don't think I rely on you?"

"That's not what I meant." He rubs her shoulders. "Meredith, I'm sorry. No buts."

She sighs. "Speaking of strong women, what do you think of your future stepmother?"

He taps his knee. The news shouldn't feel so shocking. The real question is why Oliver feels artistically stuck at thirty-nine when his father is willing to change his life at seventy. "She got him to fix up the house. I hear she's convinced him to get the driveway leveled, too. That's more than Al or I have been able to do."

"She has it out for me."

"No," he says. "Who wouldn't like you?"

"You say things like that, but you know your family doesn't get me. April's the only one who listens to me. You didn't tell me you had lunch with her in New York. I would have loved to see her."

He tenses. "It wasn't lunch. It was coffee."

"My family adores you," she says. "Our lone artist, Mr. Grammy Nomination."

"You and I both know they're still waiting for me to get a 'real' job," he says, relieved that she's moved on from the topic of April.

"You'd think over the years this vacation would get easier, but it's the opposite. Who cares if I'm written up in *Entrepreneur Magazine*?" she says. "With your family I'm still the misfit toy."

"Honestly," he says, "I don't know where you get that."

"From you, Oliver. I get it from you."

"Meredith, love." He takes her face in his hands. "From the day we met, you've been my rock star."

She rolls her eyes. "You are so freaking Disney."

"Disney?" he says, offended. "I think you meant Scorsese."

She takes off her tank top, that old mischief in her voice, distinctly Meredith. "I'm still pissed, but I'm sure you can think of ways to make it up me." She slides his shorts down and pulls him against her breasts, hoisted up by her bra. It takes him a minute to get hard, distracted by April's and Al's voices penetrating the wall. Gusts of wind assault the window until even the Coltrane washes from his mind. He wishes they had turned out the light.

11

April was in the barn unlatching a stall when Oliver's text arrived. Horse fragrance perfumed the air, oiled leather and fresh hay. As she entered the stall, the mare within stomped and nickered, pink daybreak piercing through slats of wood. "Easy, Brontë." She rubbed under the forelock, where the heat was trapped, the uncut mane dark as her own. She knew the danger of taking her eye off a skittish horse and pocketed Oliver's text unread. Wind rocked the walls and the horse sidestepped, a thousand pounds of dancing electrons. April whisked her outside, hooves clapping, nostrils flared to the scent of last night's storm.

Oliver had hatched a plan to bring a group of music students up to the farm for an overnight, city kids desperate for nature. He'd pitched it nonchalantly, as though it was not unusual for him to text her. She'd replied as breezily, implying she wouldn't even notice him on the property. Now, with logistics to work out, he'd been texting regularly. The previous day's messages were routine—how much milk to buy, favorite foods—but the early hour told her this one was different. She pictured him in his Brooklyn brownstone and wondered if he was texting her from bed.

Brontë swished her tail, bounce in her hooves, the promise of freedom in her large dark eyes. April unlatched the fence, and the mare bolted headlong into wind-bent grass. She took out her phone and read:

Too many details.
Easier in person.
Lunch Tuesday?

She read it twice. Alone? The two of them? Liquid memory shot up her spine. From inside the barn came a full-throated whinny, the old warmblood impatient for release. Apparently Oliver believed the day had arrived when they could meet face-to-face in a diner like two ordinary people. To say no would be to suggest she thought otherwise.

She climbed the slope to the barn. The six days she once spent in an Irish cottage with Oliver before their marriages had long since been erased by virtue of never being acknowledged. She rarely thought of him anymore, unless his songs popped up in her playlist or she happened upon a review: "The Oliver Night Trio is a trifecta of musical brilliance." People fell for Oliver, a man with fury in his fingers and ache in his voice. April understood how her younger self came to think of him as more than he was. Now she knew him for who he was: her children's uncle, a decent man. Sure, she'd meet him for coffee.

When April caught sight of Oliver alone in the booth, staring out at the busy Broadway intersection, static fizzed between her eyes. Even seated, his height was obvious, his hair as dark as when they were kids, and neatly cut for a musician. He was never one to cultivate image. He did not resemble his brother, not only because Al was denser, more muscular, with lighter hair and blunter features, but because Al did not stare wistfully out windows.

April slid in across from Oliver, spat gum into a napkin in a show of casualness, and picked up a menu. She pushed loose strands into her messy bun, deliberately haphazard. "Sorry. Late train." She did not add that she'd circled the block twice. It wasn't that being alone with Oliver made her nervous, only that she wanted him to know it didn't.

"Just got here myself." His mug half-empty, notepad elaborately doodled.

She caught a scent like smoldering wood, musky and redolent. It was one of life's abiding mysteries the way Oliver always smelled good. She probably smelled like the subway, or a speck of manure stuck in her boots. She'd purposely dressed down.

She asked how Meredith was and told him about his brother's recent trips—she had to manufacture the details. Once their spouses were firmly called to mind, she moved on to matters at hand, the students' meals and schedule, all the while avoiding Oliver's face, stirred by the familiar arc of his penmanship. Had he told Meredith about this meeting? To ask would imply there was something to tell. She sipped distractedly, aware that her pulse ought to have slowed. Things were going fine. Businesslike. Yet the longer they sat, the faster she talked. "Got to be at Grand Central by two."

"We have time," he said, that sonorous voice.

"I hope this won't be a bust. I don't know if the alpacas will even listen to the students practice. They like Lochlann's bass, but he is the one who feeds them. I've been trying to play Miles Davis for them, but they prefer Mozart."

Oliver smiled curiously.

She crossed her legs, squeezed back a tapping sensation in her groin, pebbles on a windowpane becoming harder to ignore. "You think I'm joking, but one squeaky trumpet and they'll turn up their snouts. I don't want the students to feel hurt."

"April, these kids will be beside themselves to see an animal that's not a rat."

Her name in his mouth was a dart in her chest. Normally they called each other nothing. "Anyway, I'll leave the schedule with my farmhand, Jorge. Al might even be home. And the kids can help once they're back from soccer and band."

"You won't be there?"

"There's an alpaca show in Pennsylvania that weekend," she said. "I need some help. I'm barely breaking even." Even if it weren't true, she'd find a way to be absent.

"If I'd known, I could have . . ." He halted. "We'll see each other soon enough at the Cape." He added quickly, "Phoebe can't wait to see Lochlann and Nula."

Aside from holidays, their annual Cape Cod reunions were the only time April laid eyes on Oliver, each vacation a year farther from the man she was with in Ireland. That man was gone forever. So was that woman, thank God.

"You could ask Meredith for financial advice," he said. "She doesn't know an alpaca from an aardvark, but she's a wizard with a spreadsheet."

"Thanks. I'll talk to her at the Cape. I'd do anything not to lose that place."

"Is that a danger?"

"Not if I stay the course."

He tilted his head, as if wondering which *course* she meant. "How's Loch doing?" he asked. "Phoebe told me about the suspension."

Outside the plate glass window, a woman maneuvered a stroller through a scurry of pedestrians. "I'm worried about him," April said reluctantly. "He sees it on my face. It must be hard to believe in himself when he thinks I don't. I wish I could project confidence. I'm afraid my dread is self-fulfilling."

"You had your own dark years," he said.

Through the blur of passersby, she caught glimpses of an abstract sculpture across the street, an *S* or a snake, both and neither. She thought back to that time in her life. "Dubious saved me." She looked at Oliver. "I owe that dog my life." She remembered the day, long before their marriages, when Oliver brought her to the pound, insisting she needed a dog for protection, only to have her pick out the most timid pup they had. A dubious choice, Oliver had said. "Who would have guessed he'd turn into such a trusting fellow?"

"Dooby was one of a kind." Sadness entered Oliver's eyes.

"I thought raising my kids around nature and animals would be all they needed. It's not."

"You've got a healing place there. Your kids benefit. So will the students." She sensed from his gaze that he was still thinking about Dubious.

"Why a field trip now?" she asked. "Why all of a sudden?"

"I thought it would brighten them up, but if you're having second thoughts, I'm sure we can find another—"

"It's fine," she said. "Just curious."

"And I thought it would be a nice way to see you. Most of my friends these days are mutual friends with Meredith—fun people, but I miss talking about music and books, you know, like we do at the Cape."

Something in her chest began to cave. "I enjoy that, too," she said.

He pushed his notepad aside. "Did you see the link I sent you yesterday, Hozier's music video?"

"I didn't understand what it has to do with the field trip."

"I only wanted to know what you thought," he said, suddenly animated. "That bass line—it's a heartbeat. And those lyrics. He's Yeats with a guitar."

"Your lyrics are just as good."

"I've lost my way. It's like I'm trapped in fogged glass," he said. "Hold on, did you just compliment me?"

"No," she said. "Yeats is overrated."

His mouth twitched in a suppressed smile.

"You're writing," she said. "That's what counts."

He glanced out the window. "The songs aren't coming lately. That's why I wanted to talk. I'm stuck."

Maybe he was mining nostalgia for a song. But she'd buried those memories so long ago even the bones had gone loamy. And digging was dangerous. "You're overworked," she said. "You're tired."

"No, something's out of alignment. It's like I've jammed together puzzle pieces that don't fit." He put his hand on his chest. "I don't know what to do."

"You need space, an artists' residency, or time at the cottage." She stopped. She couldn't believe she'd brought up Ireland.

"My dad sold the cottage." Oliver bowed his head. "No one was using it anymore."

"Oh," she said, sideswiped, disoriented.

"He offered it to us. Meredith and I decided it wasn't practical. I guess Al did, too."

"I guess he did." She fisted a sugar package.

"I'm sorry. My dad should have talked to you about it."

"Don't be ridiculous," she said. "I'm not his daughter."

"He considers you one."

"I couldn't have afforded it," she said. "I only wish you had it for yourself."

"Meredith's more logical than I am." He squinted. "That place was where my music found me again. It reminded me who I was."

"Are," she said. "Who you *are*."

"It's just as well," he said. "I can't get away anymore. I have no time."

"Yes you can. Rent a cabin somewhere, Vermont or Maine. Musicians need solitude. Meredith will understand. She loves you. She wants you to be happy."

He rotated a sugar packet, tapping each edge. "We had a blowup last week."

Her heart jolted. Was that what this was about? She would never have agreed to meet if she thought things were rocky with Meredith. She waved down the waitress. "Check, please."

He closed his eyes for a beat. "Tell me about you. Are you writing?"

"I don't write."

"Liar. I bet you wrote on the train coming in."

Her face heated.

"I don't believe in stories. You start buying into a narrative of yourself and you're padlocked to it."

"How about two people? Can they have a story?"

"That's the real fiction. It's never just two." She looked at her hands. She'd shredded her napkin to bits. "If I miss this train, I'll be late for the kids."

"Maybe we can do this again sometime. I don't think Meredith would mind."

April gazed at him, a question she'd harbored for years pressing against her breastbone. "Does she know?"

He shifted in his seat. "We don't talk about prior relationships," he said. "I mean, she knows we were childhood friends. She doesn't know about Ireland."

Of course, April thought. How else to explain Meredith's unabashed kindness over the years? She cleared her throat. "How about your dad? Does he know?"

His jaw twitched. "I've never told anyone," he said. "Have you?"

"No."

He visibly relaxed. "What would be the point, right? Ancient history. Besides, we were just kids," he said.

April narrowed her eyes. They'd been in their midtwenties. A gap opened in the stream of pedestrians. The sculpture was a kind of helix, she realized, loopy circular stairs without actual steps.

"What about Al?" he asked. "Would he mind that you're here?"

How to tell Oliver that he probably saw Al more than she did? "He was more annoyed by our Cold War years than our talking," she said.

He glanced out at the sculpture. "Why did we do that?"

Their eyes met. "Let's go," she said. They stepped into the current of pedestrians. "Ciao." She waved.

"Hey," he called out. "Forgot to talk about air mattresses for the students. I'll walk you to the subway." He fell in beside her. *Mattresses, my ass.* Her heart tripped with the quickness of their step, her movements a hairbreadth ahead of her thoughts, a film out of sync with its audio. His height, his stride, the lope of his gait, signature gestures she knew better than her own. Al had a quick stride, too, but shorter, jumpier. Her gaze fell to Oliver's hands, the graceful architecture of his fingers.

She was fine so long as she didn't look at him. But his attention on the traffic signal allowed her to catch the contour of his jaw, his Adam's apple, a shadow of growth he'd missed shaving. "So, can I?" he asked.

"Can you what?"

"Read your work?"

She stepped off the curb. His arm found her waist, yanked her back, a violent gust heating her face, a blast of choking air thundering so close she felt the spark of electricity, a flashing wall of metal. Oliver had hauled her back onto the curb.

"Holy shit," said a woman's voice as the roar of an engine retreated. April's purse swung from her shoulder, the leather gashed by the passing bus. Disbelieving, she touched the gouge. Oliver squeezed her waist, his eyes two full moons.

A tattooed teenager scowled. "Crazy bitch wants to splatter us."

The light changed and everyone moved except Oliver and April. A brush fire swept over her skin. She marched into the intersection, his hand not leaving her side, a sensation like hot wax. She ought to make some joke, defuse the terror, but words forsook her. What an idiot she was!

When they stepped onto the median to wait for a second light, she clutched her train ticket, the blaze of nettles fanned by oncoming cars. The light refused to turn, his hand on her waist radiating through her.

He exhaled as if he'd been holding his breath. "Did it touch you?" He examined her with apparent innocence, skimming her arm elbow to wrist, fingers on ivory keys. "Are you okay?"

No, she thought. *And no.* The light changed and people began to move again. The boom of the bus faded, her mind quieting to the blue of his eyes, crystalline inside a halo of indigo, flecked with turquoise and gold. Weightlessness shimmered through her. Maybe she was dead. The bus had gotten her, and the rush of death endorphins delivered this exquisite hologram. She only wanted to see if it was real, that feather of stubble under his chin, a place even Oliver, in all his caution, could miss.

Her touch released a sound from his throat, urgent and visceral. He reeled her against him as if from the path of the bus. It was like a choice made before birth, his eyes a pool she fell into, the cadence of his breath, the salted plum of his tongue. The kiss held her tight. He drew her in, her body opening to his. Noise in her skull fell silent, the stream of pedestrians parting and closing until the frail membrane that made April a separate being popped into evanescence. If this was death, she'd take it.

"Zowie," someone shouted. "Can I get me some a' that?"

They separated, looked at each other in astonishment, and abruptly turned toward the traffic. She tugged at her blouse. He straightened his hair. Chilled rivulets etched her bones. She thought of Al and Meredith at their jobs nearby, Phoebe in school, her children soon at the bus stop. At the subway entrance she whirled around to face Oliver. "Never mind," she said. "Just. Never. Mind."

"Look, I don't know what you're thinking, but I have a good marriage. The last twelve years of my life—that's not some kind of sham."

"What *I'm* thinking?"

"I mean, if this was how you felt—"

"No, I don't! I don't feel!"

"Good," he said. "Because neither do I." He cupped his hands around her face as if to profess emotion or wring her neck. "This can never happen again. Do you understand?"

"Me? You're the one who—"

He kissed her, slowly this time, the train ticket slipping from her fingers, her hands finding the ropes of his back. The first kiss she could blame on impulse. This one had drive, desire spiked with guilt, defiance, long-repressed rage. He touched his forehead to hers. "April," he said, "I want you to know I have never, for one minute, forgiven you."

She shoved him back. "Go to hell!" she screamed, shaking. He turned into the crowd and was gone. Passersby veered around her, their raised brows suggesting what she already knew. He hadn't done it alone.

12

Sunday

April cubes ripe honeydew, the dining room aglow with daybreak. She enjoys her ritual of preparing fruit for the family each morning, infusing each slice with affection. Pitch pines dance in the window frame, colors incandescent, trunks darkened by last night's rain. A paper sign on the table reads T-Minus 6 Days with a ballpoint drawing of wedding bells, no doubt Phoebe's handiwork. Nula would have added fangs. April sets the bowl on the table, honeydew perfuming the air.

On the sill over the kitchen sink, a ring holder nests a wedding band she recognizes as Hal's, worn for decades through widowerhood. In six days, he'll have a new one. Despite its age, it's shinier than April's ring, whose gold plating has begun to peel off, revealing the cheap metal below. It's surprising it's lasted this long.

Outside, she stakes a delphinium toppled by last night's deluge and tops off the bicycle tires with air. Pumping a wheel, she glances through the drape of her hair to find Oliver staring from the kitchen window, putting a cube of fruit in his mouth. She feels it dissolve on his tongue, flooding his mouth with sweetness. Meredith appears and he turns, offering her a chunk.

Last in the line of cyclers, April stares at Meredith's pear-shaped butt, Oliver's slim back—a handsome couple. Hal has stayed home, preferring to enjoy the more strenuous excursions vicariously. April doesn't mind being a third wheel to Oliver and Meredith. She likes to watch their interactions, to hear how normal married couples talk.

The rail trail traverses marshlands and overpasses, the shade of overhanging trees opening to stretches of sunlight. Pedestrians dash out of the way of Lochlann and Phoebe as they pull ahead. Nula hammers the pedals of an outgrown kiddie bike. Meredith is talking into her headset. April recognizes the pattern of her business calls, beginning with allegation—defense via offense—and only rarely ending in concession. She once asked if Meredith found these conversations traumatizing. She laughed. "Sister, it's called negotiation."

"Call me soon as you know." Meredith hangs up. "You won't believe it: Dixon says there's another case. Some lady claims our Ear Blossoms burned her ear. Maybe the first woman put it all over social media, and this one's jumping on the bandwagon." Oliver appears ready to respond when Meredith's phone rings again. She listens, curses. "Jesus. The woman went to the ER. This one's documented. She's got a burn in her ear. I have to go back to the house. Give me the car keys." They brake.

April whizzes past them. "Good luck, Mere," she calls.

Oliver catches up and pedals alongside April. "Every day a new crisis," he says.

"Poor Meredith," she says. The energy between them prickles. Nula presses ahead, though Phoebe and Loch are out of sight, possibly at the ice-cream shop by now. A wild turkey steps onto the path, head cocked indignantly, and gives a fierce *kee-kee* as April and Oliver veer to either side. The clucking fades. The comfortable silences April and Oliver earned the last few years are once again rivers to cross, stone to log, hoping none will give way. She wishes they could be at ease. Their pedaling falls into sync, and for an instant they are kids again, pumping uphill and careening down, wind in her hair. They pull up to an intersection. She looks at Oliver straddling his bike. He gives her a curious glance. The light changes and they are in motion again, swerving around potholes.

On the crowded porch of the Chocolate Sparrow, Lochlann sits alone, sweaty and windblown, eyes strikingly blue in the sunlight. "They're in the bathroom," he says. "People are staring me down for these seats."

"I'll take orders," Oliver says. "I can already guess what Phoebe wants—raspberry sherbet in a waffle cone."

Phoebe rushes toward them, breathless. "Aunt April, Nula needs you. Last stall."

In the bathroom, April hears muffled whimpering. "Honey, what is it?"

Nula's voice is thick. "I thought it wouldn't happen till I was thirteen."

"Sweetheart. Do you want me to come in?"

"This is so stupid. Why do girls say they can't wait to get it? It's the worst."

"Don't worry. I packed your swim shorts. Did it go through? I have a pad."

Nula begins to sob. April leans on the door. "Sweetheart," she says, "let me in."

By the time they return to the table, the others are eating ice cream. Raw and puffy, Nula's face looks younger than her twelve years.

"You sick?" Lochlann asks.

"Shut up," Nula says.

"We got you hot fudge," Phoebe says.

Nula pushes it away.

"Loch, let's go pick out some candy to bring back for tonight," says Oliver.

"But I'm not done eating."

"Bring it into the shop. C'mon."

Nula bolts up and follows Lochlann inside, despite Oliver's attempt to give them time alone. Phoebe goes with them. Oliver sits back down beside April.

"She doesn't want me to talk about it," she says.

"Of course," he says.

Below the porch, a pigtailed girl wails, a ball of ice cream at her feet, empty cone in her fist. A beagle stretches its leash to lick up the melt. "I was upset the first time, too," April says. "I wanted to stay a kid. I still do."

Oliver looks at her gently. "Here, I should've ordered you something." He holds a spoonful toward her. April opens her mouth and the spoon slips in. Her blood quickens, flavor gorging her tongue. She closes her eyes, lightheaded, plummeting downhill, Oliver pedaling beside her, hearts pumping. Past and present fuse. The spoon shivers, her tongue working ice cream out of the hollow, quivering against the steady pressure of his hand. He withdraws it slowly, wide eyed. She swallows, cool sweetness slipping down her throat. Inside the curve of plastic, a speck of chocolate remains. Oliver brings it to his mouth, his tongue long and dimpled, and sucks the dollop off. She barely breathes. Beneath the railing, the beagle has licked the pavement clean.

"Excuse me." Two young men stand over them, not quite holding hands, nervously touching each other's fingers. "Can we, uh, ask what flavor that is?"

Oliver clears his throat. "Amaretto Chocolate."

They glance at each other and hurry to the counter.

April collects herself. "I'd better check on Nula."

"Right," Oliver says. "I think I'll stay here and finish this."

13

April washes vegetables as the kitchen fills with dusk, her sister-in-law's voice in the next room alternately plaintive and argumentative. They have the house to themselves, the others having gone to the bay side to see Beryl's place. During a pause between calls, she comes into the kitchen. "April, Dixon and I could get sued. This crazy customer might sue us."

April puts her arms around her, a light coconut scent.

"Pray it's an idle threat. Maybe they're just gunning for free stuff." She rakes her hair into a short ponytail. "I heard about the bike ride this morning. Poor Nula."

"Womanhood's a bitch," April says. "No pun intended."

Meredith's phone buzzes. "Shit." She exits the room.

In the slanting light a hummingbird hovering at the feeder turns to stare in at April. The eggplant in her hands slips into the sink, cool water running through her fingers. The bird pivots right and left to take her in with one eye and the other, its emerald feathers shiny as wet paint. "Meredith," she calls. "Come look."

Meredith returns, but the bird has vanished. "I think I'm going to puke."

"Why don't you turn off your phone for ten minutes? Take a walk?"

"You know I hate bugs." She sits miserably. "Have a drink with me, April. The way Oliver has shoehorned the schedule, we'll never get our girls' night out. He's gotten worse, don't you think? Why is he so restless?"

"I'm married to Al. You're asking me about restless?" She uncorks the wine.

"Actually, I was eyeing Al's scotch."

"I won't tell." She takes out a wineglass and a scotch glass. "I don't do the hard stuff anymore."

"In God's name, why not?" Meredith takes a sip.

"I've told you. I busted my quota of alcohol-related disasters by the time I was twenty-five. Al does know how to buy the good stuff, though."

"Wow, this is smooth. No wonder he drinks so much of it."

April chuckles awkwardly.

"Fine, I'm taking the plunge." She turns off her phone. "Ten minutes. Set a timer."

"You're better in crisis than anyone I know. You're going to figure this out."

"Maybe if I were at the office. Oliver and I had a huge blowup over it. I was willing to compromise, said I could come for the weekend. But you know how he is about his father. It's irrational."

"Al doesn't like to disappoint Hal, either."

"We all love Hal, but come on," she says. "I need to be in the office. My partner's the only one who gets it. Plus, the internet here is crap. Why won't he get a better satellite dish?"

"Leave if you need to. Hal will understand."

"But the wedding! I'd have to come back at the end of the week. If only I'd known, I could have stayed home and driven up later. Just kill me now."

April puts her hand on Meredith's arm.

"Why are they getting married, anyway? Finding love late in life— I'm all for that. But marriage? Honestly, who would go through with it if not for kids and taxes?"

April laughs. "It's not all bad, is it? Yours, I mean."

She takes a sip, licks her lips. "Here's my philosophy. Marriage should be a lease, not a mortgage. You sign up for a five- or ten-year stint—twenty, if you have kids—then you go to a yearly renewable. That way you never take the other person for granted. You have to work to keep them. Seriously, if our lease were up next year, do you think Oliver would've insisted I come?"

"He wouldn't enjoy the week without you."

"He projects that Mr. Nice Guy thing, but he's quite dictatorial in his slippery way. You should see how he wrangles the Phoebe decisions from me."

April sips her wine, woody and dry. "Speaking from the other extreme, at least he's involved."

"They look like opposites, but the Night brothers have more in common than you think—enormous egos, for one. Oliver hides his better than Al. Of course, I've got enough ego for ten people, but at least I own it. Oliver won't admit his."

"I don't know, Meredith. He seems to live for you and Phoebe."

She sighs. "He's an amazing dad, that's true."

"And he loves you."

"Which is not the same as understanding me."

"You know what Chekhov says. If you're afraid of loneliness, don't marry."

"Ha! I have other people in my life who get me. That's enough. One person can't be the whole zip drive. You put that expectation on a marriage, you doom it." She pours another splash. "You get him, though, don't you."

"You kidding? My marriage is a Rubik's Cube with the colors peeled off."

"I meant Oliver. You get Oliver."

She fidgets. "Well, we've known each other forever. Guess that counts for something."

"Sweet that you two had coffee last month. Oliver needs more friends. He's all work."

April's gut flutters. "We met over work," she says. "The field trip."

"Dixon understands me," Meredith says, "but you can't marry someone like that. It's too much of an echo chamber."

"Guess you chose wisely."

"Don't get me wrong, Oliver's incredible. My friends drool over him. Half their husbands have sugar on the side. Half my friends do, too. Not Oliver, though; he'd never cheat."

April takes a gulp.

"Sorry, that was insensitive. Al is incurable, isn't he. Why do you put up with it?"

Outside, the feeder rocks back and forth, empty. "It would be hard to leave this."

"That's it? You're married to the Nights?" To Meredith, it must seem like nothing—this annual vacation, Christmas and Thanksgiving. To April, it's her fingerhold on family.

"To be honest, I try not to think about it."

"Al does give you those soulful eyes, though. Like the way he looked at you when he came in last night. That was intense."

"Hard to notice that sort of thing when you're pissed at someone."

"At least he doesn't seem bored with you," Meredith says.

"He doesn't see me enough to be bored."

"Maybe there's something to that. Open marriages can work."

"It's not an open marriage," April says. The room wavers. She pushes away her glass. "I wonder if you actually see how much Oliver cares for you."

"But there's always a little part of him that's absent, you know? Hypocritical of me to say since I'm the most distracted person on the planet, but here's the thing: I may give him divided attention, but he gets all of my heart. I get his full attention, but ninety percent of his heart. The other ten? Never laid eyes on it. I'm worried it belongs to that first fiancée of his. Bernadette."

"No." April pulls the cork from the bottle. "The missing ten is probably exhaustion."

"I'm not talking lately. I mean since day one. He's always held something back. But if I call him on it, he gets flustered because even he doesn't know what it is."

"You just described the entire human race. Only dogs give their whole hearts."

She laughs, yanks a tissue from the box. "You can't understand because Al's the opposite. So what if you only get five percent of his dick? You get a hundred percent of his heart."

"I don't buy that at all," April says. "I believe in a one-to-one dick-to-heart correlation."

Meredith's eyes widen. They burst into laughter, Meredith wiping her face, April holding her stomach.

"You realize that doesn't hold up." Meredith daubs her cheeks. "My parents have a faithful, joyless marriage. Who wants that? On the other hand, look at Frida Kahlo and Diego Rivera. Just because they both had bottomless libidos doesn't mean they didn't love each other."

April's smile drains. "Have you actually looked at her paintings?"

"I'm not saying they were happy. I'm saying, hands down, they owned each other's souls. Oliver's got mine, but I don't think I've ever completely—" She presses the tissue to the corners of her eyes so as not to ruin her makeup. "I hope they don't walk in right now. It's stress. This stupid allegation." The timer chimes. "Ten minutes already?"

"Ignore it," April says. "Give yourself ten more."

"Can't do that to Dixon." She kisses April's cheek. "April, you're the best."

From the kitchen April hears the girls gallop up the porch steps, Oliver greeting Meredith. She glances out the window for signs of Al and Lochlann. Oliver comes in and washes his hands. "They stayed to test out Beryl's boat," he says.

It unnerves her that he guessed her thought. "Just the two of them?"

"Yep."

"Do they know how to operate it?"

"More or less. Beryl demonstrated." He dries his hands. "You should've come. Her place is right on the bay—private dock, manicured lawn. Probably worth more than this place despite the acreage here."

Her stomach plummets. "Your dad's not planning to move, is he?"

"They're not saying."

"What about his sunrise walks to the cliff? What about the bluebirds?" Her heart constricts. "What if Beryl moves here and decides to bulldoze the meadow for a tennis court?"

"That would be soul crushing," he says. "Al would be thrilled."

"How much of a compromiser is your dad?" she asks.

"Too much." Oliver rubs his wedding band. "Not as bad as me, though."

She decides not to touch this.

"Meredith wants me to ask if they're keeping their assets separate. She says Al and I can lose this place if my dad passes first." He rolls up his sleeves. "I won't ask, of course. It's his business." He picks up a zucchini.

"It's not your night to cook," April says.

"Nothing better to do."

He's showered and changed since the bike ride. April catches the scent of aftershave. Her peeler squeaks against the skin of the eggplant. Beneath the gloss of purple, the meat is cream colored and tender. Since New York, she hears things differently in his presence, feels everything more acutely, even her blouse moving against her skin when she breathes. Only now does she realize the radio is on, a susurration of voices. The Coast Guard is searching off Nantucket for a fisherman swept from his vessel. The setting sun breaks through branches, bathing them in sienna light. A splash of iridescence hovers at the hummingbird feeder. She feels Oliver's nearness, an intoxicant breeze sifting her clothes. "Did you notice?" She gestures toward the ring holder. "He wore it longer in widowerhood than he did in marriage."

Oliver touches his heart. She looks down to see she has involuntarily mirrored him, her fingers wetting her blouse.

When there is still no word from Al and Lochlann by nightfall, April curls in a chair, straightening the pages of Al's manuscript, bargaining with her panic. *Too soon to worry,* she tells herself. Oliver picks up a novel he's been reading.

"I loved that book," Beryl says. "What part are you up to?"

"She just danced with Vronsky for the first time," Oliver says.

"Mommy read it, too," Nula says. "She said it wrung her out like a dishrag."

"You two read the same books?" Beryl asks.

"Just a coincidence," April says.

"It's nice to read together," Beryl says. "To be in the same world at the same time."

"Mommy's writing a novel, too," Nula says.

"Oh?" says Hal. Oliver closes his book, leaning in.

"Not really." April harpoons Nula with a glance.

"I'd love to read it," says Beryl.

"It's nothing." April riffles through Al's manuscript, having lost her place.

14

April takes the fish out to the grill, a shimmery salmon snatched from the ocean the previous day. She pictures Al and Lochlann trying to find their way back to the dock in darkness.

"Did you text your brother?" Hal asks Nula as they sit for dinner.

"They can't get texts if they're still out on the boat," says Beryl.

"But it's been too long," says Phoebe.

"Probably enjoying the stars," Hal says, his voice dry.

Meredith sits down. "This is the most vile day of my life." Oliver soothes her arm.

"Worst case scenario, you go bankrupt," says Hal. "Not a tragedy."

April glances at her watch. Al normally has a good sense of direction, but open water changes everything. Plus, the Lochlann factor.

"But the bank loan." Meredith moans. "The apartment."

Phoebe halts, fork halfway to her mouth. "We're going to lose the apartment?"

"No, sweetheart." Oliver pats her hand. "Definitely not."

"You took out a personal loan on the business?" Beryl asks. "With your apartment as collateral?"

Hal taps the back of her hand, some sort of signal between them.

"But putting up personal collateral for a business loan is—"

"Banks don't hand you three million dollars for nothing," Oliver says. "Obviously they have complete faith in Meredith."

"Three million?" Phoebe puts her fork down.

"Angel," Meredith says, "it's not like we'd owe that back. That's what bankruptcy means. They clean your slate."

"Why are we talking about bankruptcy?" Oliver says. "Two customer complaints can't bring you down."

"Look at the Tylenol case," says Hal. "People died and the company survived."

"Oh my God." Meredith squeezes her eyes shut.

"No one's dying," Oliver says.

April shudders. The empty seats at the table seem to fill the room. "I wonder if we should call the Coast Guard."

"Where would we go if we lost the apartment?" Phoebe asks.

"Nothing will happen to the apartment," Oliver says. "Get that out of your head."

"Every start-up has bumps in the road," Beryl says. "Your mom's earpieces are bound to be a hit, Phoebe."

Meredith bows her head. Oliver clenches his fist.

A crush of gravel sounds from the driveway. April's rush of relief is quickly supplanted by dread. Car doors slam, and the screen door bursts open. Lochlann tears through the living room and up the stairs. Al comes in leisurely and hangs up his windbreaker. "Smells divine." His eyes have the strained look of sobriety.

"What happened?" April asks.

"Good ole father–son time." He sits down with a biting smile. "Whoever thought that up is brilliant."

April's face burns.

"What happened?" Hal asks.

"You want to know what, Dad?" His jaw tightens. "Your grandson got suspended from summer school and can't apologize for it. Caught in an empty classroom with—"

"That's enough," April says.

"By the time I was fifteen, I had two jobs, bought my own mini-bike. He's never even had a paper route."

"Daddy," Nula says, "that's not a thing anymore."

"Did you get lost?" April asks.

"Of course not. I never get lost."

"Why can't you ever admit—"

"Why can't you admit you coddle him? I could get him a job as a ball boy in Citi Field, and instead he's farting around in the barn. He's fifteen and hasn't worked a day—"

"I don't have a job, either," Phoebe says. "I'm fifteen."

Everyone turns to look at her.

"That's different," Al says gently. "We all know how responsible you are, Phoebe. You play soccer. You're a math wizard. You take AP US History."

"Lochlann took that class, too. He got a four," Phoebe says. "And he plays the bass better than anyone I know. And by the way, I suck at math."

Silence envelops the table, Phoebe's face crimson.

Al turns to April. "I thought he dropped that class."

She puts her head in her hands.

"He's taken several AP classes," Hal says. "Right, April?"

"What's the point of this?" Beryl says. "Would he be a lesser person if he weren't in AP? Honestly!"

"Can I remind everyone that the walls are thin in this house?" April says.

"Second that," says Meredith.

"Who cares if he hears us? This is what I mean," Al says. "Always protecting him. The last thing he needs is babying. He's got to quit taking up new instruments, start earning some dough."

"Fine." Phoebe shoves back her chair. "Why don't me and Loch drop out and get jobs? Then I can help pay back the loan so we don't lose the apartment."

"Phoebe, don't get fresh," Meredith says.

She runs upstairs. Meredith calls after her, but Oliver motions to let her go. "This may be news to you all," he says, "but the last thing you should bring up with an adopted kid is the idea of losing her home."

Nula fidgets.

"Sweetie," Hal says, "why don't you go look up a movie for us to watch later?"

Nula closes her sketchbook and brings her plate to the kitchen. Hal turns to Al.

"Dad, I don't want a sermon."

"I see. So you only like to give them."

"I know what you're going to say. But I can only be the father I am. I can't be anyone else."

"And the person you are—that's fixed in stone?"

"Now you sound like April and her pop psych books. You honestly think people change? I don't see evidence for it. And why should I if this is who I am?"

"That's one way of going through life."

"Why can't you trust me? I owe it to him to apply pressure. All I'm asking is that he be half as responsible as I was."

"I do remember your minibike and paper route," Hal says. "I also remember your mother beside herself with fright for most of your adolescence because you'd come home late or not at all, and sometimes when you did, it was worse than if you didn't."

Al folds his hands on the table.

"And I remember girls' fathers calling the house to say they weren't allowed to see you."

Al cranes to peer into the kitchen, Nula eavesdropping behind the doorframe. She goes outside, letting the screen door bounce.

"I get it, Dad," Al says. "But you've got to admit that was different. I may have been sneaking out, but at least I was having a good time. He's sullen and rude and—excuse me, Beryl—so fucking arrogant."

"So," Hal says, "Lochlann thinks he knows everything at fifteen, but in your case you actually did."

"That's not what I said. Why is everyone defending him?" He turns to April. "What have you been saying to them?" She jolts.

"Al," Hal says, "*April* is private about your kids."

Al wags his head, looks at Beryl. "Sure you want to join this family?"

She folds her arms under her bosom. "If you didn't care about each other so much, this house would be a lot quieter and a lot duller."

One by one, people get up to scrape their plates. April glances at her remaining bit of salmon. She isn't hungry but doesn't want to throw away something plucked from life for her. She puts it into her mouth, moist and salted, and dumps the mutilated scales.

"April," Hal says, unsmiling, "it was splendid."

"Don't do the dishes," she says. "We'll clean up."

Al shovels the rest of the fish into his mouth and walks over to the television. The Sox are playing the Yankees. He watches standing up, so close he has to move his head side to side to follow the action. April goes to him and glances back at the dirty dishes.

"Right, my night."

Beryl wipes down the table, and Hal puts leftovers in containers.

"Please leave everything," April calls out.

Al pours himself a scotch and sniffs it.

"If you leave it for later, your father's fiancée will do it," April says.

"I said I'd get to it." He keeps his eyes on the television.

She tosses his manuscript on the coffee table. When she retreats to the kitchen, she hears running water. Through the doorway, Phoebe and Lochlann stand shoulder to shoulder at the sink. Oliver must have sent them. Phoebe hands Lochlann a plate, and he slips it into the drainer. From where April stands, Lochlann's hood conceals his face, but Phoebe gazes up at him, listening with full attention. Hal comes up beside April to see what she is looking at. "She's got Oliver's expressions."

Hal takes out his phone and snaps a picture.

April brings out the trash, leaving behind the clamor of the television. A whoosh of breeze envelops her, a dense river of stars gleaming above. "Nula," she calls out in the direction of the tree house. "No clouds."

Nula emerges from darkness onto the porch, shivering. April takes a towel from the railing and wraps it around them, hugging Nula from behind as they scan the sky for meteors. "How's your period? Heavy?"

"How am I supposed to know what heavy is? Two pads so far."

"Sometimes the first one's light."

"What was your first one like?"

"My mom took it harder than me. I think it made her feel old. She didn't call it a period, though. She called it 'your friend.' Every time I got a little moody, she'd ask, 'Do you have your friend?' She had a euphemism for everything."

"*My enemy* is more like it."

"It doesn't have to be that, either. Whatever relationship you decide to have with it, that's what it will be."

In the distance, a wave booms. April pictures the tide washing in along the endless beaches of the Outer Cape, drenching the sand, etching away fragile cliffs. Last year's hurricane took three houses; this year's nor'easter, two more. Over time, roads will dissolve. Lighthouses twice moved back will finally be swallowed. From inside the house drifts the sound of the piano.

"Did you get along with your mom?"

"No," April says, "but I knew she loved me."

"How about Daddy and Loch?"

"Teenage boys and their dads—you know how it goes."

"Does that mean I'll hate you soon?" Nula asks.

"Maybe for a while. I'll try not to take it personally."

"Is that why Daddy doesn't come home anymore? 'Cause Loch hates him?"

"No, honey," April says. "Daddy's been busy with work."

Nula bristles, too old for sugarcoating.

"The truth is, I don't know," April says. "He has his reasons."

"His cough sounds bad," Nula says. "Why won't he stop smoking?"

"You've heard of Stockholm syndrome, when a hostage bonds with their kidnapper? Addiction is like that. You think the thing that hijacked you is on your side, so if a SWAT team comes to your rescue, you shoot 'em."

"But that's like saying the cigarettes decide. It's Daddy doing it to himself."

"Our minds do all kinds of things to keep us feeling small and numb," April says, "because if we had any idea how big we really are, it might blow our circuits."

"Is that why you don't send your book out?" Nula asks. "To stay numb and small?"

"What?"

"Didn't you say that lady in your writing group wants you to send it to her agent? You always tell *me* to do brave stuff."

April hugs her to steady her own tremor. "You're honest, Nulie. I admire that."

"So will you send it to her?"

April stares at the sky as if the answer is up there. Nula gives up and goes inside. In the next instant, a fireball streaks over the treetops.

April goes in. Soon she'll have to get into bed with the porcupine now watching the game with the sound muted. The adults are lounging around the coffee table, absorbed in books or devices. April settles in an armchair and leafs through Al's manuscript, hoping to hate it, wanting to tell him his writing is as insufferable as he is, that Lochlann's insolence comes from him. But the story moves her, saddens and enrages her, vibrant young men who joined the NFL only to have their nimble brains pounded into dementia. Autopsies show reductions in brain weight, atrophy of the brain stem and cerebellum, neuron loss, classic CTE. Al will surely get backlash on this book from his own following, but he's writing it anyway. She looks up at him, his face slack. How can the same man defend these athletes so eloquently only to dismantle his own son at the dinner table? She flips back to the dedication page. *For April.*

After standing for five innings straight, downing more than the usual drinks needed to shake out his unease, Al sits on the couch beside

Nula. April sees by the glaze of his eyes that he is only superficially engaged in the game. "Tell me when you think they should go to the bullpen," he says to Nula. "I want to know if you call it same as the manager."

"Not yet. Only gave up one run." She puts down her sketchbook, burrows closer. "When are you getting me deGrom's autograph?" she asks.

"Soon." He nestles his drink on a coaster and tilts his head to hers, their cinnamon hair blending. For the balance of the inning, they hoot and groan in unison.

In the kitchen, April finds her father-in-law standing at the window. "Hal, you should go to bed. We're exhausting, aren't we?"

"Only one of you." He turns to her. "Al is in a bad way. I can see that much."

"He's in his own way, like usual," April says.

"It's detrimental to the kids, all this turmoil."

"I'm sorry," April says. "We'll try to—"

"That's not what I'm asking," Hal says. "I don't want you to pretend. I want to understand. All these years, and still I don't know how to be the father he needs."

"Funny, that's how I feel about Lochlann. How to be the parent he needs?"

"But you are," Hal says. "I wish Al would treat you better. If Avila were here, she'd be heartsick."

"Thank you, Hal, but Al does love me, you know."

"Yes," he says, "but love isn't the whole picture, is it."

15

April sits on her stump in the dark, the circle of tupelos swishing around her. Through branches she glimpses windowlight from the house on the hill. One day down. Two, if she counts their arrival day. Her son and husband are still alive. She tells herself to be grateful. When she left the house, Hal and Al were speaking privately in the kitchen. Al has always wanted his father's approval, though he finds strange ways to seek it. She remembers the day he called Hal to break the news of their so-called wedding. She had been sitting cross-legged in their Vegas hotel room, unraveling loose threads from her nightshirt. "If this is just temporary, why are we telling your dad?" she asked.

"All the more reason to enjoy it while it lasts," Al said.

"He'll tell Oliver," April said.

He dialed, stretching the phone cord, an uncharacteristic quaver in his voice. "Dad, you'll never guess what happened yesterday. I got married." Through the plate glass window, garish neon lights blinked red and green on Al's face. "To April," he said. "Me and April got married." Above the headboard, a tacky print of clashing drunken letters formed the cockeyed word LOVE. "April, Dad. April Simone. Oliver's friend." April rocked, hugging herself. "It's all good," he said. "But if you want to say one of your novenas, that's okay by me."

Three weeks later, April pulled into the driveway of Hal's Long Island home. Digging in the yard, he lifted his head when he spotted the Jeep. It had been months since she'd last seen him, a new touch of gray at his temples. He dropped the shovel and came over, surprise on his face. "What a delight," he said. "Let me rinse my hands. I was burying a robin. If only my neighbor would keep his cat indoors." He went to the hose and patted his hands on his pants.

"I should have told you I was coming," she said.

"Nonsense. I like surprises. Mostly." He glanced at her wedding band. "Forgive me, I had no idea you and Al were even dating. Is he with you?" he asked, though the answer was obvious. "I mean, congratulations. I should have said that first."

"Your garden is more beautiful than ever." She walked around the flower bed, buttery lilies bobbing beside blue salvia and purple alyssum, buds aglow with honeyed sunlight.

"Avila had more skill than I do," he said.

They walked around to the back. In the sky hung the tall, deformed skeleton of the apple tree she had climbed as a kid. Her heart constricted.

"They're not long lived," Hal said. "I've been trying to get the boys over to help me cut it down."

Her eyes burned. She recognized the thick, level branch where she and Oliver had hung out. Avila would call them inside, offer macaroons and milk, and gingerly comb out the knots in April's hair. The gentleness of her touch put April into a trance, meditatively still, savoring the sensation of being cared for. "What happened to your eye?" Avila would ask. "How did you get that bruise on your arm?"

"The monkey bars," was April's stock answer, and Avila would cast Hal an incensed glance.

April touched the dried trunk, bark crumbling in her hand.

"Come, have tea." Hal opened the back door. "Daughter-in-law. I still have to wrap my head around it."

She colored, adjusting her scarf. They sat at his kitchen table, sunlight pouring through the window while the kettle heated. Avila's absence filled the room. April stared at a wall of old photos. She and her brother were in one, along with other neighborhood kids. "I always loved this house," she said.

"The house loved you back," Hal said. "How's the apartment? Is there enough room for both of you?"

"It's great." She rotated her ring. "Everything's great."

"Tell me, did you get married in a church? Maybe a photograph will help it sink in."

"Graceland Wedding Chapel." She blushed. "Wax Elvis as our witness."

Hal winced.

"It was only a ceremony. We don't actually have the license yet."

"I'm sure it will arrive in the mail. The important thing is that you stood across from each other. You made vows." He paused. "Right?"

"'With this ring, I thee wed.'" She looked at her hand. "Except we borrowed the rings from the people in line behind us. Got this one yesterday."

His brow furrowed. "How is Al treating you?"

"Al's good to me," she said. "Al's amazing." She wrung her scarf. "The thing is, Hal, apparently, it looks like—I mean I am. Pregnant."

He leaped up, clapped his hands. "Goodness. So soon?"

She wound the silk around her fists like a choke hold as the kettle began to scream.

He turned off the burner. "My first grandchild. I can't believe it."

She lowered her head, scarf yoked behind her neck. He poured the tea shakily and placed it before her. "Mothers get frustrated. Mothers get mad," she said. "Who knows what I'll do?"

"I do," he said. "You'll be as loving and caring as you've always been."

"Some people aren't meant to be parents."

"That's true. You're not one of them."

"You don't know the real me."

"I saw you take care of your brother and grandmother. Actions don't lie." He touched the loose end of the scarf. "What does Al say?"

"He's absorbing it."

He soothed her hand. "April, why are you telling me this when you know how I feel about—"

"I'm keeping it." She glanced at the wall of photos, a backyard shot, she and Oliver grasping hands, spinning so fast the image blurred. "I just don't know how."

The force of his relief stirred vapor from his cup.

She picked up a key chain that had been left on the table. "Hal, I know this is unfair to ask, but if Al and I mess this up—"

"You won't. And yes, I'll be here one hundred percent for any grandchild."

The leather key chain was embossed with the word ON, as if announcing the purpose of the fob.

"Please try to have a fraction of the faith in yourself we have in you," he said. "Have you told Oliver? I'm sure he'll be a big support. You two were always so close."

She looked away, clenching the keys.

"Stay awhile. Have lunch with us."

She glanced at Avila's portrait. "It's so sweet how you still refer to her as here."

"I meant Oliver and me."

She squinted, mind scrambling. "Oliver went back to Baltimore," she said, "to see Bernadette."

"No, he's been home two weeks now. If you stay you can see pictures from his months in Ireland. I have some leek soup I can heat up."

She stood, knocking the tea into its saucer. "Oliver's here?"

"Until he moves into his new apartment. He's out signing the lease right now."

She looked at the keys in her fist. ON. Oliver Night.

"Parking's a nightmare. He took the train."

She stepped back from the key chain as if from a hand grenade. "I need to get home before rush hour."

"It's Saturday, dear. And it's noon." He followed her to the door. As she accelerated down the street, she heard the trail of his voice: "What about your tea?"

A gust stirs the tupelos, eddying leaf litter in a circle around her. The houselights are out except Al's. She can't stay on this stump forever.

16

On the small rolltop desk, Al's laptop is open to his manuscript, cluttered with tracked changes. He must have gone to the bathroom. Beside the laptop is the hard copy April marked up. She edits better with a pen in her hand. She sees he's been using her suggestions. She puts on her nightshirt and gets into bed. Maybe she can be asleep before he returns. But the door pops open. Al takes off his shirt and unzips his pants.

"Can you close the door?" she asks. He has a habit of never quite sealing things—jars, toothpaste, relationships.

He shuts it and strips down to his boxers, rubs his exhausted face. She sees by his demeanor that his team has lost.

"Look." She tries not to sound rehearsed. "I do not talk about you behind your back."

"I know you don't," he says.

"Lochlann's in trouble. He needs us. That doesn't give you permission to take him down in front of the whole family."

"You're saying he's like this because of me?"

"No, but you're not helping. He needs consequences, not lectures." She wishes he would turn to look at her. "What happened on the boat?"

"He hates my guts. It's irreconcilable."

"He's fifteen. It's his job to hate our guts. It's not our job to hate him back."

"He used to like me, didn't he?" he says. "We used to be good."

"You can't disappear for weeks and then expect him to cozy up to you."

"Why did we buy the farm to begin with?" Al asks. "Why didn't we all stay in Manhattan?"

"That apartment was too small for all the people in our marriage."

He looks into his hands, the ringless finger. Oliver's and Meredith's voices come through the wall, muffled and indecipherable. "Here's the real question: Did you choose me to keep him in your life, or did I choose you to stick it to him?"

She stands, reels on him.

"Shh," he says before she opens her mouth.

"Convenient, isn't it, to make this about him. But when it comes to you and me, there's only one of us who shows up."

He looks at the floor.

"I chose you. If we don't start there, we're nowhere."

He exhales heavily. "Bum deal for you."

"Get off your pity horse." She plucks the manuscript off the desk and sits beside him. "What about my comments, you dumb ox?"

"You're still my best editor," he says. "I see you didn't mess with the dedication. That may be the only line I got right." He takes her hand. "I do appreciate you, you know."

"Al, listen to me," she says. "Reading about all those NFL brains makes me worried about yours."

He drops her hand.

"The booze, I mean." Her voice wobbles. She's said it. She breached the line.

"Christ almighty." He leaps up as if stabbed. "Am I not allowed to enjoy my own vacation?"

"I'm talking long term. Look what happened to my father."

"Jesus Christ, now you're comparing me to your father?" He stands over her. "This is a new low."

"I'm worried about you."

"Spare me." He paces, eyes calcifying.

"You have to admit, you're not setting yourself up for a long life."

He glares down at her. "Hey, the present is all we got—isn't that what they say?"

"Which means you treat it as sacred."

"So now we've resorted to new age mumbo jumbo. That's great, darling. That's swell." He turns on her, face snarled, a torrent of splintering hail from his mouth, each word sharper until he is shouting. "Is this what you've been telling them? That I'm a drunk? That I've screwed up my own kids? You have the gall to embarrass me in front of my own father?" Each syllable a blade of airborne debris. She wants to turn away, curl up, yet forces herself to face him, unblinking. But the eyes—two glinting shards—are not his. He's been replaced. "This is priceless, April. You, who run the kids off the road, threaten to kill them, stand here accusing me. That's right; Loch told me everything on the boat. I've got it all on voice memo."

"Why do you record private conversations?" Her voice quivers. "Are you building a case against me?"

His mouth is moving but she can no longer decode the words, only their thrust, the clenched face, the explosion of sound disassembling her like a wind tunnel. Her father's voice. He shoves his legs through his pants and opens the door. "This is why it'll never work, April." His voice booms through the house. "This is why you drive me fucking crazy!" The slam of the door rattles the walls.

His footsteps descend. The clink of a glass. The hum of the television. She dresses, hands trembling, her body a shredded leaf that whisks down the stairs and out the back door, so light she hardly casts a footfall. An assault of stars teems down through light-years of space, passing through the universe unhindered until her retina stops it. The tupelo grove isn't far enough. She stumbles down the woodland trail toward the ocean, breaking through shrubbery, unsure of her way in the dark but following the sound of the surf.

For an instant she thinks she hears Dubious pattering behind. The dog has been gone for over a decade, yet a sudden longing pressures her ribs. During her last trimester with Lochlann, when she was too big to accompany Al on his trips, Dooby's sweetly tilted face helped her claw out of bed each morning as if from a grave. No matter the sleet on the windowpane, slush blackening the sidewalks, Dooby's torque at the end of the leash hauled her into daylight. Strangers smiled. Dubious always got looks. "A dog for the movies," Nana once said, "and I don't mean *Lassie*." By the third block, the cold on April's cheeks began to feel good. She wants to feel him now, tail wagging, ferrying her through darkness.

The moon has not yet risen, the path hard to make out. She hears the scramble of things in the night, small animals, the switch of feathers. She means to take the left trail, which dips through hollows down to the shoreline, but finds herself on the right, looping over ridges to the top of the outer cliff.

There are no railings or signs to indicate the edge. If April was moving faster, she might launch off the top and tumble headlong down the hundred-foot drop. This is Hal's favorite spot, Dawnland, a different place in darkness. She looks down at the white luminescence rising and receding, eating away the shore. There's a rope ladder somewhere nearby that descends the clay precipice to the beach, but if she goes down, she doesn't trust herself to return. She sits on the cliff top and hugs her knees.

She was six months pregnant with Nula when the dog began to faint. A congenital heart defect, the vet explained. It might strike suddenly or never. Every trip Al took, April prayed Dooby would not die while he was away.

She was strapping Locky into his high chair for lunch when Dubious wobbled softly on his feet and sank to the floor like a deflated balloon. April drew him into her lap, his face on her thigh. "Dooby." She stroked him. "Dooby, wake up." Locky looked down in astonishment. Dubious exhaled a long, slow breath and melted into her lap.

It was hours before she was able to reach Al in Seattle. He was one game into a series and would not be home for days. She never bothered him on trips, so he guessed immediately. "What did you do with the body?" he asked.

"Brought him to the vet for cremation." Her voice felt small and tight.

"How'd you get it there?"

"Subway. I wrapped him in a towel and put him in the snuggly."

"And Locky?"

"On my back," she said. "Al, this is hard. I can't do this alone."

"Aw, Rosie." She heard ache in his voice, love pouring through the wire. "I'm here, babe," he said.

"But I wish you were home."

A muffled knock. "Hold on. Room service."

The creak of a door, a woman's voice. "Forgot my belt."

April inhaled sharply.

"April?" Al said. "Me too. I wish—"

She hung up, staring at the phone as if lowered into ice water. She ought to have known. It rang immediately. She watched the receiver vibrate in its cradle. Next her cell lit up and went dark.

She wandered around the apartment, unable to remember her normal routine. Once Loch was asleep, she sat in the dark, staring at the phone. Her therapist's voice filled her head, as high pitched and enunciated as a first-grade teacher addressing a child who had sat in poison ivy. "When your brother-in-law calls, really examine your temptation to pick up," she said. "Ask yourself why you'd want to go back for more when he already rejected you."

But it was Oliver who had long ago persuaded April she needed a dog. At the time, she had no idea how right he was. She punched in the digits. Oliver's voice materialized, that deep timbre. "You have reached Oliver Night and Meredith Fontaine. Please leave—" Before the beep sounded, she depressed the hook. "Oliver," she said into the dial tone. "I wanted to let you know that Dubious—" She let the phone clatter to the floor.

On the horizon, only the onset of stars distinguishes sky from sea, the two blending into a vast abyss, a chasm between worlds. April looks behind her to see if anyone is coming, if other people even exist. A terrifying isolation pulses through her, but at the same time intense, pulverizing beauty. Far below, the wind shears off the tops of combers, hurling spray in billowy manes. No one will come for her. She is alone. This is what it feels like to have no name, no age, no gender, no history. Or maybe she only wishes to be free of all that. She lies on her back and listens. Breeze moves hair over her face. In the woods behind her, an owl mewls. She closes her eyes. It was pointless to bring up booze. An animal trapped in barbwire will snap if you try to help it. Yet Al believes himself free. He drinks to prove it.

By the time Al had returned from that trip, it seemed he'd been gone for months. She heard his key in the lock, not caring that the high chair was smeared with food, laundry on the floor, stagnant water in the dog bowl. Lochlann had dragged a chair to the windowsill and was plucking leaves off a houseplant. "Locky," she said, pulling him off the chair, "you're killing it."

He pattered to Al in a gleeful rush. "Dada!"

Al squeezed him. April pivoted the plant so that its two remaining leaves faced the sun. It didn't have a chance.

"Dada," Loch said. "Dooby goed ouch." He made a show of going limp.

"Sorry, Locky. We'll get you a new one." He kissed his head. "Where's your baby sister? Still in Mommy's tummy?"

"No baby!"

"Baby's coming. Time to ditch the diaper. Where are your big-boy undies?"

Lochlann wrestled out of his arms and scampered to the bedroom.

"April," Al said. "No excuses. I'm sorry."

"I just didn't think it would be so soon."

Al winced. Loch returned, Superman undies in one fist and Mousy in the other.

"Snazzy, but they belong on your butt." Al picked him up. He giggled, stuffing the mouse in Al's pocket and the underpants on his head. "April," Al said, "I swear it meant nothing."

"I can't stay here," she said numbly. "I almost called him the other day."

Al stiffened. "Why is it, April, that 'him' can only mean one person?"

"I walked by his apartment. I thought about ringing his bell."

"Who cares? Talk to him if you want."

"I need to get out of New York."

"I'd rather not have him dictate our lives."

"I don't mean us," she said. "I mean Lochlann and me."

"April, just because I messed up once—" Al put his hands in his pockets. "Okay, look, it's been more than once. But I can stop. I promise."

"We can see each other on your days off. I can't stay here." She sat on the chair.

Al knelt in front of her. Lochlann put shredded leaves in his hair. "Shouldn't we wait till the baby's born? I don't want you alone."

"I *am* alone."

He put his forehead on her knee, the mouse falling from his pocket.

"It's okay, Al," she said. "We never said this was real."

He exhaled as if struck. "April, you're realer than anything else in my life."

She rested her hand on his head. She wished it were true.

They framed it as a second home, a chance for the kids to grow up in fresh air, and remained a couple in all ways except the closing of her heart.

If she leaves him, she'll lose the farm, the view from her kitchen window, the alpacas and horses. This would be her last summer here. Her children will come without her. Maybe Al will bring another woman, a future wife or seasonal girlfriend. April will no longer be Phoebe's aunt or Hal's daughter-in-law or Oliver's anything.

17

Childhood

Long Island was pool table–flat, but April and Oliver knew where to find the hidden hills. Pumping the inclines, she felt invincible. Careening down slopes, she felt freer than she'd ever been. They went farther from home than their parents knew. One afternoon, after hours away, they barreled into Oliver's driveway, sweaty and sunburned, hoping to find Popsicles in the freezer. The sound of backyard music stopped April short. His parents were having one of their spontaneous neighborhood barbecues. A boom of joviality overpowered the music, a familiar cutting laugh. April froze. "Are my parents here?"

"My folks invite whoever's around."

She rounded the side of the house, catching the scent of lighter fluid and burnt meat. A string of lanterns illuminated the dusky patio, Seal's "Crazy" throbbing from a boom box. Loud voices. Rosy cheeks. The party had been going on for some time. Al, fifteen, was wearing his football jersey, two teenage girls tittering around him.

"Ah, Oliver's here!" Hal beamed. "Have you all met my youngest? He just won a youth piano competition. Number one in the state."

Al rolled his eyes. The girls giggled.

April caught sight of her mother at a picnic table, her hairdo stiffly sprayed, makeup perfect, hands trembling. On her face was a plastic smile, eyes glued to April's father as he climbed the ladder to the aboveground pool. People hooted, egging him on. He did a cannon-ball, dousing everyone nearby. The earthquake of hilarity riveted April, the smell of chlorine. Hair darkened by water, her father pinwheeled something over his head around and around, a bright-orange whir. He let go, his airborne swimsuit splattering onto the table where Hal and Avila sat, knocking over their drinks. People howled. Others gasped. April's mother rushed over to clean up, that impervious smile on her face. "He's such a riot," she said, her voice as tremulous as her hands.

"Who's coming in?" Her father called out the names of the neighborhood women. "Avila, how about it?" he said, a tinge of desolation in his voice. "I'm lonely here by myself."

Hal's face was crimson. Al doubled over in laughter. A few people stood to leave. In her hands April found a blood-soaked rag. No, wine. She had rushed to help her mother clean up. Hal picked up the drenched swimsuit and threw it back into the pool. "Pal, we've got kids here."

"Nah, our little guy is at camp. April's a big girl," he said. "But fine. I'll get out if you insist." He hauled himself backward onto the ledge of the pool, revealing the white flesh of his haunches. Shrieks of laughter pierced April's ears. It was clear the ledge was not meant to bear weight, the side undulating, waves of water dumping onto the lawn. A woman screamed. He jumped in again, the pool snapping back into shape.

"More, more!" someone shouted. "Full frontal, baby!"

He jumped up and down in the water, each time higher, revealing his chest, his paunch, the dark hair at the base of his abdomen. One teenage girl yelped. The other covered her eyes. April's mother was a statue, her smile chiseled in ice.

"Mademoiselles," he called, hauling himself skyward. "Who's hungry for a baguette?"

Hal rushed over, arms aloft, and blocked the spectacle, a gush of water drenching his shirt.

April's father burst out laughing. "If only Avila had done that! C'mon, doll. I bet no one can do a wet blouse like you."

Avila clicked off the music, her face a tomato. "Good night, every-one," she yelled. "We'll be cleaning up now."

People filed out, some snickering, others fuming. April's father put on his swimsuit, humming David Rose's "The Stripper," a tune he often sang when he'd had a few. He descended the pool ladder face out, doing little Rockette kicks from each rung. Only Al laughed.

"Thank you for having us," April's mother said, leading her father toward the gate. His swimsuit was on backward. "Thank you for having April over every day. She talks about you like the sun and moon."

"She's a treasure," Avila said, unsmiling.

"Didn't mean to be a showstopper." April's father swept a flop of wet hair off his forehead, flashing his brilliant grin. "All in fun, right?"

"Safe home," Avila said, though they lived around the corner.

April rinsed the wine-soaked rag with the hose, hands shaking. "I'm sorry," she whispered, but Oliver didn't seem to hear over the rush of water. She bent to turn off the spigot.

"Whoa, talk about legs!" Al called. "Your dad's got the moves, but you've got the parts."

"Allen," Avila said viciously. "She's a child."

"I was only stating a fact," he said. "You got to admit, she's a giraffe."

April looked down at her cutoff shorts, bruised shin, sock tan.

"Don't listen to anything my brother says," Oliver said. "Ever."

Hal and Avila went into the house.

April helped Oliver collect paper plates. "Simone," Al yelled. "Why you still playing Barbies with that chump when you could be smoking joints with us?"

The girls did not laugh. One elbowed him.

"Come on," Oliver said, tying up the trash. "I'll walk you home."

April did not want to go home. She wanted to be back on her bike with Oliver.

18

April shakes out her sweatshirt, sandy from the cliff top, and enters the house quietly. The static of headphones soughs through the darkened living room, Lochlann alone on the couch. "It's two in the morning," April says.

His face is stone, arms wrapped around his middle. "Where were you?"

"Out walking. You should go to bed."

"It was your fault, that boat trip. You put the idea in his head."

She sits heavily beside him. *Secrets of the Sea* is open to a swarm of baby seahorses emerging from their father's pouch. "Tell me what happened," she says.

"Him giving me a lecture on how to treat girls. Seriously?" he says. "Nothing I do is good enough for him. He thinks band is a waste of time? Fine, I'll quit band. I'll quit school. No one will even notice. Think how much easier your life will be when I'm gone."

"Loch, please don't say that. Are you thinking about hurting yourself?"

"I hate when you ask that."

"That's not an answer." She measures his eyes. "Have you gotten into Grandpa's liquor cabinet?"

"I hear another 'don't' coming."

"Here's the thing: Drinking is like a box of bonbons. If the first one doesn't satisfy you, the second one never will."

"My mother, the fortune cookie."

"I'm trying to tell you something important. Take it from someone who's been there. I was lost at your age."

"Boo-hoo." He pulls his sweatshirt snug. "Does he even know that I feed the alpacas and muck the barn every day? I guess grooming horses isn't good enough for Mr. Big-Ass Reporter."

"Dad cares about you, Loch. He loves you."

"Spare me," he says in the exact tone Al used earlier.

"Look, I know you drink. You smoke weed. You have a box of condoms in your bathroom. That's a bad combination for any fifteen-year-old." She draws a breath. "Not to mention the chain saw. Where the hell is that thing?"

"You claim all this shit happened to you—but look, you turned out okay."

"No. I made mistakes that changed the way things might have gone."

"Like what?"

She hesitates. "Bad relationships."

"Don't worry, Mom. Just because I screw girls doesn't mean I have relationships with them."

Faster than she can form a thought, she snatches his headphones and strikes him with them.

"Ow! Don't go all ballistic." He shields himself. "Did you break them?"

She steps back, a ghost of rebar cracking her chin, her father's lightning hand. How quickly she'd hit the floor. How insolent she'd been. She told herself that above all, hitting her children was the one thing she would never do. She sits down, covers her face. "I shouldn't have done that."

"Lunatic." He slides away, rubbing his shoulder. "I'll tell him you're an unfit mother."

"Listen to me. Don't have sex with anyone you don't love. I know you think it's old-fashioned. I know it's a hookup culture, but I'm telling you firsthand it can be damaging in ways you'll never know, to you and the girl."

"Okay, Mom," he says. "Can I have my headphones back now?"

She walks away to prevent herself from belting him. "No privileges without civility."

"The hell with it. I'm going for a walk."

"Not at two in the morning."

"You did."

"I'm an adult."

"That's questionable." He pulls up his hood. "Besides, you can't stop me."

"When you get back, your laptop will be gone."

"Who says I'm coming back?"

"Lochlann, please."

The stairs creak. They turn to see whom they've awakened. "Hey," Oliver says with strained nonchalance. "Nice to know I'm not the only insomniac in the family."

Lochlann looks away.

"Thought I'd take a walk on the beach rather than lie awake in bed," Oliver says. "Any takers?"

Lochlann hugs himself.

Oliver picks up a foam ball Nula left on the couch and tosses it to him. Lochlann catches it by reflex. "Might want to zip up." Oliver opens the door. "Getting chilly out there."

April doesn't know what time it is, the couch coarse beneath her cheek. "Hey," a voice says. Her hand flies out. "Mom," Lochlann says. "It's me."

She sits up, disoriented. Behind him stands Oliver.

"Sorry I was rude to you," Lochlann says woodenly.

"Thank you, Loch." She stands, brushing back her hair. "I'm sorry, too."

He gives an obligatory hug. So tall. He hasn't hugged her in months. He goes quietly up the stairs. She turns to Oliver. "How did you do that?"

"I didn't do anything."

"But what did you say to him?"

"We called whales, if you must know."

"You did what?" she asks.

"Let's sit on the patio."

Her eyes widen.

"Just for a sec."

She follows him out, opening and closing the slider. Three thirty a.m.

"I know what you're thinking. You smacked him. So what? He deserved it," he says. "It's not the same as your father clocking you."

"I wasn't thinking about my father." Her skin prickles. "Why are you bringing up my father?"

He picks up a twig, snaps it in half. "Loch doesn't have a concussion, for one thing."

"I never had . . ." She stops. "Fine, let's not argue."

"All hatred is self-hatred. He's got some dragons to slay, that's all."

"Unless they get him first. He disappeared overnight twice this summer, scared the shit out of me. And get this: he brought a chain saw up here, and now I have no idea where he's put it." The relief of confiding overwhelms her. "What if he hurts someone with that thing? What if he hurts himself?"

"The orange case?"

"You've seen it?"

"Is that what he takes when he disappears?"

"I hadn't thought about it. You think he might be using it in the middle of the night?" She looks into the woods. "No, Lochlann wouldn't hurt a tree. A mailbox, maybe. Someone's front porch."

"That's your worst fear? A mailbox?"

"No. That he'll kill himself."

"With a chain saw?" He raises an eyebrow.

"Do you know the satisfaction he'd get? Me finding him in pieces?"

He smiles. "What makes you think there's actually a chain saw in there?"

"What are you saying? Is it full of pot?"

"Follow me," he says.

"Wait, I don't think—"

He's already walking into the yard. She trails him, pine needles squeaking beneath her soles as they descend to the old beech tree. Each step away from the house, from the others, spikes warning signs from her heels up through her skull. He ascends the rickety ladder to the tree house, a black cutout against quaking limbs.

"It's up there?" Her need to know is too strong. She hoists herself up the uneven rungs and sits on the roofless platform enclosed by driftwood railings. Leaves tatter and quell. Before her is the case. "How did you know where to find it?"

"We took it down to the beach just now." He unsnaps the bolts. She kneels beside him as he lifts the lid. Faint moonlight catches spines of metal, spikes like a rib cage.

He reaches in where the chain saw blade should be and pulls out something narrow and arrow-like, a scythe or machete—no, a violin bow—then withdraws the metal cage. Water burbles in the darkness. She cannot fathom what she is seeing until he touches bow to spines. It's the eerie instrument he gave Lochlann for his twelfth birthday—an ocean harp. She releases a breath, not wanting to show the depth of her relief. "What's this doing in my chain saw case?"

"He didn't know how else to carry it," he says. "I asked him to bring it."

"You? When?"

"We text once in a while, Lochlann and me."

"But why is he hiding it?"

"Young men need their secrets." He smiles. "Not-so-young men, too." He tilts the waterphone on his knee, liquid sloshing inside, and strikes it. The instrument shrieks a banshee wail.

"Jesus, it sounds like something from *Poltergeist*."

"It's popular in horror flicks, but it can also do this." He caresses the bow over the ribs. Notes bloom like fragrance, whale song reverberating out over the treetops toward the faintly visible ocean. The plangency, the water, the breeze—something inside her begins to collapse, a liquefied sandcastle. The song pulses out, more sonorous the farther it goes, not so much waning as traveling on. Above them the negative space between branches dances in a fluid kaleidoscope. He puts the waterphone down, its echo a strange fusion of beauty and terror.

"The reason he wanted Spotify back is because he's been listening to whale songs." He props his feet up on the railing and lies on his back. "He found it on YouTube, though. Don't tell him I told you."

"Whales? And that's what I take from him? See what a brilliant mother I am?"

"Stick to your rules. They need consequences. Makes them feel safe."

"He'd disagree." Beneath her sternum, a balloon of pressure begins to release. Talking about Lochlann is a drug she needs more of. "What about his suspension? Did he tell you anything?"

"Yeah." He hesitates. "This has to be between us. Even Phoebe doesn't know."

She swallows back her dread.

"He said the girl cornered him. He didn't want anything to do with her."

"And you believed him?"

"She tried to make out with him. He told her he had to catch the bus. She got pissed and kneed him in the groin. He was too embarrassed to tell the principal."

"He must have done something to provoke it." April freezes. She can't believe what she just said.

"That's exactly why he hasn't told you," Oliver says.

"But it doesn't make sense. Lochlann's no pushover." She shudders. People might have said the same of her at that age. "You know how he is with girls."

"April, it's all talk."

"No way. He's got a box of condoms in his bathroom."

"Opened?"

She flusters. "He just told me tonight what he does with girls. Why would he say that?"

"Um, to upset you?"

She looks at him, dumbfounded.

"You've never lashed out at the one person you knew was safe?"

She flushes. She remembers the day, not long after what had happened to her in her father's bar, when she beat Oliver in his backyard hammock with a Frisbee. "Oh God," she says.

"He was worried about his testicle, but the pain went away after a few days."

"He needs to tell the school," April says. "What if the girl has done this to other boys?"

"He'll never tell. He has too much shame."

She lies on her back and covers her face. How stupid of her.

"He'll be okay. Deep down he's a very solid kid. I think what you said in the diner is right. We have to look at him with confidence, let him see his goodness in our eyes."

We. The word makes her woozy.

"The girl claimed he was the one who locked the door. He was too mortified to dispute her. He's afraid everyone at school thinks he's a dick."

April presses her hands to her face. How could she be so blind?

"April," he says, that old softness in his voice. "You couldn't have known."

She wipes her eyes. "It's nearly morning. We'd better go inside."

"In a bit." He folds his hands over his chest. "It's so beautiful out here."

His elbow brushes her arm. Suddenly she's aware of his nearness. "How's Meredith?" she asks quickly. "What a week she's having. I wish there was something we could do for her."

The breeze abates, rustling leaves falling into quiescence. "To be honest, it's always like this," he says.

She turns to him, his face closer than she realized.

"One life-or-death crisis to the next; that's how it is when you run a start-up. Every day you wake up in a burning house."

"I'm sure it'll all be worth it when—"

"She thrives on it, even the terrifying parts. Safety bores her."

"Well, you have to admire her guts."

He rubs his face the way Al does when exhausted. "I'm a disappointment to her, if you want to know the truth. Before me she dated bankers and lawyers. I think she thought a musician would be more of a risk-taker."

"You take risks."

"Selectively." He turns to her.

She looks at her watch.

"What I'm trying to say is that what happened in New York wasn't about you."

She gets up on her elbows. "What a coincidence. It wasn't about you, either."

He laughs dejectedly. "Two people kiss on a city street and it isn't about either one of them. Now there's a story."

She sits up. "I wouldn't call it a kiss. More like a pastrami sub you wish you hadn't eaten."

He eyes her. "For a sandwich you didn't want, it sure went down fast."

Her stomach fists.

"It was a wake-up call, that's all. I thought I was the last person something like that could happen to."

"'Happen to'?" She stiffens. "The hoagie didn't fall from the fricking sky."

He laughs so hard he spits. "It was two hoagies," he says. "And we caught them both."

A blade of horror washes through her, followed by something gurgling, rising up, a burst of laughter. She can't help it, all the pent-up anxiety about Loch, the terror of being caught here with Oliver. She lies back again, hands over her mouth, and tries to stop. He covers his face to muffle the sound. She wipes her eyes, hoping no one has left a window ajar.

They fall into silence, breeze filtering the leaves.

"Let's put it behind us," he says. "I like where we got to these last few years. I want that back."

"What happened to 'I'll never forgive you'?"

"I haven't," he says.

She meets his gaze horizontally, a rush inside her like an incoming wave. "We should go in," she says.

"First tell me about the book you're writing."

"I'm not writing a book. Nula was exaggerating."

"I thought about your idea," he says. "The artists' residency. Turns out there's one upstate about an hour north of you. They accept musicians and painters and writers."

"That's great. You should apply."

"You should, too."

"With what, my grocery list?"

"Everyone gets their own cabin. We probably wouldn't even run into each other."

She barely breathes. "You mean to go at the same time?"

"I'm not saying you deserve credit, but for some reason the songs come faster when you're around." He registers her expression. "Why do you always think the worst? Never mind. It was only an idea. Residency or not, you should keep writing. The pastrami thing—that should go in your book," he says. "But you should also mention that sometimes a kiss is not at all like a sandwich. Sometimes it's more like a Mozart sonata, a seat at the Bolshoi, something that dismantles you at the core." He blows out a breath. "Sorry. Forget I said that. Look, I don't want to blow up our lives. I just want a conversation."

Her teeth grit. "What do you think we just had?"

"You know what I'm talking about. The conversation we never had."

Stars swing between branches, the sky tilting. A wave collapses in April's chest, heavy and thunderous. She flies down the ladder and up the lawn, fireflies scattering around her.

19

Al's familiar snores give rhythm to the quiet. April slips into bed, heart pounding. Through the blinds, moonlight falls like cell bars over her body. As her eyes adjust, a frame emerges on the wall, three shadowy smudges posed on a couch—baby Nula wedged between four-year-old Phoebe and Lochlann. April's mind drifts back to that first reunion. She remembers turning up the long driveway, not as rutted back then, to see the pine forest sloping down from the house like a dancer's twirling skirt. Parked beside Hal's old Honda was a late-model Audi with New York plates and a car seat. "What?" She gripped the door handle. "They're here?"

"It's only a week," Al said. "The kids need family. They've got zilch on your side."

"Are you crazy?"

"For God's sake, April, how long is this going to last?" he said. "Everyone gets jilted once in their life."

"Al." She lowered her voice. "I'm going to kill you."

On the porch, Locky flung himself at Phoebe, and they fell down laughing while Oliver swept sand from the entranceway. He glanced at April. "Hey," he said offhandedly. She had no words. The script had been delivered. For seven days, they would feign normalcy.

Within minutes, Hal's tidy house fell into deafening disarray—unclosed drawers, gummy floors, the squeaky helium voices of toddlers abrading the walls. Al disappeared upstairs to work. Meredith typed emails at the dining room table. It was left to April and Oliver to wipe countertops and replace couch cushions, unwilling draftees on the same squad, cooperating to the degree necessary without making eye contact. If April had known he would be here, she might have brought better clothes, a little makeup—not to impress him but to spite him. Instead, her shoulders were daubed with Nula's spittle, hair sticky with jam. Al was distracted during their outings, stepping away for a smoke, then reappearing with a horseshoe crab shell over his face, pretending to be a sea monster. On the third day, when Oliver suggested taking the kids to a salt marsh visitor center, Meredith announced she had to stay back at the house for a conference call. Al's eyes lit up. "Rosie, I've got to finish a column by four," he said as she changed Nula's diaper in the bedroom. "You'll have to take the kids yourself today."

Arctic air rose inside her. "You think I'm going alone with him?"

"April, I pay the bills, remember?"

Frozenness was not a static state, she realized. There were infinite degrees.

"I'm sorry." He softened. "But if I spend another day in this din, I'm going to hate the children I love."

"Al, there's no loving kids without being with them," she said. "It's one thing for me to keep them busy in London while you're covering Wimbledon, but this is your own family vacation."

"You'll be fine," Al said. "Pretend he isn't there."

At the salt marsh, Locky played with Oliver's hair, untied his shoelaces, monkey-hugged his legs. Oliver responded by putting him on his shoulders, carrying him like a football, turning him upside down and pretending to shake him down for money. It irritated April how easily these gestures came to Oliver. She worked hard to plumb her maternal instincts.

On the way to the house, Locky and Phoebe made up a song in a secret language and giggled uncontrollably. Nula chortled her baby laugh. Oliver glanced over as if expecting to find Meredith beside him, his face lit with habitual affection. Unguarded, April's eyes met his. She sipped a sweetness not meant for her.

They lifted Locky and Phoebe from their car seats into the bleaching sun of the driveway and watched them scamper to Meredith at the door. April reached in for Nula and Oliver for the diaper bag. Across the shaded enclosure of the back seat, he met her eye. "How's Dooby?" he asked, his first nonrequired attempt at conversation.

"What?" she said.

"Dubious. How's he doing?"

It had been a year. It shouldn't hurt so much. The landslide of emotion on his face reflected what must have shown on hers.

"Oh, April." For an instant everything was forgotten. He moved as if to hug her, but it was impossible from their opposite doors, Nula between them. She lifted the baby in her arms. "I'm so sorry," he said.

She nodded, lip trembling, and carried Nula into the house.

In the living room, she sprawled on the sofa, Nula on her chest, while Lochlann and Oliver sat on the piano bench. She felt a nudge, Al staring down at her. "You okay?" he said. "How was it?"

"The usual mayhem." She yawned. "They didn't want to come home."

Al wavered, unmoored, it seemed, by his miscalculation. "Let me hold the baby," he said.

"She's asleep."

"Just for a sec. I feel like holding her."

"Sure, Al, as if parenting is about what you *feel* like."

Oliver glanced over from the piano.

"I'm sorry, Al," she said. "Here, sit in the recliner." She placed Nula on his chest, all softness and down, dovetailing tongue-and-groove to his breastbone like she'd been hand-beveled to fit there. He caressed the only wisp of hair on her bald head.

"I don't deserve this kid." He kissed her tiny fingers. April appraised him, a puzzle she couldn't solve. Lochlann scampered over.

"C'mon, Locky." Al nestled the boy under his armpit. "We can all fit."

April's eyes misted. "I'll take a picture."

"Oliver," Al called out, "take one of all of us."

She knelt beside the recliner. Oliver looked through the viewfinder, an unreadable expression on his face. Locky started to squirm.

"Quick," Al said. "It won't last."

20

In the dining room, April spots a handwritten sign: T-Minus 5 Days. Phoebe pops grapes into her mouth from the bowl April has set out. "Kid in my class keeps texting." She frowns at her phone. "He says I'm *exotic*."

"Ugh. Sorry, Phoebe," April says. "Don't let him ruin your day. We're heading to the beach."

The family weaves single file through pitch pine and scrub oak, branches deformed by wind. The trail snakes down from the yard, winding and dipping in a quarter-mile groove toward the sea, a deer path widened over the years by Hal's steps. When the kids were younger, they would spend two weeks alone with him every June, a big undertaking for a single grandfather. He taught them to dig for clams and quahogs. He introduced them to the important people in town—the librarian, the harbormaster, the shellfish constable. He showed them the phases of twilight: astronomical, nautical, and civil. He would ask, "Which is moving more, the waves or the sunlight?" When they claimed it was a silly question—the waves could knock you flat, the sunlight weighed nothing—he explained that despite the force moving through the ocean, the individual water molecules stayed more or less in place. The photons of sunlight, on the other hand, were bombarding their skin at the speed of light. Lochlann and Nula would return home elated, telling April the details. But now, with summer classes and college prep, they no longer have that time alone with their grandfather.

"Phoebe," Oliver calls out, "tell me if this breeze is coming or going."

"Daddy, they'll get there before us," she says, but closes her eyes. "I don't feel it, so the breeze must be headed away." A tuft of wind lifts her hair. Oliver makes a wrong-answer sound like a game show buzzer. "Can we go?" Phoebe says.

"You relied on your other senses. If you just listened, you would have gotten it."

She puckers her cheeks and looks at April. "Every time a door creaks, he asks me the pitch."

"I'm training your ear," he says. "You'll thank me later."

She waves him off and continues down the trail. When the surf sound penetrates the woods, Oliver calls back, "Phoebe, listen. Is the tide coming in or going out?"

Impossible. No one can tell without looking. Nevertheless, Phoebe closes her eyes as if straining to tease apart the collapse of breakers from the breeze gusting through pines. "Rising high tide."

"She's a prodigy." He puts his hand on his heart.

She glances at April. "I looked at the tide chart before we left."

He swats Phoebe with a towel, and she runs down the path.

The trail forks and drops, the sound of waves growing louder. Between boughs of pine, an expanse of ocean sparkles. April sprints the rest of the way, heart lit with anticipation, ready to burst with feeling for this place, this ocean that awaits her return. She can't explain it, but the sea recognizes her. She's sure of it.

Cool ripples douse her toes, splashing her ankles. Nula bends to touch the water. Lochlann surges past them, crashing his body against a wave. The girls laugh nervously. "Get back here," April shouts. "Five feet, remember?"

"Relax!" he yells. "I can touch bottom."

"Nules," Al says, "let's get out past the breakers and bodysurf in. Ten bucks says I beat you."

"Don't go in, Daddy—especially in those swim trunks. You know what shark experts call that color? Yum-Yum Yellow."

"I'll be in and out in five seconds." He jumps in.

"Al!" April yells.

"Good Lord," Hal says. "What on earth is he doing?"

Lochlann follows Al out beyond the breakers. April shouts, but they can't hear. "Goddammit." She yanks off her beach dress and wades in. The shock of cold penetrates her bones, waking up marrow. Her skin tingles in the bracing swells, brine filling her nostrils. She spots Lochlann and swims faster, salt water tickling her scalp, the ocean enveloping her. The sun winks in and out, the sea playful and glittery one minute, opaque and reckless the next. Beyond the breakers, Lochlann is doing a leisurely backstroke, staring at clouds, a contentment on his face she hates to break. "Back to shore," she calls to him. "The gannets are diving." He groans but obeys.

Al is out far, swimming hard like he's got something to prove, but she can catch him. Her muscles have the confidence of routinely hauling hay bales and digging drainage ditches. She closes in, hears him pause to cough. She wonders if she would remember what to do in an emergency. In high school Oliver once asked her to help him practice for his lifeguard test. "Will you be my victim?" he asked. "Your job is to try to strangle me. It's a reflex people have when they're drowning. You wouldn't believe how often panicked people end up drowning their saviors."

"I won't be your victim," she answered. "But you can be mine if you teach me how." It turned out getting out of a death grip wasn't so easy.

When she reaches Al, he's treading water, recovered from his hacking fit. "April Simone, swimming to me from across the sea." He smiles. "What a vision."

"If you want to lure a shark, please don't do it with your children watching."

"You know there's a better chance of dying from a fall in a bathtub."

"Unless you're swimming with baitfish." Flecks of silver arc over the waves.

They face each other, buoyant on the swells, "Rosie, I'm sorry about last night. I didn't mean what I said."

"You have no idea what it's like to be on the other end of your barrel," she says.

"I'm an idiot." He touches her shoulder. "You look so beautiful with the ocean all around you."

"Let's get back. Nula's worried." She glances at the distant beach, a slim silhouette standing at the water's edge.

"Just be with me for a minute," Al says. "It feels so good out here, just us." He kisses her tentatively, sun on her face, water lapping their bodies. If only she could hate him for more than a day. He grins as though everything is fine between them. She turns back. They swim side by side and emerge from the surf together. April wrings out her hair.

"This is ridiculous," Lochlann says. "People swim here every day."

"With sensible precautions," Hal says, handing them towels. "Do you know how many pings the shark buoys have gotten this week? And only a fraction are tagged."

"Nula, imagine Mom and Dad gone in two chomps?" Loch says. She shoves him.

"Can't live your life afraid," Al says, drying his face. "Did you see me out there? Hammerhead jumped out of the water, and I punched it in the nose."

"Hammerheads don't live here," Lochlann says. "And they don't breach."

"So glad everyone here has a sense of humor." Al reaches for his shirt.

"What's that?" April points to a curved white scar on his rib cage. He tugs the shirt down.

"There's another one on your back," Nula says. "Same shape."

"Must be scars from my old shark bites."

"Not funny," Nula says. "That lady on the news last year? Guess what? She's only got one foot." Her eyes brim. "Do you know how grumpy you'd be with one foot?"

"Aw, toots." He tries to hug her, but she pushes away and starts picking up beach trash. April casts Al an exasperated glance. He sits and opens a beer.

"No service," Meredith says, returning to the blanket. She's been searching the beach for reception.

"Good." Oliver puts his arm around her. "Let's walk." He looks cheerful in the sunlight, April thinks. More at ease than last night. Perhaps he's given up on the idea of a conversation.

Meredith pulls off her sundress, and they start down the beach, Oliver with his feet in the water, Meredith gathering her hair in a stubby ponytail. They hold hands.

"Aunt April, can you do my back?" Phoebe hands her the sunblock, and April massages it in. "I won't be as tall as them," Phoebe says, watching her parents grow small in the distance.

"Height isn't everything." April rubs her shoulders.

They switch, April lifting her hair. "You have goose bumps from the ocean." Phoebe laughs, rubbing in the lotion. "You're not as fair as my mom. No one is." Her touch on April's back is delicate. "People have strange words for skin. Have you ever seen a yellow person or an olive one?"

"Not yet," April says.

Nula returns carrying plastic bottles, a soggy Mylar balloon, and rope from a lobster trap.

Phoebe caps the lotion and begins braiding April's hair, a ritual of theirs. April closes her eyes, the gentleness of her niece's touch reminding her of when Avila used to plait her hair. "Your hair's so thick," Phoebe says. "My mom's is so wispy, like touching a butterfly." She faces April to appraise her work. "I made the part uneven."

"Convention is boring," April says.

"I don't know anyone but you with eyes darker than mine, except one Korean girl and two Black boys at school."

"You have beautiful eyes," April says. "Dark like the universe."

She looks at the shoreline. Oliver and Meredith are on their way back. "I wonder how tall my birth parents are. I wonder if either of them has a freckle on the bottom of their left foot like me."

"One thing's for sure," Lochlann says, biting into a sandwich. "They're not exotic."

She gives him a playful punch.

Oliver and Meredith return, heads bowed. April notices his hands are fisted.

"That was quick," Hal says, closing his book.

Oliver smiles tautly. Meredith reaches into her bag for her phone.

"Meredith," Oliver says, "if there wasn't cell service a few minutes ago—"

"I have to get back to the house. How long were you planning to stay?"

"The tide's perfect for a sandcastle," he says.

"Aren't they getting a bit old for that?" Meredith says.

The kids glance at each other. "I'm not too old for it," Hal says. "But I'm sure someone can walk you back if you don't know the way, dear."

"Thank you, Hal. I've been coming here for a decade. I'd better know the way." She glances uncertainly toward the trail. "Maybe I'll take the road." She looks impatiently at Oliver. "I have a conference call at three. Are we cooking tonight?"

"I want the four of you to go out for dinner," Hal says. "My treat. Beryl's coming over. She and I can make the kids their favorite dinner."

"Pancakes!" Nula says.

"No, Hal," April says. "That's too generous."

"I insist," he says. "You all work too hard. Time to go out and relax."

Oliver rubs his forehead. April muffles a groan. Only Al brightens. "Why not?" he says. "Thanks, Dad."

Oliver turns toward the ocean and pitches an imaginary ball. April is certain he does not want to go out as a foursome any more than she does.

As soon as Meredith is out of earshot, Phoebe asks, "Dad, any news from the finder?"

"What are you trying to find?" Hal asks. "Buried treasure?"

"My birth parents."

His tone drops. "Is that possible?"

"Phoebe, you know the odds. It might be different if it had been a small village, where the local people might remember something from fifteen years ago."

She looks at her feet. Lochlann offers a towel, which she bunches to her chest.

"How about we visit instead?" Oliver asks. "A trip to China to test out our Mandarin. What do you want to see? The Great Wall? The Temple of Heaven?"

"The Dalian bus station," she says.

Hal laughs, but Oliver signals him with a glance.

"That's where I was found," Phoebe says. "One week old."

"Phoebe." Hal puts his arm around her. April hears the ache in his voice.

"Sure, Bee, we can go to the bus station," Oliver says. "Why not?"

"They did it to save me," Phoebe says to Hal. "They probably already had a kid and weren't allowed to keep me. I wouldn't have had any legal status, no rights to schooling or anything, so they gave me up because in Dalian, there was a good record of foreign adoptions. They wanted me to be happy. Right, Dad?"

"That's right. Instead of one set of parents who love you, you've had two."

She gives the ocean a penetrating look, as though she might see all the way to China.

"Let's sculpt," Oliver says. "How about a giant squid this year?"

They find the right distance between dry and wet sand and begin troweling, the sand squishy between April's fingers. Oliver works animatedly, his demeanor lighter now. He starts to hum, and she wonders if he's working out a new song.

"Hey, what's this?" Nula asks. A smooth knob of driftwood protrudes from the sand. They try to shovel it out, but the plank is harpooned into the earth.

"From a ship?" Lochlann asks.

"Could be," Hal says. "Thousands of wrecks here. They call this stretch 'the Ocean Graveyard.'"

"I think you should leave it," April says. "It's part of the beach now."

"We've gotten this far," Oliver says.

The wood doesn't budge. "Look. It's telling you it wants to stay buried," April says.

The brothers ignore her. They kneel on opposite sides and heave-ho the wood, jaws clenched as they lever the plank back and forth, more like battle than collaboration. Al grunts, falling backward as the wood comes free in his grip. April shudders. The wood is sun bleached and silky, with sea-worn irregular ends. Even the craggy parts are honed.

"Perfect for a sign," says Hal. "I can finally name the house."

"The Osprey Nest!" Nula says.

April touches the wood, smooth as a baby's skin. She wonders if it's from a wreck, who touched it last, how long it drifted unseen, and how many storms polished it before it tumbled onto the shore. Al carries it to the blanket like a trophy.

Oliver remains kneeling in the sand, head bowed.

"Son," Hal says, "about dinner tonight—should I have asked you first? Is there some reason you'd rather not double-date with your brother?"

April folds her arms. *Dear Hal can't see the obvious.*

"Of course not, Dad." Oliver stands and brushes himself off. "We'll have a blast."

21

The booth is snug for four. April would have preferred a table, but as usual Al took charge. Alcohol oils each of them differently: Oliver more sentimental, Al freer with his roaming eye, Meredith giddily slapping a mosquito. April knows she tends to get more volatile after a few drinks. She tells the waitress nothing for her.

An older couple shuffles to the dance floor. She wonders how long they've been married, what their lives are like now that their kids are gone, if he ever screams that she drives him "fucking crazy."

"Oops, got to take this." Meredith leaves to answer her phone.

Al's gaze follows her swinging hemline as she laces through tables. He's been staring at her boobs all night. April heads to the restroom. On her return, she slows down to hear the brothers talking.

"How do these people get my number?" Al says, looking at a text. "Some chick wants advice on getting a book contract."

"Maybe she's looking for more than just advice, depending on what you've served up in the past," Oliver says.

"You love pretending I sleep with everything on two legs, don't you?" Al says. "Anything to sharpen your sense of superiority."

When April sits down, they go silent.

Meredith slides in across from her. "Our lawyer suggests we have the two devices examined in a lab. I think that's risky," she says. "I'd rather settle. But what if there's a third complaint? A recall would kill the company."

"How bad are the burns?" Al asks.

"One is just the customer's word. The other is documented first-degree."

"Not serious enough," says Al. "Wait for a third."

"Still, you want to find out why it's happening, don't you?" April asks.

"What if another nut wants to sue?" Meredith says. "I've attracted two in a week."

The conversation bounces from work to sports to politics until plates are cleared. "Cognac to help us digest?" Al says, his voice growing more elastic.

"God knows I need it," says Meredith.

"Let's toast to Dad and his new squeeze." Al holds up his glass. "To Professor Eldridge." He takes a swallow. "Can you believe he went for a blonde?"

"Al," April says, "what does that have to do with anything?"

"Well, my mother was auburn. People do have preferences, you know. Take Oliver, here. For him, it's been nothing but blondes. Dazzling ones. Meredith takes the cake—blonde like a Finn, hair like a snowbank. Who cares if it's from a bottle? Those dark eyebrows only enhance things."

"Al!" April says.

"It's okay." Meredith smiles. "The rest of me is real."

"You should've seen his first fiancée. What was her name? Antoinette?" Al says.

"Bernadette," Meredith says. "I know about her."

"All summa cum laude and save the whales," Al says. "That would've been mind-numbing for you, bro. Meredith here, she's got some brass, some edge. Thank God he waited." Al grins, that old flirtatious silk in his voice. Meredith's spaghetti strap slips, and she waits a beat before pushing it up.

April massages the bridge of her nose.

"Of course, he's probably still pining. Oliver can carry a torch for decades; we all know that. Me, on the other hand, I can barely keep a fricking match between my fingers." Al downs a gulp of cognac.

April presses her eyes closed. "Anyone got an Advil?"

"You kidding? I'm living on these babies." Meredith hands her two from her purse. "So, Al, what's your type? Brunettes, I take it?" She winks at April. "Enigmatic ones."

April wants to answer that Al is not so discriminating. Why is Meredith encouraging him? The two of them reduced to adolescents by a few glasses of liquor.

The outdoor dance floor has grown crowded, the volume drowning out the rippling bay below. Brisk scintillating piano chords come through the speakers, followed by a blast of horns, the first unmistakable trill of Duke Ellington's "Take the 'A' Train," the nonprofit's anthem.

"Hey, your song," Al says to Oliver.

"I wish I knew how to swing dance," Meredith says. "Looks like fun."

"Oliver knows how," Al says.

"We've tried. I'm hopeless," Meredith says.

"I can teach anyone," Al says.

"It's true," April says. "You'll feel like Ginger Rogers."

Meredith looks at Oliver. "Fine with me," he says. "Go ahead."

On the dance floor Al spins Meredith out and draws her in, his steps swift and athletic. She laughs hard, stumbling a bit. Oliver stands and extends his hand to April. Her heart skips. "If we're not going to have a conversation, let's at least have a dance," he says.

She hesitates.

"We'll be back before they are," he says.

She stands uncertainly. He ferries her around tables through a blur of noise and lights, his hand a hot coal in hers. By the time they reach the far end of the dance floor, the booth they left feels like a distant country.

She glances over his shoulder. "I don't see them. Maybe they sat down."

Oliver is already inside the song, moving to its rhythm. He twirls her out, draws her in, her body answering his, equal and opposite, the way they used to lock arms as children and spin themselves dizzy. His face shines, the glow of mosquito torches an aura around him. *"Hurry, get on, now it's coming,"* he sings. *"Listen to those rails a-thrumming."* The lyrics, the tempo, the steps—their bodies know this song, know each other. They separate and unite, a murmuration of blackbirds gliding as one, until the final note scatters her heart like a thousand wings.

New chords begin, the Hozier song Oliver sent her last month, "Movement." Hair lifts on the back of her neck. They said one dance yet remain on the floor. Oliver sways to the notes, his body a willow awash in a breeze. She watches him, all surrender and glide, and closes her eyes, letting the music penetrate. They move around each other without touching, merging into a flow so vibrant she can almost remember the lost parts of her, layers that went underground before she had words to name them. The music ends. Oliver puts his hand on his heart.

Without warning, an ache splits her brain, blinding pain. She spins away, steadies herself. How could he have left her? No, it wasn't *her* he'd abandoned but the thing that came alive between them. On the way back to the table, perspiration licks her back. A breeze cools her cheeks while the curtain of hair at the back of her neck traps a pocket of heat. With each step toward the booth, she collects her energy, neutralizes her face, reels herself in, but the table appears too soon. She expects to find Al absorbed in Meredith, but they sit, silently watching.

"Well," Meredith says. "Who knew you two were such a sensation?"

"Anyone can freestyle." Oliver straightens his collar. "How did you like swing?"

"Oliver," she says, her voice loose with liquor, "you know how I dream of swinging."

His face turns red.

April's throat goes dry, head pounding. She sips water, feeling Al's eyes on her, hand cupped over his mouth, a stillness about him that chills her. Moisture evaporates from her hairline, her breath shallow and quick, pulse sprinting as though still on the dance floor. He holds her with his eyes, taking in every nuance. She ought to have gone to the restroom to regroup.

"Still got the moves, darlin'," Al says.

She starts to answer with something glib, but he slides his fingers to the back of her neck, finding the damp place where the heat is hidden, and pulls her face to his. She laughs in surprise. He keeps his lips on hers, lightly at first, deepening into insistence. She knows what he's after. He smells it. He tastes it. He wants what Oliver has lit.

Across the table Oliver and Meredith go silent. April puts her hand on Al's chest in a gesture that could be construed as tender but that Al surely understands by the pressure of her fingers as a warning. It's a setup. She cannot turn away his kiss after dancing with his brother. She presses her fist to his chest, but Al settles in, the kiss flavored with rosemary, cognac, and cigarette ash. Her face stings with the incineration of stares, her body overheating, getting wet, Al gaining confidence.

They have not been intimate since early summer, when he found her in the barn one night near midnight. He'd missed two weekends at home, and she wasn't expecting him. She was down in the stable, checking on a horse who had shown signs of colic. She didn't see Al's headlights in the driveway, didn't hear him walk the dark field toward her. She was inside the stall, ear pressed to the mare's flank, listening for gurgles. The digestive sounds were more fluid than earlier, a steady blend of healthy grumbles, the horse finally at ease. The bolt slid on the stall door, and she turned in alarm. Al closed the door behind him. Brontë's skin twitched, tail looping. "Don't spook her," April whispered. He didn't know how to be around horses, how to read them. He kissed her without a word, drawing her to him. She kept one hand on the mare's withers to reassure her, not wanting to be kicked in the head. Only when he kissed her did she realize how much she'd missed being held, how long a drought. He relished her stored-up need, a feeling he perpetuated by staying away but that backfired over time. She'd learned to handle everything on her own: broken tractor blades, flooded basements, Lochlann's troubles at school. Though she didn't consciously think about sex when he was gone—she was too busy, too exhausted—she was sometimes awakened in the night, not recalling the dream but feeling its effect. She backed him out of the stall, closed the latch behind them, the nervous horse stomping, and let Al press her against the stall door until her knees went weak. That's what he wants now, to feel her go soft, to know it's him she needs. She pushes against his chest, but he drinks her in as if to swallow her, driving toward that moment when her need will rise to meet his. The electricity of the dance is too close to the surface. He feels it. He wants it. Her fist opens and a small sound escapes her throat. His fingers sift through her hair with a tenderness she could almost believe if she didn't know this is the same tongue he gives to all the women he seduces.

Meredith clears her throat.

Al separates from April with a wet sound, intentionally loud. Without hesitation he puts on his reading glasses and picks up the check.

Oliver takes out their father's credit card, pretending he hasn't noticed since clearly the demonstration was for him, and both brothers leave absurdly large tips.

"I don't know about anyone else," Meredith says, adjusting her shoulder strap, "but that sure made me horny." She downs the last of her cognac. "I think we should do this more often."

April exchanges a glance with Oliver, his eyes steel, her throat a burning coal. "Wonder if the kids are asleep yet," he says routinely.

April wipes her mouth with her napkin and follows Al out of the booth. She gets behind the wheel.

"April." Al reaches for her hand. "I've missed you."

The house smells of caramelized peaches and toasted piecrust. "How was dinner?" Hal asks.

"Eventful!" Meredith says, sitting at the table.

"It was fine," Oliver says. "Thanks, Dad."

"Everyone, have a slice," Hal says. "The peaches are from April and Al's farm. Phoebe and Nula rolled the crust. Lochlann and Beryl peeled the fruit."

April tries to picture Lochlann peeling a peach. He liked to bake with her when he was little, a century ago. She glances over at the couch, where the kids are huddled around cat videos. April wishes she could sit with them. But Beryl is describing her vegetable garden, string beans and tomatoes, the challenge of gardening in the Cape's sandy soil. Oliver listens with polite detachment, his face a stone, exhaustion setting in from the previous night in the tree house. Al does not pretend to listen, sipping his wine, eyes roaming to Meredith's painted nails, her cleavage. Too drunk to be discreet, he rests his gaze on the pale, freckled chasm where curve descends into shadow. Catching his stare, Meredith offers a sumptuous smile. Heat stings April's face. Beryl meets her eye as if to say *Do you see your husband?*

Al pours himself more wine, but the bottle goes empty.

"Finished it off?" Oliver says. "What a surprise."

"No one's driving," Hal says. "Oliver, grab a bottle from the pantry. Hopefully there's one left. I'll shop tomorrow."

"Maybe we should call it a night," April says.

"Light bulb's out," Oliver calls from the pantry. "Which side?"

"Left, I think," Hal says. "Up high."

April escapes to the bathroom, underwear damp, a small, persistent throb searing her with shame the way it did when she took the train home from New York. Thirty-nine, with a son in high school, she sees how much of her life has run out, how fixed and unchangeable things are. Yet a decade from now, on the cusp of fifty, she might remember this night and think, *I was young, and I didn't know it.* The hand soap smells of lilacs. She touches her lip, tender from Al's ardency, and reapplies her lip gloss.

"April," Hal says, "no one can find the last bottle. Can you take a look?"

Worried that Lochlann took it, April enters the pantry. She smells a scent like rosewood, an arm grazing hers. She gasps. "Oliver, you scared me."

"It's not here. I've looked everywhere." His voice cold. But was it her fault? Isn't he the one who set the fiasco in motion by asking her to dance?

Her eyes adjust to the dark. "It's behind you, over your head. Move."

He does not move, his cologne scented with the musk of perspiration. "Quite a show," he says. "You two should take that on the road."

"Get out of my way." She reaches over him for the bottle, trying not to brush against him. His chin grazes her nose, air passing from his lungs to hers. He props his hands on the ledge behind him as if to uphold the pretense—just a narrow space, a wine bottle—his body a hairbreadth from hers. She tries to coax the bottle into her hands, his exhalation on her cheek scented with wine. It wobbles on the shelf. Just when she thinks she's clear of him, his chest touches her breast. The jackass moved. She hears his breath catch, a shock of current.

"April." The ache in his voice shakes her brain like a dice cup.

"Shut up before I kill you."

A distant burst of laughter erupts from the living room. April lurches back, nearly drops the bottle. The pantry door flings open to blinding light. "Find it?" Hal asks.

"Got it." April rushes out.

She turns back to see Hal staring in at Oliver, assessing him. "Son," he says curiously. "Find us some chocolates, will you?"

Upstairs, April says good night to the kids and avoids the adults. She thinks Al will linger with the fresh bottle, but he follows her into the bedroom. As soon as the door is closed, he presses her against the wall, unzipping her dress. The smoky licorice of his nightcap fills her mouth. "Al," she says, "we have to talk first. There's so much—"

He pops her breast out of her bra and puts his mouth on it.

"Listen to me. There are serious things—" But her head swims and everything in her body begins to swirl. He cups her backside and carries her to the bed. In fifteen years, their lovemaking has followed numerous scripts, Al loath to repeat himself too often. This is the one where he sets her down and puts his head under her skirt. She wants to say she's not going to be his port of call girl on vacation; that they need to talk about who they are to each other; that it's embarrassing to have him flirt with Meredith in front of everyone; that what he did in the restaurant was humiliating; that if they are going to stay together, he needs to start taking care of his health, but in less than a minute, April is inside out.

22

Oliver waits for shouting from the room next door but instead hears a piercing cry that could be a call for help if it wasn't followed by a suppressed withering moan. Meredith stares, saucer eyed. Oliver sits on the bed, mind ringing with unfamiliar notes, a melody assembling itself quick and forceful as an incoming storm. He tries to hear the harmony, one strand overlaying another. Meredith rivets her gaze on the wall, silent now except for a creaking percussion. She snaps off her bra and holds it aloft with one finger. "Do you think we'd have a better sex life if we fought more?"

He looks up sharply. "You don't think we have good sex?"

"I was joking." She pushes him back on the bed. "That scene in the restaurant—that was like something from a movie."

"You didn't keep your interest a secret."

"Me and the whole restaurant. I know he's an asshole, but my God, that kiss." She climbs over him.

"Meredith, I need to write down a song."

"You're kidding, right? Do you know how hot I'm running? I could burn down this house."

"It won't take long."

"Are you pissed that he looked down my dress? I can't control your brother."

"You weren't in a rush to fix your strap."

"Of course. It's always the woman's fault."

"I didn't mean that. Ten minutes, I swear."

"Listen to me. I don't need this like I need a brownie. I need it like I need air."

"I'm going to forget if I don't—"

She rolls off him. "You're serious."

"I'll make it up to you." He stands. "I'll be quick."

"It's never quick." She groans and pulls up the sheet. "This is unforgivable."

He tears a page from Nula's sketch pad and sits at the piano with the lid closed. Upstairs, his brother's heavy steps move toward the bathroom—already done, the fool. Oliver scribbles notes with the ebony pencil. Rarely does a song come to him so complete. He smells the cedar pantry, the shock of contact. The paper is indented from the pressure of Nula's pencil. Only when he finishes an hour later does he notice the ghostly embossment revealed by the notes, the shadow of Nula's Gorgon.

When Oliver returns to his room, the door is open, Meredith naked on the bed. A wave of irritation courses through him. He knows what she'll say: *No one can see her in the dark. She needs cross ventilation. If only Hal would use the freaking air conditioner.* Oliver wishes she'd cover up, but it's the wrong time to argue. He closes the door and gets into bed. The cadence of her breath tells him she's awake.

"Love," he says, "I'm sorry, but I got the whole thing. It came to me in one massive download." He stops himself. He's said it again—*I'm sorry, but.*

"Oliver, we're not good lately." She sits up, her loose breasts angling away from each other. "What's happening to us?"

"How about we take a trip, the two of us?" he asks. "A weekend getaway."

"Hmm," she says sleepily. "We haven't been to Paris in a while."

"Paris could work," he says. "I was thinking more like Bryce Canyon or Glacier Bay."

Her mouth twitches. "Sure, Oliver. We can do glaciers."

"Fine," he says. "Paris."

"You're still disappointed we didn't keep your dad's cabin in Ireland. You have to admit, it was rustic."

His chest pangs. "Of course not. What could be more romantic than Paris?" He looks at the darkened ceiling, the invisible corners of the room. Until tonight, no song has come to him since the sale of the cottage. How stupid of him to let the place go.

"I don't mind Rice Canyon," Meredith says. "Does it have a Club Med?"

"I'm sure there's one in Cannes. Let's do France." He kisses her, catches a whiff of citrus-scented night cream. "How can I repay you for tonight?"

"Well, I was thinking," she says tentatively. "Lisbeth and Cole have been asking us to dinner again."

He bows his head. He can't believe she's brought them up.

"This is what I mean." She pulls the sheet over her chest. "Why can't you be more open-minded?"

"Dinner out, I don't mind. It's back to their apartment I object to."

"What was the harm, Oliver? They stayed to their side of the room. It was exciting."

"I've never felt more embarrassed in my life. Seriously, you want to do that again?"

"Forget I asked." She slumps down.

"If you enjoyed it so much, why don't you go there yourself?" he says bitterly. "I'm sure they'd love the audience."

"You'd hate me for that."

"You set me up that night. You knew what they were planning."

"I want us to loosen up, Oliver. I want to go with you. That's the whole point."

"Maybe you're more evolved than I am. The idea of sharing you does not excite me."

She sits up. "Lisbeth finds you incredibly hot."

"Jesus, Meredith, why would she tell you that?"

"Why not?"

"And I suppose you think Cole is hot?"

"They both are."

"Exciting fantasy makes for disturbing reality."

"Just dinner, then."

"I didn't even like them when their clothes were on."

"I'm willing to go to an iceberg for you. We're all work, Oliver. We don't have any fun."

"Isn't that what this week is for?"

"And look at the ball we're having."

He rubs his face. "I'm sorry I'm not enough for you, Mere."

"You're everything to me. That's why I want us to enjoy life." She moves closer. "Tell me you'll think about it. Call it my birthday present."

"Fine. I'll think about it," he says, but the lie feels ugly in his mouth. He can't be someone he's not.

She lies back, pulls him close. "Oliver, you're a gorgeous man. I want people to drool for you and know that you're mine."

Darkness fills him, devoid of a single note. He closes his eyes and holds her.

23

Al's broad chest warms April's back, his hand cupping her breast the way they used to sleep. "I can't believe we just did that," she says.

"Tell me you didn't enjoy it."

"It's not good to pretend everything's fine."

"April." He nuzzles closer. "What if you and the kids move back to New York?"

She can't see his face, his breath in her hair. "Seriously?" she asks.

"We'll hire someone to manage the farm, give you a break."

"Live together?"

"We've done it before."

"Barely," she says. "Loch's going into junior year. I can't think of a worse time."

"He'd be closer to Phoebe."

"What about the dogs?"

"We could get a bigger apartment."

The last thing she wants is to leave her land, the horses, the quiet breezes. She can't picture giving up Brontë. "What would I do?"

"I don't know. Have more time to write?" he says. "Think about it."

"I'm supposed to believe you're going to change because I'm around? You nearly hit on the hostess tonight. You nearly hit on Meredith."

"I did not."

"This is what I mean." She pulls the covers. "If you've been doing it all your life, there must be some part of you it serves."

"No, April. The only thing it serves is this lamprey on my brain," he says. "What about you? You changed after the kids were born. How'd you do it?"

Her life before seems like someone else's past. At the time she didn't recognize the shift, like canoeing along an estuary unaware she was making the final turn that would lead to open water. "I didn't have a choice. Suddenly I was a mom."

"And you rose to it. Hell yes, that was a choice," he says. "What about me? I had a dad saying rosaries for me. What's my excuse? I'm sick of myself. I think if we lived together, I'd have a chance."

She wishes he were right. "How about you spend more time on the farm, we visit the city more? Start there?" she asks doubtfully.

"What I'm trying to say is, I'm trying to ask you to marry me, but for real this time, license and all."

She turns to look at him, his eyes hollow and exhausted. "Are you feeling okay?"

He laughs. "I try to say something romantic for once and you think I'm sick."

"I mean your cough. Have you seen a doctor?"

"It's not about that."

She touches his face, the bristly growth, swollen eyes fighting sleep.

His voice grows sluggish. "I mean it. I'm at the end of something. I can't explain it." His eyelids flutter. "Marry me, April."

"Al, will you remember this in the morning?"

He's already out.

24

2002

When Oliver had been in Ireland for six months, his note arrived in April's mailbox with nothing but the address of the cottage. After his engagement to Bernadette had exploded, he quit law school and went abroad. April flipped over the card. It was like Oliver to be cryptic, but the absence of words unnerved her. Was it an invitation to visit or to write? Her life was going well; she was back in school, working, taking a break from men. For once she felt strong. Why not visit? They could sit in a pub and talk like the old friends they once were.

As she stood in the bow of the ferry, Galway Bay misting her face, a sea eagle glided over swells, supple and elegant, steered by precise movements of its wingtips. Suddenly it plunged into the water and emerged with a fish writhing in its claws. Beneath mammoth wings, the fish rose into a world it never knew existed, twisting desperately, enveloped by the mighty talon. The bird grabbed the fish with its beak, positioned it headfirst, and swallowed it in midair. April clutched her throat, picturing it descending blindly into the bird's gizzard.

The island emerged on the horizon, treeless and bleak. Maybe it was the missed night's sleep that made it look like a mirage. She had never taken a red-eye before. She didn't know the hour here or at home or if time was a concept she'd made up. She disembarked, woozy, and showed the address to a fisherman on the wharf. He directed her at length, his brogue so thick she could not make out a word, his cracked hands gesturing with surprising grace. She slipped her small pack onto her back—she wouldn't be staying long—and set out in the direction he pointed, bypassing the pony traps and climbing a footpath out of the village.

Fissures sliced the landscape, crevices that deepened as she approached the cliffside, open ocean roaring beyond the edge. Along the way, dwarf shrubs hid in the grikes. In large swaths, enough soil coated the limestone island to support pasture, baying sheep hemmed by crumbling stone walls. A dappled gray horse lifted his head to appraise her.

A white cottage appeared. Beyond the cliff, the North Atlantic carved sea caves out of stone in steady percussive booms. Wind rushed at her from all directions, shadows shortening as the sun got higher, her pulse drumming. The austere beauty struck at her heart. This was the place Oliver had chosen to be alone.

The red door was weather beaten, bits of thatch from the roof dusting the doorstep. What would she say? Why had she come? He was here for solitude, after all. Or maybe he had met someone traveling. Maybe they were, at this moment, together, inside the cottage.

If she sprinted, she might catch the ferry before it pulled back. She turned to make a break, gasped to see someone behind her, tall and unshaven. The uncut hair and windburned skin told her it could not be him, but the blue eyes passed through her like dye.

He dropped his grocery sack. Air vacuumed into her lungs. He stepped toward her as she stepped back, her shoulders meeting the door, the scruff of his jaw lit with sun. He smelled of peat smoke and salt air, his hand moving to her face, the wild tangle of hair. She wished he would say something—an accusation, anything—but he looked at her agape, fingers testing reality.

"April," he said. "Tell me this isn't a dream."

She opened her mouth, but no words came.

His lips touched hers, a tingle of mint. Time warped the way it did when she once jettisoned off the highway on a varnish of ice, the gully hurtling toward her. The dominoes she tipped boarding the plane could not now be stopped, his hands slipping the pack off her back, her breath choked because she didn't mean for this—did she? She didn't know. Didn't know how to respond, because despite her litany of screwing, the only thing April knew about making love was what she gleaned from movies too syrupy to believe. She had to stop him, unfreeze herself, but he drew her inside, her lungs locked, vision pixelating though her eyes were closed. She could not watch what was about to happen, her body countering, meeting tender with rough, gentle with frenzied, her pacing off, her movements crude. His hands told her to relax, savor; it was a first kiss, but his fingers on her skin were coal irons, lightness too excruciating to bear. He was going to kill her.

She knew how to end it. He resisted, tried to soothe her. "Let's slow down," he said. "I want to enjoy—" But his pent-up need made her job easy. This was one thing April knew how to do. Within minutes of meeting him on the doorstep, he lay on the bed extinguished beside her.

"Wow." He panted, hand on his chest. "I didn't see that coming. No pun intended."

She laughed, heart racing because she couldn't tell if he was pleased or put off. She buttoned her blouse.

"Hold on." He rolled on his side, taking her in with crystalline precision, eyes glacial in the center, storm gray at the edges. "Your turn."

The two syllables hit her like a foreign language. She let out a jittery laugh. Some men needed a woman's sounds to help them along, but no one asked for it after the fact. Once she grasped his seriousness, she knew what to do. She closed her eyes and let loose her voice.

Catching her breath, she turned to find him looking at her with one brow cocked. A wildfire of shame spiked through her. Their first time, a lie from her body to his.

He stood uncertainly and pulled on his jeans. "I'll make tea."

They talked about innocuous things—her classes, his travels, Dubious—tongue-tied for people who'd just had sex. He suggested walking. They hiked to a Bronze Age fortress, an overgrown graveyard, the ruins of a chapel, and, wearied, stopped for a pint.

In the next booth, musicians were finishing a session. For a moment April was invisible, Oliver's gaze fixed on the tin whistle and fiddle, a beautiful concentration in his brow. She began to relax. He sipped his beer, wiped froth from his beard. "I've decided I'm not going back to law school," he said. "I've been writing songs."

A smile filled April toe to head like water poured into a glass. She hugged him. It felt like their first true contact.

"You encouraged me," he said. "I owe you."

"You don't. But I'm happy."

He left a few euros on the table. "That condom this morning had been in my wallet for six months. I'll need to stop at the pharmacy." He glanced at her. "Unless you brought some."

She blushed. "I didn't think it was going to be that kind of visit."

"Oh." He gave a start. "It doesn't have to be."

"It does now."

"Are you sure?"

She leaned over and kissed him, briefly, clumsily. He looked into her eyes with such depth she worried what he might find. "Let's go," she said.

They walked back holding hands, twilight fading to darkness. "There's a cot in the closet." He lit a lamp. "I don't want you to feel pressured."

She dropped her purse, slid her hand inside his pants. He stopped her. "I didn't satisfy you this morning." He kissed her palm, her wrist, her neck. "I will tonight."

She steeled herself, told herself not to worry. She knew how to be more convincing.

Over the next two days, they went to greater lengths—he to make it happen, she to persuade him it had. No man but Oliver had ever seen through her. The more he tried to get her to relax, slow down, the more she began to hyperventilate. One morning, when they were done, she went into the bathroom and quietly threw up in the toilet.

She fell back into bed and remembered emptying her father's house after his death—moldy ragù jars in the fridge, dirty utensils in random drawers, a grimy blender on a bathroom counter. Her mother's clothes still hung untouched in the closet, dusty and yellowed. In her dresser, April found crotchless panties, disintegrating fishnet hosiery, a drawer brimming with dried-up cosmetics. She picked up a rusted can of Aqua Net, which her mother had used as both hair spray and roach killer. The spritzer was clogged, but a drop leaked out, pungent with the scent of April's childhood.

Sheets rustled beside her. She turned to find Oliver looking at her. He had his mother's eyes. She remembered Avila, fierce and smart, always kind to April. He touched her hand. "What are you thinking?" he asked.

She pulled up the woolen blanket. "I was remembering the cutlery organizer in your parents' kitchen—knives and forks in separate slots. What a mindfuck that was."

She'd meant it to be funny, but he didn't laugh.

"Oliver," she said, "when you sent the address, did you know I'd come?"

"In my dreams."

"But why now? Is it because it didn't work out with Bernadette?"

He turned to her. "It's always been you, April. That's the problem."

She laughed uncomfortably. "I've always been your problem."

"I didn't mean it like that." He pulled her hand to his heart.

"Why did this never happen before, when we were younger?"

"I've wondered that, too." He looked at the stove, the smolder of peat. "I was repressed. You were self-sabotaging."

"I don't think that's it," she said. A cloud darkened the window. "Your dad was a professor. Mine was a bartender. You were a prodigy. I was a dishwasher. You left for Stanford and never looked back."

"That's not true. I wrote to you. You never answered."

He was right. She'd been on a bad roll in those days.

He brought her hand to his mouth and kissed it. "I don't pretend to understand what's happening between us. It has its own timeline."

She withdrew her hand. "I'm not right for you."

"Love, maybe you should let me decide." He traced a circle around her belly button.

She stopped him. "Most men don't care if a woman comes as long as he does."

"That's not true. Who can enjoy it alone?"

He was even more naive than she'd thought. "I'm enjoying it. Just not the way you want."

He moved a strand of hair out of her eye.

"It doesn't happen for me, okay? I can't go there."

He weaved his fingers between hers. "Is it because of what happened to you?"

She pulled the blanket tighter. "I don't know what you mean." It was a mistake to have confided in him all those years ago. He misunderstood. She wasn't traumatized. On the contrary, she mastered the art of smothering reflex—sneezes, blinks, breath, screams. She could suppress anything, plunge her body into cold storage, snip buds before they popped. To keep one part of her intact, she had reached into the part that was expendable and wrung its neck. "There's no reason," she said.

He leaned on his elbow, facing her.

"I need to go home."

"No," he said. "We're here."

Outside the window a jagged stone wall framed a luminous pasture, colors so vivid they looked fake. "This is who I am. I'm sorry."

"I get your need for control. I respect that. But this is me now. This is us."

She looked away, the heady perfume of the peat stove filling her lungs.

"Tell me what you're afraid of."

Above the pasture, roving clouds darkened and rolled. "You," she said.

He placed his ear to her breast. Oliver, connoisseur of sounds, was listening to her heart. "What if you just rest, don't try for anything?"

"I'm not your mission. I'm not something for you to fix."

"I don't want to fix you. I want to go somewhere with you, a place I can't go alone." He traced the arc of her brow. "Close your eyes and let me touch you."

"I can't close my eyes. My eyes won't close."

"Open, then. We look each other in the face."

"I would explode."

"April," he said, "that's the point."

"Not the way you mean."

In the dimming light, his eyes darkened like stratums of sky, smoke blue with flecks of indigo. "How about we just look at each other? Feast our eyes. We don't have to touch at all." He moved the blanket down gently, plumped his pillow, and settled beside her, his gaze moving down the slope of her waist, up over her hip. "I could look at you all day."

His brows were dark and dense, beard flecked with red, soft mouth, ears the shape of question marks. To her, everything about him was perfect—the ledge of his collarbone, the dots of braille encircling his nipples, the raised seam on his balls vanishing into the sleeping curl of his penis. She loved the sculpt of his ankles, the length of his toes, the intoxicant musk of his armpits. He'd had a goatee years ago but shaved it for his fiancée. "Will you keep the beard?" she asked.

"Do you like it?"

"It makes you look untethered."

"Then yes."

"Your eyes are the color of the sky," she said.

"Yours are the ocean at night."

"Another reason we can't work. The two can never meet."

"Just the opposite," he said. "They can't not touch."

It was hard to look into such blue eyes. She felt too seen. Yet she couldn't stop looking. "I want to kiss you," she said.

"Only if we make it last. A daylong kiss. Nothing else." He put his lips on hers slowly, lingeringly. She opened her mouth, let her tongue touch his, the taste of him lighting up her abdomen, her thighs. She let out a long breath, felt his mouth smile beneath hers. The room darkened and brightened as clouds came and went, a quick rainfall followed by a burst of sunlight. The kiss deepened and sweetened. She grew sleepy and then vividly awake. She pulled his face against hers, felt the full shock of his tongue in her mouth. She tried to pull him on top of her.

"Easy," he said. She gripped his hair, sucking his tongue. The bed convulsed, the sound of a woman weeping. He would never be hers. She was condemned to know what she would never have. She groped for him, but he held her hand, pressing his tongue deeper. She was plummeting back through time, sucking her mother's breast, clawed by hunger, extracting nothing. Wind rocked the cottage, the distant boom of sea against rock, gales wailing like a voice in her ear: *You will lose everything. Your brother, your parents, your nana, your friend, your dignity. Do you still want to be born?* A weight of ocean pressed down, violent spasms dilating and contracting before releasing into waves of bliss, mists rolling across the hills, dissipating into nothing. *Yes,* she said. *Yes and yes, if only to have this moment now.*

She saw herself strewn on the bed, limbs at slain angles, eyes fluttering in a dream of seeing herself in bed, body shimmering like limestone after heavy rain. Beside her, Oliver's eyes shone. She wondered if he was done with her now. He got what he wanted in only three days. He always was a quick study with a new instrument. But he kissed her, drew her against him. "Love," he said.

"Oliver," she breathed. The shape of his name inside her mouth was rapture.

❧

April awakened to the aroma of melting butter. Naked and shivering, she pulled on his Aran sweater, coarse against her nipples. Humming and bare-chested, Oliver was cooking her breakfast.

"Morning, Simone," he said, that soothing baritone. He cracked an egg one-handed and reached for her. The yolk hit the pan, a frantic sizzle. The dam that took her a lifetime to build had washed downstream as flotsam. His eyes glowed with success. He had blasted away the distrust she needed to survive in the world.

He served her ripe plums, dewy and cold, crusty bread warm from the oven, and strong tea. Beneath the table, their knees grazed. An inch apart felt too far. She asked about the songs he'd written. He showed her one he'd been struggling with. She glanced at the lyrics, suggested he cut one word so the last syllable landed on a stressed beat. "It won't make sense on paper," she said, "but our ears will make the leap."

She saw him play it in his mind. He looked at her in disbelief. "Do you know how long I've been wrestling with that?"

"I'm a genius."

He guided her onto his lap.

On the second-to-last day, they walked a cow path up to the cliff, the wind fiercer as they ascended. A ewe brayed at them to keep their distance, her newborn lamb struggling to its feet. The path dissolved into bare limestone cracked by giant faults. The savage crash of waves got louder. Mist moved in swift currents, blurring the edges of the landscape and shrinking the visible world. Out of the ether, hoofbeats approached, an ash-white donkey emerging into form, the same hue as the fog, eyes hooded by a shaggy coat. It meandered, sure-footed on the craggy rock, and stopped in front of them as if to deliver a message. "Maybe she's looking for food," Oliver said. "Sorry, love. My pockets are empty."

April made a mental note. "Love" connoted kindness, nothing more.

The ass vanished ghostlike into the brume. April imagined it had roamed there for eons, trying to deliver a message humans failed to perceive.

Oliver took her hand as they bridged crevices, blasted by wind. The landscape was prehistoric, a planet without inhabitants. Up ahead, a curved wall of boulders girdled a strand of cliff jutting out over the ocean. "The only way in is over," Oliver said, and began to climb the wall.

"Is this safe?"

"I come here every day," he said. "This place is why I'm here."

They scaled the fortress and descended the other side. The ruins of a dozen womb-shaped dwellings hugged the wall, carpeted with moist grass. "This is where people hid," he said. "The Vikings came through every ten years or so, raped the women, enslaved men, and left just enough for people to rebuild so they could come back and plunder all over again."

April shuddered. "You come here every day?"

"The threshold spaces are where the juice comes through. Terror is the price of admission." He smiled, brought his lips an inch from hers. "Like this space here." She wanted to lie down with him inside one of these dwellings, feel his weight holding her down, safe from the Vikings. His lips brushed hers. "Let's go to the edge," he said.

"No way." The point cantilevered over open ocean, waves pounding below. The mist thinned and the contour of the island became visible. A nearby precipice stood cleaved from the mainland, seeming to teeter. "I'll wait here."

"Okay," he said. "I won't be long."

His form grew hazy, disappearing. "Oliver!" she yelled out. "Wait for me."

He couldn't hear. She caught up, heart battering her chest, and gripped his hand so hard she thought she'd break it. Wind ripped her hair. "Safer if we crawl the last few feet," he said.

They slinked combat style, dragging their bellies, and peered over the edge. Mammoth waves surged inland, exploding against rock. She wondered how deep the sea cave extended beneath them, how long before the ground that held them tumbled into ocean, what sound it would make. She wondered if their weight alone was enough to trigger the fall.

"I never imagined anyone would be here with me." He looked at her, that penetrating gaze. This was as far inside the real Oliver as she'd ever been, light shining from his eyes. "When I found this spot, I realized my whole life was leading me here, and catastrophe was the only way I'd find it." He took her hand. "And now you're here. It feels like we've been summoned. Do you feel that, too?"

She answered by pulling him close, scooting away from the edge, and rolling onto her back. He straddled her, eyes blazing. She unzipped his fly.

"I didn't bring a condom," he said.

"We'll be careful."

She pulled off her sweatshirt. Snatched by wind, it sailed over the edge. She laughed in fright. Desire changed the contours of his face. He pulled up her shirt, eyes like blades, and sucked her nipple. Her breath choked. Waves glutted the sea cave below, trembling the rock, surging over rubble from long-collapsed ledges. Limestone scraped her back. She could no more refuse him than stop her heart. A cry released across the ocean, her voice an animal set loose from a cage. He was obliterating her, his eyes like a drowning man she hauled down and down until the last clench of fight in his face gave way to stunned surrender.

They lay motionless on their backs, life pulsing through her so hard she could not move even to track the clouds whooshing overhead, each wisp crossing her field of vision without source or destination. Her mind distilled into arresting quiet, her breath so subtle she wasn't breathing. She was a floating cloud of ecstasy. She wished to never move from this spot.

He touched her hand. The wind had died down, sun burning through fog. "What was that?" he asked, as if a tornado had touched down. Even if she could speak, she had no answer.

The night before she left, rain swept horizontally across the fields, flattening grass and battering windowpanes. The little stone island, an improbable dare to the sea, battened down. They intertwined on the bed, the heat of the peat stove fading. Tomorrow she would get on a plane and return to her life. She was beyond saying no to him, her entire being blasted open by yes. Words in her sternum pressed for release, an unspoken voice announcing she loved him, had always loved him, would always. A brick of peat collapsed inside the stove, imploding into heat and ash, filling the cottage with fragrance.

He tapped notes on her hand. "Since you arrived, the songs are coming faster than I can write them down."

She could almost hear the music strumming in his mind. Her heart felt physically outside of her body, ejected, exposed. "You know this can't last," she said.

He looked at her.

"Nothing good in my life lasts."

"Just because you've lost a lot doesn't mean you have to push things away."

"I'm not pushing," she said, "just noticing."

"That's a refrain you're telling yourself. You can change the lyrics."

"Things happen that are out of our control."

"True, one of us could fall off a cliff," he said. "If that happens, I'll crawl back to you." He closed his eyes, breath growing deep and heavy.

When she was sure he was asleep, she eased her fingers out from where he held her hand to his chest and tore a page from her journal. *Dear Oliver.* She let the avalanche slide, certain that once she was done, she would drop the letter into the stove.

138

On the pier, Oliver's hand in hers was warm, the morning air cool and salty. The ferry appeared on the horizon, a glint of light growing larger. She wondered what it must have been like to catch a glimpse of a Viking ship approaching. How much time did they have to gather their things and run?

"How's Al?" he asked.

"Al? He's okay, I guess."

"I hear you both moved to Boston and then back to New York." He chuckled awkwardly. "Who's following who?"

"Coincidence," she said. "He was in Boston. I was in Nahant. *Newsday* offered him a promotion to come back. Meanwhile my rent got jacked up and a friend needed a subletter in Queens. Al's in SoHo."

"Do you see him often?"

"Once or twice a week, maybe," she said. "Why?"

"Just wondering, you know, with me gone if he's made any moves."

She laughed. "I know he'd sleep with a goat if he was desperate enough, but no. He's got plenty of opportunities."

"He's always had a thing for you, you know."

"The way he does for every woman till he has her," she said.

"No, not that way."

She looked at him. The rumble of the ferry got closer.

"He told me once that he'd never get married unless it was you."

She snorted. "That's ridiculous. He'll never get married, period. Besides, we're friends," she said. "Ordinary friends. Not like you and me."

"But does he hit on you?"

"Who doesn't he hit on?" she said. "Why are you asking this now?"

"Are you going to tell him about us?"

"I don't know. Are you planning to tell people?"

"I'll have to tell Bernadette," he said. "She and I have been in touch."

April chilled. Water churned against the pier, the ferry roaring in.

"It ended so abruptly," he said. "We needed to talk."

"Oh." April's voice barely made sound.

"She's living in Baltimore with her parents. Her mom is sick. They moved her to hospice last week."

The feeling in his voice made April release his hand. "I'm sorry to hear." She wiped her palm on her pants. The ferry ramp clanked onto the dock. She remembered the letter beneath his pillow. Her muscles twitched.

"It's over," he said. "We just needed some closure."

"All aboard," a deckhand called out.

Oliver embraced her the way he had on the cliff when they slow-danced in blasting wind, singing Etta James in her ear. "I'm moving back to New York in a couple of weeks. I'll stay with you for a few days while I look for an apartment, if that's okay," he said. "We're good, April. Trust me."

The boat rocked, but it seemed it was the land beneath her feet that moved. "Trust me" was what her father had said when he threw her in a pool to see if she could swim. "Trust me" was what his partner had said when he locked the back room of the bar. Oliver embraced her. "I'll write to you, love."

25

The intoxicant fragrance of freshly cut mango fills the kitchen. If April isn't here next summer, will anyone miss her daily offerings? She sets the bowl beside Phoebe's sign: T-Minus 4 Days. In the laundry room she pulls warm sheets from the dryer. Footsteps surprise her. She whirls around to find Oliver leaning in the doorway. "Why do you always sneak up on me?"

"I'll help you fold."

Reluctantly she hands him one end of the sheet, a twin-size sailboat print from Nula's bed. "She thought she didn't have to wear the pad at night. Something about gravity." She puffs out her cheeks. "I'm a terrible mother."

"They don't come with manuals."

They shake out the static and step toward each other. He takes her corners and hands them back, a crackle of electricity. She glances beyond him out the door. "Listen, it would suck if we did something that would make us have to stop talking again."

"We're back to normal now, right?"

She shields herself with a stack of towels. "Maybe we should define *normal*."

"Texting, yes. Dancing, no."

"Diners, no. Pantries, no." She grips the linens, waiting for him to move aside.

"What about the residency? What if we agreed not to cross paths?"

"Are you deranged? Besides, I'd never get in."

"Of course you would."

"How do you know? You've never read anything I've written."

A curious focus sharpens his gaze. "Fine. Best to forget."

She steps back. "What are you talking about?"

"After my dad sold the cottage, I started reminiscing about the songs I'd written there. Went searching through my files for those old handwritten sheet notes. I found the folder." He lowers his voice. "Found something else I'd saved, too."

Her fingers go numb.

"Longhand. Four pages," he says. "I know you remember."

Her breath grips.

"There you are," Phoebe calls from the doorway.

Oliver turns.

"Dad, what time are we canoeing?"

26

From his bedroom window Al watches the kids climb into the pickup.
His father and Beryl left earlier to have lunch at her place. April and
Oliver talk across the hood of the truck, eyes guarded, mirror images of
each other. They switch sides, close their doors in unison, and disappear
down the bend of the driveway.

He could have gone with them. With the amount he has to do on
the manuscript, one day won't matter. Plus, the house is oppressive with
the AC off, his dad obsessed with his carbon footprint. But canoeing
isn't Al's thing, too static and languorous. The prospect of spotting some
raptor isn't a draw. On the other hand, sating his restlessness here doesn't
look promising, either. He feels the urge for a cigarette, finds his pack
half-empty. A noise startles him—Meredith on the phone, a quick, fiery
tone that means she's talking with her partner, Dixon.

He pictures the kids settling into their electronics while April and
Oliver discuss the day ahead. He wonders if there's a chance they forgot
something and will turn back.

Meredith's voice ripples, giddy and charged. If only she'd close
her door. Al steps into the hallway. "Haven't told you the half of it,"
she says. "The restaurant could've charged tickets. I'm telling you, my
brother-in-law's a trip."

He halts. Through the gap in the door, he catches a lightning glance
of her pacing, phone to ear, that jittery gate of hers, naked. He pivots
away, but the afterimage throbs. Smoke-white skin, ample in the right

places. Logically he gets why she's attractive, yet to him she's oversaturated, trying too hard.

"Naturally Oliver got all indignant," she says. "He can be such a prig."

Al heads toward his room.

"But I might've gotten him to agree to see Lisbeth and Cole again," she says.

Al stops to listen.

"The trick will be to have him get into it. He's so buttoned up."

Al pulls his phone from his pocket and taps the voice memo, a journalist habit of his when things get weird.

"You should've seen him that night, sitting on the couch like a prisoner in the gulag. He knew what it would have meant to me to join in, but he didn't care." She exhales audibly. "Then for the next few days, he wouldn't look at me. Wouldn't talk about it. If he expected me to feel ashamed because I enjoyed watching, he had another thing coming."

Cement churns in Al's stomach.

"So the next weekend, when he had a gig in Philly, I went back to their place by myself. You know I love Oliver, but I can't live in a fishbowl," she says. "It was a little disappointing, to be honest. The real turn-on would be getting Oliver to let loose. If only he liked vodka."

Al goes rigid. He taps off the voice memo and retreats to his room, head in hands. How the hell do marriages get made? Why are people—even smart ones like his brother—so horrendous at finding the right person? In all his years Al has never seen a marriage of so-called soulmates, a term invented by wishful thinkers.

"Not planning to smoke in the house while the cat's away, are you?" Meredith leans in the doorway. She's put on Oliver's robe. She must have heard Al in the hallway. "Thought you were going to the pond."

He clenches his cigarette pack. He's far worse than Meredith. He knows that. "You want to know the difference between you and me?"

"Uh-oh."

"I know April deserves better; you think Oliver's lucky to have you."

"I'd be offended by that if I didn't know you must have a hangover that could split an atom. Rough night, lover boy?"

He looks her over, the loosely tied robe suggesting she's game. He understands her voraciousness, her need for novelty. She parts her lips, head tilted. Why not invite her in and close the door? April's style of infidelity is more egregious than Al's. Yet he cannot bring himself to betray his little brother.

"You and April might consider turning down the volume," she says. "The whole house knows someone got laid last night."

He stares at the floor. "Maybe we should do them a favor and drive off a cliff, you and me."

"Speak for yourself," she says, those copper eyes hard and bright. "I don't know what you're trying to imply, but I love Oliver with all my heart."

"All your heart. What's that, five ounces?"

"You are in a sour mood. How does April put up with you? If Oliver cursed me out in the middle of the night for everyone to hear, that would be game over right there."

"I lied at the restaurant. Oliver could've done better."

She folds her arms under her breasts. "Let's get this straight: Oliver didn't choose to have you in his life. Siblings are inherited baggage. Me, he chose."

"Get out of my room," he says. "Before I tell Oliver about your little phone chat."

She gasps. "You looked in my room?" She pulls the robe closed. "Pervert."

"April knows I'm a shit. Oliver's a goddamn golden retriever."

She starts to leave. "I'm going to pretend this conversation never happened."

"Wish I could."

She whirls around to face him. "You're a selfish, arrogant excuse for a human being. I don't care what you tell Oliver."

"So I can tell him about your cozy nude chat with your business partner?"

"Dixon is gay, you idiot. And even if he weren't, it wouldn't matter. Oliver would never leave me."

She's right, of course. Every other weekend with Phoebe would never be enough for Oliver, unlike Al, who even on vacation is staying behind while his kids go out with his brother. He glances toward the window, thinks of them climbing into their canoes. So what if the kettle ponds are boring? He missed the point. He could be in a boat, talking baseball with Nula. "I have a friend who writes for the *Wall Street Journal*," he says. "Nothing he'd love more than a leak about a potential earbud recall."

She spins back.

"I'm not going to tell Oliver. You are."

"Tell him what?"

"About your little romp while he was in Philly."

"*You're* accusing *me*? That's rich. Go ahead, Al. You have no evidence."

Her door slams. "Oh, Meredith." He turns back to the window. "Wrong thing to say to a journalist."

27

The narrow fire road is overgrown with bayberry and beach plum, yet Oliver shaves seconds off his pace, leaping ruts and ducking branches, hoping to clear his mind before his performance. In Brooklyn his route cuts through Prospect Park and across busy intersections. Here he runs miles without encountering anyone. Meredith urged him to jog on the shore to avoid ticks, but even a few chance beachcombers seem like too many right now. He tries to hear the poems and the notes that will accompany them, but his mind falls back to the song he wrote the night before, that avalanche of notes.

At the kettle pond they rented two canoes—one for Lochlann and him, the other for April and the girls—the distance across water casting them into silence. Forced to leave phones behind, the kids lifted chin from chest to take in a great blue heron, hooded mergansers, and a wake of vultures eviscerating a carcass in the reeds. How to explain to Meredith that those minutes of sluicing quietude already made this whole discordant vacation worthwhile? He wondered if their ideas of a perfect moment would ever align.

A sprinkle of rain dappled the pond, concentric ripples converging into fractals. Bigger droplets disrupted the design, the way a good song needs conflicting notes. On the seat in front of him, his nephew stared at the bouncing surface. In the beats between raindrops, Oliver heard the depth of his own aloneness. His life was rich, yet he was unknown even to himself. The truth of him hid in the silence between notes. To have a partner more aligned to him was the wrong wish, he decided. Every day his ripples merged with his wife's and daughter's to form complex radiating patterns, the farthest reaches of which he would never see. April, near the opposite shore, was creating her own patterns with those around her. This was where life had dropped Oliver, and he knew why. Even from this distance, he could spot her sleek black ponytail springing from the back of her pink visor, the child who had kicked out the walls of his heart and swelled his capacity for love. The rain ceased. April's faraway laughter mingled with the girls'. Beneath the surface an invisible current flowed between them.

Calves aching, he enters the kitchen and downs a glass of water, cool in his throat. Al types at the counter. Phoebe grabs a banana. "Dad, you're sweating on the floor!"

"Sorry. About to jump in the shower." He glances at his brother, typing rapidly. "Why do you never sit down?"

Al gives him a bruised look. "Why do you sit down so much?" He picks up a basketball someone oddly propped on the trash can. "Come on. Quick game."

"I'm beat."

"C'mon, guys," Al calls out. "Pickup game." Lochlann ignores him. Nula hugs her stomach. "Phoebe, you and your dad against me. I'll cream you both."

"Sorry, Uncle Al. We're all pooped from rowing."

"Okay, bro, you and me." He tosses the basketball at Oliver.

"I've got to get ready for my performance."

"It'll limber you up. Let's go."

Oliver reluctantly follows Al outside. The hoop in the driveway is rusty, the net gone. They haven't played in years. Oliver leisurely bounces the ball, and Al instantly steals it. "Wake up, asshole." He bounce-passes it back.

"Okay, relax." Oliver starts dribbling.

Al punches it out of his hand, makes a fast break, and finger rolls it into the hoop. "Planning to show up?"

"Fine, I'm here."

"Man-to-man. Pay attention, little brother." Al V-cuts around him and sends it through the hoop. Normally they're better matched, but Al is fierce, determined, increasingly irritated. Before Oliver can get his bearings, Al takes a jump shot. In it goes. Al retrieves the ball and chest-passes it. "Possession, Oliver. Never gonna win if you keep losing possession."

Oliver tries to spin toward the basket, but his brother's hands are blocking him. He throws a prayer. It circles the rim and falls out.

"That's all you got, man? A toilet bowl?" Al goes in for the layup, sends it in, and throws it savagely at Oliver's head.

He snatches it. "Damn."

"One life. You can start playing anytime now."

Oliver cuts back, sends it off the backboard, but it ricochets off the rim.

"Beautiful. Another brick." Al catches it on the rebound and dunks. "What's your five-year plan, bricklayer?" He shoves the ball at him.

"Well, I hope to get a basket before I'm forty."

"What are you doing after Phoebe goes to college?" They loop around each other, Oliver dribbling, Al charging.

"I haven't even figured out what I'm wearing tonight." He tries to keep the ball from him, makes a banana cut to the basket.

Al snaps it away. "Too slow, asshole." He thrusts the ball so hard Oliver nearly falls. Al's jaw clamps, tendons throbbing in his neck. His words come out sideways, twisted and tight. "Think, Oliver. Think!"

He tries to steal, but Al elbows his ribs, sends the ball through the hoop, and hurls it at Oliver's head.

He catches it in time. "Christ, Al. It's just a game."

"That's exactly your problem," he says. "That soft do-gooder brain of yours, save-the-world brain, do-the-right-thing brain—your fucking stupid, full-of-shit brain." He fakes, dunks, catches it again. "You were the big-ass talent. I was the joke. But you know what? I went for the jugular. And you? You frittered your time teaching scales to kids. Gave up the girl you loved to make sure you didn't offend the one you didn't. Sold your soul to the god of niceness. Open your eyes, shithead. It's not a game."

Oliver spins, leaps, and sends the ball through the hoop. All net. But when it lands, Al is doubled over in a coughing fit.

"You okay?" he asks, breathless, a spike of panic in his chest.

Al spits into the flower bed and walks into the house.

28

"Feels like a church," April says, staring up at the hammered glass windows of Preservation Hall.

"Our Lady of Lourdes, repurposed," Hal says. "The old gal had gone to ruin."

Yet April catches a scent like vesper candles. Gallery lighting illuminates the piano on what looks like an altar. The laundry-room conversation circles back to her. How could Oliver have kept her letter all these years when she burned his postcard after reading one line? *Dear April, I'm in Baltimore with Bernadette.* She didn't need to know more. She crosses her arms and legs.

Beside her, Al's seat is empty. He promised to arrive by intermission, but the last time they went to a musical performance, she had to poke him when he began to snore. "I wasn't asleep," he said loudly, and the row behind them snickered.

Loch leans forward, eyes on the baby grand. He has changed into a black T-shirt like Oliver, hair tied back for the first time all week, revealing the chiseled jawline of a young man. The angles of his face, at once strange and familiar, stir a question she can't name.

Robert Pinsky reads a poem about the myth of memory as Oliver weaves the piano through the lines, magnifying their depth. He performs with his whole body, foot tapping, shoulders rocking, his face transfigured. He is elsewhere, nonexistent, melded into the music, his absorption like a meat tenderizer soaking her chest.

"Shoot, got to take this." Meredith slips out of the hall.

April looks at the empty seat, astonished, and slides into it for a better view.

Pinsky comes to a poem called "Whale," a translation of an Anglo-Saxon story about Phasti-Tokalon, a creature that lures sailors to camp on its back only to plunge them into the sea.

"Lucky for us," Pinsky announces, "we have a young man here tonight to accompany us for this poem on an ocean harp."

Lochlann goes to the stage. April sees it's been planned, the water-phone covertly brought by Oliver. She glances back at the entranceway. No Al. Lochlann props the instrument on his knee, shoulders squared, and smiles at Pinsky. *Smiles.* The flash of openness in his face, sincere and unguarded, swells her heart. She had almost forgotten the boy beneath the armor.

As the poet reads, Lochlann draws his bow across the rods, angling the instrument to shift the water within, bending tones into frightening sub-sonic throbs. The spooky sound evokes the terror of the poem, fishes lured into the whale's mouth by the ambergris perfume it emits, sailors who set up camp on its back suddenly drowned as it plummets. When the poem is over, they wait a beat for the eeriness to settle. The audience roars. Lochlann shakes Oliver's and Pinsky's hands, a beam of warmth between them, and skates back to his seat. April glances back at the entrance. Al has missed it.

"That was way cool," Phoebe says. "Gave me goose bumps."

Hal slaps Lochlann's knee. "Spine chilling."

Lochlann quietly takes in the rest of the performance, shoulders at ease, face calm. April can almost picture the adult he will become. How beautiful he is. How little he belongs to her anymore.

The poets' words blur. She is immersed in Oliver, carried along by the current of music until the final ovation ends and the notes sink away like the back of the whale.

When people shout, "Encore," Pinsky returns to the mic. "Let's give the final word to my brilliant accompanist, Oliver Night," he says, and steps off the stage.

Oliver runs his fingers over the keys as if deciding what to play. Let it be instrumental, April prays. She steels herself, but her folded arms cannot keep his voice from entering her body, a baritone deep as the sea, with a range that plummets and soars.

Two pillows whispering darkness,
Night mingles ocean and sky.
Beginning and end have no edges.
Hearts black with memory's lies.

She is hurtling downstream toward a waterfall, nothing to hold on to. She looks up to see him glance her way, the bottom dropping out, her body in free fall. "Sure, one of us could fall off a cliff," he once told her. "If that happens, I'll crawl back to you."

He finishes, head bowed, and the audience thunders. Hal, Beryl, and the kids pop up, but April stays in her seat, collecting herself. She listens to the buzz of conversation as Oliver chats with admirers and signs programs. She likes watching him this way, invisibly, the music echoing inside her.

He spots her and comes over, looking tired but energized, color in his face, electricity pouring off him. "Meredith?" He sits down.

"Had to take a call. But she was here for most of it."

He looks at his feet.

"She enjoyed it. I could tell." The room slowly empties. "If being an uncle were an Olympic sport, you'd get gold."

He frowns at the comment.

A thirtyish woman approaches, shuffling sideways down the row in suede heels. "You were phenomenal," she says. "I saw you last spring in Chicago. You're my fav— Excuse me. Is this your wife?"

"Yes," he says.

"Nice to meet you." She vanishes.

April flushes. Clearly he wanted to announce he was married, that's all. She gathers her things.

"Stay," Oliver says. "How did I sound?"

She shields herself with her purse. "Wide and deep," she says. "All in."

He looks at his hands. "That's how it felt, like the room fell away and it wasn't me playing anymore. The song was playing me, like it wanted to hear itself." He turns to her. "That's all I want. To be the space the music comes through."

"Oliver, you are."

"What if the music's too big and I'm too small?"

"Stretch."

He looks at her curiously.

"Al's right. You need a better manager. You should be touring more. Why not line up some gigs in Europe?"

He rubs his hands.

"Phoebe's old enough to stay home alone. You need more exposure."

"What I need is time to write. Another farm trip would help." Elbows on knees, he looks into her eyes. "The students want to go back."

"Don't get their hopes up." She lowers her voice. "I don't even know how long I'll have the farm."

He straightens. "What do you mean?"

"It's appreciated so much. I could never buy Al out."

"Wait." He glances over his shoulder. "Are you two—"

"I don't know. We're talking. Don't tell the kids."

Oliver's jaw drops. "Well, if you split, you get the farm, he gets the apartment, no?"

"The farm is in both our names, sixty-forty his. The apartment is all his."

"You need a lawyer. That farm is part of you," he says. "Where would you go?"

"Like I said, we might still work it out." She shouldn't have brought it up. She turns to him, more emotion in her voice than she wants to reveal. "You were amazing tonight. You should be focusing more on your career."

He arches back in the chair, covers his eyes. His throat makes an anguished sound.

"Hey, babe." Meredith stares down at them. "You played your ass off."

He stands and returns her embrace.

Outside the hall, the kids run to Oliver and Meredith's car, petitioning for ice cream. If April doesn't follow, will they notice her absence? Her pickup is in the far corner of the darkened lot. These are the moments she hates, more often now as her children get older, when she must get into a car without them to go someplace they're not, the abysmal emptiness catching her off guard, showing her how much she depends on the filigree of family.

She gives her bag a violent jerk and riffles through for her keys. Inside the cab, bleakness shudders through her, Oliver's lyrics moving in her veins. She pulls a tissue from the console but gets a tuft of down. She forgot about the stowaway mouse. She stuffs fiberfill back into a hole, straightens a bent ear. As a toddler Locky had smuggled Mousy everywhere, including to Oliver's wedding. April settles into the creaky driver's seat and lets the day rush back—Oliver's tuxedoed shoulders, Meredith's satin bodice, Lochlann scribbling in his coloring book. As the couple processed, April stayed riveted on a stained glass window, broken fragments of color, heart battering her ribs like a caged bird in a fire. All she had to say was one word: *congratulations*. Eye contact not necessary. But the receiving line was sluggish, Oliver incapable of generic phrases. Her feet began to swell.

"Three years apart?" A man in python shoes gestured to April's belly. The bride's relatives looked like they'd arrived by private jet.

"Yup." She glanced toward the vestibule for Al.

"Mine, too. They're in college now. May I?" He placed his large freckled hand on her stomach, hairs sprouting from his knuckles. "Hey, felt a kick."

She had slugged men before. What she lacked in power she made up for in speed. She caught a glimpse of Al's cinnamon hair, plucky smile. She tried to meet his eye, but he was engrossed in conversation with one of the bridesmaids. By the time April approached the vestibule, they'd disappeared outside, probably on the pretext of needing a cigarette. Maybe the bridesmaid was a smoker, too. Maybe she had, at that moment, decided to become one. Al was a persuasive man.

Oliver's bride turned to April, gown falling like a snowdrift. "You look so beautiful," April said. "Oliver's mother would have loved to meet you." A mistake to bring up Avila, to position herself as someone from Oliver's past, and worse, to put his name and *love* in the same sentence.

"Thank you so much," Meredith said. "Sorry, who are you?"

"I should have introduced myself. I'm April." She paused. "Al's wife."

Meredith's pretty mouth swung open. Perhaps she was about to wish April a happy birthday. She turned to Oliver, who was absorbed in another conversation or simply avoiding April. "Oliver." She poked him. "Get out! You never told me your brother was married."

Cinders erupted beneath April's skin. Yet her name had been on the invitation, *Mr. & Mrs. Allen Ignatius Night*, in Oliver's own script, though *Night* was not her name—April Simone erased.

Meredith's child popped out from the folds of the wedding gown, black hair threaded with daisies. Locky shrieked in delight, and the two of them tore into the church with madcap leaps. April lunged after them. Oliver surpassed her, reaching the children as they mounted the sanctuary, and lifted Phoebe in his arms. Lochlann launched himself onto April's belly. Oliver faced her on the altar, his gunmetal eyes pulverizing her bones. She wished she could disappear.

She marched down the aisle, smiling tightly, her face ablaze. Oliver matched her stride. She fell behind, not daring to walk on the white runner beside him. They were almost to the vestibule when Lochlann hurled Mousy at Phoebe, bouncing it off Oliver's shoulder. He got down on his knee to retrieve it.

April's breath stopped, Oliver kneeling before her. Eyes agleam, Locky removed his shoe and tossed it down. From the rear of the church, an eruption of laughter. Oliver handed her the mouse and the shoe. She had no choice but to take them. Their fingers brushed—a jolt of neurons. Her lips formed the required words, *thank you*, but without enough breath to push them out.

Outside, Al ground a butt into the pavement with the toe of his oxford. No bridesmaid. Another case of April's hyperactive imagination. *Why was she so fricking insecure?*

"Rosie, you shouldn't be carrying him," Al said, taking Loch in his arms. "What's wrong, babe?" he said gently, seeing her eyes.

"Just hormones," she said.

He held Loch with one arm and hugged her with the other as the couple exited the church to a shower of birdseed. Through the limo window, April caught Oliver glimpsing her wrapped in his brother's embrace. She nestled closer.

The chirp of her cell phone startles April from reverie, Nula's name aglow. A bubble of relief rises in her chest.

> Uncle Oliver says to tell you we're
> at Chocolate Sparrow. Come.

29

April puts on a smile and finds them inside the cheerful frenzy of the ice-cream shop, highly refrigerated, overly lit. Nula hands her a take-out cup. "Uncle Oliver said you'd want the Amaretto Chocolate."

April blushes.

"I didn't get you a lid. It was plastic."

"No problem."

Outside, Nula moves toward Oliver's car with the others. Oliver tucks his hand around Meredith's waist, kissing her temple. What must it be like to be the landing pad of that affection? April knew once. Even as a kid, he'd been kind. She ought to be grateful for that. She is grateful. But now the empty cab of her pickup awaits her.

"Nula, want to ride with me?" April calls out. It's wrong to ask. Parents are supposed to look out for their children's needs, not the other way around.

Nula hauls up into the passenger seat beside April. She's tall enough for the front now. "Don't you want to eat your ice cream first?" Nula says. "I'll wait with you."

"Thanks, Nules." She reaches over and kisses her head, not wanting to show her relief. "You're my favorite daughter."

A worn-out joke, but Nula smiles anyway. She looks down at her T-shirt, pulling it taut over the nubs of her nipples and letting it loose again. "A guy in there was staring. Do they show?"

"I guess they're starting."

"I don't want to wear a bra. Bras are stupid."

"There are alternatives. Sports bras. Undershirts."

"Boys don't have to wear that stuff." She frowns. "It's solids that are the problem. I need patterns or decals or something to camouflage the pointy parts. A girl in my grade has C cups already. She parades them around like a couple of poodles."

April chuckles, eats a spoonful.

"Will I be your size?"

"Don't know. My mother had enough for three women, but my nana was more or less average like me."

"Aunt Meredith has big ones."

"True."

"She seems to like them."

"Might as well enjoy your body."

"Well, I don't enjoy these stove knobs." She looks at her shirt.

"'Stove knobs'?" April laughs. "Where'd you get that?"

"You know, the bumps on a humpback's head, how you ID them. Fine for whales, but I don't want these things identifying me." She crosses her arms. "He was looking at my backside, too, that man. At first, I thought my period had gone through."

"I'm sorry, Nula."

"Are my shorts too short?"

"No. You're perfect. People stare at young women. You can think you have the right clothes or the wrong clothes or you're too fat or too skinny, and really it doesn't matter. People stare."

"Men, you mean."

"Mostly."

"Phoebe was crying in the car. Some boy wants to know if her pubes are straight or curly."

"I hope she tells her mom."

"I don't have hair down there yet."

"You will."

"What if I don't want to be a teenager? What if I want to stay like this?"

"I'd like to stay the way I am, too, but our bodies think otherwise. They're hardwired for change. It's their manifesto."

"The older kids at school are all so stupid. They talk in fake voices. They laugh forced laughs. It's all bullshit. Sorry to curse, Mommy, but it's true." She picks up April's lipstick from the console. "People still stare at you, you know. Some people, especially."

"I wouldn't know."

"Daddy says I'm not like you when you were my age."

"Thank goodness."

"He says you wore microscopic skirts and skyscraper heels."

"I was older then. Daddy says too much sometimes."

"He said once your skirt was so tiny your father's friend did bad things to you."

April jolts. She puts down her spoon.

Nula fidgets. "Sometimes I wish I had a pocket sketchbook. Maybe I'll ask for one for Christmas."

"He said what?" Her voice shakes.

"I'd just come home from the lake and, well, I guess my swimsuit looked different on me than it did last summer." She folds her arms. "He looked kind of panicked. Told me to be careful what I wear. That's why I brought my swim shorts."

"Sweetie, there's nothing wrong with your swimsuit."

"But is it true what he said?"

April puts the ice cream on the dashboard, chest tightening. "I was planning to tell you eventually." She had constructed a script for this moment, every word of which eludes her. "I'm sure Daddy didn't mean it like that. No matter how a girl dresses, it doesn't give men permission to do whatever they want."

"But some do anyway," she says. "Isn't that what happened to you?"

She reaches for Nula's hand. "I didn't know it wasn't my fault. Your generation's smarter. *You're* smarter."

Nula pulls her hand back. "You mean 'cause I carry pepper spray?"

"It wasn't because of the way I dressed. It's because my father couldn't see it was dangerous to have a fourteen-year-old girl bus tables in a bar till two in the morning."

She sits on her hands.

"I'm not saying all men are predators given the chance. Absolutely not. I'm saying a situation like that increases the odds of one finding you. And one did."

Nula screws up her lip. "Plus, you were pretty. You had nice hair and all."

"No. I was vulnerable," she says. "Nula, when did Dad tell you this?"

"Last time he was home. June, I guess."

"Is that when you cut your hair?"

She massages her scalp. "Maybe."

April's chest hurts.

"But it's only made people stare more. I need to get it long enough for a ponytail again, to look more like a kid."

"Honey, you can wear it however you want. Don't worry about other people."

Nula hugs herself. "But why did you dress like that?"

"The only reason anyone does anything is to get love. That's not what it got me, though."

"Is that true?" Nula asks. "Like eating ice cream or playing Monopoly or Daddy yelling at Lochlann—all that is to get love?"

"I'm not saying it works."

"So what works?"

April thinks for a moment. "Listening. Listening works."

"Listening to what?"

"Trees. Birds. Waves. Your heart. Other people's hearts. Not so much their words, though. Words can't be counted on."

"You always go all goopy on me."

"All I'm saying is, dressing a certain way doesn't work."

"But you're dressed up tonight." Nula raises an eyebrow.

April straightens her skirt, a bit clingy, but with enough springy movement to make walking feel fun. "When I was your age, I dressed for other people. Now I use my canvas the way I want. I was thirty before I could look in a mirror and feel okay. There are benefits to getting older."

Nula holds the lipstick like a pencil. "Grandpa says I look like you."

"You have Daddy's coloring."

"But my nose, the shape of my face."

"You look like an artist. An athlete. You look like someone who is super focused."

"I'm just okay at basketball. I'm getting better, though." She tugs down the hem of her shorts. "At least long legs are good for something."

April kisses her head and turns over the ignition.

When April returns, the family is already heading down the lower trail with flashlights and beach chairs. "Help them carry the firewood," she tells Nula. "I'll catch up."

She finds Al in front of the television, bases loaded. The batter chalks up and spits. Her rage snaps the room into ferocious clarity. She catches the Band-Aid scent of scotch, sees Al's fist cocked on his hip, eyes on the screen. She grabs the bottle, hears the crack of the bat, a line drive rocketing into left field. She's already through the slider when he calls out, "Whoa." She runs, the roar of the crowd portending a grand slam.

He catches her at the edge of the woods, but she manages to hurl the bottle. An explosion of glass. The pricey perfume of single malt fills the air, twelve-year-old 80 proof dripping down a tree. "Mother of God," he says, though she's certain he has a spare.

"How could you tell Nula?" she says. "It wasn't yours to tell. I wanted to wait till she was older. No wonder she's afraid to grow up."

"What are you talking about?"

"You've paralyzed her," she says. "No kid should have to picture her mother—"

"What? No, April. I'd never say something like that. Swear to God."

"Of course you don't remember," she says.

"Rosie, if I told her, I'm sorry. I didn't mean to."

"That excuse is dead, Al. Do you hear me? I've forgiven a lot, but I can't forgive this." She races down the trail.

April rests in a beach chair as close to the pyre as she dares, the night having chilled. The family sits around the bonfire, the snap of flames blending with the hissing seep of waves. Her pulse is jumpy, fury still burning in her veins. She takes a deep breath and exhales. On the way down she heard coyotes howling off the trail, the piercing yelps of a pack defending a kill. Now motes of ash float above, the air sweetly charred. Even the children are reverent, taking in the crackle of cinders. Only occasionally do they joke about the primal terror of it all, the possibility of a freak wave curling over or a burst of flames leaping out to engulf them. The circle of feet around the fire is visible, but the faces recede into gloom. Hal and Beryl hold hands. Meredith drapes her leg over Oliver's. Lochlann and Phoebe huddle close, whispering, and Nula draws in the sand with a burnt stick. April looks from one shadowy face to another, this cluster of people her only kin.

"I have the perfect poem for this moment." Hal takes a paperback from his backpack. "'Go to the Limits of Your Longing,' from Rilke's *Book of Hours*." He shines a flashlight on the page, his voice intermittently audible. April hears the words *beauty* and *terror*. A heavy wave empties itself. Hal closes the book and smiles with satisfaction. "Some of us have to get up early for a fishing charter." He folds his chair.

"Let's take the road back," Meredith says. "I don't want to run into any more wolves."

"Coyotes," Phoebe says. "And they're scared of us."

Meredith heads toward the road, the kids dragging their chairs.

"What if Al shows up?" Hal asks. "If he comes by way of the trail, we'll miss him."

"I'll wait a few minutes," April says, though she's certain Al won't show.

"Alone? Oliver, stay with her. And make sure the fire's out before you come back."

"Will do." He glances at April across the flames. In the dim ballet of light, she feels the energy shift.

"Where's Dad?" Meredith asks, her voice receding.

"Grandpa told him to put out the fire," Phoebe says.

When it's just the two of them, Oliver drives a stick into the pyre, rearranging until it leaps in size. She eases back in her chair, listening to the hiss and crackle. Notes from his performance surface in her mind. Oliver brings his chair around to her side so they're both facing the sea. Earbuds in, he's probably listening to Mandarin, as he sometimes does at night. He closes his eyes. April closes hers, too, feeling the nearness of him. In his presence she becomes more aware of her physicality, the almost imperceptible weight of her upper eyelids resting on the lower, lips lightly touching. She crosses her legs to make sure her knee does not fan out to touch his. "One of your lyrics was a little corny," she says. "'*Two pillows* whispering darkness'?"

"Tupelos." He smiles. "It's a kind of gum tree. My dad's got some on his land."

"Oh." She startles, thinking of her secret grove.

"What would you say are the chances?" he asks. "Of you and Al splitting?"

The flames dance and lick. She pictures her land, the kitchen window that overlooks pasture, the baby alpacas she cradled from birth. Lochlann and Nula know no other home. She read to them in the hayloft, taught them to ride bicycles and horses, to bottle-feed orphaned fox kits. "I'm trying not to think about it."

"Even if you split, we'd still have these vacations." The sand at their feet appears liquid in the shifting light. "I mean, you'd still come here, right?"

She lets the absurdity of the question stand. Firelight illuminates their legs, everything beyond them falling into shadow. Light shimmies his face. She doesn't want to go back to the house, doesn't want to think of a future without these trips, Hal's kindness, Phoebe's hugs. Him.

"But we'd still text," he says. "We'd talk."

A thunderous wave rushes toward them. She holds a breath, wondering if it will reach the fire. It recedes in time. "What lesson are you up to?" She gestures to his earbuds. "Can you order from a menu yet? Are you beyond *hello* and *where's the bathroom?*"

He takes out one earbud and hands it to her, keeping the other in his own ear.

"I won't understand a word," she says. "I don't even know thank you or goodbye." Salty breeze stings her eyes.

He touches the screen of his phone, perhaps changing the lesson to something simpler. She takes the earbud uncertainly, pushes the node—still warm from his ear—into her own. It slips out, her fingers fumbling. He kneels on one knee, cups a strand of hair behind her ear, and pushes the bud in. Her breath stops. Not Mandarin. Sound floods her brain, a human voice, a long vowel sound like cosmic noise, the birth of the universe ringing through space, vibrating through her. She shuts her eyes, the other earbud connected to him, his hand on her ear pressing the song in deeper. The *A* crests like a wave, the foamy crown forming a *T*. The voice is resonant and soulful, simultaneously pining and sated. April cannot look at him knowing he hears the same notes. Even before her brain registers the peak of the word *at*, the curl and treacherous slide into *L*, a jolt seizes her, a net dropped head to toe. *At last . . .* Etta James's lyrics in her ear dovetail ache with relief, outset with arrival. *Wrapped in clover . . .* It's a trap—these words, his voice, a long-ago dance blasted by wind, the limestone cliff revolving in quarter turns beneath them. Oliver has pried open her palm and placed it on the seething griddle of memory.

She yanks the earbud out. "Doesn't look like Al's coming." She stands.

"Go back if you want to." He pulls his chair closer to the fire and pokes the flames. "This isn't out yet."

30

April had been back from Ireland for two weeks when she abruptly stopped answering Al's calls. He drove the Midtown Tunnel rather than endure the lethargy of the N Train and found the entrance to her apartment unbolted, as usual. Her cheapo sublet had bought her a good-for-nothing super. Al bypassed the buzzer and bounded up to her door. The last time they'd talked, her voice was aglow with neon intensity. Oliver, she said, was coming home soon and would stay with her a few days. Al pictured her buying silk sheets, scrubbing the bathtub. He knocked, heard the dog whine within, yet she didn't answer. "April." He pounded.

The door cracked open, April gripping the doorframe.

"I hope you checked the peephole before you opened," he said. Through the sliver of light, he made out a strand of dark hair, pale quivering chin. "You okay?"

"Busy," she said, steel in her voice.

The scraggy mutt nosed through; leave it to April to have a dog no one else would want. It sniffed Al's leg and, delirious with recognition, pushed open the door. Al stepped in. April covered her face, the spindly hound prancing at their feet, begging Al to fix things. To hear her cry was shocking, let alone with such force. He sat her on the couch, put his arm around her. "Let me guess," he said. "Oliver's not coming."

She turned away.

Aw, shit. Al had warned her that her sinkhole of nostalgia had no relationship to his real-life brother. As kids, he never understood why Oliver would want to hang around the same dirty-kneed, tangled-haired girl 24-7. Until later.

"This was bound to happen," Al said. "No one lasts on a pedestal."

"I did not put him on a pedestal." She shrugged free from his arm.

"It's because he's been living in your head. You can't idolize someone who's actually around."

"I did not idolize him. Can you leave?"

"I told you before you left. Whatever void you got inside, Oliver's not gonna fill."

"My God. For the least introspective person on the planet, you sure like to analyze everyone else. Go home."

He stood to leave. Through the kitchen door, something caught his eye. The white eyelet curtain over the sink hung in charred shreds. "You burn something?"

"Accident." Her shoulders convulsed like something big wanted to bust out.

His gut did a little loop-de-loop. "Maybe I should stay here tonight."

She shook her head like he knew she would. Fine, he could say he tried.

"Call if you want to come to my place," he said. "The fleabag can come, too."

When Al opened his eyes the next morning, metallic dread soured his tongue. He should not have left her alone. By 10:00 a.m. he was knocking on her door, twelve hours since his previous visit. He heard movement inside, but oddly no whimpering dog. "April," he called. "Let me in or I'm ramming the door."

The latch released. She peered out with a vacant smile, eyes raccooned in black, lips garishly red—her high school look. He let out a rush of breath he didn't realize he'd been holding. Skintight skirt, stiletto boots, dizzying cleavage—bizarre for this hour of the morning. "Early Halloween?" He stepped inside.

"Really?" She looked at her clothes. "Who am I?"

"Dead ringer for your former self. Got any coffee?"

She walked unsteadily into the apartment. He looked around for the dog, relief supplanted by a cold, hard chill. "Where's Dubious?"

"Neighbor's."

"Going somewhere?"

She took a swig of something on the table.

"Doll." He laughed. "Are you loaded?"

She reached into her blouse, pulled each breast up so it rested higher in her bra and appraised them. "Surprised *you* haven't made a move yet, Allen. What's keeping you?"

He had, of course. None she took seriously. "Maybe you should slow down on whatever's in your glass."

She knocked it back.

"April, you put a lot of effort into getting your life together. Done a damn good job, too. Not sure you want to flush all that down the crapper."

"Clock's ticking." She plopped down on the couch, tossed one leg over the armrest so he caught a glimpse of dark pubic hair against pale skin. "Better get a piece before the pie's gone."

He bumped into a wooden chair in the middle of the room, drew her leg off the armrest, and closed her knees. "Fine, drown your sorrows for a day, but tomorrow it's back to school and work." He sat beside her.

She looked up at the vaulted ceiling with the glass suspended between two fingers. "I ever tell you about my first time?"

His hands went numb. He glanced at the empty dog bed, the near-empty whiskey bottle, paperbacks on the coffee table beside a coil of rope.

"We used to call him Uncle Quincy, but he was no uncle. He liked to keep me late busing tables."

Al's gaze circled the spiral of rope.

"He told me I had the best legs in Nassau County, and I thought he meant for running. I was fourteen and had just joined track. Quit the next week, though. Turns out I wasn't such a good runner."

The wooden chair belonged to the desk in her room.

"I'm nothing special, of course. I know lots of girls whose first time wasn't a picnic."

Above the chair in the middle of the room, a rough-hewn beam spanned beneath the raised ceiling.

"Only person I ever told was your brother. Big mistake."

Al grabbed the rope.

"See, Oliver knew before I did that I'd only gone to Ireland to get laid." She laughed. "Life-size blow-up doll boards a 747."

He squeezed the rope. "What the hell is this?" He yanked her up from the couch, his breath hard and fast. "You think I'm going to let you check out? Go change. You're coming to my place."

"Of course he couldn't go for me no matter how good the sex. Anyone can spot damaged goods once you open the box."

"I'll wait here. Bring a few sets of clothes."

"If I hadn't flown to see him, I'd have gone on my happy way."

"You're still on your way, April. Oliver's no prize. Compared to your previous scumbags, anyone with a set of balls and no brass knuckles would look like Prince Charming."

"How about you, Al?" She put her arms around his neck. "Scumbag or prince?"

"Not like this." He pushed her back. "Go change."

"But, Al, you always loved my skirts." She swiveled her hips against his.

"Stop it, April. It was never the skirts."

She wagged her finger in disagreement and turned precariously for the bathroom.

"Don't lock the door," he yelled.

While she was in the shower, he put the wooden chair back in her bedroom with a shudder.

She came out in a terry cloth robe, skin scalded pink, steam rising ghostlike from her hair, and stumbled into the bedroom. When no sound emerged, he looked in to find her asleep atop the coverlet, hair soaking the pillow. *Damn, were there pills in the bathroom?* He opened the medicine cabinet. Dumped the wastebasket on the tile floor. Nothing, but she was crafty enough to have hidden the bottle. He climbed onto the bed, reached into the pockets of her robe. Empty. He lay down, her eyes pressed shut, fists clamped in sleep. He listened to make sure her breathing didn't falter, counted a dozen breaths, two dozen, his eyelids heavy. If she got up before him, there was a 100 percent chance she would split. He took a pillowcase and tied their arms together.

Her Hula-Hoop years with his brother had gone to hell when she got breasts and he got awkward. Oliver started busting on her for the cigarettes and miniskirts, and she made fun of his Eagle Scout badges even though she helped him earn them. One night when she was maybe fifteen, she showed up at the back door glassy eyed, with her blouse askew, and asked for Oliver. Al, home from college, thought she looked like a sorority girl who'd overnighted in a frat house. He told her the good little soldier was at his SAT-prep class. Al made sure his parents didn't see her like that—they'd always fawned over April—and drove her home though it was only around the corner, the car heady with perfume and bourbon and the brine of damp skin. He pulled up in front of her house, with its missing shingles and misshapen shrubs, and offered a drag on his cigarette. She got out without a word and disappeared in the gaping maw of the front door. He wasn't the brother she wanted.

Al woke with a start, afternoon light slanting into the room. He found April staring at him, eyes so hollowed out he could see right down to the dark center, gouged and marauded by the scalpel of loss. She held his gaze, allowed him to see her like that, blasted open, terrible to witness yet beautiful without her armor. "April," he said. "You need help."

Her breath rose and fell. She blinked slowly.

His heart swelled, doubling, quadrupling, until his chest hurt. "What you told me, that's too much to haul around on your own."

"What did I tell you?"

"Quincy."

She cringed. "Thousand years ago."

"No, something like that's never going to be farther than your back seat. The point is, to keep it away from the steering wheel."

"I was fine till I went to see your brother. I had myself back."

"You were held together with Elmer's. Oliver just melted it." He slipped his wrist out of the pillowcase. "You want me to call him? There's no phone at the cottage, but I have the number for the post office. They might be able to get him a message."

"He's not there anymore. He sent me a postcard. He's in Baltimore with his ex-fiancée."

"Seriously? A postcard?"

"I burned it in the sink, set the curtain on fire."

"He's back with her?"

"Obviously being with me made him realize what he'd given up with her. It's my doing. My wiring's screwed. Let's face it. There's a reason I've got no one."

"You've got the only person that counts. Yourself."

"Lot of good she's done me."

"April, if you think I'm going to let you do this—"

"I'm okay now." She turned on her side and looked at him. "You're a good friend, Al. I'll call you—"

"Quit the bullshit." He leaned on his elbow, facing her. No way was he going to let this be the last time he saw her. "I'm covering a game in Vegas tomorrow. Either you come with me or you pay a little visit to the psych ward."

"Both cost a grand a night. What do you think I'm made of?"

"We can get married in Vegas. Only for a few months. They hand out divorces just as easy." He heard these words as if someone else was saying them, the idea voicing itself before it registered in his brain. He had often, after a few drinks, suggested they elope—not a joke he made with other women. But this time he meant it seriously, albeit temporarily. "Just to get you on my health insurance. You need someone who specializes in this shit. Quincy was your dad's age. Don't go calling it your first time when you know that's not the word for it."

"Married?"

"Just on paper. It's not like you'd be holding me back. I'm never getting married, anyway, and you always said you wouldn't, either." He looked at her, this person he'd known most of his life—pesky kid, wildcat teen, always a churn of contradiction, always tethered to Oliver. He wanted to throttle his brother for touching her. "Don't let Oliver fuck with you like this. You're sad when you should be mad. Why are you so attached to him? I'm the one who talked you into community college. I'm the one who calls you late at night to make sure some scary dude hasn't cornered you in your lobby. You could've died last night while Oliver was busy boning his ex."

She winced. He touched her cheek. Her desolate gaze, the sweep of hair on the pillow, combined to melt something deep in his chest. He couldn't help it. He leaned down and kissed her. Tentative. Brief. "I'm sorry." He wiped his mouth. "I shouldn't have done that."

Tears squeezed from the corners of her eyes.

"I said I'm sorry. Look, the marriage thing, you wouldn't owe me anything. We'll get separate beds in Vegas. I think you need serious—"

"Al, I did something I can't live with. I left a letter under his pillow. I told him how I felt."

"That doesn't mean anything. Those are just words."

She covered her face. "Please leave me alone. I need to be alone."

"Like hell you do." He removed her hands, kissed each eye. "You don't have 'no one,' April. You got me." He kissed her cheeks. Her lips. The phone rang. He reached behind the bed and yanked the plug. The taste of her tears hit him like the first drink after three days dry. He wondered if she was too distraught to refuse him, but she returned the kiss. He was sure of it. Fairly sure.

Al had never slept with anyone he knew as deeply as he knew April. In that way, the kiss was like his first, Al—ironically—a virgin. He rolled onto her, felt the silk of her skin, the softness of her breasts beneath his chest. "God," he said. "What am I doing?" He'd left his wallet in his car, along with his Trojans.

Eyes closed, her tears came fast and silent. The question wasn't "What am I doing?" but "Why?" This wasn't about his brother, Al thought. It wasn't spite. This was about them, Al and April, their long history, their dance of flirtation, their genuine friendship, his long-held lust. "April." His voice came out hoarsely. "I know for you, it's always been Oliver. But for me, it's always been you."

Her eyes opened, dark and moist. She touched the stubble on his cheek, looked into his eyes. Rubble, that's what he saw—a crater where her life should've been. Not the eyes she gave his brother, that much Al knew. "Aw, hell." He pulled her robe closed. "This isn't right. I'm sorry."

He told himself one more kiss to close the moment, to breathe life back into her, to let her know he was not abandoning her. But the kiss refused to end. It was the taste that held him, tart and electric. Her face gripped in pleasure or pain. She arched back, her lips forming a word he was sure was not his brother's name.

31

Huddled in bed, April ignored the drone of the buzzer. With the entrance lock busted, no one used it except some neighborhood kid who pushed all the buttons for kicks. But a knock on the door made her eyes fly open. The room was dusky, her apartment shades drawn. Beside her slept a man with his back turned, thick shoulders, snoring lightly. Oh God. Al. What had she done? She sat up, heart pounding. The knocking got louder. She forgot to pick up the dog from the neighbor. She rushed to the door. On the coffee table sat the rope, the empty bottle. She tied her robe, unbolted the lock. No pawing or whimpering. Maybe something terrible had happened. "I'm sorry, I meant to get him last night." She opened the door. Her breath stopped. Oliver stood before her, freshly shaven, a bouquet of flowers in his hand. His face contorted. "April?" he asked, as though he wasn't sure.

"You shaved," she said stupidly.

"Are you okay?" He stepped in, but she continued to hold the door open.

"What are you doing here?" she asked.

"What do you mean? I wrote to you. I tried to call you all day yesterday. Did something happen to Dubious?" He looked around, his gaze moving from the bottle to the rope to the burnt curtains. He dropped the flowers, put his hands on her shoulders.

"Don't touch me," she said.

He let go, wide eyed.

"It's okay, Oliver. I don't blame you."

"Blame me for what?"

"She's your fiancée. I get it."

"What? No, April. I wrote to you about her mother."

The room started to turn. She tightened her hold on the doorknob.

"And yes, she and I needed to talk. We needed closure."

Her voice trembled. "You had to sleep with her for two weeks to find closure?"

"I did not sleep with her," he said. "Her mother was dying. I stayed for the funeral. I wrote you this."

The doorknob barely kept her upright.

"Bernadette was the one who wanted to try again. I had to at least wait till her mother was in the ground."

The sound of the woman's name filled April's mouth with dry sand.

"Yes, I went for two days and stayed for two weeks. I'm sorry, April. I'm sorry I didn't call you. It didn't feel right calling from her mother's deathbed."

"I don't believe you."

"But I told you—"

"Don't mess with me. I know what happened."

"No," he said. "Please."

"I'm a liability. It's obvious. No one ever really gets their shit together, not someone as screwed as me."

"April, you've got this all wrong."

"Sure, you wanted to have me across the ocean, where no one would know, but the minute you got back—"

"You know how I feel," he said.

"You mean, because we fucked our brains out for a week? Trust me, a girl can't infer anything from that."

"It wasn't fucking, April. We made love."

Her ribs locked up. She couldn't breathe.

"Please, close the door," he said. "Let's sit down."

"No."

He whistled out a breath. Angry honking rose from the street below. "Fine. Let's de-escalate. We moved too fast. We'll take it slow. Rebuild." He glanced at her wrist. "What's that?"

The pillowcase was still tied to her. "You don't know me, Oliver. Every day I wake up trying to hold a thousand marbles in my arms. I take one step, I get on a plane to see you, and everything scatters worse than ever. You don't want to be with someone like me. No one would."

A cough emerged from the bedroom.

Oliver made a guttural sound—a laugh, or a gasp. "Is someone here?"

April hugged herself, the apartment door falling shut. Al emerged from the bedroom, buttoning his shirt. Oliver jerked back.

Al picked up his keys. "I'll let you two talk."

"No, Al." Her voice quavered. "You can stay."

He squeezed her waist. "Let me know if we're still catching the plane."

The door shut behind him, and she was alone in the apartment with Oliver. He stared at her waist where Al's hand had been. The wall clock ticked. In the lapse between seconds, she sank into oily darkness. "Please tell me this is a joke." Oliver put his hand on his chest. "April, did you sleep with my brother?"

A strange sound came out of her, icy and foreign. "Yes."

He gripped his chest. "But your letter," he said. "What kind of person writes a letter like that and then—"

"An evil one." A voice in her head whispered, *I got spooked, Oliver. I'm sorry. Give me another chance.*

"I don't believe it," he said. "You wouldn't." His eyes sharpened to knives, her father's eyes the instant before his fist flew. She almost wished he would strike her. "I need space," he said.

"I'm going to Vegas with Al," she said. "Today."

He looked at her incredulously.

Her face burned. She could not risk opening up to Oliver again. She wouldn't survive it.

"April, don't do this."

"It's done."

"If you get on that plane," he said, "I will never forgive you."

She didn't want him to see her cry. He stepped toward her. She stepped back.

He took her face in his hands. "Listen to me. Don't do anything drastic. If we can't work this out, you can go to Al or whoever you want. Slow down. Trust yourself."

She was the last person she trusted. "Goodbye, Oliver."

He crushed her in his arms until she began to sob. "Love," he said, "try to remember."

The donkey materialized in her mind, ghostly and mute. She opened the door and shoved Oliver out.

32

At the dining room table, April tries to write, savoring the morning hush. Etta James lights her mind like the glow of last night's bonfire. A drawing of wedding bells has been propped against a bowl of oranges with the words T-Minus 3 Days.

The screen door opens, Hal shaking out his poncho. "Ah, another early bird."

"Did you go to the cliff in the rain?" April asks.

"Sun comes up, rain or shine." He sits across from her. "Orange?" He tears thick cushiony peels from the fruit.

"The kids ask what you do out there."

"Not much." He chuckles. "I guess it's like that Rilke line, being sent out beyond your recall. When I'm out on the cliff, I can almost recall."

"Recall what?"

"I said *almost*." He winks. "My mind goes quiet out there. Most of the time I'm not thinking at all. I take it in. I let myself be stirred." He smiles. "We'll all be there in a few days for the wedding. You should have seen the priest's face when I told him five a.m. And way out there. Good thing I'm paying him well."

The rain slows. April likes being here with him in the dusky light. "Why is it called Dawnland?"

"It's the Wampanoag name. This is their land, after all. They're the People of the First Light. Of course, they're feeling pretty invisible nowadays. If only you were staying longer, I could bring the kids to the tribe's dugout-canoe demonstration next week." He hands her an orange piece. "They helped the colonists survive their first bleak winter on the Cape, and then, in only three years, ninety percent of the Wampanoag died from diseases they had no immunity to. They called it the Great Dying. Bones everywhere. Nine out of ten people. Picture that. Of all of us here this week, only one would survive. And who would want to be that person?"

"Oh, Hal."

"Sometimes when I'm out there at twilight, I can almost feel them. I wonder if some are still wandering."

"You mean spirits?"

"You might be the one person in the family who won't think me cuckoo." He looks at the stairs, the house silent. "Years ago, I was out there watching the last stars fade when I felt a presence—a young boy, nine or ten years old. I hope I'm not scaring you," he says. "Let's sit on the couch. We'll bring the oranges."

They settle on the sofa. On the coffee table, the giant tome *Secrets of the Sea* lies open to a sea turtle caught in a ghost net.

"Each day as I walked to the cliff, I could feel him from a hundred feet off, and by the time I got to the edge, I was overcome with grief." He hands her another orange segment. "It was beyond me to help him. I cried out for one of his elders to find him. A tremendous gale came off the ocean, violent at first, then tender. So intimate. In an instant, he was gone. The absence was so complete I thought I'd imagined the whole thing. Maybe I did."

"Maybe you didn't."

"All I know is that breeze changed me forever. It passed right through me. Touched every cell. The boy was the first. Then came a pregnant woman. Followed by an old man," he says. "It stopped for a year, and I thought it was over. Then a teenager showed up, a modern kid. He told me he'd fallen from a billboard. I googled him and found his name. He hung around for a good two weeks. Wanted me to call his parents, but how could I? They might've thought I was some charlatan taking advantage of their grief. I wrote an anonymous note instead. Told them he was fine, that he loved them and wanted them to know it wasn't their fault." Hal chokes up. "Weirdest thing. When I finished, the penmanship didn't look like mine, blocky and uneven, like it had been written by a kid."

April imagines what it would have been like to get such a note after her brother died. "I'm sure it meant the world to them."

"You of all people would understand," he says. "You're too young to have lost all your family."

"You were like my family, too. You and Avila," she says. "Have you ever felt her?"

"She's the one I've always wished for—but no, I can't control who shows up. Maybe my grief was too dense for her to get through."

"What do you think happens when we die?"

"Anyone's guess. Our trappings go through the woodchipper, like passing through a black hole. And what emerges on the other side? No idea. Maybe it's like a musical tone, the single note that begins a new composition. Not some generic soup, mind you, but the personal recipe you've simmered on your heart stove, your essence. That's what I wish I could feel. Her essence." He wipes his eyes. "Gone like a note in a symphony."

She touches his arm.

"Don't go thinking I'm some kind of psychic. It's the spot. Any porous person standing there at that hour will feel something big." A breeze moves the curtain, the window growing bright.

"What do you suppose makes a person porous?" April asks.

"That's a mystery. Souls are like seeds. They have to sprout in order to find out what they are. Some never break the surface. They get stymied before they even reach the light. Those are the folks who can end up hurting other people or themselves. They might seem despicable on the outside, but inside, layered under a lot of scar tissue, they're fighting a miserable battle, warriors using all the wrong weapons. Those people need our prayers." He looks at the billowing curtain. His hands go still. Footfalls creak overhead. "I'm worried about Al," he says.

"Me too."

"If he doesn't do something drastic, life might do it for him."

She shivers.

Hal gathers the peels. "Better get Lochlann out of bed. The fish bite best in the morning."

Across the table from April, Meredith wears a sundress that matches her fingernails, stirring coffee with her signature flair. Nula and Phoebe sprawl on the floor with a checkerboard between them. "Seriously?" Nula says. "Dress shopping on vacation?"

"Beryl wants to get to know us," April says. "Would you rather be fishing?"

"Not with Daddy and Loch. They've probably thrown each other overboard by now."

"Both at once?" Phoebe laughs, crowning one of Nula's pieces. "Hey, I want to dip-dye my hair. What do you think?"

"Don't do magenta," Nula says. "Everyone does magenta. Your mom's letting you?"

"She's working on me," Meredith says without looking up from her phone.

"Do blonde," Nula says. She opens her sketchbook and leafs through. "Hey, someone tore out a page."

"Maybe the Gorgon did it," says Phoebe.

"Not funny," Nula says. "I dreamt of one last night."

"I dreamt I was a leatherback turtle. I even had the beak," Phoebe says. "And the night before that, I was a mantis shrimp and could see ultraviolet."

"You're so extra. Wish I could trade my dreams for yours." Nula triple-jumps Phoebe's checkers. "Beat you. Let's wait in the tree house." They go outside.

Meredith sips her coffee. "How's the farm?" she asks April.

"Heat wave back home. I hope my farmhand remembers the fan in the barn."

"I meant your profitability. Oliver told me you're in the red."

April twitches. *What else has Oliver told her?* "Not red," she says. "Breaking even."

"Then why bother having a business?"

"It's home. And I love the animals."

"Do you want me to look at your financials? We have ten minutes before Beryl gets here. Never mind if it's too personal."

April opens her laptop. "You know what they say about small farms: you need a big fortune to make a little one."

Meredith's quick eye takes it in at a glance. "These gentleman farms are fantastic tax write-offs. I'm sure you use it against Al's income."

April lowers her voice though they're the only two in the house. "We file separately."

"What? April, that's insane. Do you know how much you lose?" She studies the screen. "Your mortgage payment's a whopper. To be expected, plum spot like yours. Fiber sales are flat. Must be a way to pump that up."

"Too many people have gotten into alpacas. The market's flooded."

"Vet's pricey. What was this six thousand for?"

"Horse with a prolapsed uterus."

"I hope it was a derby winner."

"Brontë's a rescue. Can't be ridden."

"Girl, you're not solvent enough for charity."

April pictures the mare's long eyelashes, the way she wrinkles her velvety muzzle when she smell's April's green tea. "We've had her since Nula was born. What was I supposed to do? Let her uterus hang out of her bum?"

Meredith presses her lips. "Here's the wheat and chaff of hobbyists versus real farmers. A real one wouldn't think twice about . . . Never mind," she says. "Four years ago, you sold nine alpacas for a hundred grand. Why not since?"

"They were from Draco, our champion herd sire—stud fees of five hundred dollars a pop. He died of heatstroke three years ago while we were up here," she says. "Solid black. He fell asleep in the sun and got too weak to reach the water trough."

"I didn't realize alpacas were so stupid."

"Some are smart," she says defensively. "He was a champ for fleece, not brains."

"Invest in another Draco. Focus on stud fees. That's the quickest bang for your buck. Literally." She chuckles. "Al got a nice advance on his book, didn't he?"

"We share the mortgage. The other expenditures come out of the farm's profits."

"Better yet, agritourism. Build a little gazebo and lease the farm out for weddings. Invite schools for field trips. Do what you did for the nonprofit, but for actual dough," she says. "I don't see your own salary here."

"I don't draw one. The pumpkin and Christmas tree sales are cash."

"No, no, April. That's all wrong. Here, I'll give you a prescription. Ready?"

April picks up a pen. She can already picture where the gazebo will go.

"First, start drawing a salary. Even if you can't pay yourself each month, keep it on the books as money owed you. That way, when you sell the farm one day, it comes to you as back pay."

"That's smart."

"Not to mention social security. As it is, if things go bust, you can't even collect unemployment. Second, sell your horses and use the stalls for boarding. Save your sentimentality for all those books you read. Loss aversion is the biggest reason people fail. That goes for companies and relationships. If you can't cut your losses, you're cooked," she says. "Listen to me—women have to look out for ourselves. Right now you've got more savings for your kids' college than you do for yourself." She scrolls. "Puny IRA. I hope you're not counting on Al."

"I'm not."

"Dependency is prison. You wouldn't believe the shithouse one of my divorced friends is in. Death, disability—you don't know what's around the bend. Here's the real question: If Al leaves or, God forbid, croaks, can you afford the place on your own?"

April shivers. "If we split, he has the money to buy me out, but I don't have the money to buy him out. If one of us dies, the other inherits everything."

"Then you'd better hope that man gets hit by a bus." Meredith laughs.

April shudders, a wall of metal screaming in her face, Oliver's arm around her.

"April, I was kidding," she says. "Bottom line, you've got to wake up. You have ten idyllic acres ninety minutes from Manhattan. You can make a killing. Forget everything I just said. Weddings, that's your ticket." She closes the laptop.

"Ironic." April pictures a bride posing beneath the weeping willow, the spare barn remodeled as a reception hall. She sees it. She can leave Al and keep her home. It would take years, though. Or would Al simply sign the farm over to her for the sake of the kids? April knows him, and she doesn't.

"I'll walk you through it. Let's meet once a month for lunch. Better yet, drinks. I promise you can turn a profit. Five years from now, you'll have the cash to buy out Al or sell the whole thing for a fortune, a real one."

Beryl's car sounds in the driveway.

"Meredith, you may have just saved me." April hugs her.

April turns through racks of clothing, fingers swishing nylon and silk, her daughter moping beside her. "Muzak kills the soul," Nula says.

"You brought earbuds, didn't you?"

"If only I could plug up the perfume stink in here. Isn't this a little old-fashioned? Boys fish, girls shop?"

"Beryl wants our input on a wedding dress. Or pants. Nothing too Cinderella-like—second marriage and all."

Meredith's phone buzzes. "Hey, Dix." She steps outside.

"He calls a lot, that guy," Nula says into the clothing rack.

"That's normal." April pulls a dress from the rack. "They run a company."

"They don't just talk about work." Nula looks her in the eye.

"Let's not worry about other people's business," April says.

"I'm not dressing up."

"No one's asking you to."

"It stopped, you know." She folds her arms. "You said it would last five days."

"If you're like me, it might be a week one month and two days the next. Hopefully you'll be more predictable than I am." She tousles Nula's hair. "In that way, I mean. Stay unpredictable in other ways."

"You always wear blue to fancy things," Nula says. "And black is too sad. You should go for the white. It looks nice against your skin."

"That might be weird, me wearing white instead of the bride." April holds the sundress in front of the mirror, not cream or eggshell but pure blazing white.

"What was your wedding gown like?"

"Jeans and platform shoes, probably. I don't remember."

A woman at a carousel beside them turns through maternity clothes, her puffy hand resting on her stomach, and waddles to the checkout. Nula gives her head a violent shake. "I hope it never happens to me."

"Nula, pregnancy is a choice," April says. "It's not like catching the flu."

"But you had Loch before you finished college."

"Yes, but that was my doing."

"But did you want a kid then?"

"Not a kid in general, but him specifically, yes."

"And me?"

"I wanted you since I was born. I just didn't know it until I had you."

"You always say mushy things."

"But it's true."

"What does it feel like to have a kid inside you? It must be like a house with a squirrel in the walls."

"It felt good. That was when I could protect you most. All I had to do was eat right and not fall down the stairs. Once the baby's out, suddenly there's a lot beyond your control. Germs, bullies, windmills." She smiles. "*Don Quixote*—you'll read it in high school."

"And don't forget predators."

April's smile fades.

"That's the word you used in the car yesterday."

"Nula, please don't think of my childhood as normal."

"But you did. You thought it was normal."

"Until I realized it wasn't."

Nula picks up a dress, teal green with swirls of sapphire, and holds it to her chin in the mirror. "Let's do the hair game. With lipstick this time." She reaches into April's purse, and with the precision of a drawing pencil, paints her own lips.

April bends down ear to ear and drapes a lock of her own hair over Nula's forehead, another falling down her shoulder. The image in the mirror quakes April's heart, a landslide of feeling she can't name. Nula is a woman. And a child. Both and neither, a shimmering hologram. Yesterday's leering man in the ice-cream shop will not be the last. Baggy shorts and chopped-off hair will not protect her much longer. What do most mothers feel when they catch this glimpse? Pride? Tenderness? Jealousy? Grief? Is April alone in her terror? She smashed Al's bottle in vain. He wasn't the one who instilled their daughter with fear.

Nula pulls the dress taut over her nipples and studies her reflection. "I wonder if they sell bras here."

33

Oliver stands beside his brother in the stern of the small charter boat rocking on the swells. He reels his line a few inches to test the resistance. In all their years of vacationing, he has never admitted his distaste for fishing to his father, now sitting in the bow with Lochlann. The boat's all right. It's the bait that repulses him, the stink and the slime, not to mention having to witness each catch die a desperate death. Despite seeing a school of tuna skitter across the surface, they've caught only a few stripers and a pollock.

"Sorry I missed your performance last night." Al adjusts his line.

"I might have played better if not for a bruised rib." Oliver lifts his shirt to reveal a welt from their basketball game.

Al gives him a side-glance. "Would've been nice if you'd told me my son was performing."

"He didn't want me to say anything in case he backed out."

Al frowns, looking out at the water. In the bow, Hal and Lochlann are talking, the boy pointing to something on the horizon. Al tweaks the drag on his line. There's no smoking on the boat, and his hands are starting to twitch. "I'm rewriting my will," he says. "I need you to re-up as my executor."

Oliver turns to him.

"Just some adjustments. No big deal."

A wave slaps the side of the boat, and they hold on for balance.

"Got a small medical thing going on. I'm taking care of it. April doesn't know."

"What kind of thing?"

He pulls on the line. "Like I said, nothing serious."

"When are you planning to tell her? Does Dad know?"

"Only you. I want to keep it that way."

"Might be useful if I knew what it was I'm not supposed to tell."

"I don't need your questions, just your signature."

Oliver puts the rod under his armpit and wipes seawater from his sunglasses. His brother is the last person he'd ask to be his executor.

"Just so you know," Al says, "I'm planning to stick around."

"You'd better."

"Rooting for me?" He tugs on the jig. "That's touching."

Oliver groans.

Al rebaits his line, pushing the hook through the mackerel's eye and base of the tail. "Tried to teach Loch how to do this. He's too squeamish. Wouldn't even do the frog dissection in biology last year. Teacher could barely get him to prick his finger for a lab report."

"I didn't think that was allowed in schools anymore."

"Unorthodox teacher." Al loads and casts with a small motion of his wrist, dropping the lure off the port side.

"Testing for lead?" Oliver feels a tug on his line.

"Blood types and heredity," Al says. "Loch had to text me for mine. Of course April didn't know." He straightens abruptly, as if he's turned down a one-way street. The line screams out of Oliver's spool. He didn't set enough resistance. "Better close that bail before you're out of line."

Oliver snags it, so heavy he can't turn the handle.

"Almost lost it."

He cocks the rod in his holster. The thing, whatever it is, begins to pull.

"Something towing us?" The captain makes his way toward them. "How much frigging drag you let out?" the captain says. "Thing's a mile away. Who's got strong hands here?"

"I do," Al says. "Give it to me."

Al settles into the draw. Maybe it's obvious Oliver lacks the requisite spleen. The captain wraps a Velcro brace on Al, asks if he's okay. "Got a sharky feel," he says.

Hal and Lochlann maneuver unsteadily from the bow as the boat pitches. Al cranks and leans back. "Come on, fish," he says. "I own you now."

Oliver stares at the spot where the line disappears into water. The more Al grunts and curses, vein throbbing in his neck, the more Oliver begins to sweat. Al cranks, drawing the invisible force steadily closer. "Give me the rod," Oliver says. "I'll take it from here."

Al ignores him. After forty-five minutes of hauling, the first surface splash appears off the stern, something long and narrow like a silver machete. "Sweet Jesus," the captain says. "That there was the tail. Thresher shark. Nice catch! Reel her in. Don't let her take more line." He turns to Oliver. "You gave up a good one."

Beside Al, Lochlann hangs over the side of the boat, riveted. Oliver watches him, the lanky frame, long calves, shoulders he has yet to grow into. The boy turns to look at him, eyes catching the sun, startlingly blue. "Uncle Oliver, you see it?"

He doesn't answer.

"Keep breathing," the captain says. "Making headway."

"Come on, sucker," Al says.

As it approaches the boat, the line attaches to an underwater shadow, molten and refracted in the shifting currents. A fin flashes and everyone leaps back. Al reels, jaw clamped, the thing twisting and writhing. The upper tail lobe slices the air.

"Oh baby," says the captain. "Sitting on the grill tonight."

Lochlann's head whips around, meeting Al's eye.

Al nods, sweat staining his shirt, face so fatigued he looks on the brink of collapse. He leans back with a grunt of exertion and launches into a coughing fit.

"Let me." Oliver reaches for the rod.

Al shrugs him off, recovering himself.

"Attaboy," the captain says as a gleam of pewter skin surfaces alongside the boat. "Young thresher. Dang, that's a nice-looking fish. Get the gaff."

"No gaff," Lochlann shouts.

The captain looks up.

"Cut it loose," Al says.

The captain laughs, confused.

"Give the boy the clippers. We only wanted to know what it was."

"Hell of a lot of work for a look-see," the captain says. "Would've been awful pretty hanging on the dock." He bends down to snip the line.

"Let the boy do it," Al says.

"Thing's still thrashing—"

"He knows what he's doing. Give it to him."

The shark lists upside down, revealing its pale belly and pointed fins. Lochlann's face contorts. "Don't tell me we killed this thing." Clippers in hand, he bends over the side of the boat so far Oliver grabs his waistband, knuckles braced against the knobs of his spine.

"Watch the teeth, boy," the captain says. "Thing's still got fight."

As Lochlann reaches down, a vertical line on the horizon catches Oliver's eye, a triangular blade hurtling toward them. "Get back," the captain shouts. "Back, back!"

Oliver yanks Lochlann up as jaws the length of a ripsaw emerge from the water. A thump rocks the boat, a wild thrashing, the water boiling red. The thresher's tail rises out of the churn, clamped in a larger shark's teeth.

"Holy Christmas," the captain yells. "Second time this summer."

The water quiets. Blood billows from the stump of the missing tail. Lochlann gags.

"He'll be back," the captain calls out. "Did the snips go overboard?"

An enormous shadow passes silently beneath them. The captain opens a box, scrounges for the spare snips. What's left of the thresher snaps back to life, writing wildly, frantically slapping the hull. Jaws break the surface, grasping the thresher by the middle and shaking it like a rag. The thresher twists and thrashes, the water roiling, red droplets spraying their clothes. The rod bends and Al struggles to hold on. The water quells. The rod springs up. Al reels rapidly and the thresher's head pops free of the water, decapitated. For an instant the gills appear to move. The captain snips it and holds it aloft. "Souvenir?"

"No thanks," Al says.

As the head sails overboard, the eye holds Oliver's gaze. The murky silhouette reappears, swallows the head without altering its glide, and sinks into the crimson gloom.

"Eighteen-footer," the captain says. "This is getting out of hand. I ought to ditch the fishing charters and start charging to see the great whites."

The clippers fall from Lochlann's hand. He'd been holding them all along. He buries his face in Oliver's chest. Oliver embraces him, his bony back convulsing.

"Don't worry, son," the captain says. "You may have lost the catch, but you got yourself a hell of a video. Your grandpa was filming."

Lochlann's heart pounds against Oliver's.

Al tears off his Velcro belt, forehead gleaming. Hal touches Loch's shoulder. Instantly the boy abandons Oliver and squeezes his grandfather. "It's okay, Locky," Hal says, leading him back to the bow. "You tried to save it."

The captain starts the motor. They're late getting back. Al coughs something up, spits overboard, and snaps open a beer. Oliver stands over him. "Back hurt?"

"Everything hurts." Al takes a swallow. The surface of the water is calm, the only evidence of the fight are the abrasions on his hands. The boat picks up speed.

"Al," Oliver says, "about the blood types—"

"You're right," Al says. "That teacher should be fired."

Their father sits down beside them. "Good Lord, I don't think I've ever seen anything so primal. Look, I'm still shaking."

"Can't blame the white, though, can we." Al wipes his face with his shirt. "Thing's got to eat."

When they arrive at the house later than expected—sweaty, sunburned, and stinking of fish—Oliver finds Meredith setting the table. "Sorry we're late," he says.

She splays her fingertips under her chin and gives a sarcastic curtsy, but her batted eyelashes tell him she's only pretending to be annoyed.

"Let me shower real quick, or we'll have to fumigate the place." He bounds up the stairs, still rattled from the boat. Seeing the bathroom door ajar, he pushes in.

April startles, her back to the mirror, holding up her hair to see the rear of her dress, white eyelet with the tags still on. A soapy bouquet fills the air. He wavers, breathless, the dress falling over her hip in a way that makes him remember its shape. "Sorry," he says, catching his breath.

"How did it go? Did Lochlann talk? Was he involved?" She drops her hair. "Is that blood on your shirt?"

He looks at the spatter. "Al can tell you about it. I'm never fishing again."

"You say that every year."

"Do I?" Their eyes meet in the mirror. She looks as clean and pristine as he feels grimy and disgusting.

"Have you seen Nula?" she asks. "I only wanted to see if it fit, and now the zipper is stuck."

He clears his throat. "For the wedding?"

She reddens. "Beryl's wearing pink."

"Nula's in the tree house. I'm filthy, but I can give it a try." *His brother wouldn't think twice, so why should he?* He scrubs his hands up to his elbows, the water reddish brown, as if he's a murderer washing away evidence. "I'm usually good at zippers. Phoebe's backpack always jams." He dries his hands.

She hesitates but lifts her hair. Close up, the ring on her finger looks tinny and dull, thinner than the soda can pull tabs they used to marry each other as children. He examines the zipper. "Just some fabric caught in the teeth."

"Maybe I should find Beryl," she says.

His fingers tremble. "Fishing was horrific. Did I already say that?"

"Be quick." She glances at the door. "Snag's near the top."

"I see it." He tugs the zipper.

"Don't get blood on me," she says.

"It's dry," he says. "Hey, did Loch have to do a fingertip prick for a school report? I think that's banned."

"He didn't tell me." She holds the front of the dress. "Never mind. I'll find Nula."

"Maybe if I bring it all the way up." He pries threads out of the teeth, and the zipper glides. "There."

"Thank God."

"Hopefully that's it." He nudges the door closed with his foot and coaxes the zipper down farther.

"I'm sure it's fine," she says.

He tells himself he'll halt at the first glimpse of a bra strap, but none materializes. A sensation comes over him like when he once lost his place during a performance, a complete free fall out of the score— terror and exhilaration—until he remembered to breathe, and the beat caught him on its wings. He navigates past her shoulder blades, the arch of her back, her waist, until he reaches the stop. Down in the shadows within the garment appear twin curves and a dark hollow bridged by a waistband. Her eyes press shut in the mirror. He raises the zipper a little without taking a breath. "All set," he says hoarsely.

"Thanks." She bolts out the door.

Oliver strips and gets into the shower. *Ambush*, that's the word he's been searching for, the great white's predatory strategy. But it's the thresher who writhes in his mind, the savage way it fought even after its tail was gone, that mighty desperation to live. Oliver braces himself against the tile and lets the water blast him.

He finds Meredith in the kitchen, searching the fridge. "Out of milk again?" she asks. "Do you notice everyone in this house has an enormous appetite?"

He lifts her flaxen hair and kisses her neck, downy and coconut scented. She shimmies back against him and draws his hand between her legs. He presses closer, chilled by the open refrigerator. "And we haven't even had the oysters yet," she says.

They hear movement in the dining room and separate.

34

The white dress feels alive as April slips it off. She shuts it in the closet and pulls on shorts. The family has assembled at the table except Al, who slumps on the sofa in leaden sleep, hands open as if lifeless. Between his thighs stands a glass of scotch.

"He should've let us take turns," Hal says.

April takes the glass from between his thighs, buttons straining across his chest, face sunburned except for his eyes, a raccoon in reverse. She opens his top button and brushes hair from his forehead, still damp from the shower. His face is flushed, skin hot. Even passed out, his energy feels prickly.

"Come eat," Hal says. "The steamers are out of this world."

April sits, glancing at Nula's worried face. "You know Daddy. Can't do anything halfway," she says.

Thunder explodes over the house. Al rouses, looking disoriented. He makes his way to the table, stumbling, and pours a glass of wine. Beryl appraises him. "For a man who got a big catch today, you don't look happy."

"Was Oliver's catch." He rubs his face. "Even for me, it was a bit much to watch a thing with no chance of escape get brutally mauled." He takes a sip.

"I would have puked," Meredith says.

"Goodness, we're eating," Beryl says. "The mussels are divine, Meredith. Not too overdone."

"That's a miracle," Meredith answers.

"How are things?" Hal asks. "Did you resolve the customer complaint?"

"I need to think about something else," she says.

"Yet you still keep your phone on the table," Beryl says. "Oliver, how on earth do you get her attention?"

"We take a candlelit bath once a week," Meredith says. "No devices in the tub."

"Theoretically," Oliver says. "You still text."

"Only when I have to." Meredith touches his arm. "Oliver's brilliant that way. Thirty minutes of bathtub conversation is worth a week of distraction—isn't it, babe?"

April brings her napkin to her mouth.

Meredith chases an oyster down with wine and turns to Hal and Beryl. "Let's hear how the lovebirds met."

"We've been friends for years," Beryl says. "It's best when it happens that way, don't you think? You can see how the person treats store clerks and librarians. You know what you're getting."

"But we still don't know how you met," says Meredith.

"Hal used to go fishing with my husband, Ed. Was very good to him when he got sick, especially that last year." Beryl's voice thickens. "Once we got the hospital bed in the living room, most people stopped coming by. Not Hal."

Al shifts uncomfortably. "Pass me the whole-belly clams."

"He kept coming till the end. Didn't mind the one-way conversations. He knew Ed could hear him." Beryl's eyes redden.

Hal slips his hand in hers. "Ed showed me where the best oyster beds are. We used to drive each other to Boston for our colonoscopies. Now *there's* a friend."

Meredith leans in. "Would your husband have minded you marrying his buddy?"

"Ed was the one who asked Hal to look after me—not that I'm a woman who needs looking after, mind you. Ed told us to find each

197

other after he was gone. That's the kind of man he was." She dabs her eyes.

Al locks eyes with Oliver, silent as a beach draining before a tsunami.

"But why marriage?" asks Meredith. "Can't you enjoy each other this way? Who's giving up their house? What about finances? Wouldn't it be simpler to—"

"Because we love each other." Hal caresses Beryl's hand.

"I like you, Meredith," Beryl says. "We have a similar style, don't you think? Get it all out there. No pretense. I appreciate that. What's your story? How did you two meet?"

"I was head of philanthropy at Bose, looking for causes to sponsor. I met Oliver at the music nonprofit."

"Hal showed me your wedding pictures. That dress looked fit for an empress."

"Feels like ages ago, doesn't it, babe?" Meredith leans on him.

"No wedding shots of you two, though." Beryl turns to April.

"Eloped," she says. "Saved a mint."

Across the table, Al's expression hardens.

"But how did you meet?" Nula glances up from her sketchbook. "That's what she wants to know, Mommy."

"Al and I knew each other growing up." April shifts back to Nula. "I said to put the sketch pad away."

"Yeah, but what made you get married?" Nula lifts an eyebrow.

"It goes like this." Al pushes aside his plate, a cue he's about to hijack the conversation. "Before we got married, when she and I were just pals, April and this old flame of hers had this secret rendezvous in Ireland."

Oliver drops his knife. April freezes. "Al." She lowers her voice as if admonishing a dog to untooth someone's wrist.

"I encouraged her to go," he says, "because before this guy, April hadn't had a good run with the men she picked out. At least this one wasn't packing heat." He laughs grimly. "But soon as her plane took off, I had this sick feeling, like, if she could go for this dude—no gold teeth or rap sheet, just some flake trying to find himself on some godforsaken island—then why hadn't I made a play for her myself?"

Lochlann stares, transfixed. Meredith puts her phone down. Oliver's jaw twitches. April tries to find her voice, but she's a car stalled on the tracks, train barreling toward her.

"So off she goes, comes home like someone turned on a floodlight inside her—a walking meteor shower, all shimmer and spark—but wouldn't talk about it. Wouldn't say a goddamn word," he says.

April flashes a look at Oliver. She wants to murder them both.

"Not what I expected," Al says. "See, I had this theory about your mom that she was addicted to the badass type, like a DNA imprint, probably from her father. No offense to your heritage, but your Grandpa Simone was a piece of work."

"Allen!" Hal turns to Nula and Loch. "No one's perfect. Your grandfather would have loved you if he'd had the chance."

"Dead by what, fifty-five?" Al says. "You know why? 'Cause he treated his body like a vacuum bag, filled it with crap that never got emptied."

Nula gives a start. "How old are *you*, Daddy?"

"He died from injuries from a car accident," Hal says. "Get your facts straight, Mr. Reporter."

"Technicality," Al says. "He was loaded."

A sob lodges in April's throat like a cannonball. She grips her fork.

"For goodness' sake," Hal says. "Enough!"

But April knows Al. He cannot stop himself. No one can.

"When your mom gets back from Ireland, she's too busy to see me. She's shampooing her rugs, washing the curtains because Charming is planning to visit. You'd have thought this guy was Leonardo DiCaprio," he says. "Only problem? The prince is a no-show."

Oliver goes crimson. Volcanic heat mounts in April's spine, pressuring the plates of her skull.

"Allen Ignatius Night," Hal says. "That is sufficient."

"By the time I knock on her door, she looks like a Giacometti sculpture, all teeter-tottery," Al says. "Like those people who jump from burning buildings because the pain's so bad you'd rather take death in one slam than have your skin scalded off a layer at a time."

Lochlann jerks. Nula looks at April wide eyed. She wants to defend herself, reassure her children, but she's a rabbit frozen beneath a diving hawk.

"Turns out she left a letter under DiCaprio's pillow, poured out every last cog and gear in her heart—not her usual style, see; your mom likes to play her cards close to the chest—but it was the spell of the place, all that ocean and sky. She got carried away. She's pretty sure that's what did her in. You know how guys get all spooked by that shit."

A glacier cracks in April's chest, fear collapsing into roaring rage. She pictures plunging her fork into Al's back.

"That's when I ask if she'll go to Vegas with me to eat sushi and get married," Al says, "and she doesn't say no."

April's heart pounds in her ears. Meredith's phone rings. She doesn't reach for it.

"Take your call, sweetheart," Hal says. "We are most certainly done here."

Meredith gives Oliver a glance and goes out to the patio. The weight in the room makes it hard to draw a breath, everyone speechless. Al looks into his glass, swishing the wine. "I thought he'd blown his chance and if I treated her right, maybe I could turn on those flood lamps, too," he says solemnly. "Won a hundred bucks from the slot machine and got a honeymoon baby out of it, too." He raises his glass to Lochlann. "Happiest man in the world, for a night." He knocks back the drink.

"Yeah, right." Loch's voice quivers. "Like you even care if I'm yours or the other asshole's."

April winces. "Lochlann, please," she says, her heart a rattle of artillery. "That's not true. Dad loves you." She puts her hand on Loch's, feeling him tremble. She skewers Al with her eyes. *Say it,* she thinks. *Tell the boy you love him!* But Al's eyes are glossed over. He's not in the room.

"The guy wanted her back," he says, looking in his drink. "But it was too late. She'd already flung herself out the window."

Lochlann bursts up the stairs, sobs echoing down the stairwell, a grating blend of childhood abandon and adult anguish. Phoebe runs after him. April feels a stab in her heart, her ribs imploding, pain so sharp she can't breathe. Hal slips into Loch's seat and puts his arm around her.

Meredith returns from the patio and clicks off her phone. "My God, is that Locky crying?" She looks upstairs in astonishment. "What on earth?"

"Your brother-in-law knows how to ruin a perfectly beautiful meal," Hal says. "Meredith darling, everything was delicious."

Al plays with an unlit cigarette. "The thing is, I could have called him myself. I could've said, *Hey, asshole, you're about to lose her.* I even had the phone in my hand."

Oliver's eyes turn icy. Al's words scramble April's brain. The storyline she's been living in sways on buffeted pylons.

"Put your regrets where they belong," Beryl says. "Obviously that other man was a heel. Some men will say anything to get you in the sack. Remember that, Nula."

Oliver makes a fist on the table, knuckles bulging.

Al laces his fingers. "See, Beryl, the thing you got to understand about April is that the black hole in her heart—that's her default. That's why she can't let herself be happy. That's why she married me."

"No, Daddy." Nula straightens. "Mommy gets up at five and she's outside all day and she sings in the barn. She's got her book club and writing group and chickadees who eat from her hand."

"Nules," he says gently, "busy ain't the same as happy."

Her jaw drops. "Dad, you're the one with the black hole."

Al startles. He turns to April, eyes seething.

From the stairway the sound of Loch's cries slows to a whimper. "You didn't have to be so mean to him," Nula says. "He only wants to know you care."

Al fixes on April, each word a lit fuse. "You turning my own family against me?"

The fork slips from her hand.

Oliver stands, circles the table, and looms over Al. His height fills the room, his muscles taut. "Get out," he says with chilling control.

Al looks up in astonishment. "What?"

"Get out of the house."

"Look at you." Al laughs. "Little Ollie, standing up."

Oliver yanks Al's chair back from the table. Wine leaps from Al's glass.

"About time, bro." Al daubs his shirt. "But guess what? It's not your house."

"Get out before I drag you out." Oliver grabs Al's arm and pulls him up. "Come back when you can treat your wife with respect."

No one moves. Nula's chin trembles. Al looks from one face to another.

"Your brother is right," Hal says. "Come back when you can apologize."

Al rolls his shoulders. He gives Nula one last glance, but she's staring into her lap. He fumbles for his windbreaker on the hook, gets one arm in, and struggles with the second. "Ciao," he says, and lets the screen door slam.

35

After dinner, Phoebe tucks into the sofa and pretends to play on her iPad while she watches each person acclimate to the weather in the room. Her father plays ferocious piano, armpits dark with sweat, getting alarming sounds out of the old Baldwin. Nula hunches over her sketch pad on the floor, drawing frantically. Grandpa turns the pages of a newspaper, every so often glancing at the door, a furrow between his brows Phoebe has never seen before. Lochlann stays in his room. Phoebe hasn't heard him cry like that since they were little and a bee got trapped in his shirt. Footsteps descend the stairs. Aunt April snatches her raincoat and goes out. Without breaking the music, her father turns to watch her go.

Phoebe's battery dies and she runs upstairs for her charger. Her mother comes in behind her and closes the door. "What did I miss?"

Phoebe sits on the quilt, running her hand over the puckered seams. "You were there."

"Not for the last bit. Everyone looks like a bomb dropped," she says. "Why was poor Locky crying? What does he have to do with any of this?"

"I don't know. I'm pretty sure it wasn't stuff Aunt April wanted us to hear."

"He's an idiot, your uncle. Mr. Radical Honesty, always on his high horse." She goes to the dresser and looks in the mirror.

"But he's not all bad, right?" Phoebe asks.

"Phoebe Fontaine." She whirls around. "Never settle for 'not all bad.' You don't have to tolerate a man who demeans you. Find someone like your father, someone who would never violate your privacy at a dinner table just because he's loaded."

"Okay, Mom."

"There's no excuse to stay with someone like that. She should be stronger."

"She's strong."

"No, that's the wrong kind of strong." She hugs Phoebe tight. "Pick a good career. Put that first. If someone comes along you want to be with, let them follow you. You call the shots. It's been the other way around for too long." She flops onto the bed. "Come rest with me, angel."

Phoebe lies beside her. The pictures are tilted on the walls, as if a temblor shook the house. She wonders how long before Uncle Al returns. Her phone vibrates. "Stupid kid in my class won't quit texting."

"Watch out for white guys who only date Asian girls. That's a red flag."

"For?"

"Fetishizing."

"But what about all the boys who only date white girls or girls with big boobs?"

"Just as bad."

"That rules out a lot of boys!"

Her mother chuckles. "Whatever happened to Alex Liao? He was cute."

Phoebe groans. Last winter, Alex invited her over for Chinese New Year. She thought it would be fun, until she got there and realized his family was speaking Cantonese. Even her few words of Mandarin were useless. When she said *no thank you* to a turnip cake, his mother explained in loud, enunciated English how delicious it was, as if Phoebe were illiterate in both languages. "I've told you, Mom. He's nice and all, but I don't like him that way." She bristles. "Did you ever date someone Asian?"

"Yep, sweet guy from Sri Lanka, investment banker separated from his wife. He ended up going back to her."

"Were you sad?"

"Not really. It was mostly convenience. He lived down the hall."

Phoebe pictures dating for convenience, like her friends who have hookups to get the experience. She'd rather wait for someone she likes, like Tommy Rodriguez from orchestra. "What about dip-dyeing my hair?" she asks.

"Angel, you know it's okay to embrace your Chinese identity. You don't need to change anything about you to fit someone else's idea—"

"White girls dip-dye their hair. No one accuses them of not embracing who they are," she says. "Besides, you dye your hair."

"That's true." She touches her roots. "I apologize."

"I want to do my whole head, streak it all blonde."

"Really." Her mother swallows. "It's just that your hair is so magnificent."

"And it's mine."

"You're right." She twirls Phoebe's hair. "Let's do it properly, then. I'll make an appointment at a salon. You can tell them exactly what you want. We'll go tomorrow."

"Really?"

Her eyes moisten. "Let's cuddle. You're growing up so fast, Bee." Her mom's body is warm and soft.

Phoebe looks at her phone. "I haven't answered his texts. He's going to tell the whole school I'm a bitch."

"In business, I get called that. It just means they're afraid of your power."

Phoebe snuggles closer and pictures her hair fluorescent blonde.

Past midnight, she rouses at the sound of the back door, the rustle of a windbreaker—Uncle Al returning to his room. A murmur of voices. She slips out of bed and listens at their door. Aunt April whispers fierce and fast, her voice shaking, "No right . . . my story!" Footsteps approach from within. Phoebe darts back toward her room, but their door opens too quick. Her aunt looks at her without surprise, eyes puffy, a pillow under one arm and a balled-up sheet in the other. She turns and descends the stairs.

Unsettled silence slinks through the house as Phoebe gets back into bed. The moan of distant waves blends with the ghostly thrum of the ocean harp—Lochlann in the tree house, filling the night with sorrow.

36

At the click of a door, Oliver sits up in bed.

"What's wrong, babe?" asks Meredith.

"Thought I heard Phoebe."

"Probably in the bathroom looking at herself again. She wants to go blonde."

He settles back beside her. "I hope you said no."

"She's old enough to decide."

"Blonde? What is she thinking?"

"Who keeps turning off the air-conditioning?" Meredith kicks off the comforter.

"Sixty degrees out."

"Are you accusing me of having hot flashes?"

"I'm not accusing you of anything. I'd like to keep my half of the blanket, though."

She turns over her pillow. "What's that noise?"

The house is too quiet, as if something that was writhing and gasping all week has abruptly died. "The waterphone. Lochlann is in the tree house."

"Probably can't stand to be under the same roof as his dad. Who can blame him?"

Oliver can't come up with a response. All night he's been tossing around in bed, trying to create a small space for himself. Al's portrayal of events could not be true. Clearly he and April had been sleeping together the whole time Oliver was in Ireland. It was the only explanation. No one gets married in a week. Oliver smells Meredith's night cream, feels the coolness of her foot against his calf.

"I've never seen you stand up to your brother like that." She glides her toes down his leg. "That was hot."

"Not what I was going for."

"Your dad let him go on and on. What's wrong with this family?"

"He tried. He doesn't speak Al's language."

She touches her ear. "Shoot. Forgot to take off my earrings." She drops an earring onto the end table with a clink. G-sharp. "I think I lost one. Do you mind if I turn on the light?" She feels around in the sheets.

"If only you kept them someplace safe."

"That's helpful." She clicks the flashlight app on her phone. "I hope I didn't lose it at the dress shop."

"Can't we look in the morning?" He shields his eyes.

"April looked so humiliated. Why did Al bring it up? It was so long ago."

"He's unraveling," Oliver says. "That cough sounds like death."

"Who do you think the guy was in Ireland? Did you ever meet him?" She feels around his side of the bed. "Can you shift over?"

He stands, balling his hands.

"I didn't mean you had to get out of bed."

He turns on the lamp. "Just find it, will you?"

She squints.

"There." He points.

She grabs the earring, looks up at him. "You look like death yourself."

"Maybe because it's two in the morning and I was trying to sleep."

She studies him, her eyes adjusting to the light. The lamp was a mistake. He tells himself to intercept whatever realization is assembling in her mind, but seeing him there, kneading his temple, her finely threaded brows lift. Nothing gets by Meredith.

"Can we turn off the light now?" He gets back into bed.

"Oh my God." Her glare narrows. "Your dad's cottage. The guy she slept with in Ireland. It's you."

He winces.

"No." She throws off the sheets. "I'm going to throw up."

He tries to find his voice. The smart thing would be to deny it.

She whips off her eyeshade, throws her earplugs across the room. "You and April? Are you kidding me?"

Words scatter as he reaches for them. Outside, the ocean harp reverberates, haunting and dissonant. He throws his legs over the side of the bed. "It wasn't the way he made it sound."

"Well, you'd better explain how the hell it *was*."

"We never discussed the men you were with before we met. Or the women, for that matter."

She stands, hands on her hips. "That's a cheap shot."

"I'm saying there's lots I could have asked."

"The whole human race is going to be bisexual a hundred years from now. No one will care what people are labeled. It's a higher state of consciousness."

"You know I respect your bisexuality. I love all of you."

"You're dodging." She walks over to his side of the bed. "I want to know why you never told me."

"It was before we met." He turns out the light and lies down.

She looms over him. "If I'd had a prior relationship with your future brother-in-law, you'd sure as hell expect me to say so."

"It wasn't a relationship." He pulls up the blanket. "It was a week."

She steps closer, staring down at him. "A week of what?"

He rolls over, turning away from her.

"That's not going to fly, Oliver."

"Meredith, please."

She crawls over him on hands and knees. "What are you telling me? You boned her and handed her off to your brother?"

"Stop," he says, his teeth a vise.

Moonlight gives her face a metallic sheen. "Now it makes sense how weird you were at the wedding. Stupid me never dreamed she was a bang buddy gone bad." She stares down at him. "And look, it's happening again. You're falling for her all over."

"That's ridiculous. Yes, we had hard feelings, but we moved on. We're family now. End of story."

"You are a colossally bad liar." She compresses his chest as if the husband she married has flatlined.

"I was young, Mere. I had an embarrassing fling. Why would I want to share that?"

"It's what's in here I'm worried about." She flattens her hands on his chest.

"I married you. I've spent my life with you. Doesn't that speak for itself?" He draws her face down to his. "Whatever came before, you erased." Her lips part, but he stops the words with his mouth. He's exhausted, unsure if he can get hard, but can't risk the possibility that her next question will be about timing. He closes his eyes, pulls her against him, and lets himself picture the dark hollow his eye should not have entered.

37

Each time Al slept with April, he waited for the usual urge to move on, but every sip of her made him want more—the arc of her neck, the weight of her hair, eyes like volcanic ash. Their sex was a liquid poured into a sieve, the instant of fullness, the onset of depletion. When he stepped outside for a smoke, the memory of her sad sashay unhinged his knees. He couldn't drink her down fast enough.

In Vegas he took her with him to the press box, the locker room, not trusting her to be alone, then to the Elvis wedding chapel, where it turned out she had forgotten her birth certificate. He bought her private health insurance, not cheap, and started looking up shrinks. Her zombie eyes came to life only when she called the neighbor to see how the dog was doing.

Back home, they stood in his SoHo apartment, sorting through a box of cookware, weeding out the extras. If Al didn't find a way to keep her, his brother would be back.

"I don't know why I'm so tired," she said. "I feel like I'm made of bricks."

Al held up two spatulas, his and hers.

"Shouldn't we be saving the doubles for when this arrangement's over?" she asked.

Arrangement. Was that the word he'd used? "We don't have room." He tossed out the spatula with the melted tip—his, no doubt—and held up two ladles. No way was he letting her go back to that shady sublet.

She put one in a drawer, the other in the donation pile. "What's wrong with me?" She yawned. "It's only nine p.m."

He took the remaining items from the box—a tea strainer, a corkscrew, a pair of tongs. "Are you late?"

"What?" A fierce laugh. "I've only been here a week."

The dog, resting its chin on her foot, looked up.

"Plus, a week in Vegas," Al said. "How long do you think it takes?"

"We've been careful."

"Well, there was that first time."

Her face creased. "Didn't we?" The dog tilted its head.

"No," Al said. "We didn't."

She studied the utensils like a riddle. Al was certain that their first time, the most vivid minutes of his life, never registered in her memory. He wanted to ask if she was careful with his brother but knew Oliver would never be reckless.

"Al." She clicked the tea ball open and closed. "You know I can't. I mean, I wouldn't trust myself to—"

Al did not trust himself, either. Children were never on the docket. Too much responsibility and weight. Yet he sometimes had weird dreams. In the empty space where a football had fit snug in the pocket of his forearm, something new appeared—warm, heavier, and softer than the ball, breathing against his chest. But wasn't freedom his most valued possession? He pictured a runaway hot air balloon drifting without ballast. He could never do a conventional marriage, he thought. It would have to be someone who understood his essential nature. His needs. He looked at April. "You're probably not sleeping well here. Forget I mentioned it."

"I know you don't want to, either; you've always said. Besides, this isn't a real thing." She gestured to the apartment, the infuser rolling off the edge.

Al caught it in midair. "Well . . ." He hesitated. "It could be. If we wanted."

Her dark eyes widened, bottom lip catching a quiver of fluorescent light. He wanted to kiss her there, suck that trembling shimmer deep into him, the soft curve of her mouth, distrustful eyes, dark brows lifting now like two startled ravens.

"Let's pick up a test tomorrow to put our minds at ease," he said, closing the drawer. But he suspected neither result would ease him.

38

Al parked outside the church before the baptism, Locky gurgling in his car seat, mesmerized by bare tree branches moving in the wind. "He's going to be smart." Al glanced in the rearview. "Look, he notices everything." April massaged her palm, staring at the church door. It was a cold March day, crocuses poking through mushy snow, yet she wore a floral spring dress, legs bare, breasts round with milk. "You look nice," Al said.

She reddened. He didn't mean to insinuate anything, but the blush told him whom she'd dressed for. "He'll need to nurse in an hour." She adjusted her bra. "I hope the ceremony doesn't go over."

His father entered the church, followed by other guests. "We should get in there," Al said.

She visibly flattened against her seat. Oliver was trotting briskly up the stone steps in polished shoes and a regimental tie, looking a lot different, Al supposed, than a year ago in the Irish cottage where he'd cloistered himself, wild eyed and unshaven like a Celtic monk. She kneaded her hand. "I don't think I can do this."

"For Christ's sake, it's our kid's baptism," Al said. "Does everything have to be about him?" He didn't mean it as harshly as it came out. He knew she did not want Oliver, whose name she refused to speak, to be their kid's godfather—did not want him in the same country, no less the same church. But family was family, and here they were.

"You're right." She puffed out a breath. "I'm sorry." She kissed Al distractedly and lifted Lochlann from his car seat. The moment his tiny face touched her neck, the kid was out cold.

At the altar she stood beside Oliver, their mutual nonchalance so convincing no one but Al seemed to notice the cable of tension between them, two towers of a suspension bridge concealing the strain that connected them. Her hair draped over her shoulder and the baby's wrap, her skin flushed with suppressed feeling. She exuded radiance, bent on showing his brother what he'd given up. Killing it, too, her head held high. Damn proud of her, Al was. Standing across from her, he observed the scene with his journalist's eye, fascinated and detached, confident that her hatred of Oliver would preclude any rekindling. Having a child with Al would forever be a stronger bond than a few ill-fated days in Ireland.

The godmother, some gum-chewing friend of April's in tie-dye and chaps, claimed she had a cold and could not touch the baby. Looked more like she was afraid motherhood was contagious. The priest instructed Oliver to hold him. April's eyes begged Al to take Lochlann and pass him to his brother. But victim of his own curiosity, Al pretended not to understand. Oliver stammered, looking at the priest. "Uh, I've never held one before."

"Nothing to it." The priest smiled.

April speared Al with a glance. Was he really going to make her stand face-to-face with his brother, pass the baby to him with her own arms? Al feigned oblivion, not to cause her pain but to see firsthand what his brother had over her.

To make the transfer without waking the baby, they stood like interwoven trees, the infant cradled between them, April's breast grazing Oliver's forearm. Al followed the brush of skin, her hands positioning Lochlann's head in the crook of his brother's elbow, their eyes on his squished little face. "Is this right?" Oliver's voice cracked.

She nodded. They managed the pass without waking him. April grabbed Al's hand, her palm a jellyfish, her face so green he thought he'd have to catch her before she hit the tile. Man, that would've pissed her off, fainting in front of everyone. But she stayed on her feet, smile glued to her face. That was Al's girl. That was April through and through.

After the ceremony his brother, confident now of his hold on the baby, sauntered down the aisle and sat in the last pew, humming to Lochlann. The humming spooked Al, as if Oliver were casting some spell on the boy. April kept her back turned, laughing a little too loudly with her friends, who, in their badass boots and studded vests, looked ready to bolt. With each passing minute, distress tightened April's smile. Finally she turned to Al, whispered viciously, "I'm going to soak through."

He walked down the aisle to the final row. His brother's eyes were closed, the baby asleep. "He needs to nurse," Al said.

Oliver opened his eyes. With all that happened in the past year, Al's only conversations with him had been terse exchanges about sports, politics, and repairs on their father's house. His brother stood to his full height, looked at him with an expression Al had never seen on his face before, a cobra fanning its hood. "I want a paternity test."

A blade of terror sliced through Al. He let out a harsh laugh. At the distant altar April half turned to look at them. "You're a year late, asshole. I already did one." Al took the baby. "You think I'd be standing here if it wasn't mine?" It was only half a lie. He'd bought a kit but never mailed it in. His certainty that Loch was his rested on the obvious assumption that his Boy Scout brother would never have unprotected sex. Lochlann writhed and began to scream. Al headed back to the altar. Behind him, the exit door swooshed.

Al felt April's stare as he returned to the altar. "What did he say?" She took the baby.

"My pick for March Madness," Al said. "He's putting down money."

Her eyes said she did not believe him. But she had a baby to nurse.

After a small reception at Al's father's house, the baby cried all the way home, a noise like extruding metal. They wound up the five-story walk-up, she with the screaming infant, Al with the diaper bag and carrier. Inside the apartment, the dog pranced excitedly while April paced, cooing and swaying, patting Locky's back too quickly. Al took him, nestled him on his shoulder, and he immediately calmed, grasping Al's shirt in his teeny fist. April sat on the ottoman and covered her face, a torrent erupting. The dog rested his chin on her knee. Aside from framed photos of April's grandmother and brother, there weren't many traces of her in the apartment, as if she hadn't fully committed yet. She continued to bawl, Al's sternum aching like when a hard tackle had once given him a contusion. "Wow," he said.

She blew her nose. "What did you expect?"

"It's not about what I expected. It's about what I hoped." He sighed, settling into the couch. "Who knew I'd end up the chump at the three-card monte table?"

Her face glistened. She swallowed back emotion. The tear spigot—padlocked for most of her life, blasted open for the past year—was clamping shut again. Al felt her grandmother and brother staring at him from within their frames. April was tarring over something too raw to stay open. "What did you hope?" she asked.

The ache in his ribs made it hard to breathe deeply. "That eventually, for you, I'd be the one. But it'll always be him, won't it."

She kissed him with salty, swollen lips, pulled a blanket over them, and nestled her head on his shoulder. "You'll always be the one, Al. But let me hate him."

He pulled her closer, her leg draped over his, the baby asleep between them, and decided to believe her.

Al had no idea how he got from that moment, when he would have done anything for April, to a few months later, when he spotted a woman with a heart-shaped ass waiting outside a locker room and asked without the slightest tick of hesitation who her favorite player was, his stock lead-in. At the airport, regret landed in his stomach like a cheesesteak left in the sun. He changed to a later flight to get home after she was asleep.

He'd thought he was done with hookups, but hookups weren't done with him. Restlessness of all kinds—sexual, culinary, locational—was as fundamental to him as blood type and eye color. The women he met on the road, usually groupies for the athletes he covered, were caffeine, nicotine—a craving that bit and clamped down, the promised relief, always a lie. Those encounters were fueled more by the need that preceded them than the momentary gratification that followed, the actual sex consumed distractedly, the third cup of coffee of the day.

His career choice—with its endless hotel rooms and restaurants, one arena after another packed with tipsy, revved-up fans—only deepened his grooves. He was up front with the women he approached. Single-entry visa was all he applied for. No exchange of numbers. He had more luck with women whose team had lost, the empty hole of disappointment opening out into need. Unlike men who fantasized about cheerleaders and would gladly get laid by any one of them, female fans tended to fixate on a particular player. They wanted to know if Al had interviewed them, what their demeanor was like in the locker room, if they seemed like genuinely nice people. He answered honestly even if it cost him the hookup. Once, in a hotel room, a woman asked if he'd shaken the hand of A-Rod. When Al said yes, she put his hand inside her bra. That alone nearly gave her an orgasm. He didn't care that those women were thinking of someone else when he touched them, only that April was.

Quietly he let himself into the apartment. Dubious frolicked but didn't bark—an affectionate companion but worthless protector. Al gave him a piece of cheese, and he curled up beneath the crib. The light on the answering machine was blinking, his brother's number on the caller ID. Their father had been asking them to repair a fence. When Oliver's number appeared, April never picked up. Her therapist said not to; they were working on "self-preservation." Al had never been to a shrink, had no intention of going, but could imagine what one might say, that the only reason he'd pursued April was because he could never have her. It was only a matter of time before his brother called and she picked up. Even a violent argument would be an intimacy both would relish. Al wondered how long he had.

He downed a glass of scotch to settle his mind—two because he forgot to savor the first—and slipped in beside her, she hugging a pillow. It touched him to know she missed him when he was gone. He cautiously caressed her. Once, when he climbed in too quick, she clocked him in the jaw. Old ghosts. "Hey," he said softly. "It's me."

She groaned. "Just got to sleep. Locky was awake all last night."

He moved on top of her, the scotch swirling in his gut, warming his brain. "Rosie," he said. "Let's make another one."

She laughed, pushing him off. "Are you out of your mind? I'm barely surviving this one."

It was the hundredth time he'd asked, because surely a deliberate child would solidify them more than an accidental one.

"Too soon," she said. An improvement over her previous "No," but for Al, it wasn't soon enough. A door was closing, and all his strength wasn't enough to keep it open.

39

April awakes disoriented, the sound of breath from the floor causing her to think she's home, the dog asleep beside her. She feels the roughness of a couch cushion, hears the faraway sibilance of ocean. Hal's house. A pink strand of sunrise slices the darkened room. She looks at the floor, sees Al's broad shoulders. At first, she thinks he's fallen or passed out, wedged between couch and coffee table, but a pillow is stuffed beneath his head, a sheet draped over his legs. He followed her down to sleep beside her.

The sensation of being observed fills her. She sees the screen door close, the silhouette of Oliver leaving the house for an early-morning run. Shame sears through her. If not for her children, she'd get in her truck and drive home.

She looks at Al jammed between furniture. Soon Hal will be down for his sunrise walk, or perhaps he's already seen them. She sets her phone timer for five minutes, places it beside Al's head, and goes up to shower.

By the time she's done, she estimates he'll be out on the porch for his morning smoke, but when she slips into the bedroom with dripping hair, he's waiting in the wooden chair by the rolltop desk. "Hey," he says softly.

She goes to the closet.

"I need to talk to you," he says. "Just for a sec."

She grabs clothes to change in the bathroom. "You're lucky I didn't kill you in your sleep."

"What stopped you?"

"Two children. Maybe you remember them."

"Doubt they'd be heartbroken. At least one of them."

"I see what you're doing. You want me to say it's over so you don't have to."

"No, Rosie. I don't want to lose you."

"Brilliant way of showing it."

"I'm unforgivable. I get that."

"You can take your self-pity and shove it up your ass."

He straightens.

"I looked up your scars," she says. "Three identical marks on your back, underarm, and rib. When did you have the thoracoscopy?"

"That didn't take you long." He looks at his feet. "End of June. Thought by now the scars would fade."

"That's why you didn't come home? Because you've been getting medical treatment?"

"It's done now. I'm good."

"How long were you in the hospital?"

"Five days for the surgery—there was a complication—then just outpatient stuff."

"And it never occurred to you that I might want to be with you?"

"To change my bed pan? No thanks."

"Imagine when your mom got sick if she refused to let your dad—"

"Stop it." His voice goes cold. "That was completely different."

"That's just it, isn't it, Al," she says. "You never need anyone, do you."

"My dad doesn't know anything. I don't want him—"

"Lung cancer? Is that what we're talking about?"

"Shh." He glances at the door. "Precancerous. I dodged a bullet."

"And tough guy that you are, you think it's fine to keep right on smoking and drinking no matter what meds you're on."

"You've been looking through my toilet kit?"

She flings the alarm clock at him. He blocks it, knocks it into his lap. "Ouch." He rubs his arm. "I told you I don't want my father to—"

"Sure, let's protect *your* privacy."

"I'm sorry about last night. I don't know why I said all that."

"I've never met anyone so smart and so stupid at the same time." She hurls his cigarettes at him, his keys, his wallet. She reaches for the lamp.

"Whoa." He leaps up and grabs it from her.

"You don't stop killing yourself, swear to God, I'll do it for you."

He sets the lamp down. "Stupid's not the problem. Heartless— that's the problem."

"Forget the saga about keeping us in your life. I don't want to hear another goddamn epiphany. Just do something." She turns for the bathroom. "Do it today."

April is halfway down the hall, her own words ringing in her head, when she realizes she's talking to herself. She's the one who has to do something drastic.

40

Al showers at length, scrubs fish scales from beneath his fingernails that he missed the day before, sunburn stinging under needles of water. In the mirror he combs his hair, thinner than summers past, and shaves for the first time all week. His back aches from reeling in the thresher or sleeping on the floor or both. A blister swells on his thumb. He puts on a clean shirt, thinking of the cigarette he didn't have upon waking, his missed time on the porch getting mentally prepared for the day. One skipped smoke and his mind is already a rat maze.

Someone raps on the door. "Boat leaves in an hour. I need to get in there."

"What boat?" He opens the door.

His brother stands in the frame, sweaty from his run. "Whale watching."

It impresses Al how the family sticks to a schedule as though everything is hunky-dory, a perfect family vacation.

Oliver lowers his voice. "So good at painting things with your own brush, aren't you."

"I'm making my apologies where I need to. You're not one of them."

"How much have you told Dad?"

"That's your worry? Your reputation with Dad? Always did have your priorities screwed." He steps out of the bathroom. "All yours."

Oliver stops him. "Meredith figured it out. Do you realize what you've done?"

Al wants to tell him there's so much more he and Meredith need to talk about. He shrugs his arm free and moves down the hall.

Meredith is trotting up the stairs as Al heads down. She blocks him on the landing. Her eyes without makeup are tender and pale. "I need the truth, Al. Is there something going on with them?"

"Them? Maybe tonight I'll let loose about your little threesome."

She shoots a look up the stairs. He brushes past her, but she takes his arm. "You think you have any credibility left after last night? I'm not afraid of you. You've got nothing on me."

He pulls free and descends the stairs. His clueless brother doesn't know his own wife. If Al tries to tell him, Oliver will only defend her. She's got to confess herself.

The room smells of burnt toast and strong coffee. At the dining room table the kids are picking from a bowl of sliced watermelon, discussing a local news report about an osprey tangled in balloon strings. "Same thing happened last month to an eagle," says Nula.

Al circles the room. On the coffee table Meredith's laptop is open to a purchase order. She must've run upstairs for something quick. He pulls a thumb drive from his briefcase, slips it into her port, and types a command.

"Hey, son." His father assesses him.

Al turns quickly. "Morning, Dad."

Two descending beeps sound from the laptop. Nice quick machine, Meredith's. Al figures he has what he needs. Earbuds don't burn for no reason. He plucks out the thumb drive just as Meredith jogs back downstairs.

When he approaches the dining room table, the conversation halts. Lochlann pulls up his hood. The girls hug themselves. Al's chest tightens. The kids are scared of him. "I shouldn't have said those things last night," he says. "I'm sorry."

His niece gives him a fleeting glance. No eye contact from his own kids.

"Everyone deserves privacy. I said stuff that's between your mom and me."

Nula eyes him warily and returns to her drawing, a fanged monster. Phoebe glances at her mother across the room as though to see if she should leave the table.

"I'm apologizing to all of you, the whole family," Al says.

Nula eyes him.

"I was out of line. Plus, I'm pretty sure I got it wrong. It was so long ago." He spots April through the window beside the hummingbird feeder, hands cupped as if beckoning one to land on her. "Here's the thing about memory: When I was in college, I helped a friend move cross-country. We thought we'd packed up the van real careful, but it was too big, not enough stuff to pack it snug. We get to California, look in the back, and not a single thing is in the same place. A bureau we'd stood upright is on its side. Broke a mirror, too. My point is that the longer you travel with your memories, the more they jumble up. The things I said last night are as good as lies."

"You didn't have to go to California to figure that out," Lochlann says. "If it wasn't packed right, everything was a disaster by the time you turned the first corner."

"True that." Al sighs. He ought to have gone upstairs last night when the kid was bawling. If only his son knew how Al had changed the trajectory of his life just to have him, how he would do it all over again. But Loch glances at him with poison in his eyes.

"Daddy," Nula says, "are you coming whale watching?"

"Got some things to straighten out today. I'll come with you tomorrow, whatever you do."

She frowns and returns to her drawing.

41

On the porch steps, Oliver sits waiting for his wife beneath rolling clouds, a vast unfurling darkness. Normally Meredith lets arguments go, but this one feels different. He looks at his watch.

Lochlann's voice booms from indoors. "Not getting on another boat."

"Fine," April says. "Stay home."

"Who else will be here?"

"Just Dad. Grandpa's gone food shopping."

Lochlann pitches open the screen and hurtles into the pickup. Nula and Phoebe follow, zipping their raincoats. "Dad, I'm going with Aunt April," Phoebe says.

"Okay. See you there."

April comes out of the house, tying up her hair, and sweeps past Oliver. Since last night's fiasco, she has not so much as glanced his way. Jouncing over ruts, the pickup flies down the driveway, stirring a wake of dust.

He looks at the time. Meredith is cutting it close. She pops out the door, talking into her headset, just as an email lights up his phone, subject line: Response to Ad. The finder in Beijing. As they walk to the car, he scans it, scrolling to a grainy photo of a Chinese couple with a boy, ten or twelve years old. Damn.

He pulls onto the road. Meredith argues with Dixon over what settlement to offer. One customer would be satisfied with free merchandise.

The other threatens a lawsuit. To Oliver, her calls all sound the same. The content may change, but not the energy. He turns the radio on low and strains to hear the newscast. A fragile dune cliff collapsed overnight, plunging a condemned cottage into the sea. And the search for the missing fisherman has switched from rescue to recovery.

Meredith pulls off her headset. "How far ahead are they?"

"Ten minutes. We'll find them on the pier."

She rubs her forehead. "All these years she's acted like my friend."

"She is your friend. Nothing's changed." He taps the steering wheel. "I got an email from the finder."

"What?"

"In Beijing, the agency conducting the search."

"Oh God."

"I haven't read the whole thing yet, but there's a photo of a fortyish couple." He pauses. "With a boy."

"Older than Phoebe?"

He swallows. "Younger."

"Shit. You can't show her that. We don't know if it's them. And if it is, there goes your heartwarming story of parents who gave her up for a better life because they weren't allowed to keep a second kid. Instead, she gets ones who held out for a boy. You think that's going to help her? You think you're doing her a favor?"

He searches for a parking spot. "Phoebe understands that people can be overwhelmed by societal pressures. She's smart."

"It has nothing to do with intelligence. This isn't about the brain. It's about the heart. She's going to be crushed."

"So we don't tell her?" he asks.

"What can I say? I know you will."

"No," he says. "We have to decide together. I trust your instincts."

"Dear Phoebe." She bows her head.

"I'm sorry I set this in motion. We should have talked more." He looks at the street jammed with tourists.

"Fine, tell her," she says. "It'll make her stronger. She'll value her womanhood even more. That's how we'll pitch it."

"I'm glad you're coming with us today. She'll want you on board."

"It's fine," she says. "I realized even though it's a three-hour trip, it really only costs me an hour since it takes two hours there and back to reach the fish."

"Whales." He hesitates. "But you know there's no internet on the boat."

"You're shitting me."

"What about your personal hot spot?"

Personal hot spot is a bedroom phrase of theirs, but she does not smile. "I've already exceeded our data plan." She looks at her phone. "I'm sorry. You'll have to go without me."

"Seriously?"

"I did shopping yesterday, the beach the day before. I can't afford three more hours. I shouldn't even be here this week." She stuffs her things into her bag. "Forget parking."

He rolls his head, turns on his blinker.

"Don't act like you'll suffer any, driving home with her."

The words sting. The opposite is true, he thinks. Being with April *is* a kind of suffering now. It's his fault. He's got to dial back, return to the cordial homeostasis they achieved as in-laws. The last thing he wants is to blow up his marriage. He won't do that to Phoebe. He pulls over. "Meredith, I'm sorry. I hope we can put this behind us."

"You know how stressed I am. This couldn't happen at a worse time."

"Nothing's happened. Please, it's old news." A pang in his chest tells him he's lying. More has happened than he knows how to name.

They open their doors. Between swift-moving clouds, a brief blast of sunshine drenches them. She buckles into the driver's seat. He leans through the window, relieved that she lets him kiss her. "I'll wait to talk to Phoebe."

"Don't wait. This is your thing. Just let me know how it goes."

"I think she'd rather have you there," he says. "She might be upset."

"I'll talk with her later. Just do it."

He touches her cheek. "Fingers crossed for no more complaints," he says.

She puts the car in gear.

"Love," he says, "was it good last night, at least?"

"As make-up sex goes, you've got a lot more payments."

"The interest will be worth it." He kisses her, feels a tentative smile on her lips, that old stunning resilience. There's a chance she will forgive him.

Phoebe's face falls as Oliver approaches the queue without Meredith. "I'm sorry, sweetheart," he says. "You know what a bear this week has been for her."

The line moves and April hands out tickets, chill pouring off her like morning fog. The girls clank down the metal gangway, dash into the cabin, and claim a table, though they needn't have rushed. The threatening forecast has left the boat half-empty. Lochlann slides into a booth by himself. The horn blasts and the ship eases back. April keeps her eyes on the window, taking in the passing lighthouse and receding contours of land. Her neutral expression fails to conceal a roil of emotion.

Nula glances up from her drawing—the images are becoming more ominous—and studies April. The girl's antennae seem extra sharp today. "When you were outside this morning, Daddy said he was sorry."

April touches her hand. "I know he is."

"He said it wasn't true." Nula squints, awaiting her reaction.

"Never good to let someone else tell your story," April says. "That was my mistake."

Oliver pretends to focus on the pamphlet, illustrations of whales, shearwaters, a number to call if you witness entanglement.

"So what is it?" Nula asks warily. "Your story?"

She gives Nula a serious, adult-to-adult look. "Your heart's not a thing to give away like a free appetizer. Remember that."

Oliver's chest spasms.

Nula chews her cheek. "Can we get fries?"

April hands her a five-dollar bill.

The girls head for the concession counter, leaving Oliver alone with April. His pulse thumps. She opens a book. He scans his pamphlet— gannets, scoters, widgeons—and lets himself glance at her book jacket. No bookmark. It seems to him she's opened to a random page. He studies her fingers on the cover, the chisel of her wrist, the strength of her arms, age making her more distinct in ways that deepen his attention.

"There was no shampooing of rugs," she says without looking up. "Let's get that straight."

He puts down the pamphlet.

"And I didn't even own drapes, let alone wash them for anyone." She turns a page. "Complete fantasy. I hope you get that."

"Obviously," he says, "because I know for a fact the asshole wrote to her explaining what happened."

"Right. A postcard."

"Of a thatched cottage, a picture a person might find romantic if she had a heart in her chest."

She looks up, eyes like black ice. "Nothing prettifies *Dear John*."

"That is not what it said. Did you bother to read it?"

"You're right. *Dear John* implies a relationship. The girl got laid, is all."

He crushes the pamphlet, lowers his voice to suppress the tremor. "You're not the first person to go for one last fling before getting married, but you might've mentioned that's all it was."

She angles away from him.

He glances at Phoebe and Nula paying for their fries. "All these years, I assumed you two were busy screwing while I was in Ireland, but maybe you skipped that part and went straight to your casino wedding."

She looks at Lochlann in the booth across the aisle. "I'm not talking about this."

"Later, then."

"Not later." She turns another page. The book might as well be upside down.

Phoebe and Nula return, filling the booth with the aroma of french fries. "Want some?" Phoebe offers.

"No thanks." He tries to smile. Bullets of rain strike the window.

"I'm going to get some fresh air," April says. The girls stand to let her out. Phoebe gives a backward glance at April and looks at Oliver quizzically. The rain slashes sideways.

"Maybe the chop is getting to her," he says. "They say it's best to get outside."

The girls start chatting. Oliver tries not to stare at April huddled in the deluge. He pulls out his phone. He almost forgot about the email from Beijing. He looks from the gritty framed faces to his daughter's. She has large eyes, a delicate nose, and a smile that could melt an ice cap. The photo is shrunken and imprecise. She glances up and, seeing his expression, asks, "What?"

"There's a first bite on the ad," he says. "The one the finder put in the newspaper."

She pushes aside her iPad, face pale.

"It might be the only response or the first of dozens."

"Is there a picture?"

"We'd have to get a DNA sample to find out if it's a match."

"Can I see?"

He hands her the phone. She stares into it. "Xu? Their name is Xu?"

Nula looks over her shoulder. "No way. They don't look like you."

"He's a tempering operator at the No. 2 Flat Glass Factory, and she's a production clerk," she reads haltingly. "How old is the boy?"

"Not clear when the picture was taken," he says.

Her face screws up. "Younger than me?"

"Like I said, we have no idea if it's a match."

Her chin trembles. "It was probably because of the heart murmur. If they were factory workers, they probably couldn't afford medical care."

"Could be." He does not wish to explain about socialized medicine.

"Or the girl thing. Could've been that."

His heart hurts. "I suppose it's possible."

She hands back the phone. "Send it to me."

Nula nudges her. "You don't even look like them."

"Do you want to get their DNA or wait for more responses?" he asks.

"Wait."

He looks at her gently. "Should we pull the ad?"

She stares out the window, lip quivering. "No. I don't know. Let me think."

"Take your time."

"All I wanted was to see them. If it's even them." She stares at the whitecaps, the sea getting rougher.

He touches her fingers. "I'm sorry if—"

"It's okay, Dad." She withdraws her hand.

"Sweetheart, I can only guess what this feels like."

She wipes her eyes. "Where's Mom?"

"Remember, she had to go back."

She looks at Loch in the booth across the aisle, but his headphones are on, eyes closed. "Where's Aunt April?" she asks.

"Outside, but it's raining, sweetheart. Stay here with—"

She hurries onto the deck and pulls herself along the railing, struggling against the wind. He watches as April folds her into her arms.

Lochlann straightens up and slips off his headphones. "I told her it was a bad idea."

"She needs time to absorb it." Oliver swallows, wondering how much the boy has overheard.

"You think knowledge is always a good thing," Loch says. "Sometimes it's not."

Oliver looks into his eyes, storm gray in this light. "Yes, I know."

"You try to candy-coat. Why don't you listen to her? Being adopted sucks." He folds his arms straitjacket-style and burrows into the booth.

"You're right," Oliver says. He's botched this.

The ship's engine slows. The rain eases to a drizzle.

"I think I see a blowhole." Nula pulls on her poncho. "Loch?"

He shakes his head.

Oliver and Nula file outside with the other passengers as the ship lists. They work their way to the bow, where Phoebe stands cocooned in April's raincoat. Oliver stands behind Nula, wrapping his arms around to warm her. "Anything yet?" he asks.

Phoebe doesn't answer. April gives Oliver a questioning glance. He pats Phoebe's shoulder, but she nestles closer to April.

"I see one logging out there." Nula points to a whale sleeping quietly at the surface, its back barely visible like a floating log.

"Good eye," April says.

Near the bow three humpbacks break the surface, two adults and a calf, the blow from the baby half the height of the adults.

April glances back at the cabin. "Where's Loch?"

The whales sound, the massive tails of the adults springing airborne, followed by the half-size tail of the calf. The crowd *ooh*s. Through her loudspeaker, the naturalist predicts the whales will surface on the other side. "One of the adults has ensnarement scars," she says. "Look for the ruts."

"That's what I want to be when I grow up," Nula says, "one of those people who cuts whales free." She takes Phoebe's arm and pulls her starboard, leaving Oliver and April at the rail.

She looks away. "What's up with Phoebe?"

"Meredith's right. I let her go too far with this birth parent thing."

She appraises him. "Phoebe likes truth."

"That might depend on what the truth turns out to be."

A rocketing turbulence churns the water, a barnacled head and pleated underside hurling skyward, landing with a massive splash. The boat rocks. The whale rotates on its side, spy-hops its head out of the water to gaze at them. The crowd falls into hushed reverence. A burst of exhalation shoots up, reeking of rotted eels, a pong worse than the bay at low tide. A collective groan rises from the passengers, laughter and revulsion.

Nula wedges between Oliver and April. "Mommy, I got sprayed!"

"We stink!" Phoebe says. "Did you see the breach, Dad?"

The return of her smile warms his chest.

"But Lochlann." April glances back at the cabin.

Shearwaters skim the surface, wings catching the chilly drizzle. On the distant horizon, a gush of exhalation lifts higher than the rest. The naturalist reports rumors of an endangered blue whale sighting, the first in a decade, too elusive to be identified. Oliver imagines it out there, the largest creature ever to live, its heart wider than his outstretched arms.

April stares in the direction of the spume. Though he cannot see her face, the softening of her shoulders tells him she's moved.

Inside the cabin, Nula slides into Lochlann's booth. "You should've come. We saw the awesomest breach." He doesn't open his eyes.

"Hey." Phoebe pokes him. "Let's go outside. Rain's letting up."

"We're heading back," Loch says.

"Come anyway."

He trudges behind her to the rail. Beads of water etch down the glass. Lochlann seems to be asking something. Phoebe answers, eyes cast up to his. He puts his arm around her, Phoebe holding back her windblown hair to meet his eye. Oliver's heart warms. At least she has a cousin to talk to when her father has blown it.

"I hope they recycle." Nula collapses the empty french fry box and heads to the counter.

Alone with April, Oliver's pulse quickens. In the distance the giant green bell buoy rocks in the waves, clanging its message of danger. April fans the pages of her paperback as if rolling a question in her mind. He searches for a single arrow—a word—and takes aim. "Yes."

She looks up curtly. "Yes what?"

"The letter. I still have it."

She blinks. "I don't care. I didn't mean it. I was being theatrical."

"You forget," he says. "I know when you're faking."

Her eyes seethe. "Christ, I thought we put this behind us," she says. "Why now?"

He looks out the window. The cottage materializes in his mind. The finality of its absence staggers him. He could have explained to Meredith its symbolic importance to his music, but symbols unused turn to dust. He spins his wedding ring, the boat picking up speed. Meredith has her own cliff edge. She wants him to go there with her. He pictures her face as she watched Lisbeth and Cole. Was it the same rapture he felt seeing the Atlantic surge into sea caves? To Oliver, the savagery between ocean and rock was a timeless intimacy. The mist on his face was alive. Lisbeth and Cole were a cliché reenactment of a cheap porn film, loveless and predictable. He wonders if Al has ever asked April to participate in anything like that. No. Al likes his sex private if not monogamous. And even if he did, April would say no. Oliver understands this because despite his frustration and rage and resentment, he knows her, this person who went with him to the edge of the world and peered over. "I need to understand what happened." Oliver turns to her. "All it will take to put it behind us is one conversation."

"Oliver," she says, "it's been behind us for years."

Nula slips back in the booth. "Yep," she says. "They recycle."

42

April swings the truck out of the dockside parking lot, silently cursing the poor suspension, grateful for the girls' chatter. In the passenger seat Oliver rolls down his window and taps out notes on his thigh. Warm air whistles through her hair, the letter a fire in her veins.

As they pull up, Meredith hops off the porch. "You'll never believe it." She leans in Oliver's window. "They accepted the settlement, both customers. It's a miracle." April cuts the engine.

"That's great," Phoebe says from the back seat. Meredith flings her arms around Oliver as he steps out. He lifts her and sets her down. Phoebe rushes out, leaving the door open. "Mom, that's amazing." The three of them hug, Meredith rattling off details.

Has April ever exchanged a hug like this with Al and the kids? Comparisons are quicksand. She gets out. "What a relief, Mere," she says. "You can finally enjoy your vacation."

"Of course, it might be useful to know what caused the burns to begin with," Al says, sitting on the porch steps. "Like, I wonder if the marketing outpaced the supply chain. Maybe the booming orders meant resorting to substandard suppliers, ones with leaky battery acid." He perches Nula's ebony pencil behind his ear.

Meredith whirls around to face him. April sees he has something on her, the weasel.

"If that were the case, let's hope the secondary supplier conformed to the label: Made in America." Al sniffs. "That would be fairly important. Legally, I mean."

Meredith's eyes narrow as if peering through a gunsight.

"Mommy, guess what? Dad got an email from the finder." Phoebe hides her face in Meredith's shirt.

"Angel." Meredith looks down in surprise. "What happened?"

Phoebe covers her eyes, shoulders shaking. Meredith gives Al an incinerating glance and leads Phoebe into the yard.

When Oliver and Lochlann have gone inside, April stands before Al on the porch. His arm is bruised where she hit him with the alarm clock. "How are those journalistic ethics holding up?" she asks.

"I'm not on the job," he says. "She's not straight with her customers."

"Nothing like fixating on someone else's problems to avoid your own."

He sticks out his lower lip.

"How she runs her company is not our business."

"Wasn't sure there was an 'our' anymore."

She can almost see the throb of his headache, his shirt pocket empty. She's seen him try to quit before. A few hours in and already he looks like he's been dragged by a snowplow. She tries to imagine what it would mean for the kids to see him quit, but her hopes won't make an iota of difference. This is between Al and his Marlboros. She goes inside. Oliver is at the window, watching his wife and daughter in the yard. Even from behind, April can feel the ache in his heart.

Phoebe rushes in and flies upstairs. Loch follows her.

April expects Meredith to chastise Oliver, but she wipes her eye, rests her head on his shoulder, and he puts his arms around her, ritual gestures April recognizes as the call-and-response of their marriage, the ingrained comfort of repeated action, the way April's father on his deathbed had, over and over, lifted an invisible glass to his mouth. Oliver and Meredith rock as if soothing each other were a way to soothe Phoebe.

April retreats to the kitchen. Living relationships look nothing like ink on paper. What's a yellowed letter compared to a shared bed; care of a child; an accruement of decisions about schools, orthodontic work, which movie to watch, what flavor to buy, cursory kisses, and petty annoyances too minor to threaten a decade of vows? The needle April and Oliver threaded and dropped was nothing compared to the tapestry he's sewn with his wife. The fabric of their affection for Phoebe makes of them a shared being. April doesn't want to remember what she wrote. It was too much, too fast, a levee collapsing. Still young, she had somehow believed love was a thing that happened to you like rain.

Meredith and Phoebe return from the salon just as April and the others sit for dinner. April expects a niece as fair as her sister-in-law, but Phoebe's hair has only streaks of light brown woven into the black, the tips white as a palomino's tail.

"It looks great, sweetheart," Oliver says, a tenderness in his eyes that soaks April's heart. He has a good life, she thinks. So does she. Al will let her keep the farm if only for the kids' sake, won't he? She can use Meredith's advice to make it profitable. Nothing is wrong with her life, except one thing—she needs the letter back.

Phoebe nudges Loch, the only one not staring at her hair. "Well?"

He looks up from his phone, eyes softening. "It's dope, Beebee," he says, his childhood name for her.

Al removes the wineglass from his place setting and sips seltzer through a paper straw, his body shaking like a revved engine.

"You okay there, son?" Hal asks.

Al answers by lifting a hand, a one-armed surrender. Drops of sweat dot his forehead. April leans in and discreetly feels his pulse, faint and erratic. "You may be excused," she tells the kids, though they haven't asked. They cast side-glances and pick up their plates.

"Anyone got a Valium? Benzos? Anything for sleep?" Al asks when the kids are gone.

Meredith considers him with a smirk and, to April's surprise, withdraws two pills from her purse on the side table. "What's that?" April asks.

She shrugs. "Been a hell of a week." She gives them to Al.

April startles. "Is that a good idea?" But he's already swallowed.

"Don't say I never gave you anything," Meredith says. "I'm going to relax for once. Who wants to watch a movie with me?" She fills a bowl with popcorn and sits on the couch. Phoebe snuggles close without taking her eyes off her phone. Al navigates unsteadily to an armchair, the quake in his limbs tugging at April's gut. She's seen him try to quit smoking but never booze, not to mention both at once.

In the kitchen she sinks pans into a basin. Oliver comes in, picks up a towel, and takes a steaming dish from her hands. She turns off the water and, seeing no one behind them, looks him in the eye. "I want it back."

"You want the letter; I want a conversation," he says. "Let's barter."

"We tried talking in the diner. Look where it got us."

"You know what I mean. The conversation we never had."

"Because there's nothing to talk about," she says.

"No deal." He hangs up the towel and goes into the dining room, where he takes out his planner. The week is winding down, everyone starting to look ahead.

She sits across from him and opens her laptop. Nula wanders over and wedges into April's chair. "Daddy ate my M&M's," she whispers.

"I'll buy you more." April makes room for her. "Let's see your sketchbook."

"I saw a nicotine patch under his sleeve. Last time, he got super cranky."

"To be expected." April flips pages. "Yikes, these are getting creepier. Don't they give you nightmares?"

Nula tilts her head. "It's the other way around. They come from my nightmares."

"Oh God. Why didn't you tell me?"

"But that's what I've been doing." She gestures to the sketchbook and leaves.

April massages her temple. Why can't she get a single part of motherhood right? She feels Oliver glance at her, but she doesn't look back.

Lochlann appears. "I decided something on the boat today," he says.

She looks at him in surprise.

"I'm not going back to school. I'll do homeschool or something."

"Honey," she says, "homeschool isn't easy at this stage. Physics, calculus—I can't teach you that stuff."

"I'll do online courses. I can't go back there."

Oliver glances up from his planner.

"We'll talk about this when your father's feeling better," April says. "This isn't a good time."

"You mean 'cause he's sober?"

April girds her voice. "That's not what I meant."

"You always make excuses for him. You're part of the problem, you know. You *are* the problem."

"Lochlann," Oliver says. "Don't be rude to your mother."

Loch casts April a searing look, as if it's her fault Oliver admonished him. He goes upstairs.

"It's not that I make excuses," April says quietly, eyes on her keyboard. "Children see parents as extensions of themselves. To trash the dad is to trash the kid." She finishes an email, the clicks of her keyboard like pellets of hail.

"Dad!" Phoebe leaps off the sofa. "I got it! My ancestry results!" She leans on the table beside him, her hair smelling of salon chemicals. "Wow, it's here!"

"Let's see . . . 99.5 percent East Asian, 78 percent of which is Chinese; 13 percent Korean; and 7 percent Japanese," he reads from her phone.

"Did you think it would be like that?" she asks, breathless.

"I had no idea, but Dalian is up toward that part of China."

"One percent Southeast Asian and half of one percent broadly European." She scrolls through the results. "I wonder how that compares with most Chinese people. I mean, do you think that's normal?"

"Not sure there is a normal. Pretty cool, though." The cheer in her eyes warms April's heart. Finally, a happy turn to this week.

April reaches across the table and touches Phoebe's hand, fingers painted like her mom's. "Exciting, Pheebs."

Nula comes by, chomping on a pretzel, and looks at Phoebe's screen. "How about your DNA relatives?" she asks. "Here, click this."

"What's that?" Oliver jerks. "I didn't know that was a feature."

"Dad, look! I have relatives in Ohio and Canada and—oh wow, all over the place. Can I contact them?"

Meredith's head pops up. She puts down the popcorn bowl.

"Mom, I have a cousin in Cleveland."

Meredith comes over and shoots Oliver an aggrieved glance. "It says third to sixth cousin," she says. "Do you know how distant that is? Look here, they share less than one half of one percent of your DNA. The deckhand on your boat today probably had more."

Oliver massages Phoebe's arm. "Mom's right, sweetheart. The word *relative* here is, well, relative. Maybe if a closer one turns up, we'll see about contacting them."

"Anyway, it's very cool, Bee. Look at all those influences." Meredith kisses her cheek and goes back to her movie.

"How about your results, Dad?"

"Didn't get mine yet, but I'm sure they won't be as interesting as yours," he says.

April turns her attention back to her mail.

"How about Lochlann?" Nula asks. "Did he get his?"

April jolts, hair rising on the back of her neck.

"We had an extra kit," Oliver says. "Meredith didn't have time to spit."

She closes her laptop. "Lochlann's doing DNA testing? Don't you need parental permission for that?"

"I assumed he must have . . . anyway, it's just ethnicity. Nothing medical."

"Let's go see if he got it." Phoebe tugs Nula upstairs.

Hal sits at the head of the table and unfolds a newspaper. Oliver takes out his phone. "Guess I do have my results." He taps the screen.

Phoebe comes back downstairs. "Where is Loch, anyway? I saw him go up."

"Probably the tree house," Nula says.

Oliver taps rapidly. "Phoebe," he calls as she opens the door, "how do I opt out of the relatives thing? What if I want that part private?"

"But that's the fun part," Phoebe says.

"Go to your settings," April says.

The screen door slams, hurried footfalls descending to the tree house. Oliver's eyes widen, his face bloodless. His gaze travels to the corner of the ceiling, out over the ocean, the stratosphere, a place so distant she doesn't know if she can call him back. "Oliver," she says.

He turns to her as if waking from a dream. "I opted out," he says.

"Oh," she says, voice quavering.

"But I got a screenshot first."

April's mouth goes dry. She doesn't ask of what.

Hal turns a leaf of his newspaper, shaking out the page.

The bathroom door opens. "Where'd everyone go?" Lochlann asks.

"Tree house," Hal says. "They want to know if you got your ancestry thingamajig."

Loch pulls out his phone and comes over to Hal—sweeping stride, gangly legs. April hardly breathes. "Hey, I did. Cool." He bends behind Hal and puts his chin on his shoulder. "Grandpa, what's Iberian?" He hands him his phone.

Hal puts down his newspaper. "That's from your Spanish great-grandmother, your mom's nana. She was a hot ticket. Let's see what else. Plenty of Irish—no surprise there. One percent Ashkenazi Jew and Middle Eastern. Touch of sub-Saharan African. I bet if the whole world did this, we'd realize how connected we are. Three percent Neanderthal. Does that explain your behavior at dinner?"

Lochlann musses Hal's hair and rests his hand on his shoulder. Long fingers, sculpted knuckles.

"What about your DNA relatives?" Hal asks. "I think I have some distant cousins in North Carolina."

"No Nights yet," Loch says. "But Uncle Oliver will show up."

Oliver stares at Loch, frozen.

"No results yet?" Loch asks.

Oliver's lips part but no words come out.

"Yes, he got them," Hal says, scrolling.

Loch looks to April for an explanation, his silver-blue eyes slicing through her, parting flesh from bone.

Oliver splays his hands on the table as if on a keyboard, that broad finger span. "I'm not doing the relatives thing," he says. "For now."

"Oh." Lochlann scratches his head, a glaze of confusion in his eyes. He looks at his own hand.

"McDermott," Hal says, reading. "That's a name from your grand-mother's side."

Loch's gaze ping-pongs from April to Oliver. His face whitens. "I think I'll go to the tree house," he mumbles, retrieving the phone. "Thanks, Grandpa." He hurries outside.

Oliver looks at April with the eyes of a man who has come home to find a tornado has taken his house. He taps his screen. Her phone chimes. The screenshot materializes.

Lochlann Night
50.0% DNA shared, 24 segments
Strength of Relationship: Son

243

Something clatters to the floor behind her. Her chair. She is standing bolt upright with the phone in her hand.

"Oh!" Hal lowers his newspaper. "Are you okay?"

Her voice comes out thinly. "I think I'll take a walk."

In an instant she is flying down the trail, branches scraping her legs.

43

Darkness amplifies the sound of the surf. April sits near the base of the rope ladder, hugging knees to chest, shivering on the cool sand. A squeak jars her, feet straining rungs, followed by a scritch of footsteps. How could he find her when even she didn't know where she was going? She shields her head, crash position. "Go away."

He looms over her. "Every time I think I know who you are, you show me you're someone else."

She keeps her head down.

"How could you do this to me?" he says. "You had no right."

"If we'd known, you would've married me to do the right thing and resented me all your life."

"April," he says through his teeth, "I *have* resented you all my life."

She lowers farther, clutches her hair the way she used to in the back seat when her father swerved between lanes.

He crouches beside her. "I can sue, you know." He's closer than she realized, eyes phosphorescent in the darkness. "You lied about the paternity test."

"What test?"

"The one Al did when Loch was born."

"He never took a test." A creeping numbness fills her. "He would have told me."

"I asked him at the christening. He said Loch was his."

Her mind scrambles to make sense of this. Can a DNA test be wrong? Maybe Oliver's result was faulty. "Did he show you the numbers? What did it say, exactly?"

He rubs his brow.

"Oh my God." Her fingertips ice. "You took his word." Her thoughts ricochet, chuting out. "What about me? You never asked me for a test."

"You could have done it yourself. You could have insisted."

"Why would I want to know when you'd disappeared off the planet?"

"You married my brother. What did you expect me to do?"

"Don't turn this around. I wasn't the one who went AWOL."

His eyes widen. "Are you serious? You're making this into I abandoned you?"

She looks away, the shoreline dissolving.

"I have rights. Don't you see what you've done? You robbed me of my son."

"Me? I robbed you?" She springs to her feet. "You opened my heart so you could stick a dagger into it."

"I did not go back to her. I told you that."

"You got on the plane, didn't you? You spent two weeks with her. Maybe for a normal person, that would be fine, but I wasn't normal. You knew that." A swarm of sandflies erupts in her skull, stinging thoughts she cannot swat. "Admit it. I was too high-risk for you."

He whistles out a breath. "You knew how I felt," he says.

"Because we fucked like rabbits? No, Oliver. It's the opposite. *You* knew how *I* felt because I gave you that stupid letter."

His eyes spark, a glint of teeth. "It wasn't fucking. Can we at least for Lochlann's sake admit that we made love, that we were in love, that he came from love?"

The horizon judders. A twist of vertigo spirals through her, tunneling her vision and muting sound. The churn of the ocean, the serration of his voice, the raggedness of her breath meld together and drop into

246

silence. She plants her feet, stays upright. "Al, on the other hand—he thrives on risk."

"Fine," he says. "You chose him. I get that. But it didn't give you the right to cut me off. I should have been there for Lochlann's first steps, the bedtime stories, the Suzuki lessons. All that should've been mine, not Al's."

Her eyes salt. Al was not there for those things. She hugs herself. "Lochlann idolizes you. Be grateful for that. It's more than we get."

"No, I'm done being the nice uncle. All the angst between a father and son, the arguments and pushback—I want that. When I visit colleges with Phoebe, Lochlann should be there. I want to be the one to talk to him before his prom, tell him how to treat a girl. I want to teach him how to drive."

"Are you out of your mind? That one you can have."

"I've lost too much time. You owe me."

"I owe you? You flip me like a fricking jigsaw puzzle and—" She shoves him. Catches herself. Folds her arms. Always a mistake to touch him.

He stumbles and rights himself. "Fine, I could have communicated better. But never in my wildest dreams did I think I'd come home to find you getting *married*? Two weeks later? To my own brother?"

She winces, hands ablaze from having pushed him.

"Do you know what you put me through? How close I came to—"

The words *I'm sorry* slip down from the whir of her mind and dissolve unspoken in her mouth.

"And then I find out you're expecting? Al a father? Anyone could've predicted how that would go."

"And me a mother? Be honest. That made you shudder twice as much."

"Yes, I thought you two would screw it up. I almost said no to the whole godfather sham, but I figured I owed it to the baby, my nephew, at minimum." He picks up a rock, turns it over in his hand. "I told myself you two wouldn't last six months." He hurls the stone in the

247

direction of the sea, a plop puncturing water. "But when I heard you were pregnant again, I realized you two might actually stick. Not that I wanted you back." He hurls another rock, harder this time, the splash followed by a seep of backwash. He bows his head, thinking or searching for another stone. Something is shifting deep in her body, a sand pit caving. With each hurl of his arm, her heart plummets. She tries to picture a Lochlann raised by Oliver. It's suddenly so clear. Fifteen years ago, she reached into the hand of cards her son had been dealt and removed the ace.

"I need these next two years with him before he goes to college. I want him to live with me."

"Are you crazy?"

"If you don't tell him, I will."

"Slow down. What about Meredith? She doesn't even want him in your back seat."

"Because she thinks he's my nephew."

"And she'll feel better if she knows he's our son?" She shields her heart, too late, the words—*our son*—a harpoon.

"That's between Meredith and me. Talk to Al tonight."

She hugs herself, the temperature dropping, stars sharp as needles. A blade of light emerges on the horizon, gilded and shimmering, the sea giving birth to the moon. "I'll talk to him," she says, "when you give me back the letter."

"As if you're in a position to bargain."

"We made a deal. You just got your conversation. Now I get the letter."

"We never agreed on that," he says.

"Think of Meredith. Think of Phoebe. Why hurt them? Why shame me?"

"When I came across it again, I put it in a safe-deposit box."

She steps back. "Jesus, Oliver, only you would do something like that. It doesn't mean they won't see it. We won't live forever."

"I'm not parting with it."

The prickling in her feet and hands ignites through her body, mingling cold and hot, skin perspiring in icy tremors. The thought of him rereading it makes her want to die. "It's a piece of paper, wood pulp and ink, sappy words. I was dreaming. We were young. I don't even know what I wrote."

"'Sappy'? No. Keats had nothing on you, girl."

Quills sear down her neck, her breath short. The orb lifts free of the ocean, casting a luminous lane through which three seals cruise one by one, moonlight defining their horselike snouts. How can they be so tranquil when sharks traverse nearby? "Name your price," she says.

He steps closer, his chest grazing her back. A faraway bonfire scents the air. How long can she go without taking a breath? He puts his lips to her ear. "The letter is all I have from that week, and I'm keeping it."

Her eyes sting, the wind picking up sand. The moon is rising with surprising speed, the seals gone. His chest radiates heat.

"That, and the song."

She faces him.

"Aren't you going to ask? I wrote it the morning you left. All the notes came to me in a single downpour." Chilled water reaches their feet, sea melting land, the world shifting beneath them. "I thought if I played you the song, it would make it harder for you to say no."

"No." Blankness descends on her, blocking out the cold, the salt, the icy stars. Vaguely she hears the tide rising, each boom louder.

"See, the killer was that I had the idea of eloping, too—not to Vegas, though. Never Vegas. I pictured a little ceremony on a mountaintop, something like what my father is doing. Those two weeks apart, all I did was paint scenarios—how I'd ask, where we'd live, the places we'd travel. I had it all worked out."

She feels nothing, not the ash in the wind, the brine on her face. Even the rising moon goes empty.

"I see you don't believe me, but it's in the safe-deposit box, too. A Celtic love knot, size six, because I measured your finger while you slept."

Her fist flies out, knuckles to chin, a clean snap worthy of her father. Pain shoots through her hand, Oliver's face spinning. Before she can sidestep, he snatches her wrists, pulls them snug to his chest. A dark rivulet seeps from his lip.

"Liar," she says. "You would've told me."

He holds her wrists, his chest drumming against her forearms. "I wanted to surprise you."

She yanks back, hands on knees, her knuckles throbbing. He moves toward the ladder. A wave pummels her calves and empties itself with a violent rush. The groan of rungs grows faint as Oliver ascends. April goes to her knees, doused by water, and muffles the choke of her breath.

44

Phoebe lies in bed after midnight, staring at the image of the Chinese couple. She supposes they are not her actual parents but approximations, prototypes for the real thing—the dress, the hair, the serious expressions, the young boy—because for sure her birth parents, whoever they are, have another kid. She stares at their complexions, the shape of their noses, the father's cowlick. Is Nula right that they look no more like Phoebe than any Swede looks like another Swede? She can't name the feeling inside her, the ocean at slack tide, listless and stealthy and too dark to see into.

A twig snaps outside, and she lifts the curtain. A flashlight darts along the beach plum path toward the house. Aunt April. Phoebe's father came in half an hour earlier, murmuring now with her mother across the hall.

Phoebe skulks out of her room and peeks downstairs into the living room, where Aunt April's shadowy figure bends over Uncle Al in the armchair. She gives him a shake, puts her ear to his chest. She comes toward the stairs, and Phoebe slips back in her room, watching from the doorframe. April stops in front of her parents' room and knocks.

Her mother answers, pulling her robe closed. Phoebe catches snippets of her aunt's voice: ". . . cool and sweaty . . . reedy pulse . . ." Her father appears behind her mother, bare-chested. "He won't come to," Aunt April says. "What were those pills?"

"Just something my doc gave me to take the edge off," her mother answers. "He was only supposed to take one. He'll probably be out till noon tomorrow."

Aunt April's voice is soft but insistent. ". . . shallow . . . dilated . . ."

"Oliver, go down and check on your brother," her mother says. "Don't worry, April. Your man is cast iron." She goes back to bed.

Her father trots downstairs and quickly returns. "He's done worse to his body than this," he says to April, and closes his door.

Phoebe gives a start. Her dad never acts like that. She clicks off the ceiling fan to better hear whatever is going to happen next. The fan slows to a halt, one blade faintly discernible, three blending into gloom, the fifth invisible—there but not there. Nula tosses beneath the covers, and Phoebe wonders if she's dreaming of a Gorgon. Careful footsteps ascend the stairs. She gets up and cracks open the door. Her grandfather peers in. "Princess, still awake?"

"Did my mom give Uncle Al pills? Is he okay?"

"Aunt April is keeping an eye on him. He'll be fine." He pats her cheek. "Since we're both up at this ungodly hour, follow me. I want to show you something."

Bookshelves line the walls of her grandfather's study, the heavy desk adorned with photos. His focus and discernment are palpable here. She feels safer being in this room. She catches her reflection in the antique mirror, the blonde taking her by surprise.

"I made something for you." He boots up his desktop. "I'm ashamed to say how long it took. Lochlann helped. They say it's good for your brain to keep up with technology."

She sits beside him at the walnut desk. The lamp casts a dusty glow.

"Look, I made you a GIF. Actually, two."

"A gift?"

"Maybe it's pronounced *jiff*? Anyway, your old gramps made one."

The first shows Phoebe on one side and Meredith on the other, faces turned up, eyes closed in laughter, a mirror of each other. The second shows Phoebe on one side and Oliver on the other, both nodding in sympathy—a similar tilt to their heads. A strange feeling stirs inside her. "What is this?"

"I snapped these when you weren't looking," he says. "I made the GIFs to show you. Don't you see?"

"See what?"

"Who you look like. You have your parents' expressions."

She turns to the bookshelves, eyes dampening.

"Princess, I upset you. That's the opposite of what I wanted," he says. "I see their goodness in you. That's all I meant to show."

She blows her nose. "I know they love me."

"Phoebe, I can't pretend to understand what it's like to be adopted. It's traumatic for a child to be separated from their parents, no matter the circumstances. If I can help carry the sadness, I'd like that. But I'm not trying to take it from you."

She looks at the books, too dark to make out titles, imagining the stories that live inside each binding. "I just wonder if they think about me," she says. "Is it possible to have a kid and not think about them?"

He squeezes her hand. "I don't know."

She wipes her eyes. "How long did it take you to make those GIFs, Grandpa?"

"Not telling." He closes the image. "Lochlann is sworn to secrecy."

She spots another photo on his desktop. "What's that one?"

He opens an image of a seascape. "That blue whale I saw the day you arrived. Too far away to capture, but I like knowing it's there beneath the surface."

Like her birth parents, she thinks. "Can you send me that one, too?"

"Sure, sunshine." He gives her a hug.

Back in bed, she checks her phone, which she smuggled into her room, and opens the photo of the invisible whale, wondering how it ended up here so far from its birthplace. She falls asleep picturing it swimming in the dark.

45

Phoebe dreams of her birth mother's black hair flowing, supple as fins, the two of them swimming side by side through eons of ocean, a whale and her calf. The distance between them lengthens gradually until a morning arrives when Phoebe can no longer hear the vibration of her mother's song, her back breaking the surface, or the vaporous burst from her blowhole, only her own in-suck of air, sun on her back, a tingle of spray. With no fluke to follow, no wake or watery footprint, no mother sounding in unison, Phoebe's world grows strange and new. Hunger drives her from warm to cool, clear to turbid, navigating by stars and sonar and the magnetic tug of the north, a force urging her forward. She surfaces and sounds, temperature cooling with each stratum, moving from one molten amber cloud to another, vacuuming in krill, pullulating, growing in length and speed, until she arrives at the underwater plateau beneath Dawnland, a place of colliding currents and internal waves. A powerful upwelling lifts food from the bottom, sand lances and copepods. She gorges and sleeps. Daybreak filters down, illuminating an endless sandy ledge that rises straight up through the surface. The world, it turns out, has edges, beyond which the bottom of things becomes the top. She will need to return to boundarylessness, but for now she skim-feeds the surface, glutting on bounty. On a distant cliff, a salty-haired man lifts his binoculars. The touch of his eyesight glitters inside her, a warming glow. She fills her belly with the peculiar sensation. Phoebe has been seen.

46

Friday

Al awakens to first light piercing the blinds. His head is ether, his body a sack of stones. Something lies across his lap—some*one*—mink-dark hair in his fingers. April is on the floor, head cradled atop a pillow on his knees. He tries to find his voice, his throat like steel wool. "Hey."

She picks up her head groggily.

"What're you doing here?" he asks.

"Making sure you're not dead." She sits up. "What were those pills?"

"Who the hell knows? This is exactly why I don't mess with shit like that. I need to take a leak." He tries to stand but loses balance. April catches him. "Could also be the withdrawal. Hit me different last time." They walk to the bathroom. "Is this what it's going to be like when we're old, helping each other to take a piss?"

"We'll never know." She waits for him outside the door and guides him back to the living room. "What do you need? A glass of water?"

"A cigarette."

"No, you've gotten this far."

"This far ain't very."

"If I quit, you can."

He knows April believes this, but for her, cigarettes had been a high school accessory. For him, they're a requirement of his ability to think and work, even—counterintuitively—to breathe. "I'll get back on track tomorrow. Go to bed."

"You're the one who should go to bed. I'll help you up the stairs."

"Told Nula I'd go out with you today no matter what. What's the agenda?"

"Ocean kayaking. You're in no shape."

"Always some excuse. Can you make me a cup of coffee? I'll be fine."

She starts toward the kitchen but turns back. "Al," she says. The way she stands—spine erect, holding a question upright in her body—he knows something big is coming.

"That night in my apartment, when I told you about the postcard, you know, that your brother went to see Bernadette—did you know that he'd gone there to end it?" Her eyes fix on him.

"I could've guessed."

She nods slowly. "Did we have sex that night?"

It stabs him that she has to ask. She remembers the postcard, though. "Yeah, April. It was afternoon. The sun was coming in the window. That was our first time."

She rubs her forehead. "When we bought the pregnancy kit, did you already know that your brother was living back at your father's house?"

"Yeah," he says. "I knew."

She massages her finger, absorbing this. "Did Oliver . . . ? Well, he claims he asked you for a paternity test." Her face is open and raw, like she's hoping he'll deny it.

"At the christening. Yeah."

"And you said you'd done one."

"I did the swab. I never mailed it in." He braces for her to pick up the floor lamp and swing at him, but she rubs her brow, as if trying to absorb each word separately.

"But you told him you had."

"I didn't want to lose you, Rosie."

She touches her collarbone. "Oliver did a DNA test."

"I see." He bows his head. His chest hurts. His heart. He's been given everything in life and has squandered it. Always hungry, wanting more, needing what his brother has. "I've been meaning to tell you," he says. "Last spring Loch asked to know my blood type. He's a universal donor—type O, like you. Not sure if you know mine."

Her face pales.

"AB positive. I never realized that doesn't compute. Had to look it up." He lathers his hands, spooked by her calmness.

"Does Loch know?"

"He asked me next time I was home. You were at the Wool and Fiber Expo. What could I say? The kid can do math," he says. "He asked if I knew who the guy was. I give him credit for that. That's a ballsy question to ask your dad."

She shudders. "What did you say?"

"Some guy you had a thing with in Ireland."

"You mentioned Ireland?"

He rubs his face. "That was the first night he split. Came home around six in the morning."

She covers her face, perfectly still. It seems she's not breathing. He wants her to slap him in the head, kick his shin, but her sadness fills the room like a night-blooming flower, heady and funereal.

"April, I'm sorry," he says. "Look, I know there's no reason you should give me another chance, but I'm telling you the truth. This health scare shook something loose in my brain. I'm ready to turn everything around. Nothing is more important to me than you and the kids. Look, you see me here. I'm trying to claw my way back."

Her eyes are bottomless wells. "I hope you make it, Al." She turns toward the kitchen. "But do it for yourself."

When Al awakens the second time, he's horizontal on the couch, a cold cup of coffee on the table. It's after ten, and the house is quiet. "Damn." He sits up, the room undulating. He wonders if he can catch them. Nula doesn't ask for much.

He hears the tap run in the kitchen. Maybe they haven't left after all. But only Meredith emerges, a pack of cigarettes in her hand. "Ah." She sits across from him, landing on the cushions with a little bounce. "Back from the dead?"

"Not yet."

"Your life must be pretty pathetic if you'd rather hack into mine."

"Can this wait till I've had my coffee? You nearly killed me last night." He remembers April's face in the morning twilight, that crushing sorrow. He owes her. He owes his brother.

Meredith lights up. "Normally I only smoke with my girlfriends. Some of us know how to do things in moderation." She passes the cigarette to him. "I bet you're dying for a hit."

He drops it into the cold coffee. "No smoking in the house." He wipes a speck of ash off *Secrets of the Sea*. Feet like sledgehammers, he shuffles to the kitchen. On the counter, a jam-stained sign reads T-Minus 2 Days.

"If you want to make an issue over who supplies my batteries, we can start counting the ways I can make your life feel like a root canal." Meredith leans in the door.

"I've already got that down." He fills the coffee maker.

"What do you want from me, Al?"

"Simple. Come clean with Oliver about your little throuple."

"My what?" She laughs hard and bright.

The scent of the extinguished cigarette drifts from the living room. He can taste the ash, granular and intoxicating. One puff and he'll be able to think a clear thought. The coffee begins to percolate. "You two want to do orgies, have at it. But don't do it behind his back."

"*You're* lecturing *me* on fidelity?"

"Nothing April doesn't know about me. Sad but true." He sighs. "I'm trying to fix things—myself, my marriage, stuff with my kids. I don't think the odds are with me, but it's one life and I'm going for it."

She stares at him, her mouth hard.

"If she won't give me another chance, I want you to cut him loose, too. With as much custody as he wants."

Her jaw falls open with a high-pitched yelp. "You're a piece of work, Al, you know that? You're amazing."

"Laugh if you want. Mislabeling product is a federal offense. I have what I need to bring you down. Start-up like yours will never survive a recall. Even if you pay the fines, no investor will touch you again. You should've deleted those purchase orders from Guangdong Province."

She blinks uncontrollably, hands on hips. "Oliver and I have a commitment to Phoebe. That's something we're in absolute agreement on. She's already been unloaded by one set of parents, and it's not happening again."

"No one's talking about abandoning Phoebe."

"Sure, your style of parenting doesn't require a person to actually be there."

He pours coffee. A hummingbird hovering at the feeder pivots to look inside, examining Al first with one eye and then the other. Does each eye supply different information? Al tries to read Meredith's expression, covers his left eye and sees disgust, fury, and indignation. Covers his right, and those layers dissolve into terror and grief.

"What the hell are you doing?" she asks.

"I'm not judging you, Meredith. You're a far superior parent. Better spouse, too. And a damned good businesswoman. But I owe this to my brother. Come clean."

The aroma of brewed coffee fills the room, textured with the scent of his father's flowers drifting from the open window. Meredith's eyes brim. "You are a revolting human being. I can't believe you're Oliver's brother."

"I could stand to be more like him. Not worth the price, though." Al heaps sugar into the brew. "Better to fail big than be afraid of what you want."

47

In the passenger seat of her truck, April awakes to the pop of the fuel flap, a liquid gurgle, Oliver holding the nozzle. Through the convenience store window, the kids stand in line. She brushes sleep from her eyes—it's been days since she slept in a bed—and thrusts three twenties toward Oliver. He waves them off and gets behind the wheel, his profile revealing a purple lip. She squirms, the seat squeaking beneath her. It took them a decade to stitch together a thread of normalcy, one summer to unzip it.

"Talk to Al yet?" he asks.

She hugs her middle. Her body feels sore, as if she's the one who has been punched.

"I can tell him myself," he says. "I don't need you."

"We talked," she says. "He knows."

The kids climb into the back seat, Phoebe's face alert, listening.

Oliver looks in the rearview. "What'd you buy, Bee?"

She offers her chips. "Your lip's gone down. Aunt April, did you see? A mosquito bit Daddy right on the mouth."

"Some nerve," April says.

She turns to see Loch staring at the crown of Oliver's head where the dense hair corkscrews clockwise. He touches his own scalp in the same spot. Catching April's stare, he stuffs his hands in his pockets. "Do we really have to kayak?" He slumps back. "Most people actually relax on vacation."

"Our last adventure," Oliver says, pulling roughly onto the road.

Already the week is on the verge of disintegrating into memory. April pictures next year's reunion, the kids driving up in Al's car, taking excursions without her. She'll plan a trip with friends. She'll survive it. They pass an oak tree with a giant burl, the trunk having deformed itself to cordon off injury.

Phoebe sneezes. "Dad, hand me a tissue?"

Oliver reaches into the console and pulls out the stuffed mouse, head flopping to one side, fiberfill bulging from its missing eye. April holds a breath.

"What the—" Loch gasps, grabbing it. "Mousy!"

"Is that really what we called it? That's the lamest name ever." Phoebe breaks into laughter. "It looks like something from *The Exorcist*."

"Hey!" Loch cradles it, smiling. "You'll hurt his feelings."

They've barely parked when the kids leap out to pick their kayaks. Oliver lifts his chin in the visor mirror. "Impressive left hook. I was braced for the right."

As if he's expecting an apology. April gets out, rubbing her swollen knuckle. A young couple hauls kayaks onto the dock—unmarried, based on their adoring glances, vibrant in a way reserved for people their age, oblivious to the transience of that particular vitality. April pictures herself at twenty-one, hell-bent on self-sabotage, and good at it. The couple must have left before daybreak to be back already. "Excuse me." The man asks Oliver to take their picture and offers to take one in exchange.

Oliver hands over his camera and motions for the kids to line up. When April stands apart, he loops his arm around her waist, that old electric claim in his grip, and tugs her into the frame. The shutter clicks. Her fake family. This is as close as she will get.

Loch asks to see the photo, staring into the frame for a long beat.

"What is it?" Phoebe asks.

"Nothing." Loch gives Oliver a side-glance and hands it back.

Paddling last, April soaks in the scent of seaweed and salt, the hypnotic swish of water. Her eye falls to Lochlann's and Oliver's sinewy backs, the catch and release of their paddles through troughs, the way they both tend to bury the blade. They glance at each other alternately until their eyes meet. Loch quickens his pace. How might he have been different with Oliver as a father? How would Oliver be different with Loch as a son?

The wind picks up, and a pink blur hurtles above the waterline. Oliver's long fingers snatch Phoebe's visor in midair. Phoebe looks over her shoulder at him, touching her bare forehead. "How'd you catch that?" She laughs. He paddles alongside her, his eyes softening, that radiant smile. April sees the enormity of his love for her, the child who came to him as pure gift. He passes her the visor. "Thanks, Dad," she says. She doesn't know how close he came to missing it.

They lace through tidal marshes and along the bluffs of the barrier island until they reach the southern tip and drag their kayaks ashore. To find shade, they climb the forested upland and sit beneath a stand of conifers. The kids are subdued from sun and exertion. April distributes sandwiches. Oliver pulls off his T-shirt. "Aunt April and I are going to look for fiddler crabs," he announces. "Who's coming?"

"Pooped," Phoebe says.

"Hungry." Nula takes a bite of her sandwich.

Lochlann gives them a discerning look and answers by lying down.

April peers with suspicion over the rim of her sunglasses. Oliver claps his hands as though it's settled. Reluctantly she follows him over the ridge and down the other side to the water. They walk a stretch before he stops and lies on the sand. "Lochlann's right. We hardly relax on these vacations."

Hands on hips, she stares down. He crosses his legs. She sits beside him—not close. The bay laps in a gentle, rhythmic percussion, the sun baking her skin.

"He's coming to live with me," he says. "No question."

"Meredith's right. You are a dictator."

"It's got to happen," he says. "It's overdue."

"You're not the only person in the picture."

"I haven't been in the picture," he says. "That's the problem. I got photoshopped out." Above them two black-backed gulls make sky-circles, the distant sound of the children's laughter carried on the wind. "He has my hands," Oliver says, examining his palm. "Your attitude, though."

She keeps her eyes on the sky.

"It must've been that time out on the cliff," he says. "That sea cave thundering below. No wonder he is the way he is."

Her chest tightens. "Fiddler crabs," she says. "Really."

The gulls dip and loop. "I used to fantasize about murdering you."

She turns to him, glasses shiny and impervious. "'Used to'?"

"I had a plan," he says. "Several, in fact."

"Don't think you're so special."

"Got a hell of a song out of it. The Grammy nomination—that was your murder anthem."

"Wonder what it would take to get the Grammy."

"We have a son. Communicating one text at a time isn't going to cut it anymore."

"How do you think divorced people do it? Five-course dinners?"

"We're not divorced," he says.

"Right," she says. "We're less than that." The gulls rise on an updraft and separate. "So what if you bought a ring over there while that place had its hold on you? You wouldn't have given it. Admit it. You got a case of reality whiplash. We both know I would have mucked up your life."

"More than you have?"

She folds her arms. He does the same. The gulls lift out of sight.

"Does it matter? We should be grateful. Life without Phoebe and Nula would be unimaginable." Her eyes fill, her throat hard. "Besides, we never would have made it. Even if you hadn't gone to see Bernadette,

I would have sabotaged it somehow. I was pathologically insecure. I wasn't ready."

"Ready enough for Al, apparently."

The birds circle back, joined by a third and fourth. Heat flushes through her body, her gut tightening. Tears leak from her eyes. "I used him," she says. "I held on to him like a life raft."

"I can understand that, for a few months," Oliver says. "A year, maybe."

The gull calls sharpen, strident and alarmed. April clutches a fistful of sand. She feels her mother's hand limp in hers, sees herself sitting by her hospital bed, her father down the hall with minor cuts. Her mother appeared intact, the injuries internal. Even her hair was exactly as she had starched it that morning. "Mom, they say you can recover. Nothing is permanent," April said. "He did this to you. You can leave him."

"Easy for you to say." Her mother opened her eyes one last time and looked at April. "You don't know what love is yet."

April grips the sand so hard her hand is empty. Pressure builds in her chest, her throat, behind her eyes, quaking her shoulders, a throb too big to contain. It breaks out, a visceral wail. Oliver touches her arm.

She covers her face. "I'm sorry, Oliver," she says. "I've hurt you. I've done damage to your life. Loch can live with you if that's what he wants."

She hears her name from a great distance, the past calling to her across the years, getting louder, a familiar inflection. Al's voice. She straightens. "April!" he cries. Beyond the waves, she makes out a Mets cap, a floundering kayaker. "Where the hell?" he calls.

She can't believe he had the strength to find them. She wipes her face. Oliver stares at the kayak, mouth taut. "He could hardly stand up this morning. He needs help," April says, and turns for the dune. "I'll let you do it."

48

Chest-deep in the surf, Oliver waves his arms, a spray of seawater stinging the cut on his lip. "Al," he shouts. Al spots him, but each stroke of the paddle seems to require all his strength. Oliver's jaw clenches as he watches him struggle, this brother who raised his son. He remembers the first time he saw Lochlann as a baby. His father had asked him to stop by to help with repairs. Hal was out back, raking, so Oliver let himself in. His eye moved to the recliner, a woman's elbow on the armrest. A step closer revealed a strand of long dark hair. Oliver almost left right then, but he walked around to see her full on. She'd fallen asleep nursing. The cyclone inside him went still, arrested by the tilt of her face, the down of his hair, his tiny fists. Even asleep she looked exhausted, the baby sated and peaceful. Oliver went to his knees. Then he noticed her hand. He hadn't brought himself to believe it, but there it was on her finger. They were married. He can't remember what song was playing, only that he got back in his car before it was over.

When the kayak is close enough, Oliver grabs the hull and starts hauling it in. Al stumbles out onto the beach, and Oliver lurches the boat onto dry sand. It's unlike Al to accept help, especially when it comes to physical strength. He collapses as if shipwrecked. It's unnerving to see him so weak, this brother who defended Oliver from grade school bullies and once tried, to no avail, to teach him to box.

"Not easy to find you." Al shields his eyes from the sun, breath labored.

"What are you doing here?" Oliver asks.

"No one told me it was such a long way. Where's April? I saw her up there with you."

"We were talking about Lochlann," Oliver says. "I only hauled you in because she asked. If it were up to me, I'd have left you out there."

"Look, Oliver. I only found out a few months ago. None of us knew. We're all at fault."

"Are you kidding? You lied to me."

"You did it to yourself." Al struggles to his knees. "If the tables were turned, I'd have jumped on a plane and followed you to Vegas," Al says. "I'd have pounded down your door and demanded to know who gave you the right to take my girl—"

"*Your* girl? Try a woman, a human being nobody owns."

"But you had yourself a pity party."

"You act like she's a football you intercepted. She made a choice."

"For a so-called genius, you have the IQ of a marmot," he says. "Tell me this: When you scoop a drowning fly out of a dog bowl, is the fly making a choice?"

"Now she's an insect. What a charmer, Al. No wonder all the women go for you."

"I wanted you to beat my head in. I expected it. But you were a no-show. Too much wounded pride, I guess. And people think I'm the egomaniac in the family." He looks at the dune. "When I finally see you at the baptism, what do you say? Not *I'm going to tear your limbs from your body.* Not *I want her back.* Or even *How is she?* Just *I want a paternity test.* And that's when I lied to you, because you didn't have the brains to ask the right question." Al gets to his feet. "Do you know that I saved her life? She nearly killed herself while you were out banging Miss Norway."

Oliver remembers the burnt curtains. The rope. He feels light-headed. "I made a mistake," he says. "That entitles you to my son?"

"Don't you get it? He wouldn't have been born if not for me." His nostrils flare.

An uneasy memory descends on Oliver. He looks out at the spray. "I was worried she'd take her life once, too, the night of her brother's funeral. It didn't seem safe to leave her alone. I slept on her couch. The state she was in, do you know how easy it would have been for me to take advantage of her?"

Al claps sand off his hands and looks at Oliver calmly.

"Yeah," Oliver says, "I suppose you do."

"That's the difference between you and me," Al says. "One of us hesitates."

Oliver's voice shakes. "You had Bernadette's number."

"Yep," Al says. "And you had April's."

"I was staying with Bernadette's family. It would have been rude."

"Wedded to politeness. I wonder what else that's cost you."

Oliver clamps his teeth. Whitecaps spark in the distance. His high school piano teacher once told him he'd never achieve greatness if he didn't learn to get ruthless.

"All that time you and April spent together in high school, and you never did anything?" Al asks. "What was that about?"

"She was my friend, Al. I cared for her. She was fragile."

"She was powerful. She was changing before your eyes. She scared the shit out of you."

Oliver blinks.

"Remember that time I fell off the merry-go-round reaching for the gold ring, busted my nose?" Al asks. "Guess what? I got it."

"Daddy," a voice calls. Nula crests the bluff, bounding toward them. "You made it!" she says. Al walks over to her, arms opened.

Oliver looks out at the ocean, spray ripped from the crests. "You rely too much on your light touch," his teacher had warned him. "It's an insult to the score."

49

Oliver finds Meredith in front of her laptop at the dining room table. It won't be easy to dislodge her from her work, no less to talk about Lochlann. He pours two glasses of wine, test-driving sentences in his mind, trying to find the least shocking way to say it. "Let's sit on the patio." He offers a glass.

She looks up in surprise. Across the table, Al types in biting silence. "I have a few more emails to write," she says.

"There's something I need to talk to you about," Oliver says.

She cuts a glance at Al. He looks up from his keyboard without expression and down again. She follows Oliver outside, where they sit beneath the chestnut tree. Early conkers, glossy and russet, have begun to fall, along with papery tear-shaped leaves the size of human hands. "How was your day?" He leans forward, a chestnut splitting beneath his sole, the shell softer than it appeared. "No more complaints, I hope."

"The settlement's not going as smoothly as we thought. They're upping the ante." She puts the wine on the arm of the chair. "How long do you think the wedding's going to last? I have to set up the booth for the trade show, and my assistant's out sick."

"I don't know, but I'd hate for my dad to feel rushed." He sips the wine, leans back in his seat.

Hair falls from her stubby ponytail, uncharacteristically bedraggled, her eyes squinty and guarded as if she's been working out numbers. Even stressed and weary, she's beautiful by any standard.

"Meredith." He looks at her directly but can't read her expression, eyes blinking as if her contacts are dry, hands tucked beneath her thighs. "You know I love you, right?"

"Uh-oh."

"No matter what happened before, we're a team. We agree on that, don't we?"

"What's going on?"

Above them shines Phoebe's window. "Maybe we should take a walk."

"You know the woods creep me out. Just say it."

"It has to do with things that happened before we met. It doesn't touch us."

She leans away from him. "Is this about her?"

"No. It's about Lochlann, that DNA test we took."

Her mouth swings open. "Tell me this is a joke." She stands. "What the— When were you planning to tell me? How long have you known?"

"A few hours. I'm telling you now."

"Who else knows?"

"Only me. And his mother."

"His *mother*? Is that what we're calling her now?" She puts her hands on her hips. "And Al? He knows?"

"Apparently."

She looks in the window. "This is priceless."

"Meredith, we need to talk about what this means."

"I'll tell you what it doesn't mean." She points at him, trembling. "I am not paying for his college."

"What? This isn't about—"

"Of course it is. It's always about money. Why else would she tell you? She hasn't made a profit with the farm, so she's going after you. Do you know what it's like to be sued for fifteen years of child support?"

"Why is money always the first thing you go to?"

"Why are you so naive?"

He rubs his forehead. "Look, I'm sorry. I know this is a lot to spring on you, but the school year starts soon and, if he's willing—"

"They want to foist him on us? Are you insane? We don't have room. He'll disrupt our lives. He's bad for Phoebe. No, Oliver. Absolutely not."

"You don't have to decide today."

She snorts.

"Meredith, I'm not saying you owe me this. I'm not saying it makes sense. I understand it's a huge ask." He takes her hand, pulls her back down to sit in front of him. "It's not just that this would mean a lot to me. It's that it has to happen."

"I can't process this. Give me time to process. This whole week's been a disaster."

"Take your time. But not too much. I plan to talk to Lochlann before we leave."

"As in, tomorrow?"

"It has to be in person."

"You're going to tell Loch he's not his dad's kid? Shouldn't his parents tell him?"

"They will. Tonight."

"The night before your dad's wedding? This is hilarious. Let's live stream it on YouTube. Monetize it. We'll make a fortune."

"It's not a joke, Meredith."

"If only." She looks in the window, at Al typing. "This must kill him."

Oliver shifts uncomfortably. "We'll try to be sensitive, then."

She picks up her wine. "I'd better finish those emails."

"He sent me a strange text earlier. I haven't had a chance to ask him about it."

Meredith goes rigid. She sets down her wineglass.

"Something about my gig in Philly."

She throws back a swallow. "Oliver, there's something I have to tell you, too." She glances up at Phoebe's window. "Let's take a walk."

"A walk?" A shudder sweeps through him. "*You* want to—"

"I'll grab a sweater." She goes in and climbs the stairs. Oliver retrieves his sweatshirt from the dining room. Al gazes up from his laptop, a familiar expression from childhood, hard and accusatory, as if Oliver has once again screwed up. They say nothing, the shorthand of the glance sinking weight in Oliver's gut.

The surf pounds louder as Oliver and Meredith move down the path. Dusk descends in the woods with a burnt, musky aroma. She turns to face him. Bows of beach plum arch over them like a wedding arbor, the path to the sea a winding tunnel through shrubbery. "I get it," she says. "Your brother's on a witch hunt, and now I see why."

Oliver looks at her in the fading light—her moist hazel eyes, the tension in her brow. "'Witch hunt'?"

"Apparently it's not enough to destroy his own life."

A surreal sensation comes over him, a suspension of time. The trail stretches before them and away—one direction to the house, the other to the cliff. The more the branches buck and rear, the stiller he becomes. He takes in her alert posture, the fixedness of her shoulders suggesting something incalculable at stake. Her eyes glow like a turned-up burner.

"Oliver," she says, as if he hasn't been listening, "he can't stand the truth about you and Lochlann. That's why he's trying to hurt you." She's all aflame now, vibrant and crackling. "He thinks he's got something on me. Suddenly wants to defend his little brother's honor, as if he's ever been your ally."

Oliver takes a half step back. He remembers telling Phoebe to listen to the breeze. Coming or going? Something is approaching, not sound but realization, unnamable, with speed and momentum behind it. He doesn't know what expression he wears, only that it's not what she hoped.

"I see. Brother over wife," she says. "That's how it goes with men."

"What?"

"Tell me the truth." She steps toward him. "Have you ever been unfaithful to me?" Her amber eyes bronze in the failing light. He's heard her phone negotiations hundreds of times. If a co-packer thinks she's cheating him on a price, she anticipates the question, accuses him first. *Unfaithful.* His teacher once nailed him for interpreting Bach in a way that was unfaithful to the score. "Congratulations," he said. "You're becoming a composer."

"Well?" Meredith asks.

"Yes," Oliver says.

Her lips part. Perhaps she expected something more mitigated, lust of the heart. She covers her stomach. "When?"

He hesitates, not wanting something he's kept to himself to be consumed too greedily, an expensive chocolate dispatched in one gulp. "Earlier this summer. I kissed a woman on the street in New York."

"You?" She lets out a frightened laugh. "Who?"

"Someone I was walking to the subway," he says.

"From the nonprofit? A teacher?"

"It was a onetime thing."

"And then?" She draws in a breath.

He looks at the ground, a conundrum of myrtle and moss. A breeze fingers his hair, tousling his clothes, the autumnal aroma of moldering pine needles. "The light turned. That was it."

Rarely does she lose her way in a negotiation.

"I take it there's more to it in your case," he says.

"I'm not in love with anyone, which is more than you can say." Her eyes moisten. She looks down the path in the direction of the cliff. A harsh chorus of cicadas stridulates above them. "I'm not an idiot. I saw your face when you danced with her. And now you tell me you have a kid together but not to worry about it?"

"Is this about Lisbeth and Cole?" he asks. "Have you been back to their place?"

"It's your fault. I wanted us to go together."

A bullet of cold pierces him below the ribs. Wind rips through the foliage, a clash of the day's warmth and the ocean's chill sending everything around them into motion, trees, sky, cricket song throbbing his eardrums. "And did you—"

"When you're with me, you're giving it to her. Isn't that the truth?"

"Please, answer—"

"*You* answer," she says.

"You're trying to dodge—"

"Who can blame her for choosing your brother? At least he's honest."

The merlot he sipped on the patio rises in his throat with a tart burn.

"The woman you kissed on the street—was it her?"

"Did you have sex with them?" he asks. "I need to know."

"Truth for truth."

"It lasted all of ten seconds," he says.

"I knew it. Now it makes sense why you've been so distant."

"Me?" he says. "I've been distant?" But a twinge in his chest tells him she's right.

"It's because of her."

"It's not right to equate these things. Yes, I have a complicated history with her, but I'm not—"

"It's not just her," she says. "You have more allegiance to your father than you do me. Phoebe is closer to you than I am. You've never let me in."

"That's not true," he says. "I've been completely committed to you."

"I'm not talking about duty."

"Have I not been there for you emotionally?"

"You say the right things," she says.

"What more do you want?"

"Your heart."

"And that's what those two give you?" he asks.

She exhales forcefully.

"How did we end up here?" he says.

"I feel disconnected from you," she says. "That's how."

"So instead of talking to me about it, you jump into bed with—"

"I had too much to drink." Her eyes glisten. "I only meant to watch."

"Sure," he says, "but somehow you became the main course."

"We all wished you were there."

"That's touching," he says. "Let's text them now. Let's put it on the schedule."

"Why are you so goddamn vanilla? Another husband would die for it."

"Well, maybe that's the husband you need."

She covers her face. "Don't say that, Oliver."

Dusk turns the tree trunks black, patches of lichen aglow in the gloom. In the distance the ocean seethes. "I'm sorry I'm not enough for you," he says. "I tried."

"I'm sorry I hurt you," she says. "But you hurt me more. You and April, you deceived me. I can't look at her again. No more vacationing together. Next year we'll come a different week."

"I don't want Phoebe to know about any of this," he says.

"I can't have Lochlann live with us. If that's what you want, you'll need your own apartment. It's not a bad idea, anyway. Lots of married couples do it. It would give us both space."

"Space for what? Lisbeth and Cole?" The words come out sharp, yet the thought of his own apartment makes him swoon. No static of television, blow-dryer, overheard business calls. What would it be like to live attuned not to her rhythms but his own? How long would it take for his inner cadence to come out of hiding?

Her voice is thick. "Believe it or not, there are people out there who think I'm amazing. You? You think I'm shallow and self-absorbed. I'm sorry if I don't have time for Tolstoy. I've been busy busting my ass to support us."

He puts his hands on his head. "I never said—"

"You didn't have to."

"Meredith, how can you think—"

From a dead branch a crow peers down, its strident caws rebuking Oliver. What makes him think his parental decisions are wiser than Meredith's? That national parks are better than resorts? That monogamy is above polyamory? Which is more hurtful, that his wife screwed two people she cares nothing for or that he kissed a woman he's loved for years, and still cannot bring himself to regret it?

"I love you, Oliver, but you're maddening. You're superior. You're distracted. You act the part, but your head's not in the game. Now I know why." Her shoulders quake. "Don't you see? You're the one who left."

A thunderous wave breaks in the distance, what was deep spilling onto the shore. His throat thickens with something visceral. Guilt. Relief. "There's nothing wrong with what you need," he says. "The only thing wrong is, I can't give it."

"Not *can't*. *Won't*." She begins to weep.

His habit is too strong. He takes her in his arms, feels the familiar curve of her spine. "Meredith," he says, "I'm sorry." He hugs her as though Phoebe were there between them.

50

Captain Hook's, where they traditionally have their farewell dinner, is open despite a leaky roof. Behind April's chair water drips into a bucket with the steadiness of a ticking bomb. Beneath the floorboards the fitful bay slaps against pylons. Al sits unnervingly still, palms flat on the table as he sizes up his water glass. He slept all afternoon and awoke looking steadier, stronger, and eerily silent. Introspection is not his norm, but he appears to have taken it on the way he does everything—full blast. The husband April knows has been replaced by a morose and solemn doppelgänger. Oliver and Meredith avoid eye contact. The kids are subdued. Hal and Beryl exchange glances.

"Let's hear about the ceremony tomorrow." April tries to sound cheerful. "I'm surprised the church is letting you have it outdoors."

"We got a dispensation," Beryl says. "Since I'm not Catholic, they're letting us have it in my place of worship—nature." She smiles as though expecting a reaction, but everyone looks distracted. The sulfur of low tide permeates the room.

Once the plates are cleared and dessert ordered, Hal leans on the table, fingers folded. "Can someone please tell me what in heaven's name is going on?"

"Are you worried that I'm taking your father and grandfather away from you?" Beryl asks. "Because those are normal feelings."

"Of course not," Oliver says.

"No one wants to go back to school," Nula says.

"Some of us aren't," Lochlann says.

Beryl looks at Oliver and Al. "I hope you know I have no intention of replacing your mother, God rest her soul. The things in the house that belonged to her—"

"Beryl." Ungreased by alcohol, Al's voice is parched. "You're obviously the best thing that's happened to Dad in years. No one's worried."

"We're all incredibly happy for you," Oliver says.

Hal surveys their faces and settles on Phoebe, the one he relies on, but she says nothing. Nula tugs April's sleeve. "I'm going to the bathroom."

"I'll go with you," April says.

"Grandpa's right," Nula says, weaving around tables. "Everyone's being weird." She scoots into a bathroom. The other is occupied, so April waits on the battered hallway bench. Oliver appears, looks at the Occupied sign, and sits beside her, head in his hands.

"Al and I are planning to tell Loch after dinner, if that's what you're worried about," she says. "You can't blame Meredith for being upset. Give her time."

"She's not to blame." He stares at the grimy vinyl floor. "I've been thinking about what you said. I suppose I did have second thoughts. I bought the ring in Galway, but on the flight home I figured I should pocket it for a while, see how things went. I didn't know what your life was like. I wondered if your old volatility would flare up. If I could live with that."

"I guess you got your answer," she says.

"But I knew once I saw you again, those doubts would vanish," he says. "It's a habit of mine, hesitation."

"I could stand to hesitate more often," she says.

"I was scared of you," he says.

"As you should've been," she says. "Obviously I wasn't stable."

He massages his temples. "The walls of my life just got kicked out. The landscape's changed overnight. Loch is my son." His eyes are gray in the shadowy light. "He asked me before dinner why I'd opted out of the DNA relatives. Looked me straight in the eye. He's figured it out,

April. I don't want him to think I'm avoiding him. I don't want him to think I'm ashamed."

"What did you answer?"

"That I need to talk with him, but you and Al will do so first."

"That's a yes, Oliver. That's confirmation."

"I'm not lying to him. I'm done with hesitation. I'm claiming him. Do you understand?"

The bathroom door pops open. Nula takes them in with a curious expression. April slips into the restroom.

When she returns to the table, Beryl is showing Phoebe her engagement ring, made from a small misshapen pearl Hal found in an oyster. "One-in-ten-thousand chance," he says. "I nearly swallowed it."

"Let's see everyone's ring," Beryl says. "I like Oliver's. Nice and sturdy."

Nula cradles her head on the table. "Daddy doesn't wear one."

"Only because your mom and I never quite finished the job." Al reaches contritely for April's hand. "But I'm working on her."

Oliver chokes on his coffee. April withdraws her hand. Even sober, he can't keep from saying the wrong thing. Nula picks up her head. "Wait a minute. You and Mommy aren't—"

"We had the ceremony. That was the whole reason for Vegas," he says. "But it didn't count because your mom forgot her birth certificate. And then, with Lochlann coming along, we never got around to it."

Lochlann's jaw opens. Nula whips her head to look at April.

Hal laughs. "Your dad's a real card."

"We love each other." Al looks at April. "That's what counts."

"But Mommy wears a ring," Nula says.

"Nah, that's a fourteen-karat piece of armor." He beckons the waiter for the check.

Nula screws up her face. "Armor against what?"

Oliver's face drains of color. April spears Al with her eyes. He lightly pokes Nula, as if realizing for once that he's said too much.

"What about April?" Hal asks. "Whose name is the farm in? What if you drive out of here tonight and get hit by a truck? Do you realize she's put ninety-nine percent of the sweat equity into your kids? Not to mention vows, to have and to hold, in sickness and in health—"

"She's covered. We've survived fifteen years. We'll tie the knot before death do us part. Besides, I've got life insurance up the wazoo."

"It's not enough to protect your kids."

"Dad, April is taken care of. I'm not a complete jackass, you know."

"'Taken care of'?" Hal says dismally. "If your mother was still alive, her heart would be in pieces."

In the parking lot, the kids make a beeline for Hal's car.

"Loch," Al calls out. "Drive with us. Mom and I need to talk to you."

Loch darts into Hal's back seat. "Like he'll want to talk to us now," April says, getting into the Tesla.

"We should've told them a long time ago." Al gets behind the wheel.

"So you pick the eve of your father's wedding to make a public announcement?" She can't find the energy to argue. The consternation that tied her to him has run dry.

"What am I going to tell him?" he asks, buckling up. *By the way, son, your uncle is your dad.*"

"I think he's already figured it out. The point is to tell him how much we love him, that even though Oliver is his father, you'll always be his dad."

"That'll send him running."

In the beam of headlights Oliver and Meredith barrel out of the lot.

"If only we had bliss like that," Al says.

When they pull in the driveway, the house is dark, Oliver and Meredith on the patio in what looks like serious conversation. "Don't interrupt them," April says, but Al goes directly out.

"Where is everyone?" he asks.

Meredith casts him a knifelike glance. Oliver lifts his head. "Dad drove Beryl home. We told the kids to pack and get ready for bed."

"Surprise. House is empty," Al says.

"We'll find them." April pulls Al into the yard.

He draws her to him, his cheek rough against hers. "April, is Loch going to talk to me after this?"

"He doesn't talk to you now," she says. "He wouldn't hate you this much if he didn't love you."

"I need a drink first."

"No," she says.

"Listen to me, if I'd known from the get-go, I'd still have wanted him. I'd have wanted us. You get that, right?" He kisses her—a sober kiss, tentative, apologetic, a kiss that almost makes her believe. "Okay," he says. "Let's roll."

April's phone chirps, a group text from Beryl:

Cold front moving in. Dense
fog by morning. Dress warm.
See you at sunrise!

At the base of the ladder, Al calls up, "Yo, Lochlann. Get down here."

Nula peers down. "They left."

"What do you mean *left?*" Al asks.

"Loch said you're not even effing married, and Phoebe said she's mad at her effing mom, and they went into the woods. I told them not to."

"Phoebe cursed?" Al asks.

"Did they say when they'd be back?" April asks.

"Yep," Nula says. "Never."

51

At 1:00 a.m., April waits in the living room with the others. Across from her Hal fingers his rosary beads, murmuring. In the hours since the kids went missing, they've searched the trails and shorelines with flashlights and rain ponchos, April drenched in memories of Locky as a toddler. She remembers calling, "Locky!" her voice steadily more desperate, yet each time finding him safely burrowed in some adventure—examining a duck nest under the porch, petting the fuzzy new leaves of a syca-more, or turning stones to look for orange salamanders. Once, when she could not find him, she let his favorite alpaca out of the pen. Locky habitually carried chunks of broccoli stalks in his pockets, the animals' favorite snack. The alpaca found him down by the creek, watching a painted turtle.

The doorbell rings and April jumps up to answer.

A tall, heavyset man fills the doorway, hawkeyed and world weary, his receding hairline white against his dark skin. "Juvenile Detective Isaiah McClellan." He puts his badge away. "You got to do something about that driveway."

Hal appears. "So sorry. They're coming Monday to grade it," he says. "Please come in. You look familiar." He slips the rosary into his pocket. "Maybe I've seen you in the oyster flats?"

"We were both pallbearers for Ed Eldridge," McClellan says.

"Of course. You're one of his poker friends."

"Still save a seat for him. Our wives were tight."

"You know Beryl?" Hal asks.

"I hear she's getting married tomorrow. Didn't take long."

Hal looks at the doormat. "Yes. That would be to me."

"Sorry, man. I forget he's been gone, what is it, four years already? Only feels like yesterday. Wonderful gal, Beryl."

"It may not happen tomorrow, at this rate."

Oliver and Al shake the detective's hand.

"Have you sent out a search party?" Meredith asks.

McClellan calculates them, scanning the room. "Everyone sit down. We'll do a better job once we know a few facts. Has anyone disturbed their things since they left?"

"Is that a no?" Meredith asks. "No squad cars?"

"Nothing's been touched." April returns to the couch. Nula, asleep, nuzzles onto her lap.

"Keep it that way. No touching their rooms, laptops—nothing. Let's start with names, ages, physical descriptions, clothing. Who are the parents?" He takes out his pad.

"Lochlann Night and Phoebe Fontaine, both fifteen," Al says. "Loch is ours. Allen Night. April Simone. Tall, skinny, bushy eyebrows, messy hair."

As Meredith describes Phoebe, the detective stares at Oliver, studying his face. "Someone belt you, son?"

He touches his lip, hardly noticeable now. "Beesting."

"Uh-huh." He scans each person. April slips her bruised knuckle under Nula's blanket. He casts her an appraising look that makes the back of her neck bristle.

"Detective McClellan, with all due respect," Meredith says, a clause, April has noticed, that always predisposes disrespect, "our children have been missing for hours."

"They take any belongings? Change of clothes? Toothbrush?"

"Not even a sweatshirt," April says. "It's getting cold out."

"Who was the last person to see them?"

"Nula." April nudges her. "Wake up, honey. This is Detective McClellan."

"She doesn't know anything," Al says. "Poor kid just finally fell asleep."

Nula mashes her eyes.

"Can you answer a few questions for me?" McClellan asks. "I'd like to hear about the whole day, everything that happened."

Al glances at his watch in an exaggerated way.

"Allen Night." McClellan rubs his chin. "You're not that sportswriter, are you?"

"Is this relevant?" asks Meredith.

"Yes, it's him," April says. "Nula last saw them about nine forty-five, right, sweetheart?"

"So much for your Super Bowl prediction," McClellan says.

"Seriously?" Meredith says.

"He's not worried," Al says. "He thinks if every parent whose kid wasn't home by midnight called the station, he wouldn't get shit done—right, Detective? You think we're a bunch of high-strung out-of-towners who need hand-holding."

McClellan offers an unperturbed smile.

"Forgive us," Hal says. "Everyone's on edge."

"Nula, honey," April says, "tell him everything you remember from today."

Her face is pale. She digs her sketchbook out from between the couch cushions.

"Nula, this is important," Hal says, but McClellan motions to let her be.

With a razor-sharp pencil, she sketches crisp black lines. "We went kayaking off Great Island. My dad slept in, but he caught up with us later."

"Anything unusual happen on the trip?" McClellan asks.

Nula looks at April.

"Don't be shy," she says. "Any detail might help."

"Well, you and Uncle Oliver went for that walk."

April shivers. Meredith folds her arms. Hal shifts uneasily.

"To look for fiddler crabs," Nula adds, as if sensing she's said something wrong. "Phoebe told Loch she overheard you saying you had to have a talk with him."

"So Phoebe overheard your parents talking?" McClellan asks.

"No. She overheard my mom and her dad."

April tucks her arms. Oliver crosses his legs. Confusion clouds Hal's face. McClellan lets the quiet sit as if to measure it. "So your mom and your uncle wanted to have a talk with your brother?" He scratches his head in an exaggerated fashion, the way a twelve-year-old girl might expect a puzzled detective to do.

Nula eyes him. "All the grown-ups talk about Loch. Lochlann this and Lochlann that, like something's wrong with him, when really he's just doing Loch," she says. "He's disappeared before."

"I see." McClellan recalibrates, makes his voice more adult.

"It started last spring," April says. "He comes back around six in the morning. At home he has animals that rely on him."

"A punctual runaway?" McClellan rubs his ear. "Six would get him back in time for the wedding, no?"

"You don't understand," Meredith says. "Phoebe would never do something like this. What's normal for Lochlann is not normal for her."

"But they're close?" he asks. "When you're not on vacation, do they talk?"

Simultaneously Meredith says, "No," and Nula says, "Snap."

"Snapchat," McClellan says. "Have they snapped since they left the house tonight?"

"We've asked these questions already," Al says. "Wherever they are, they're either out of range or they've turned off their Wi-Fi."

Nula's pencil moves furiously.

"To me, the kids seemed quiet all day," Hal says. "Something was up."

"It's the adults who were acting weird," Nula says.

"'Weird' how?" McClellan asks.

"Daddy's been grumpy. He's trying to quit smoking, but he just smoked two out on the porch while we were waiting for you."

Al rubs his scalp.

"Aunt Meredith and Uncle Oliver were big mad at each other, which is strange, because mostly it's my mom and dad who do the fighting on vacation since that's when they get the chance. My mom was doing her nervous chitchat thing because she was worried we were going to ruin Grandpa's wedding, which I guess we have." Nula looks at Hal. "Grandpa, does Beryl know? Are we still meeting at five?"

He massages his hands.

"Let's get back to the sequence of the day," McClellan says. "You return from kayaking. Now what?"

"We hung out in the tree house like normal. Loch played his ocean harp." She nudges the chain saw case with her toe. "He does that when he gets moody."

"Ocean harp." He examines the case, which Loch brought indoors from the rain. "I was about to ask. We call something like this 'the elephant in the room.'" He winks. "Funny, I think I heard one recently at Preservation Hall. Creepy as hell."

"That was him," Oliver says. "That was Lochlann."

"He's tall for fifteen. Oh, you were the pianist. I remember now. Hey, you were swell."

Meredith casts Hal a pleading glance, eyes shifting to the clock on the mantel.

"So you're up there in the tree house. Your brother's playing his water harp. Where was everyone else?" McClellan asks.

"Grandpa was gardening. Mommy and Daddy were in the house. Aunt Meredith and Uncle Oliver were out walking, but she came back first."

"So nothing unusual? Nothing that further upset your brother or cousin?"

Nula closes her pad and gives McClellan a discerning look.

"Meredith and I had an argument," Oliver says. "Phoebe is very sensitive. I don't see how she could have heard us, but if she did, it likely upset her."

Nula picks up her pencil and opens to a new page.

"We're getting off track," Meredith says. "It's obvious what happened. Lochlann doesn't want to go back to school. He somehow convinced Phoebe to leave with him. April, you know him best. Where do you think the patrol cars should look?"

"Phoebe wanted to go, too," Nula says. "She was just as mad."

Meredith looks at her in surprise.

"'Cause of what you said on the phone in the backyard." Nula draws a thin arc that vanishes off the page. She looks up at Meredith. "You said, 'He found out.'"

Meredith casts Oliver an ice pick glance. "I've been having a crisis at work. Everyone here knows about it. Detective, please, our kids are out there somewhere."

McClellan puts out his hand to quiet everyone but Nula. "What else did you hear?"

"Maybe Aunt Meredith should say." Nula darkens the line. "We were in the tree house. I only heard part."

"Nula, honey." Meredith's voice trembles. "I'm not sure what you mean."

"Maybe I heard wrong. It sounded like, *He'll suck it up for Phoebe.*"

Oliver stands abruptly and walks over to the window.

"That's when Phoebe busted out crying," Nula says, "except she doesn't make noise when she cries."

Meredith's eyes fill, Oliver stock-still at the window.

"Hurt your hand?" McClellan asks, twirling his pen.

April turns to see he is talking to her. She fists her purplish knuckle. "I bruise easily," she says.

"Uh-huh." He writes something down. "What was it, then? The big conversation you wanted to have with your son?"

"They were going to tell him that they aren't actually married," Hal says, "except Al blurted it out at dinner."

"Well, that is big news," McClellan says. "But I thought the conversation was supposed to be with his mom and his *uncle*."

Oliver turns from the window. "It involves a DNA test we did. Can we ask Nula to go upstairs for a minute?"

Hal steeples fingertips to lips.

"Nula can stay," says Al. "That's only right."

"Hold on. Daddy, is this about you not being Loch's biologic father?"

"Biolog*ical*," Al says.

"Nula." Hal lets out a shivery laugh. "What on earth—"

"And all of you were ready to crucify *me*." Meredith blots her eyes. "At least I don't have a kid I didn't raise. It's the opposite. I raised someone else's kid."

McClellan writes something down. Hal's voice splinters. "Can somebody please explain—"

"She's talking about me, Dad," Oliver says. "The son I didn't raise, that's Loch."

"Not only that," Meredith says, "they kissed on the street in New York last month. Oliver and April. Go ahead, ask them if it's true."

April's chest seizes. She turns to see Al's laser glare. Her voice shakes. "It was a mistake."

Oliver bows his head. Hal tries to stand but falls back. "I'm sorry. I think I need some water." April rushes to fill a glass, hands it to Hal. "I'm so dense," he says. "Avila would have put it together ages ago."

"Seems Nula's the one who put it together." McClellan turns to her. "You knew this bit of news about your dad?"

"Loch figured it out last March. He asked Daddy if he knew who his real father was. You were at that fiber convention," she says to April. "The Warriors were playing the Clippers. Remember, Daddy?"

Al keeps his eyes on April, his stare chilling her skin.

"March," McClellan says. "And Lochlann's been running away since, when?"

"He said it was some guy in Ireland, but we were confused because, you know, Loch looks like Grandpa." Nula rolls her pencil nervously between her palms. "We thought maybe Daddy had forgotten his own blood type. Loch didn't realize it was Uncle Oliver until the DNA results came and everyone started acting even weirder than before."

"Just met for coffee, huh?" Al stares as if April is the only one in the room. "Did you go to his apartment?"

"Of course not." April shudders. "Let's focus on the kids."

He opens the scotch. Cold darkness rises up April's spine in sync with the filling glass.

"We've lost time," Meredith says. "The question isn't *why*. It's *where*."

"*Why* leads to *where*," McClellan says.

"Daddy's why," Nula says to Al. "Loch's been talking all week about how you trapped him on Beryl's boat and reamed him out."

"The boat." Oliver turns from the window. "Has anyone checked Beryl's dock?"

"That's it," April says. "Oh God, they've taken the boat."

McClellan straightens.

"But her place is three miles away," says Hal.

"They know the way." April looks out the window. The fog has grown thick. Her hands start shaking.

McClellan springs up and calls for a car to swing by the Eldridge dock. He turns to Nula. "If your brother took the boat, where do you think he'd go?"

She picks up her pencil. "Wherever the boat takes him."

Meredith lets out a wail.

"Let's not jump to conclusions," McClellan says. "We'll know shortly if the boat is there. You all stay put. I'll be in touch." He flies out the door.

Al stands over April. "Let's talk outside."

She casts Oliver a glance.

"Now," Al says.

Nula leaps up. "Daddy, leave Mommy alone."

April wavers. She remembers stepping between her mother and father, the crack of his fist, her clatter to the floor. This is different. Al has never raised a hand to April. He would die before touching Nula. Even this version of Al can be relied on for that much. "Sweetheart," April says, "wait here with Grandpa. Daddy and I will be back in a minute."

They go out to the porch. He lights up, fingers trembling, and takes a drag.

Her heart plummets. "Al, don't do this to yourself."

"Like you give a shit," he says. "My own brother, April? If it were anyone but him, you could claim it was meaningless."

"It was a mistake," she says. "I've forgiven you plenty."

"A kiss? Who stops at a kiss?"

She thinks of the day in her apartment when it all began. "Not you," she says.

"I can destroy you. Do you know how easy it would be for me to get full custody? I can prove you're financially pinched, you let the kids run away, tell them you're going to murder them. I've got it all on voice memos."

This is not the real Al, she knows that, yet there's no way to reach him. "Right now I'd give anything to know they're alive," she says.

"You think I can't handle full custody?" His voice betrays pain, and beneath that, terror. "Guess what? Once I sell the farm, I can afford round-the-clock nannies. You'll see them again at their weddings."

"How can you focus on this when our son is missing?" she asks.

"So he's *our* son again. Why did I ever go to your apartment that day?" He snuffs out the cigarette, hand shaking, and opens the door. "Why didn't I let you hang?" He lets the screen slam.

52

Phoebe is cold. Quiet as cat burglars, she and Lochlann slink through tall grass alongside Beryl's house so as not to be heard on the gravel driveway. From the dock, they climb into the small boat, lie flat on the bottom, and pull a tarp over them. The ping of raindrops punctuates their breath. "My dad's worried by now." She shivers. "Maybe we should've left a note."

"Go back if you want." The boat lifts and lowers, clanking rhythmically against the dock. It's dark beneath the tarp, but she makes out the shape of his face. "Who knew we had so much in common?" He taps the vinyl. "My dad's a cheater and so is your mom."

She slaps his arm. "Just because I told you doesn't mean you can diss her."

"We'd better launch before they think to look here."

"It's too rainy now. Let's just hang out." The wood of the skiff is hard against her hips and shoulders.

"They can't make me go back to school," he says.

"It might not be as bad as you think," she says. "People are wrapped up in themselves. They might not even remember."

"What planet do you live on?"

"But where will you go?"

"Somewhere." He flicks the tarp, harder this time.

The storm picks up. "What about Grandpa? What about the wedding? Your parents must be worried, too." The heat of their bodies begins to warm the enclosed space.

"They're not even married. He's not even my father. You'd better get out if you're not coming."

She throws off the tarp, rain pelting her face. "What do you mean, not your father?"

He sits on the bench. "You heard my dad's story. He left out the part about my mom getting knocked up. That guy she did in Ireland— that's my sperm donor."

She straightens. "You don't know that."

He bunches up the tarp and stuffs it under the thwart.

"Who was he, then? The guy?" She sits on the bench across from him. The downpour is cold as hail.

He scowls at the motor. "Forgot how to choke this thing."

"Why don't you tell me?"

"Because Little Bee wouldn't like it."

"Me? What does it have to do with me?"

Moisture flattens his hair. "My mom. Your dad. That's the news."

She flinches, his words like loose shale on a steep trail. "What news?"

"Phoebe, really."

Her forehead hurts the way it does when she can't unlock a sentence of Mandarin. "You're not . . . I don't under . . .'"

"Forget it."

"My father? You're talking about *my* father?"

He smiles dejectedly. "I heard your mom on the phone telling someone her husband has a bastard son, her own nephew, and what the hell is she supposed to do now?"

Phoebe lurches back, falls off the bench, and clambers back up, hands moving faster than her brain, pinpoints of rain assaulting her face. She reaches for the outboard motor.

"Whoa. You can't start her here. Beryl will hear."

She unties ropes from the dock and picks up an oar.

"Slow down, Phoebe. We have to be quiet."

"Go to hell." She pushes with the oar, freeing them from the dock, and rows.

"Jesus." He picks up the other oar.

They struggle to scull the boat over incoming chop. Her clothes are heavy, her skin electric with brisk salt air. When they've gone a short distance from the shore, she tilts the outboard motor into the water. The bay is rough and edgeless, smudging the contours of land.

"I'm not turning around," he says. "You change your mind, you swim back." He pulls the cord. "Damn thing won't catch."

"Maybe because you didn't attach the fuel line, Sherlock." She connects the hose as the boat pitches—she saw Beryl do it the other day—and pulls the cord until the flywheel roars. Soon they're in a molten abyss with nothing to guide them.

They blast through combers before reaching open water, the swells deeper than they appeared from shore, the dinghy climbing and dipping. Lochlann's eyes water in the bracing wind, his profile a knife against the sky. The swells steepen and the boat falters as it scales them, the engine spitting out water. Towers of clouds over the horizon appear prehistoric, as if she and Lochlann have passed through a portal of time, the only two humans in existence. His chin quivers, his hand a fist on the throttle.

"Maybe you heard wrong," Phoebe says. "Are you sure?"

"I asked your dad why he opted out of the DNA relatives. He said he'll explain after my parents have a talk with me. Like I'm going to sit through that conversation."

"But what does that make us?" Phoebe asks. "Are you my brother?" It's true she always wanted a sibling, but Lochlann? A wave hits them starboard, nearly pitching them overboard. "Jesus, Loch, point her into the crests."

The engine sputters and he goes full throttle before it can stall. The boat rockets up a mountainous swell and soars airborne over the crest.

Her stomach drops. They smack into the trough. The impact knocks him off the bench, his head hitting the sideboard. She grabs the tiller and decelerates. Water sloshes at their feet. They mount the next swell and slope down into its furrow. "You okay?"

He sits up, holding the side of the boat. Ahead the clouds have broken. An enormous cumulus in the shape of an anvil cleaves the horizon, lit by an invisible moon. Under the vaporous shelf, slanted striations bucket into the sea. If they turn back, the swells might capsize them. If they venture forward, they might enter the curtain of rain. But the question is pointless. They have no sense of north or south, land or open ocean. The motor stammers. "Did you check the gas?" she asks. "Make sure the oars are locked."

"Lot of good they'll do."

"What about life jackets? Look inside the bunk."

He yanks the cord on the drum and restarts the motor.

"Lochlann! Vests!"

He pulls out a life vest and slips it on her.

"You too."

"You shouldn't have come," he says. "I told you not to come."

"Put on the stupid vest." The water is up to their ankles. Ribbons of fog skirr the chevrons. In minutes they're enveloped by mist. Even the bow of the skiff is hazy.

"It doesn't matter," he says, his voice cracked with cold. "I'm never going back."

"Shut up! We're going to sink!" She thrusts the life jacket at him, letting go of the till long enough for the boat to lob sideways. She rights it, one hand gripping the till and the other gripping Lochlann's hand. They seesaw over wave after wave. She struggles to find the best angle. She's been in ocean chop plenty of times in a kayak, but never like this. Head-on is too violent. Sideways keels them over. She aims for forty-five degrees, but the waves are erratic, their trajectory shifting. She tries not to blink, eyes pinned on each curtain of water until she can no longer remember why they are here or where they came from, everything erased by the volley of waves.

Slowly, imperceptibly at first, the swells space apart, their rise and dip easing. The rain must have stopped some time ago, because half the sky is starlit. His hand in hers is a mutual death grip, but he's looking up, mouth open. She sees it then, a shooting star, and another. They watch until the swells level off, the boat hardly pitching. She isn't sure if they've been gone for minutes or hours. She wonders how long a small outboard motor can go on a tank of fuel. She pulls the kill switch. The idle sputters and dies. "We should save gas till we figure out where we're going," she says.

"Look." He points skyward. "There's another one."

Overhead, a sizzle fades.

He puts his life preserver behind his head and lies back against the thwart, staring up. She stays upright, scanning for rogue waves, but the boat sways gently, the Milky Way teeming above. "Wow," he says, his voice deeper than normal, calmer—like the voice he might have as an adult, her father's voice. She wants to ask if it's true, but the only sound is water lapping the side of the boat, the world too quiet to talk.

"What was that?" He sits up.

"What?"

"I heard something."

She looks around. "Like what?"

"A sort of drumbeat, super slow, larghissimo. Listen."

"The bell buoy?"

"Not a clang—a thump, like a bass. Once every ten seconds or so."

She listens. Her father says the Milky Way is a symphony, and if you focus on one star, you might hear its vibration.

"Pull up the motor," Lochlann says.

"What?"

"Lift the blade in case."

She tilts the motor up and sits beside him, hearing nothing but the lap of water against the hull. Without warning, a burst fractures the silence, louder than steam lifting the lid of a boiled-over pot. They clutch each other, skin dampened with spray, the smell of rotten fish stinging their nostrils. "Holy shit." He lets go of her, turns on his phone light, and holds it out. In the frail circle of light, a dark mound rises from the water. "Phoebe," he whispers. "Phoebe, Phoebe!" He takes an oar and sculls toward it.

"What're you doing?" Her breath sticks high in her chest. "What is it?"

"It's logging," he says. "I think that was the heartbeat."

A blast of air rockets out of the water, a manhole explosion—spray wetting their faces—followed by a mighty in-suck of air.

"Hurry," she says. "Let's get out of here."

"There must be a better flashlight somewhere." He opens the bench, riffles around. "I want to see it." He finds a light and shines it directly down. Beneath the surface is an endless canvas of speckled blue too big to be a single thing. Her mind clamors to make sense of the mottled shapes lifting toward the surface. The water breaks, two dark holes blasting out and suctioning in. She gasps.

"Shh," he says. "It's a blue, Phoebe. People go their whole lives without seeing one, and it's right here. Listen to that pulse. Do you know how big their hearts are? You and me, we could fit in there together."

In the distance, a splash. "If that was the tail, it's a hundred feet long."

"We're too close," she says. "Row back!"

"I want to touch it." He hinges over the side of the boat. "Paddle me closer."

"No! What if—"

"It's sleeping. Phoebe, please!" Lochlann extends his arms.

She puts the oar in the water. "Don't reach too far."

"Get me closer."

She nudges the paddle, heart pounding in her ears. She hears it now, the slow drum from the ocean, a deep resonant throb vibrating through her body, thumping her bones. The boat tilts and she leans back to compensate for his weight draped over the other side. She sees it as if in slow motion, Lochlann stretching across the bow first to his waist, his hips, reaching his hand down, feet lifting as he loses balance. The worn soles of his sneakers flash against the star-washed sky. With a subdued splash, he's gone. The boat seesaws. The submerged glow of the flashlight sinks and dies out.

She waits for him to surface, holding in her scream. She's going to kill him. Everything goes still. Movement stirs the water, rotating Phoebe in a slow vortex. She bends over the side, her vision a frantic scramble. He can't be far. Opaque blackness gives way to a sheath of dappled gray, translucent as a human iris, a delicate interlacement of fibers. A terrifying quiet fills her ears, hushed ripples slapping the hull as the boat sluices through swells on its own, swiveling. The whirlpool slows and a circle of water flattens around her, still as a mirror. She thinks of her grandfather out on the cliff, feeling things he cannot name. Something beyond her imagination is about to happen.

The water breaks with a behemoth exhalation, followed by a whistling suction of air. A dark island twice her height rises up, lifting, curling, a living wheel revolving, topped with an improbably small dorsal fin. It turns counterclockwise, an endless length of speckled steel blue revealing itself a few meters at a time until the towering obelisk comes free of the water, lifting skyward, and sinks vertically into the sea. Tail flukes twice as long as the boat vanish without a splash.

She doesn't know how long she's ceased breathing when her breath comes out as a scream, his name over and over. She didn't know she could yell so loud. When there is no response, she pitches herself overboard, blistering cold. Underwater she sees nothing but dense murkiness, salt blazing her eyes. She scrambles back into the boat, nearly capsizing. The pause between each drumbeat lengthens, growing faint. From the opposite direction comes wild splashing. How could Loch have gotten so far? She starts the motor, races toward it. A swish of luminescence flashes in front of the skiff, a neon form slicing through swells, rapid and agile, trailing a phosphorescent wake. She cuts the engine. It's Lochlann's size, streamlined, moving impossibly fast, aglow with the color of his eyes. A ghost. The luminous blur surfaces and sinks out of sight—a dolphin. She should not have moved the boat! She looks back, but the listing motion makes it impossible to tell which direction she came from. A shroud of fog approaches. She needs a way for him to find her. She ransacks the thwart, teeth clacking, and finds an orange revolver. A flare. He'll have to be looking her way to see it. With shaking hands Phoebe points at the sky and pulls the trigger.

53

Al stands at the edge of the Race Point surf, the farthest tip of the Cape, watching a predawn blaze of helicopters and Coast Guard ships circle in the distance. The news choppers are hungry. His father and April are at the house, waiting by the phone, but Al needs to be here, close as he can get, as if the boy might stagger from the waves. Oliver and Meredith are in the ER with Phoebe. Just a precaution. A touch of hypothermia is nothing compared to hours in open ocean. With each passing minute, Al calculates the odds. In sixty-degree water the average person would succumb to unconsciousness in one to three hours. Phoebe was found four hours ago. Al keeps checking the local news on his phone, which is bound to outpace the official notification of next of kin. As the last star fades, the wind picks up. His father is probably on his hundredth Hail Mary by now, April murmuring reassurances to Nula. Only Al sees reality cold and clear. Somewhere between when he arrived here an hour ago and now, time ran out.

Yet there was that NFL player a few years back who fell from his boat and swam sixteen hours to shore. That was a professional athlete in warm Gulf waters. This is a scrawny kid in North Atlantic chop. Who is Al kidding? He's doing what every parent in this spot has done throughout time—bargaining, pleading, conjuring unlikely scenarios: Lochlann sleeping it off on the deck of a yacht; Lochlann floating safely on a piece of driftwood; Lochlann, having swum ashore, hiding beneath the dock to give them all a good scare.

Faraway searchlights crisscross the water. A pink seam of light glows on the horizon, prompting seabirds to caw. Cold shudders through him. *Why not me?* he thinks. *Me whose prospects are shitty? What kind of world takes a healthy kid over his used-up old man?* Something deep in his chest splits like a calving ice shelf. He drops to his knees and calls out to the God he does not believe in, "Take me instead." Pain spikes up his shin. On the sand, the scythe of a clamshell is scarlet with blood. He rinses the cut in the surf, salt stinging to bone. He cannot stand another minute of doing nothing. Any action would be better than none. Just then a black head bobbles out beyond the breakers. There hasn't been another soul on the beach. It's got to be Lochlann. He texts April.

Think I see him. Race Point
straight up from the parking lot.
Tell McClellan. I'm going in.

He tosses his shirt and phone on the sand and lunges into the surf, glutted with the relief of action. At last, a moment he can get right.

The birds cry louder, frenzied and shrill. He swims in the direction he saw him, but there's no sign. He treads water, scanning. Gannets drop like torpedoes into a bait ball, frantic fish leaping airborne. "Lochlann!" he screams as if calling him home from the neighbor's farm, his voice so shrill it's not his own. Swells lift him and lower him. A crimson ribbon drifts from his shin—more blood than he thought. Bad idea to be out here, but he'll be damned if he lets his kid drown to save himself. The black head reappears, swivels its oily snout and darts back under. A seal.

Darkness fills him, pressuring his ribs. This is his fault. Lochlann took off because of him. He'll do anything to save him, swap places if he could. The pressure mounts until the tight kernel of Al's soul bursts like popcorn. His mind goes blank, everything abruptly quiet. The skyline glimmers, stillness spreading across the water, silent and immense. He wonders if this is how his dad feels on his predawn walks, no hamster wheel clattering the gut, no constant gnawing not-enough-ness. His father thinks there's a good person hiding inside him, but Al can't find him. He went to an AA meeting once, years ago, only because April asked.

"That *surrender to your higher power* stuff—that's not me," he told her afterward. "I'd be a hypocrite if I said I thought anything could save me but myself."

"I see," she said. "And what a great job you're doing."

A drop of light emerges on the horizon. He pictures his dad on the cliff, every morning a new astonishment. Liquid fire oozes from the ocean, oblong, as if the sea is holding on. The string snaps, the orb set free. A lane of light glints across the water directly to Al's chest. It means something—that Lochlann is alive. Or that he's dead.

The surf sound is faint, the choppers closer. Al is farther out than he realized. The sun begins to ascend. In his peripheral vision the apparition of a fin feels like something he could not have seen. He's dehydrated, sleep deprived, delirious. He avoids splashing just in case. Sharks don't go for people unless you give them a reason. They prefer less bony prey—fish, seals, their own young. How miserable to be a thing so hardwired for hunger, so without choice. Figments morph on the crests. Maybe this is one of those dreams where he turns to see that the thing stalking him has his own silhouette. A smudgy purple shadow passes beneath him so close he can nearly touch it. He's heard they like to smell you first.

The thoughts come rapidly, crisp and audible. He has everything to live for. He owes Nula deGrom's autograph, April the truth, Oliver an apology. He cannot die without saving his son.

He pivots toward land, a swift breaststroke so as not to splash, flying through currents. He's never swum so fast. He hears nothing but the heave of his breath and a vast silence of ocean. He's getting closer. Something hits him sideways, launching him laterally, a force like a car crash. The pain is so complete he can't tell where it's coming from. He resumes his stroke, slower now, hobbled, catching glimpses of the beach between waves. Some part of him is missing or not working, but there's no time to look. If he survives this, it will be the byline of his career. His stroke wobbles. He's almost there. He tries to focus on the lede: "The bloom of my own blood saved me, the water so red as to make me invisible." He feels its nearness radiating through darkness, hunger so familiar it feels like his own.

54

Noise pounds Lochlann's head, rhythmic but irregular—clang, clang, clang—the lonely sound he swam toward through darkness. Above him clappers swing to the swells, striking a giant rusted bell. He recognizes the green steel frame, the bell buoy. He's on his back on the platform, pitching in the sea. He feels pressure on his arm, a face filling his field of vision, orange jumpsuit, goggles, a snorkel attached to a yellow helmet. The lips are moving, asking him something, but all Lochlann hears is the bell splitting his skull. High above, a chopper is suspended against a pale-pink sky, wind like a gale storm, a line lowered down, a rectangle growing larger. The man winches him onto the stretcher, and at once he is aloft, alone, spinning. He feels himself sway and bank, the bell buoy shrinking, coastline appearing. He sees the contour of the Cape's outermost finger doused in golden daybreak. In the froth of the surf, a shock of red blooms and vanishes. He wonders if he's dead, if in the moments of being belayed skyward, he fell out of his body. How do you know when it's happened? Underwater he thought himself killed, yet somehow got pushed to the surface. He'd coughed out his lungs, sliced through darkness, fighting off the sting of jellyfish and the terror of luminous things in the night.

He remembers the giant eye taking him in, the feel of its skin against his palm—rubbery, smooth, cool, but also warm, subtle warmth, like the heat that comes off a light bulb, like he could feel its soul. He has to find a way to tell her. He focuses on the words and sends them out, piercing the whir of the helicopter, traversing ocean and dune to land precisely in the curved canal of her ear. "Phoebe," he breathes. "I touched it."

55

April floors the pickup through stoplights. The distant whir of a siren penetrates the cab, blue flashing in her rearview. Hal must have reached McClellan. She presses the gas. She has been awake all night, conjuring dreaded scenarios, praying every prayer she knows how to pray, petitioning saints and ancestors, her whole being frayed down to one raw nerve. She tries to picture Loch and Al standing on the beach, exhausted but alive.

At Race Point she barrels the truck up the dune until the wheels won't turn and bolts across the sand, kicking off her sandals. Al's shirt flutters on the beach, the surf empty. "Al!" she screams. Her pulse pounds in her ears. Beyond the combers the water breaks in thrashing turbulence, a shimmying tail fin, the flash of a muscled arm. The water boils red. "Oh God oh God."

She looks back. On the distant dune the shimmery silhouette of a police officer appears. Al's voice fills her mind: *Full custody. Shut out. Destroy you. Let you hang.* She stands frozen between racing back for help and plunging into the sea. Maybe he's already dead. People would say he did it to himself. They'd be right. He'd resent April for trying to save him. Attempting to rescue a drowning person without equipment is destined to fail. She owes it to her kids to stay put, not leave them parentless. She can tell Nula he died a hero, striving to save Loch. The woman who lost her foot last year survived because a stranger pulled her ashore, but she was closer, the man only dragging her a few yards.

Al's death would spare April the warfare of leaving him. Yet he'd once saved her life with a pillowcase. The father of her children. Why did she arrive at this moment, catching the arc of his arm, and not a moment later? So she could be haunted by what she fails to do?

An eternity passes with no time elapsing, as if she is simultaneously experiencing and remembering this moment. An endless comber hovers over the shore, cold and impassive. Her phone beeps. A text from Nula. Did you find him?

She pulls off her shirt and shorts and plunges in, the water frigid, and mounts swells, fighting momentum. The scrim of blood is already dissipating. She struggles to find the spot. "Al!" she screams. A sensation like sandpaper grates her leg. She kicks, her foot hitting something solid. It flails, pushing her back. She's hyperventilating. She's got to go back to shore. But a waft of blood tells her he's near. She gulps air and goes under, blind with terror, groping through darkness until she finds flesh, an arm, and hauls him to the surface. It's Al and it's not, his skin ashen. She hooks her arm under his armpit, holds his chin above water and starts kicking. A plume of red trails from his lower body. She struggles to keep him aloft. A long shadow moves beneath them. She pictures two graves side by side, her father's funeral, a neighbor's cruel whisper, "She's better off without them."

No. Nula needs her. Loch will be found. She's getting weaker. She must let go, save herself for her kids. No one will blame her. He's already dead. She jerks him violently. "Al, wake up before I kill you!"

A gush of water ejects from his mouth. He gags. She kicks harder, but he gropes for her, locking his hands around her neck, pushing her down to push himself up. "Stop! You'll kill us both!" He's not Al. He's a thing desperate to survive. She gets her arm free and clocks him in the jaw, her father's thunderclap punch. He releases his clutch. A voice tells her to swim free. A voice tells her to try again. "Stay limp. Don't hold on to me," she says. His eyes flutter closed. A cresting wave tumbles them forward, and her feet hit bottom. A dark shape appears in the surf, the officer wading toward them.

56

Wednesday

Every atom that made him a distinct human being is crushed by pain. He is being extruded through a reducing valve—bones, sinews, memories, his very name, all pulverized to powder so fine there is nothing left to grind. He hears the beep of medical equipment, the heave-ho of a respirator, but cannot open his eyes against the scorching whiteness of the room. He doesn't know who he is or used to be but prays for death. Out of the incinerating whiteness a form emerges, winged and gargantuan, like a drawing he once saw in a sketchbook, but with the face of a young girl, round and fierce, a daughter he once had. Or has. Her power quakes through what's left of him. He cannot hear her voice, but her mouth takes the shape of the words *Come back!*

Something he once called time moves around him in both directions like the give and take of a tide. He doesn't know if he's been here for hours or years or what those measurements mean anymore. Shapes emerge from the whiteness and pass away like voices. The word *hey* pierces the fog.

Al blinks. Beside him stands a young, long-haired version of his brother. No, it's his son. "Dad," Lochlann says, "I'm being released today."

Notions reconstruct themselves in Al's brain, his idea of himself reassembling. He licks dry lips. No more respirator. Behind the boy stands a pale dark-haired woman, more beautiful than anyone Al has ever seen, though right now these are the only two human forms his mind can conjure. He hears his own voice, cracked and thin. "How long?"

"You've been here four days," April says. "You had a ten-hour surgery. You'll need another one. They're trying to save your leg."

It comes back to him now—the crimson sea, the bladelike fin. What was that lede?

"Lochlann was hypothermic, but he's fine now," April says. "Strong swimmer, your boy."

Loch's eyes move over Al's face and body in a way that suggests he is unrecognizable. "Will he come back to normal?" Loch whispers.

"A new normal," April says.

"Dad," Loch says shakily, "even though it was way stupid, thanks for trying to save me."

Al nods, but even that sends shards of pain through his skull.

Lochlann cringes as though the ache is his. "Take it easy," he says. "I'll be back tomorrow."

Lochlann leaves and April sits beside Al. "You're all over the news," she says. "Producers are asking for movie rights."

"Jesus," he says. The word comes out garbled.

"Nula gave a statement. She told them it wasn't the shark's fault."

"True." Each word takes effort to push out.

"It was a juvenile, ten feet long, a single bite. Took a chunk of muscle, part of your Achilles, crushed your bone, but missed your tibial artery by a hair. You lost so much blood they didn't think you'd make it. The important thing now is to avoid infection. Marine bites are notorious."

"How. Long. Will I be here?"

"Long enough to detox from every bad habit you've ever had. Including me," she says. "Who knew a shark could save your life."

Even his jaw hurts. He remembers the blow. "Nice punch."

"You had drowner's panic. It's a reflex."

He squeezes his eyes. His whole life's been a reflex. "Rosie." He looks into her eyes, sees her depth of exhaustion. "Don't go."

"We'll always be the kids' parents." She puts a straw to his lips. Cool water lubricates his throat, the sweetest thing he's ever tasted.

"I was hoping," he says, "to get married before we divorce."

"Saved ourselves a ton of paperwork," she says.

"I'm sorry, April."

"I am, too, Al." She lowers the bed rail, puts her head on his shoulder. "I hope I didn't keep you from some greater love."

"You're my greater love. Everything that matters to me came from you." He tries to stroke her hair, but the IV restricts him. "Where's Nulie?"

"They're limiting your visitors. I'll bring her tonight. Your dad's been here every day. He prayed for ten hours straight through your surgery. I wish you could've seen his face when they said you'd pull through. He wept like a child," she says. "We all did."

His eyes fill up. He doesn't deserve this family. "The wedding?" he asks.

"Tomorrow. He wants to do it before the kids leave. Oliver will drive them home in time for school. Meredith flew home Sunday." She stands to go. "I'll stay for your second surgery."

"You don't have to."

"I know."

"Rosie," he says, "tell Nula I haven't forgotten. Soon as I'm out of here, I'll get her deGrom's autograph."

57

Thursday

April walks with the others on a carpet of pine needles, a canopy of bay-berry overhead. The last holdout of darkness that hung in the treetops when they set out fades as they approach the cliff.

The area clear of shrubs is barely big enough to hold them. The trail behind dissolves into ether. Waves surge below, foamy edges engraving the sand and receding as fizz. April listens to the prayers without taking her eyes off Venus vanishing into bright-white mist. It's brisk for August, her skin chilled beneath the white eyelet dress, her feet warm in her hikers. The sun is minutes from rising, the world already lit, colors peeking out of the gloom as vapor dampens her skin. She holds her breath, wanting to see the sun pop out of the ocean, but understanding now that she won't, the brume cloaking them layer upon layer until sea and sky are one fathomless chasm—what Hal likes to call "the Great Abyss." He reaches for Beryl's hand.

"Loch, Phoebe," Oliver says. "We're up." He uncrates his guitar.

Phoebe tunes her flute and Loch his violin, a short clamor of dissonance magnified by fog. They fall into sync, finding the storyline, moving the song along to its crescendo.

"Stupendous," the priest says too quickly. "What talent."

Nula tries again to dial Al, but April sees from her frown that there's no signal. She gives up, climbs through a beach plum thicket, and untangles a balloon string.

Hal and Beryl exchange rings and a bashful kiss. The priest apologizes that he must hurry back for 7:00 a.m. Mass.

"Just one more song," Hal says. Loch unclips the chain saw case, water sloshing inside the instrument.

"Oh my." The priest startles at the strange-sounding notes, looking around as if to see if someone or thing has crept up on them. The flute notes had melted like snowflakes, but the ocean harp's throb gains momentum, a whale song crossing the sea. When he's done, Oliver gives him a shoulder hug, his face a blend of affection and grief.

"Not your typical wedding hymn—but this isn't a typical family, is it, Hal?" The priest chuckles. "Lucky a big wind didn't take us."

Oliver links arms with the priest and guides him back down the trail.

"I think we spooked him," Phoebe says.

"Good." Beryl smiles.

The sky morphs, vapor burning off, the sun a veiled disc behind layers of gauze. Hal puts his arms around the kids and faces them toward the sea. "Close your eyes. Listen." The wind warbles and whips. April can almost hear each molecule of fog evaporate with a tiny pop. A chorus of whispers weaves through the wind like an invisible current of souls. Hal hugs them. "I can't believe we almost lost you." He lets out a sob.

"Aw, Grandpa," Phoebe says.

Hal and Beryl start down the path. April lingers with the kids.

"Do you ever feel anything unusual out here?" Phoebe asks.

"Everything out here's unusual," Loch answers.

"I wonder where the blue is now."

"Probably a hundred miles away. It saw me, Phoebe. It looked me in the eye."

She tugs his ponytail. "You're probably the strangest fish it ever saw. I bet it'll never forget you."

A salmon blush illuminates the haze, the seascape singing with color. Soon a sphere of liquid light will crest above the cloud line. April wants to see it and doesn't, because how can she absorb more than she's feeling right now?

They lug their instruments down the trail, Hal and Beryl far ahead.

"Do we call her Grandma?" Phoebe asks.

"Beryl," Nula says.

High above, a formation of geese catches light on the undersides of their wings. Honeyed sunlight breaks through fog, glowing on branches, coating everything in waxy amber, the kind of light that can't last more than a minute. April pauses to look up.

"Dreamt last night I was tumbling inside a wave, gagging on seawater," Loch says. "My dad put me on his shoulders and walked me out of the surf."

"I can picture that," Phoebe says. "Nonchalant, with a cigarette dangling from his lips." They laugh, continuing down the trail.

The pine needles are made of gold, incandescent, shimmering April's insides. She wants to remember this moment. She stands still, letting the light drench through her. The rising sun sifts through branches, touching her face, her arms, the dress glowing like a wedding gown. A smile fills her. She turns toward the dawn and says, "I do."

58

April follows Oliver and Lochlann out to the porch, music thumping from Loch's headphones. "Can you turn that off for a sec?" she asks. They've decided to talk to Lochlann together.

Loch flips the switch, frowning with one corner of his mouth.

"Let's sit." Oliver settles on a step. April, having changed into shorts, sits cross-legged on the planks.

"I'm good." Lochlann shuffles. "If this is about the paternity thing, I don't see what there is to talk about."

"I realize how uncomfortable this must be for you," Oliver says.

Lochlann looks distractedly in the direction of the trail. "I'm fine with the way things are. You're an awesome uncle."

"That might be admirable if I were your uncle."

"But you are. I mean, okay, I get that maybe you were supposed to be my father, but it's like Phoebe and her birth parents. Just water under the bridge, right?" He scratches his nose.

"No, I don't think it's quite the same." Oliver brings his palm to his chest. "I wasn't allowed to visit you in the hospital. If I die tomorrow, you'd have no claim to anything."

Loch rolls foot to foot, passes April a hooded glance. "Look, I know me and Dad haven't been getting along that great, but it's not like he's some booby prize. We'll get it back, Dad and me."

"Absolutely," Oliver says. "I only want you to know that you're welcome to stay with Phoebe and me anytime, occasionally or regularly.

I know junior year would be a tough time to change, but since you've been unhappy at school—"

"I'm not unhappy. Do you know how many texts I got this week? I'm the kid whose dad survived a shark attack. Besides, I know Aunt Meredith's super busy. It's a small apartment and all."

"Actually, we're taking a break." Oliver shifts. "Aunt Meredith and I are separating."

Lochlann startles. "Not 'cause of me, I hope."

"No. It was coming."

"Where will you stay?"

"Your dad's apartment. I've already talked to him about it. It'll be weeks before he's home, and who knows when he'll be able to do that walk-up again."

Loch gives a start. "Seriously?" he asks April. "He won't be able to do stairs?"

"Time will tell," she says. "You know him. He'll probably try to do a Tough Mudder next year."

Lochlann sniffles, staring at his feet, those long toes. "Phoebe will be there, too?"

"Aunt Meredith travels more than I do," Oliver says. "So yes. Mostly."

At the edge of the woodland, a speckled fawn nibbles on sassafras. Loch taps his sandal against Oliver's foot. "Maybe eventually we'll start to feel it, the father-son thing, but right now I want to stay on the farm. Nothing personal."

"Sure, Loch," he says. "I understand."

"Plus, my dad's bound to need help. Even if the surgery works, it'll be a killer recovery. And, you know, he's going to be a bear." Loch offers a small smile and heads inside. The screen door bounces.

April sits on the step beside Oliver. "He adores you," she says. "Give it time."

He cradles his head. "Time is what I'll never get back." Wind rustles the forest, each tree swishing in its own unique dance. "I would have liked to be there when you were pregnant," he says. "The sonograms, the first kicks, to feel him sleep on my chest—that's the part of fatherhood I never got. When Phoebe came into my life, she was already potty trained and running full tilt."

"You're romanticizing," she says. "I threw up every day. I could only eat Cheez-Its. He cried a lot. No matter how I did his diaper, he pooped up the back of his onesie," she says. "Be careful what you want. He's a bigger handful now."

"He knows what he's about more than I did," Oliver says. "At fifteen, I was still checking my parents' boxes—Eagle Scout, math camp, lawn mowing, the trajectory that led me to law school. Loch is in touch with himself. That's all the compass he needs." The shimmying trees settle into quiescence. "You've done good, April."

"Ha. Ask him about that." The trees resume their conversation, whooshing and whistling. "As maddening as he is, I'd miss him if he went to you."

"Phoebe will try to persuade him," Oliver says, gazing at the meadow. He hasn't shaved in a few days, a scruff of growth defining his jaw. "I think there's a chance he'll come around."

Late in the day, April returns from the hospital, the fresh stones of the newly graded driveway grinding smoothly under her tires. Across the sloping meadow, she catches movement through the trees. A deer. No, a person. Perhaps Hal is clearing some brush. But when she looks up toward the house, she sees his car is not yet back. He and Beryl took the kids to a daylong Wampanoag demonstration to learn how dugout canoes are burned from tree trunks. April brakes halfway up the driveway and gets out, straining to see who is in the woods. She makes out a guitar, someone sitting on a stump.

She marches across the field, grasses swaying against her legs. At the edge of the forest a bluebird swoops into one of Hal's birdhouses. It's late for chicks. She must be on her second brood. April slips through the archway of trees into the grove of tupelos. With their alligator bark and glossy leaves, the trees form a temple around Oliver.

"What are you doing here?" she asks. It sounds more accusatory than she means.

"I come here to think. How did you find me?"

"That's my stump," she says.

"Only if you borrowed it from me," he says. "I've been coming here for years."

"No way." She glances at the tupelos as if they've betrayed her.

"Don't tell me," he says.

"At night sometimes."

"I come in the day." He looks at her curiously. "Anyway, there's another stump there." He plucks a few strings, working something out. "How's Al?" he asks.

"Energetic enough to be cranky. Good sign, I guess." She sits on the other stump. She would have preferred her own. "He's listening to the news reports. Half the stories skewer him for recklessness. The other half canonize him for bravery. Leave it to Al to think he could single-handedly outdo the Coast Guard."

"Father and son medevaced within minutes of each other," Oliver says. "He gave them quite a headline." A leaf falls from a tupelo, scarlet though the tree appears green. "You risked a lot, swimming out to him," he says.

"You'd have done the same."

"I'm not sure." He bows his head, glancing at his empty ring hand. "Phoebe's taking it hard," he says, his voice thick. "I knew she would."

"You and Meredith will work it out," April says. "She's forgiving."

"I'm not interested in working it out. Neither is Meredith." He tests another string.

"Don't be impulsive. You both have a lot to absorb."

"It's not about Lochlann. It goes deeper than that."

"That's what counseling is for."

He looks up, his voice heavy. "The better we communicate, the clearer it is that we want different things." The fragrance of late-season honeysuckle drifts through the trees. "I can't give her what she needs."

"I'm sorry, Oliver."

Crickets chant in the underbrush. In the canopy above, the haunting call of a hermit thrush drops from a flutelike whistle to soft echoing tones. "Birds have been congregating here all day," he says. "The tupelo berries are ripening." A crow hops through leaf mulch, the fruit in its beak as blue black as its eye. "I'm curious," Oliver says. "How does a person go to Vegas to get married and forget her birth certificate?"

She looks up in the direction of the thrush. "I didn't *forget*." She rubs her ring. "And we didn't get rings in Vegas. I bought this on my own when I found out I was pregnant. I married myself."

He goes still, staring at her as though finding the final note of the song he's been working on. Uneasiness comes over her. She twists the ring. "I should've sprung for gold. I can't get it off anymore, my hands are so calloused."

He looks at her thoughtfully. "You're in luck. I just broke my high-E string. Got a piece in my pocket." He puts his guitar on his stump and kneels beside her, examining the ring. "Do you want it off?"

"Trust me. It needs a wire snip."

"No, I've done this for Meredith with dental floss. All the air travel swells her fingers." He slips a thin guitar string under her ring and wraps it tightly around her finger up past the knuckle, an excruciating vise. "It'll only hurt for a minute," he says. With quick precision he unwraps the string from the bottom, pulling the ring up her finger. A stab of pain shoots from her knuckle. She swallows her cry as the ring comes free. The empty spot on her finger is tender as a newborn. So easily the ring came off. She clenches it in her fist.

"Oliver," she says, "why is it so hard to live without hurting people?"

He draws her to him. His heart against hers unleashes her tears. His ocean of grief pours in through her chest, hers flows out into his. She never knew things were so big, so uncontained, she so lost within them. She remembers overlooking the Irish cliff, that impossible vastness, as alone as she had ever been, yet for an instant touching each other's aloneness.

They separate. She opens her fist, the ring like a small dead bird in her palm. "What do I do with it?"

A passing cloud darkens the woodland. "I don't know." He picks up his guitar. "Crows like shiny things." He walks through the archway back into the meadow. April places the ring on the stump and stares up at the canopy of tupelos, their crowns tossing like the manes of powerful horses.

A recent nor'easter has transformed the beach. Gnarled skeletons of dune shrubs litter the sand, high tide etchings stretching up the eroded cliff. Post-storm breakers surge inland, mammoth and crescent shaped. In the distance, surfers in wet suits get on their boards, tiny figures vanishing into roiling barrels of ocean. April and Oliver walk a long way until they reach a length of beach with no name and no access, the dune cliff towering above. Powerful combers angle in, row after row of spuming white curls. The tide is coming in, and she worries there will be no sand to walk back on. "They don't have scales," she says, breaking the silence. "The skin is like sandpaper."

He turns to her.

"I'm never going in again. Not to my ankles, not on a boat—nothing."

"I've had the same thought," he says. "The longer we wait, the harder it'll be."

"It's not a choice," she says.

"Everything is," he says.

"Leave it alone, Oliver. Never is never."

"In that case, let's do it now. A quick plunge."

"Yeah, right." She pulls her sweatshirt tighter.

"No seals. No gannets. It's the perfect time." He takes off his windbreaker. "We'll leave our clothes here."

"Not funny."

"I'll do it alone." He takes off his shirt.

"You expect me to stand here and watch you go in?"

He unbuckles his belt. "One wave," he says.

"Goddammit, Oliver." She yanks off her sweatshirt. "Turn around!" In a minute she's down to bare skin, eyes blazing tears. Blowing sand stings her calves. Her clothes start to flutter away, and she stacks her sandals on top of them. "Don't look at me." She turns to him, his back to her. He's hugging himself, head bowed to the wind. She sees the V of his back, compact ass, long legs.

"Hurry up," he says. "I'm freezing." When she doesn't answer, he turns to see her staring at him. The contours of his face shift to longing and regret, his eyes registering the wetness on her cheeks. "April." His voice drops.

They stand a short distance apart, two pale shivering human beings, naked as at birth. Her mother always said she was torn from the womb too early, the doctor having scheduled a vacation. That's when it started. Born too soon, had a child too soon, divorced before married. She is not ready for this. She has never for one minute been ready for anything in her life.

"Wading in won't work," he says. "We have to charge."

"Do you have any idea what it was like out there?" Against the cold air her tears are hot, her hair a tattering whip. "I'm sorry, Oliver. I can't."

"On the count of three," he says. "One, two—"

She bolts on two. The water hits her like ice. Oliver gasps at the shock. Instantly she sees their mistake. A colossal wall of water cascades toward them. They are going to be pulverized. The only option is to swim into it as fast as they can, try to catch the rise before it peaks. But the froth is already seething, the arc curling. Adrenaline propels her forward, her strokes fast and hard, the ocean lifting her higher and higher as if she's ascending a tsunami, so high it seems she is on the cliff top, the horizon expanding like vast unfurling wings. Poised on the crest, Oliver materializes beside her, his face flush with beauty and terror. A panicked laugh escapes her. The faraway beach looks the way it must to a gull in flight. They balance on the brink of collapsing with the wave or gliding up and over. It's not up to them now. April extends her hand, and Oliver takes it.

ACKNOWLEDGMENTS

For contributing to this book by way of advice, moral support, beta reading, inspiration, or expertise, I am grateful to Stephanie Acquadro, Andrew Alford, Remko Arentz, Valerie Block, Nicole Bokat, Maureen Dumser, Detective Sergeant Robert Feeney, Caprice Garvin, David Goldstein, Andrew Hozier-Byrne, Tina Johansen, Alina Kotova, Margo LaPierre, Heather Lazare, Alexandra Mahoney, James Marcucci, Megan McCullough, Alyssa McPherson, Mar'ce Merrell, Kirsti Morin, Holly Obernauer, Von Rollenhagen, Suzanne Roth, George Saunders, Carrie Schnitzler, Julius Tolentino, and especially Sasha Troyan.

For tough, illuminating questions, I am indebted to Alan Watt.

For countless readings and wise instincts, I am deeply grateful to Flannery James.

For choosing this book out of the pile, and for her jigsaw wizardry, I thank my editor, Laura Van der Veer.

For her dogged faith, enormous generosity, and depth of wisdom, I am eternally grateful to my agent, Anne Edelstein.

Most of all, I thank Vincent, Brendan, and Flannery for supporting me with love, meals, beach walks, and life-giving conversation. I am lucky to walk life's trails with you.

ABOUT THE AUTHOR

Photo © 2023 Brendan Paul James

Tess Callahan is the author of *April & Oliver*. Her essays and stories have appeared in the *New York Times Magazine*, *Writer's Digest*, National Public Radio, *AGNI*, *Narrative Magazine*, *AWP: The Writer's Notebook*, *Newsday*, *The Common*, the *Best American Poetry* blog, and elsewhere. Her TEDx talk on creativity is titled "The Love Affair Between Creativity and Constraint." Tess is a graduate of Boston College and Bennington College Writing Seminars and teaches creative writing and meditation. A dual citizen of the United States and Ireland, she lives with her family and number one life coach: her dog. For more information, visit www.tesscallahan.com.